MICK'SOLOGY

THE FLYNNS BOOK TWO

KAYT MILLER

THE FLYNN FAMILY

2

MICK'SOLOGY

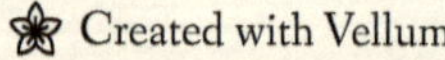 Created with Vellum

CONTENTS

1

———

MICK

As I lean over to buckle her into the back seat of the Uber, I feel fingers and the scrape of fingernails as they run across the back of my head, catching on my knot of hair. I turn to look at her as she pulls my head closer. She's beautiful for a thicker girl. Her long blonde curls are sort of a mess now, after having worked all day and spent the evening drowning her sorrows at my bar. Her eyes are hooded. She looks a tad drowsy. They're surrounded by long eye lashes. She flutters them for a second and my eyes are drawn to her full, pink lips. Lips that are on mine before I can even utter a word. They taste sweet, like the drinks she had tonight—one too many drinks, apparently.

Bent over at the waist to get her into the cab, I turn my body and place my hand on the back of her seat. I move my head a little to the side to get serious about this kiss. Her tongue moves over my bottom lip, seeking mine. I oblige because that's the kind of guy I am. I learned early on, when a pretty girl pulls you into a kiss, you reciprocate.

When our tongues meet, we moan simultaneously. I pull the hand from the back of the seat and slide it into her lustrous blonde curls to pull her even closer. It's the best fucking kiss I've ever had. My dick is hard as stone, and all I want to do is get this girl naked. But, she's drunk, and I'm supposed to be the good guy here and not take advantage of her. I'm her fucking bartender, not her date.

I pull away and see that her eyes are still closed while her lips are open slightly. She licks her lips as her eyes flutter open. She's got the greenest eyes I've ever seen.

"Wow," she says. "That was some kiss. You're hot as hell, Mick the Barkeep."

"Thanks," I smirk, still close enough to smell her sweet, feminine scent.

"It's a shame," she adds.

"Why's that?"

"Because... we could have made beautiful babies together." Her head falls back on the seat, and seconds later she's snoring.

Fuck! Of all the things she could have said to me, that one made my dick flaccid. Beautiful *babies*? What the fuck?

The Uber driver interrupts my thoughts. "Mick, Jesus, dude, time to hit the road. Where does she live?"

"Oh, sorry, Sam. I didn't.... I was caught up with...."

"Obviously."

"She's out cold. I'll see if she's got ID in her purse. You're my witness, Sam. I'm not trying to roll her."

"Be kinda hard to do; she's a big girl."

That comment pisses me off. "Knock it off."

"Oh, sorry, Mick. She your girl?"

"No. It's... just... she's a nice girl." Okay, I know shit about her, but after years of being in the bartending business, you get a sense about people. My gut tells me she's a nice girl. Too nice for the likes of me.

"Gotcha. Address?" Sam asks impatiently.

"Ah, here it is. Oh, Jesus." I snort out a laugh. "She said her name was Roni, but that must be a nickname. It's no wonder she has a good sense of humor. You'd have to with a name like that."

Sam chuckles. "I can't wait. What's her name?"

"Veronica Sue McGonigall."

"Veronica McGonigall? Shit, say that three times fast. Not possible," Sam says, laughing hard.

I can't help myself, but I laugh out loud and startle Sleeping Beauty. Not for long, though. She turns her head to the other side and starts snoring again.

"Today, Mick. What's her frigging address?"

I read it off and realize that she lives in Lincoln Square, which is the neighborhood just to the east of mine, North Park. We're neighbors. I put her ID back in her tiny purse and pull myself out of the car, wincing when I straighten my back. I shut her door and tap the roof, letting Sam know he can take off.

Sam is the guy I call when one of our patrons needs a ride. He's a good guy, a family guy with six kids, just like my family. Well, not my family, my mom and dad's. I have five siblings. That's what I'm trying to say. In any case, I like helping him out when I can.

I turn back to the entrance of Chrome and nod to our head bouncer, Steve.

Steve raises his hand up for a high five and says, "She's not your usual type, kinda a blonde Ashley Graham. She had nice tits. Way to go."

I can't leave him hangin', so I slap his hand. He smirks at me as I walk back inside. What can I say? She did have nice tits. The rest of her was pretty good too. Long blonde hair, full pink lips, plump round ass, and expressive green eyes. Remembering that kiss and the rest of her curves makes my dick twitch. Damn, she was all woman.

THE END of my day sure beats the shit out of the way it started. I was off last night, so I had come in early to get a jump on paperwork. When I walked into the bar, the first thing I saw was a fucking disaster. It looked like no one did any goddamn closing work at the end of the shift. There were empties all over the place; the counters were sticky. They left dirty dishes in the sink, and the chairs were still on the floor, which means no one mopped the floors.

I stomped into my office and picked up the phone. I called every single one of those assholes that worked last night and told them to get their ass to Chrome, or they're fired. I thought about firing them anyway. Twenty minutes later, I had seven people in front of me who knew exactly what the fuck they didn't do last night.

"YOU'VE GOT thirty minutes to get this bar in order. If I ever see this place like this again, you're all fucking fired," I shout. Then I turn to the person who was supposed to be in charge last night. "Stacy, my office now!"

She follows me back, head hanging low. She knows what's coming. I slam my door shut after she enters and say, "If you ever leave my bar like that again, you're not only fired, you can kiss any recommendation from me goodbye. We clear?"

"We're clear," she says sadly.

"When I'm not fucking livid, I'll ask you what happened last night. Until then, get out there and get that shit cleaned up!"

"Okay. Yeah, thanks, Mick." She scurries out the door like the room is on fire.

I know I should feel guilty for being such a prick, but fuck that shit.

When I walk back out to the bar forty minutes later, the

place is now spotless, and those worthless sacks of shit are gone. Good thing. I feel like yelling all over again. I turn to go back to my office but stop when I catch a glimpse of a guest at the bar. Emily. She's smiling at me, but I can tell she's tired. Still in her scrubs from, no doubt, a long shift at the hospital, she's got her dirty blonde hair pulled back in a tight ponytail and it doesn't look like she's got on any makeup. Not surprising, my little sister isn't girly. She's pretty but not overtly feminine.

"Em? What are you doing here?"

"Biding my time. I thought I'd let you cool off before I knocked on your office door."

"Yeah, so you heard that?"

"The tail end of it."

"So, what can I do for you, baby sister?" I love Emily. She and I are tight. We're just over two years apart, which means we were thrown together a lot when we were kids. As the two youngest in a family of six, we had to be a united front against the tyranny of our older, meaner siblings.

Em follows me into my office. I sit in my chair, and she plops her ass down in the chair in front of my desk.

"I haven't seen you in a couple of weeks big brother, so I thought I'd stop by to catch up. Maybe I shouldn't have come unannounced, though." Emily throws her feet up on top of my desk, getting comfortable. "From the scene out there, I was fearful I'd get caught up in the crossfire." Using her thumb, she points toward the bar. "What's up with you? You've been miserable for months." She arches her brow at me. "So, when are you gonna get happy, Mick?"

"What do you mean? I'm perfectly happy." No, I'm not.

"You're not happy. The Mick I know and love wouldn't have lashed out at everyone out there just now. Sure, he would have been pissed, but he wouldn't have been so harsh."

"Emily, you didn't see this place. It was a fucking dump."

"Stacy's dad died last night."

"What? Why didn't she tell me?" I pick up my phone and see my voice mail icon shows several missed messages. I click on it and see three from Stacy. "Shit."

"Did she leave you a message?"

"Three." Jesus, I feel like shit now.

"She had to get out of here last night to get to the hospital. The other people dropped the ball. Not her."

"How do you know that?"

"I sat at the bar and listened while they worked. They were careful not to say too much about you, but the consensus was: – you're a cranky, old bastard."

"I'm not old," I grumble even though I feel about a thousand years old right now. I stand to move around and sit on the front of my desk, the action pushing Emily's dirty sneakers off.

She huffs in irritation. "Older than most of them," she says with a smirk. "So, when are you gonna let your anger at Lauren go? It's been over a year."

"I may never get over the shit with Lauren. Look, Em, I'm doing the best I can."

"No, you're not. I mean, you've always been a moody asshole, but this last year you've become... completely unfun."

"Unfun? That's not even a word."

"It fits, though, doesn't it? You used to laugh with me, tell jokes, make fun of our older siblings, but whenever we're together, you're sullen and angry. It sucks. I want my fun-loving brother Mick back."

I sigh, knowing it's true. I haven't been able to shake the anger and sadness from all the shit that went down with my ex, Lauren Sly. Fuck, her last name fits her perfectly. She's a deceitful bitch. "Yeah, I know. I just didn't realize how far I'd slipped. Now that I know, I can make a conscious effort to do a better job. I can try to fake it."

"Jesus, Mick. I don't want you to fake happiness. Just get happy. Maybe it's time you met someone."

"No way. No fucking way. I'm never gonna be in a relationship again. I'll just stick with hookups."

"Having sex with these stupid barflies is a bad idea. You need a good woman. Look at what a difference Sophie's made in Hank's life. He's actually a joy to be around now, and we both know that's a miracle."

My brother Hank fell head over heels in love, and it shocked the shit out of all of us. He'd divorced his bitch of an ex-wife a long time ago and swore he'd never remarry or even have a serious relationship. But then he met Sophie, and all of that shit went out the window.

"Sophie's different."

"I know. She's cool. She's sweet, funny, and she loves all of us probably as much as Hank does. I never thought he'd get remarried after she-who-shall-not-be-named," she says ominously. Emily loves Harry Potter. She uses quotes from those books on a daily basis.

I chuckle. Lauren deserves that moniker too. "I'll think about it. Okay? That's all I can give you right now. I'll think about it."

"I guess that's all I can ask of you. I love you, big brother. We all do. You deserve to be happy, and you're selling yourself short if you let what Lauren did to you keep you from finding a good woman."

"Jesus, did Mom send you? You sound just like her."

"I know. It scares the living crap out of me too." She laughs. "But she has a point. She and Dad have been happy for decades. They've set an example for the rest of us—that it's possible to be in a healthy, long-term relationship and be friends as well as lovers."

"Please, do not say the word 'lovers' when referring to Mom

and Dad." I exaggerate a shiver. "While I'm at it, what made you all Miss Fucking Romantic? Is there something you need to tell me? Did you meet 'the one'?" I say sarcastically.

"Maybe. But I'm not saying a word about it to anyone, and neither are you." She points at me and looks serious. "What you and I talk about stays between us, or have you forgotten?"

"Of course, I haven't forgotten. I still have a scar on my thumb from when we made that stupid blood oath. You're such a bitch. I can't believe I let you talk me into that stupid ceremony and got me to let you use a knife on me."

"I was practicing," she smirks.

"Well, it's a good thing you're going to medical school. At least now if you cut someone open, you can sew them back up."

"True dat, bro. True dat. All right, I'm out. I've got a date with a textbook."

I stand up and walk around my desk to give her a hug. "I love you, Emily. When you're ready, I want to hear about the love of your life," I say sarcastically.

But she's serious. "I will. When you get fun again, I'll tell you about him."

Jesus, she's met someone? Damn. "Okay. That's a deal. Love you."

"Love you too," she says walking out of my office.

Stop being "unfun"? "Good luck with that," I mutter, picking up the phone to call Stacy so I can tell her how sorry I am about her dad.

2

―――――

VERONICA

"Oh, Jesus," I mutter to myself. It feels like someone is beating my head repeatedly with a sledgehammer. "Why did I drink so much last night?" I look at my clock and see I still have fifteen precious minutes in bed. I lie back on my pillow and close my eyes as the memories from the previous night flood back.

―――――

"Can I get you another one, sweetheart?"

I look up and see the most gorgeous man I've ever seen in real life. He's tall, probably over six foot two. His blond hair is pulled back into a bun at the back of his head. I can only imagine how long his hair is because the bun is a decent size. I sigh thinking about seeing all of that hair flowing around his broad shoulders—and those are broad shoulders. They are attached to thick, muscular arms, and those are barely encased in a tight gray T-shirt that reads: Real Men Wear Kilts. I peek over the edge of the bar to see if he is in fact wearing a kilt.

He smirks at me as he backs up.

Nope, he's wearing jeans that are torn at the knees and tight in all the right places. At least that's how it looks when he turns around for me.

His face... his face could launch a thousand orgasms. Seriously. His eyes are the color of a clear blue summer sky. They're surrounded by thick brown eyelashes, and his arched eyebrow tell me he knows I'm checking him out. His lashes flutter as he winks at me. I don't care; I've had a couple of drinks. It's given me the courage to shrug my shoulders and say, "Yeah, I'm lookin'." A woman would have to be dead not to appreciate all that is this bartender. When my eyes fall from his strong nose to his full lips, I feel a funny tingle in my lady parts. I can just picture myself doing things to those lips and those lips doing things to me. And it's a nice picture. His scruff of a beard would add nicely into this story as it scrapes on my inner....

Ah, shit. What am I doing? Get over yourself, Roni. I'm a twenty-six-year-old woman fantasizing about a man who would never go for a woman like me. I'm too full-figured. I snort out loud at my use of "full-figured." I'm fat, but it's so much nicer to say curvy or thick or plush. Oh well, it was a fun fantasy while it lasted. I give him my best smile and say, "Yep. Keep 'em comin', barkeep."

I'm getting more than a little drunk. This will be my fourth Old Fashioned. I should stop, but I just want to wallow in self-pity at a bar where no one knows me or cares that I'm wallowing.

"Here you go, darlin', another Old Fashioned. You may want to take it easy; those are potent cocktails," he says, smirking.

"Thanks for the tip, but I'm fine," I say, flipping a rogue chunk of hair back over my shoulder. I should cut my hair completely off. Why do I keep it long? It certainly does nothing to attract the attention of the male persuasion. Yeah, a pixie cut. That's the way I should go. No muss, no fuss hair would save me at least an hour on my morning prep.

Lost in my thoughts, I almost miss the hot-as-hell bartender say, "So, what's a pretty girl like you doing here alone on a Wednesday? You waiting for someone?"

I snort. "You're good. I've just had a bad day. I wanted to drink it away."

"Bad day? What happened? Anything I can do to help?"

"Not unless you can make a guy at work finally take notice of me. No? I didn't think so." Okay, why the hell did I just say that out loud? Crap. I need a drink. I pick up the glass and take a large gulp. Getting drunk faster is my new goal.

"What?" says the barkeep, feigning shock. "You've got a guy who hasn't noticed you? I can't believe that. The guy must be an idiot. Or gay. Is he gay?"

I look at him like he just sold me some swampland in Florida. "You don't need to stroke me, bartender man. I know how life works. I'm big... bigger than the average girl. But I'm not hideous. Plus, I'm nice, thoughtful, and I'm frigging hilarious," I add with a laugh.

"You are definitely not hideous. I'll have to take your word on the rest of it. What's your name anyway?"

"Roni. What's yours?"

"Mick."

"Seriously?" I laugh. "That's like the perfect name for a bartender. Is that your real name?"

"Nope. It's Michael, but only my mom calls me that."

"So, Michael, what's a hot guy like you doing working in a place like this on a Wednesday? Are you being punished?" The place is d-e-a-d, dead.

"Nah, I manage the bar down here on the main level, and my Wednesday guy called in sick, so I drew the short straw, as they say."

"I'm sorry to hear that. Now you're stuck talking to me. Your life sucks." I laugh again.

He laughs too. "My life's okay. So, tell me about this idiot at work. What's his deal?"

Letting out a deep sigh, I shrug. "I've worked with him for over a year and a half. I'm not very assertive, so I haven't told him how I feel about him—even if I did, I'm afraid he'd turn me down. Then, I'd have to work with him all day every day, and that would be even worse than now."

"True. Have you tried to give him small hints?"

"Oh, yeah! Let's see, I've been his secret admirer at work for a year. I leave him things on his desk like candy and snacks. One time, I finally got the courage up to leave a note with a bobblehead doll of Anthony Rizzo. You know, the first basemen of the Cubs? He loves the Cubs."

"The Cubbies are awesome," he interjects.

"I agree. Anyway, I wrote a note—my confession, if you will—and set it next to the bobblehead on his desk. As I was walking out of his office, I heard his voice, and I freaked. I thought, 'What the hell am I doing? I can't leave a note!'"

Barman nods. He's waiting for the worst part.

"So, I turned and grabbed the note off his desk, but

his voice was loud enough for me to realize that he was seconds away from walking into his office. If he saw me, he'd know I left the bobblehead. My only recourse was to hide, and the only spot to hide was behind his office door. So, I slid in between the wall and the door and waited. Thankfully, I was partially obscured by a big leafy plant, or he would have seen parts of me that didn't fit behind the door."

"Wow, good save," he mutters.

"Yeah, so there I was, hiding behind his door. Waiting. Just waiting for him to leave again. But you know what?"

"What?"

"He didn't leave. Not for Two. Fucking. Hours!"

Mick, the hot bartender, throws his head back and laughs so loud I think he scared the guy at the other end of the bar. He places his hand on his stomach—an amazingly flat stomach that I can picture with those ridges all hot guys have—abs that are covered by a snug T-shirt and jeans that fit his ass perfectly. What can I say? A girl can't help but notice when a man like that walks away.

I'm laughing too but not at my story. No, that's a sad-ass story. I'm laughing because he's laughing. "My feet were numb, and my legs were shaking from standing still for so long. Plus, that day I had decided to wear three-inch heels. Bad idea."

"Well, I like the sound of those shoes. Jesus, I haven't laughed that hard in fucking forever," Mick the hot bartender says.

"Yep, that's me. I'm *hilaaaarious*," I deadpan.

"So, what did you do?" he asks, wanting the rest of the story.

"What could I do? I waited. Our boss finally called him out of his office, and guess what he wanted?"

"What?" Mick leans on the bar on his elbows until he's close enough to smell.

Mmm, yummy. Damn, this man should be in movies—he's that smokin' hot with his blond man-bun and beard.

"He wanted to know if he'd seen me! So, they both set off on a search. Once they moved far enough away, I slipped out of his office and ran to the ladies' restroom. I had to pee like crazy, but I thought the bathroom would be a good cover.

"Good cover? How so?"

"Well, when they found me, I could tell my boss was pissed. I was late for a meeting. So, to smooth the way, I told them both I was having 'lady problems.' That works every single time with you guys. Men won't touch a menstrual cycle discussion with a ten-foot pole."

"That's very true." He laughs again. "Very true."

As I reflect on the events of the night, I realize that this part of the evening wasn't that terrible. I mean, I confessed a few of my office secrets to him, but he doesn't know Chris. However, the part that's making me cringe began when I nearly fell off my barstool. He had to run around the bar to keep me from falling ass over tit onto the floor.

After that, I remember him telling me he called me an Uber. It was sweet. At least I hope he was just being sweet. What if he was trying to get rid of the annoying drunk? "Ugh." That thought makes me even more depressed than I was yesterday. Maybe I should call in sick? I haven't missed a day in months, and that was due to a funeral.

Then it hits me. The memory. "Oh, God... I kissed him. That's so humiliating. That poor guy. Why did I have to pick that bar? Why did I have to drink so much? Why? Why? Why?"

Okay, Roni, stop talking to yourself. Instead, I should get my big bottom out of bed and into the shower. If I stay home, I'll spend the entire day reliving the nightmare that is my life instead of focusing on work. That will take my mind off of... what was his name again? Matt? Mike? No! Mick! Mick the hot bartender.

I get out of bed and drown my sorrows in a long, hot shower. My head still throbs, but it's better after I'm clean and have taken some ibuprofen. With minutes to spare, I grab my cup of coffee and head out the door to work.

3

———

MICK

Chrome is hopping tonight, and it's not even eight o'clock yet. That's not surprising since it's Friday and the first of the month. Something about first Friday's gets people out and about. I peer around the space, making sure everything is running smoothly. The cocktail servers are bustling around like it's New Year's Eve. I've got three other people on the bar with me tonight, and we're still really busy thanks to the after-work crowd.

I take a minute to check on our supplies and yell for our barback to bring up several more cases of imports from the cooler in the basement. It's unseasonably warm for October in Chicago, which makes it a beer kind of night. While I wait for the brews, I wipe down the counters, restock the olives in each station, and cut limes.

"Yo, Mick. Your girlfriend is here," shouts Steve, the bouncer at the far side of the bar.

I look at him with that expression that says, *Huh?* "No girlfriend for me, man," I reply.

Steve smirks and replies, "Yeah, you do. It's the one with the amazing tits. You put her in an Uber a few weeks ago."

Oh, yeah, I remember her—blondie with the nice rack and fucked-up name. The one who kissed me like a porn star. As I slice, I raise my head and see a familiar face waiting to be served. Shit, I hope she's not here for me. I've got no time for a clinger in my life. When she gets to the bar, her face shows very little expression. Doesn't she remember me? I smile at her. She smiles back, but I can tell it's just a polite smile. I don't think she remembers me. What the hell? We'll see about that. "Veronica! It's great to see you again."

She blinks at me and blushes. "Oh, hi," she says nervously.

Oh, yeah, she remembers me. "Long time no see. I was hoping I'd run into you again sometime."

"You were?" she says, sounding sincerely surprised.

"Sure! It's not often I get a kiss like that in the back of a Uber. How could I forget you?" Her face turns a shade of red I've only seen on roses. "Shit, babe. I didn't mean to embarrass you."

"You didn't. I just don't remember a lot from that night. Sorry about that."

"No need to apologize. As drunks go, you were one of my favorites," I say, winking. "You look good, Roni."

She looks down at herself. Her long, blonde locks are pulled back into a high ponytail. She's wearing a white blouse and a tight skirt in a deep red color. She reminds me of a fifties pinup girl. Pencil skirt—that's what they call it—and it hugs her curves nicely. She's damn sexy. No jewelry, no scarf, no nothing. The blouse isn't even that daring. She's only got the top button undone. Veronica's got a great rack, so she doesn't need to have anything unbuttoned. When she looks back up at me, I can see her mood has changed from embarrassed to confident.

She ignores my compliment. "Can I get an Old Fashioned?"

I chuckle at her nonresponse. "Sure. Give me a sec."

Old Fashioneds are a pain in the ass to make with their eight ingredients, but I don't mind. It's for Veronica. The fact is, I enjoy making these classic drinks now and then, but creating new drinks is my calling. That's why I've been dubbed a mixologist.

What's a mixologist? It's a person who's been trained to mix drinks—more specifically, to create new drinks. I love using new combinations of liquor, mixers, and other elements to make something unique. Some mixologists even have college degrees in chemistry. Not me. I just know what tastes good together.

As I muddle the sugar cube, water, and bitters in an old-fashioned glass, I look back over at the blonde who ordered this drink. I wonder what her deal is? She's a pretty woman—a bit on the bigger side of the spectrum, but she's still gorgeous. I haven't stopped thinking about that mouth of hers. Those lips. I know how those luscious lips feel too.

I slide the glass over to her as she starts to pull out her wallet. "It's on the house, babe."

"No. I insist—"

"I said it's on the house, Veronica." I ignore her look of irritation. "Are you here alone?"

She lifts her head after putting her wallet back in her bag and gives me a dirty look. Not the good, sexy dirty. She shakes her head and says, "I'm here with friends from work."

"Is the guy here?" I say as I scan the room.

She blushes again.

Oh, he's here. "What was his name again?"

"Chris," she says quietly, looking around, probably making sure he's not in earshot.

"So, you haven't told him yet?"

"No! Shh, I don't want anyone to hear about that."

"Right on. I get ya. My lips are sealed." *Unless she wants to unseal them with a kiss.* I chuckle at my joke. I really shouldn't toy with her. She's not my type. She's curvier than I usually go for; plus, this girl's the marrying kind. The one who wants a fuck-ton of kids, a big house in the burbs, and a man to take care of her. I have a feeling she'd fall pretty hard and fast for me, so I'd best lay off.

Roni grabs her drink and turns, getting lost in the crowd. I'm dying to see the guy she wants, so I yell to the guys that I'm taking a walk around the bar to see how things are going. It's my prerogative as the boss, right? I make my way around the club, checking on the servers, asking if they need anything. Things seem to be running smoothly when I see Veronica with a group of people dressed just like her in uninspired office wear. I stop at a few tables, checking on our guests, and then stop at her huddle. I slide my hand down her back to rest on her waist. She stiffens at my touch.

I lean down to her ear and, in a low voice, ask, "Hey, Veronica. You doing good here?"

She turns her head and looks into my eyes. There was fear there at first, but once she sees me, she softens against my arm. "Yeah. My drink is delicious. Thanks."

I start to speak again, but a woman I recognize interrupts me. Well, let me rephrase that; I don't recognize her specifically. I just know the type. This woman is always about five feet nine with long hair; this one is a brunette, no boobs, no ass, and no personality.

She scoots in close to me and coos, "Roni, is this a friend of yours?" She's made no eye contact with Veronica because she's looking at me like I'm lunch.

A shiver runs down my spine. Yep, I know her.

"You going to introduce me to your friends, Veronica?

Tentatively, Roni says, "This is Mick. He works here."

"You work here? What do you do?" asks Brunette—I'm calling the brunette Brunette from now on.

"I manage this level of the club," I say as monotone as I can.

I don't want to engage this woman. I don't think it matters, though. She's salivating.

"Roni, you should have told us you have a friend here," says another woman. This one isn't quite as assertive as Brunette here, but she's working up the courage to engage as well. "Can we get free drinks?"

I ignore the free drink question. That always pisses me off when people ask for free shit because drinks at this place are ten bucks a piece. I'm not giving away my profits unless I want to. "Veronica? Didn't you tell them about me? Wow, I'm hurt," I say, placing my hand over my heart. "You wound my ego, baby." I lean in and kiss her on the temple. Sure, I'm a dick, but one, I want these chicks to forget about me, and two, I want Chris to see what he's missing.

Ah, and there's Chris. How to describe him? Let me just say he's a typical cubicle guy. He's about as tall as Brunette, five feet nine or ten. He's wearing gray polyester pants and a white button-down shirt. He still has a pen in his breast pocket. What the hell does she see in him? More importantly, what is wrong with this guy? He's got this fine-lookin' woman panting for him, and he's too busy checking out Brunette's ass. Typical.

Chris reaches out with a hand to shake. "Chris. Chris Smith. Nice to meet you."

He shakes hands like his fingers are wet noodles. Yes, there is moisture. Fucking gross. My dad always told me you can tell a lot about a person by their handshake. A limp shake equals untrustworthy and/or lazy. A shake that's too firm, almost painful, is untrustworthy. That guy is gonna screw you over. Then there are people who have to shake your hand like twenty times in rapid succession. Those are the nervous ones. You can't trust them either because they've got no balls. No, there's a fine line between handshakes. You want a firm, dry shake but not too firm and three shakes tops, then you let go.

Chris falls into a couple of categories. He's got a limp shake, it's moist, and he shakes too many times. So, that means he's a pussy who'll throw you under the bus first chance he gets. Nope, this guy isn't good enough for Veronica. No way.

"Yeah, nice to meet you too," I say casually.

When I look at Veronica, she's beaming at the fucker. He gets her smile, and I seem to get her scowl. I suppose it's because she doesn't know me. But one thing is for sure; Chris Smith has suddenly found Roni very interesting. Not surprising. Men are territorial as fuck. If this guy thinks I'm pissing where he sleeps, he's going to make a play. Even wimpy douchebags like this one have that in their DNA. When Chris slides his scrawny arm around Veronica's shoulder, pulling her to him, a feeling of something I can't explain runs through me. Jealously? I'm fucking jealous?

Then the assclown says, "V, babe, I didn't realize you went out to party. Glad to hear it." He winks at her, then looks back at me with a smirk.

Fucker. V? Babe? What a tool. I've never wanted to punch someone so much in my life. And I'm a Flynn. Flynn's like to punch shit. Before I can toy with the little douchebag, my barback approaches.

"Mick?"

"Yeah?"

"We need you. Three of the kegs blew."

"Be right there." I turn to Roni and say, "Duty calls, sweetheart. Be sure to stop up and see me before you leave, okay?"

"Sure. And thanks again for the drink, Mick."

"No problem." I wave to her coworkers, intentionally scowling at Chris, and head back into battle. I shouldn't have left my post, but I'm glad I got to see the players in this deal.

Just as I turn to head back to the bar, I hear Roni say, "Oh my God, I love this song. Anyone want to dance?"

It's Meghan Trainor's song called "Me Too." They play it constantly, so I'm used to tuning it out like most of the music here, but I can't help but take notice of Roni's excited voice. Almost to the bar, I turn to watch her. Holy fuck, the woman can dance. "Jesus," I say under my breath.

We get a lot of talented dancers in the club—men and women. When it gets slow, I'll check out the dance floor so I know who's got it and who doesn't. Roni's got it. The song is fast-paced, and it's kind of an anthem for girls, or women, I guess. The gist of the song is about feeling self-confident. Watching Roni out on the dance floor, I can tell she's confident. She's a fucking rock star out there. I watch her body move. My eyes slide down from her long blonde locks, down over her amazing tits to her ass that just won't quit, and farther down her long legs. On her feet are some serious fuck-me heels in animal print. My eyes move back up; her hips in that tight skirt moving back and forth, in and out, mesmerize me. My dick is taking notice. So when my barback taps me on the shoulder again, I'm annoyed.

"Give me a second, damn it."

"Sorry, Mick," he says sheepishly.

I pull my eyes from her to get back to work when I see someone walk up behind her and grasp her hips. Some douche is trying to press his dick into her back as she moves her ass. She's oblivious. I start toward the dance floor to push the guy away from her, but that asshole Chris beats me to it.

4

___

RONI

"Roni! Let's dance," Chris shouts over the loud music.

I'm already into the song and dancing, so I just nod at Chris. He takes hold of my hand and leads me to a more open spot on the dance floor. I watch as he attempts to dance. I snort out a laugh as I see him do the white-man overbite. Google it. You'll see what I'm talking about.

My eyes don't stay on him for very long because once I hear the chorus again, I'm lost in it. I love to dance. I know I'm the fat girl on the dance floor, but I'm not a terrible dancer. I used to take dance lessons with my sisters when I was young. I quit when I was ten and both my sisters were encouraged to join the traveling dance teams. I overheard the dance teacher tell my mom, that "a girl her size should probably stick to the piano." My mom defended me, but the dance teacher wouldn't budge. Mom threatened to pull all three of us out of dance and take us somewhere else. My sisters threw a fit. They didn't think it was fair to make them quit because I was fat. So, I convinced her I hated dance and was glad to quit. Besides, dance was expensive, especially with three girls involved. I think she was relieved there would be one less bill to pay. The sad part is my mom and dad always told me I was the best dancer out of the three of us, and I really did love it. I guess it's just the way it goes. So, I focused on school and my friends, and I was okay with that, I guess.

As I dance to Meghan Trainor's "Me Too," I close my eyes and let loose. Chris is in his own world too. He's turned so he's no longer dancing with me. He's found two other women. I don't care; honestly, I don't. I'm just glad he asked.

As I move my body, raising my arms to the chorus of the song, I feel hands slide over my hips and up to my waist. Next, I feel a warm body move in close to my back. Whoever this is, he can move. His hips mimic mine as we sway back and forth. I reach my arms up to wrap around this guy's neck. His hands slide farther up my torso until they rest right below my breasts. They pull me into him so close we're touching from ass to chest. I finally peer up and gasp. It's Mick.

When he smiles down at me, I smile back. I should be embarrassed, but I love to dance. The fact that I'm dancing with the sexiest man in the place is just a bonus. I'm one who firmly believes that we should dance like nobody's watching. When the song ends, he takes my elbow and leads me back to my group of coworkers.

"Don't forget to give me a goodnight kiss before you leave, Roni." Mick winks as he turns to make his way back to the bar.

"Wow, Roni, you didn't hold back, did you? A girl your size should probably skip the dance floor, sweetie. It wasn't pretty," cackles Trisha Kepler. She's a marketing assistant in our office who works for one of the other analysts at P&P Advertising, and she is not a very nice person, obviously.

Ignoring her jab even though it hurt, I laugh it off. "Yeah, well, I can't help it. Dancin's in my blood, bitches."

The three of them laugh weakly at my self-deprecating joke. I know Trisha's making a jab at my weight, but I choose to pretend she isn't. It makes life easier. I also recognized her attempt to get Mick to notice her. I should have encouraged it. She's pretty and seems to be more his type anyway. But I didn't. Why should I when his attention was on me? Stuff like that never happens to me, so I chose to enjoy it.

I've tried my best to like Trisha, but she doesn't make it easy. Sure, she's pretty. Some might even say beautiful. Trisha's tall and very thin, with long, dark brown hair that she wears stick straight. My opinion is that she'd be prettier if she had some curves, but if I said that to her, she'd probably implode. I've seen what she eats. Her typical lunch consists of tiny snack bags each with a few carrots, celery, and a tablespoon of hummus. It boggles the mind. How can she survive on that?

The other woman with us tonight is Barb O'Brien. Everyone calls her Barbie except me. Even though she resembles a Barbie doll with a slim figure, shoulder-length blonde hair, and blue eyes, she doesn't act like you'd expect a Barbie doll to act. She's down-to-earth, modest, and friendly. She's an administrative assistant at P&P, very professional, and likeable. I consider her my only real friend at work.

Barb interrupts my ponderings by saying, "You guys ready to go? I'm beat."

We all nod in agreement. I finish the rest of my drink and turn to walk behind the group. As I walk past the bar, I hear my name.

"Veronica?"

I turn to see Mick looking at me. People asking for drinks surround him, but he's ignoring them and looking at me. I smile and wave. He holds up one finger—the one that means wait. So, I wait, because a girl waits for a guy like Mick. As he rounds the bar, he says something to one of the other bartenders who then rushes to his old spot to take drink orders.

"You leaving?"

"Well, yeah. Everyone's tired after a long week."

"I thought I asked you to say goodbye before you left?"

"I did. I waved," I say with my flirtiest smile. To be honest, my flirty-face sort of resembles a constipated person. I've got no game.

"So, did Chris get more interested tonight?" he whispers in my ear.

A shiver runs down my spine to my center at the sound of his soft voice in my ear. He's so close I can smell him, and let me just say, he smells wonderful with a touch of musk and something else woodsy.

Forcing myself back to reality, I think about his question. It's true. As soon as Mick showed interest, Chris became much friendlier. "Yeah, he was."

"Guys are territorial. I was making a play for you. He didn't like it. But I've gotta say, you can move, babe. I enjoyed dancing with you. You're talented." Still close to me, he slides his bristled jaw over my cheek.

I choke out a laugh. "Well, everything I know about dancing I learned playing Just Dance 4 with my nieces. So... yeah." Sure, I took dance lessons, but downplaying that part of my youth is easier than getting into all of that.

Pulling back, he looks into my eyes. "You got nieces?"

"Three. You?"

"Two. They're both only about four and five months and fucking beautiful."

I smile at his obvious love of his nieces, then look over at my group and see their impatience. "Well, I should go. Thanks for the drink."

"Give me your phone," he asks with his hand out.

"What? Why?"

"Give me your phone, babe."

Sighing, I reach into my purse and pull out my iPhone, type

in my security code, and hand it to him. He types away and then hands it back. "My number's in there, and I called myself, so I have your number."

"Why do you need my number?"

"So I can help you out with 'the love of your life, Chris.' Why else?" He says "love of your life" with air quotes and a touch of sarcasm. Either he thinks I'll never catch Chris's eye or he thinks love is stupid. Either way, it's troubling.

"Oh, yeah. I guess that makes sense." Why else would he want my number? Sometimes I'm seriously pathetic. "Okay, well, see ya, Mick."

I feel his hands slide from my waist to my hips. I'm shocked—I mean we aren't on the dance floor. He pulls my hips toward his quickly. I place my hands on his hard chest to brace myself, feeling his pectorals beneath my hands, and they feel perfect.

He leans down and rubs his lips gently over mine once, then steps into me, deepening the kiss. His tongue touches mine, and I feel my legs almost give out on me. He pulls away slightly, then murmurs huskily in my ear, "That guy's an idiot, beautiful." As he turns back to the bar, he adds, "I'll be in touch."

I say nothing and turn to my friends. Trisha looks like a fish with her mouth gaping open. Barb is smiling from ear to ear, and Chris? He looks pissed. *Good.*

5
———

MICK

I watch Veronica leave the bar with her group. My eyes fall from her long ponytail and trail down to her waist and ass. Sure, she's a bigger girl, but she's curvy in all the right places. As far as women are concerned, I've always had a type—the overly confident, slim, leggy blonde with ample tits type. I guess you could say I'm a breast man.

Roni certainly has that going for her. She's got to have double Ds at the very least. But the thing that surprises me about her is how much I like the rest of her. Pulling her against me during that dance felt good. Her ass fit against me like a puzzle piece. Jesus, the woman can dance. I'm still hard from having her against me. Roni's beautiful, sure, but she's got a sweetness to her that comes through her green eyes. She's sincere and somewhat shy—my total opposite.

I get back to work after I see my employees look at me pleadingly. Two out of the three behind the bar are relatively new. This is their first busy night, and they're floundering. I hope they don't quit on me. That would suck.

Back in the fray, I lose myself in the job. I love tending bar. It can be exhausting. Plus, dealing with drunken assholes sucks sometimes, but there's nothing like the rush of a large crowd like this one. I don't even mind the hipsters tonight. Why has my mood improved over the last couple of hours? Hell. I'm smiling. I'm actually fucking smiling. Jesus, what's wrong with me?

As I sling drinks, I think about Roni. Damn, the girl can dance. It blew my mind when I saw her out there. Chris was hopeless. I don't think Roni cared. She had her eyes closed—lost in it. She must've known the song too. Her lips were moving to the lyrics.

I could've watched her all night but was pulled from my trance. Before I joined Roni on the dance floor, Brunette had slithered up to the bar, twirling her hair around her finger and attempting that coy look. Fail.

She'd interrupted my current customer when she said, "So... Mike."

"Mick," I corrected.

"Oh," she giggled. "Sorry. So... Mick. What are you doing later?"

Not you, I wanted to say. "I close tonight. I won't get out of here until dawn."

"Oh, damn. When are you off next?"

This one isn't going to give up. "Look, I appreciate the attention, but I'm spoken for," I said, turning back to Veronica.

She laughed. "You're joking, right? Roni?"

"What's wrong with Roni?"

"Well, nothing's *wrong* with Roni. She's cute. She's just, you know... fat."

"I think she's beautiful." I wished that was the end of it with this chick, but it wasn't.

"There's no way a guy like you"—she pointed at my stomach—"would date a girl like Roni. You're just messing with me."

I turned back to Brunette. "You believe what you want. I

don't give a fuck." That's when I headed out to dance, probably shocking the shit out of Roni.

I'm a little surprised by it myself. I don't dance. Besides, why is it so hard to believe? Hell, now I've gotten myself entwined in her life. I didn't mean to insinuate that we're dating. But maybe that's what Roni needs me to do so she can get with that Chris guy—to make Veronica's dreams come true. She's a cool girl; I can help her with that. What the hell else do I have going on right now. Nada. Now, I just need to convince her.

Before she left for the night, I pulled her aside and told her how much I enjoyed watching her dance. I watched the blush run up her neck to her cheeks. It was adorable. When I told her to give me her phone, she was perplexed. Honestly, if I asked any woman in the bar right now to give me their phone, they'd have it in my hands so fast it'd make your head spin. But not Veronica. No. She questioned why, and I'd had to insist.

After I'd entered my number and then called myself, I leaned in to kissed her lips while her friends were watching. Brunette had a scowl on her face, probably not uncommon, while Chris looked pissed. Roni just turned and walked away from me without another word.

By midnight, Chrome is surprisingly dead. Where'd they all go? I think a lot of them went up to the third level. Chrome is broken up into three different bars. My level, the first floor, is the dance club. The second floor is more of a swanky lounge, and it's also the location for our VIP rooms that look out over the dance floor. The top and third level is a sports bar with huge televisions everywhere and comfortable seating. That level gets packed whenever any Chicago sports team is playing. I know there's something going on, but it's not the Cubs. Playoffs don't start until midweek.

"Tony? What's going on tonight? This place cleared out fast," I ask.

"Replaying last night's Cub's win. It started at ten."

"Makes sense." That means the crowd will filter back down in a couple of hours. Times like this, when it's dead, I'd love to do something else. Keeping busy is key right now. "I'm going to my office for a while. Yell if you need me."

"Sure thing, boss."

I head to my office, sure I've got things to do in there. When I slide down in my seat, I look at the pile of invoices on my desk and sigh. I don't want to do paperwork. I pull my phone out of my back pocket and see a missed call from an unknown number. That's when I remember I called myself from Roni's phone. Sweet! Time to send a text.

Me: Did you get home safely, beautiful?

Veronica: Who is this?

Me: Funny. You know I programmed my name in there for you.

Veronica: But who's *Michael Flynn, hot bartender extraordinaire?*

Me: That's me, Veronica McGonigall.

Veronica: **groan** How do you know my name?

Me: Driver's license. Gave your address to the Uber guy that first night. So, are you alone?

Veronica: And you remembered?

Me: How could I forget? You're unforgettable. So... you didn't answer me. You alone?

Veronica: Hardly unforgettable, and of course I'm alone. Who would be with me?

Thank fuck. I was hoping she didn't take that tool Chris home.

Me: Your one true love.

When she doesn't respond to my snide comment, I try again.

Me: Hello?

Veronica: Still here.

I take her silence to mean she didn't appreciate my comment about her "true love."

Me: I'm glad you stopped in tonight. You've been on my mind.

Veronica: Ha-ha. Funny.

Me: Not joking. I've thought of you. Did you have a good time tonight?

Veronica. Whatever. I had a semi-good time.

Me: Speaking of semis. You looked hot tonight.

Veronica: You did not just reference your dick, did you?

Me: Maybe. Are you offended? If not, I could send you a pic to prove it.

Fact: this girl has me hard whenever I think about those full lips and that ass on the dance floor.

Veronica: No! Pervert.

Me: LOL. I'm not a pervert. I'm just a red-blooded man. You're hot, Veronica. It's too bad I'm not a relationship guy.

Veronica: Why not? Did a girl ruin it for all others?

Me: You could say that. Anyway, back to tonight. Why didn't you have a full-on good time?

Veronica: **groan again** IDK. Trisha is hard to take sometimes. Please don't reference dick again. I know I said "hard."

Me: LMAO. You're fucking funny.

Okay, I could seriously be friends with this girl. I never thought I could have a woman who was just a friend, but maybe I can with Veronica. She's funny, clever, and a smart-ass. Just like my brothers and sisters. She would fit right in at the Flynn house. I should take her over for one of the weekly family dinners at Mom and Dad's. That would certainly stir things up. Maybe I'll do that.

Veronica: So I've been told.

Me: You are talking about Brunette?

Veronica: Brunette?

Me: Yeah, the scrawny brunette. That Trisha?

Veronica: She's not scrawny. She's slender. She probably looks scrawny compared to me. You need to see her on her own. She's gorgeous.

Me: I did see her on her own. She came up and asked me to hook up with her later. And she's just average looking.

Veronica: Average? Ha. That's funny. The woman is gorgeous.

Veronica: Wait! She hit on you? That's not cool. As far as she's concerned, you and I are together (even though you were just trying to make Chris get off his ass).

Me: I know. Chicks be crazy.

Veronica: This "chick" isn't crazy. I'm as levelheaded as they come. Oh, God...

Me: Damn, all of your sexy innuendos are making me hard. Again.

Veronica: Seriously, stop. I don't need to read about your boner.

Me: LOL. I'll stop. You're fun to tease, though.

Veronica: Good. Now, don't you have work to do? Cuz I'm going to bed.

Me: Yeah, I do. Before you go, let me ask you something.

Veronica: ...What?

Me: What are you wearing?

Veronica: I'm torn. Should I tell you the truth or lie?

Me: Don't lie to me, baby.

Veronica: Okay then... I'm wearing pajama shorts and a tank top.

Me: How short are the shorts? How tiny is the top, and for the love of all that's holy, tell me you're not wearing a bra.

Veronica: Believe me when I say you'll never know, Mick Flynn, hot bartender extraordinaire. Good night!

The hell I won't.

Me: Night, beautiful.

6

RONI

As I lay in bed in my pajama shorts and a tank top, (Yeah, like I'd tell him a lie.) I think about my night. There were some surprising occurrences. First of all, the fact that Hotty McBartender remembered me would have been enough to sustain me for weeks, maybe months. But, on top of that, Chris acted like he was interested in me. Holy smokes! I think that was the best night of my life—as it relates to men, anyway—so far. I need to forget about Mick Flynn and focus on the guy who's actually attainable. Chris. What is it about Chris that has me so determined to make him mine? The events of the last few hours have sort of made me forget. Maybe it's his dedication to his work? A guy with ambition is always attractive. It could be the way he relies on me at the office, though. He's always stopping in to ask me questions or to discuss projects. It's like we're a team at work already. Why can't we be one at home too?

Sighing, I close my eyes and picture everything that happened tonight. As we were leaving, Chris put his hand on my elbow again. Then he walked me to the taxi stand and waved one over. Sure, he could have ridden with me since we both live in Lincoln Square, but he decided to catch a ride with

Trisha in her cab. I won't read too much into that, but at least it was something.

It must be true what Mick was saying about men being territorial. Makes sense if you think about it. They're full of testosterone, and with that comes the need to hunt and gather. Forgive me, I'm gleaning that information from Anthropology 101... oh, and *Cosmo*. With that knowledge in my arsenal, all I need to do is figure out a way to make Chris jealous. That's it. That's all I need to do. Ha! Good luck with that, Roni.

I sigh and fall asleep dreaming of hunky bartenders and guys named Chris. If I could construct a perfect man, it would be half Mick and half Chris. Two-thirds Mick, one-third Chris? Hmm, maybe it would be three-fourths Mick, one-fourth Chris. Yeah, that'd be good.

I WAKE up bright and early Saturday morning. I'm naturally a morning person, but today I'm especially energetic. It makes me want to go out for a run. *Snort.* Just kidding. I could call a friend and do some yoga. I could take a walk in the park or, ooh, I know... I could swim! I have a membership to a club over in North Park that I never use. Who has time to work out anymore? It seems like my days are filled with sleeping, eating, and working. Then, I repeat it. It's a shame, really. I love to swim. I took swimming lessons at our local YMCA from age five until I was fifteen. I quit when I could no longer get myself to wear a swimsuit in front of people I knew. I've always relished in the feeling of weightlessness you get in the water. Plus, it's great exercise. I'm always sore all over the next day. That tells me I'm working muscles that I haven't been using. I really should start swimming on a regular basis. I'll see what I can do.

After I drink my coffee and eat a piece of wheat toast with

grape jelly, I grab my gym bag and fill it with my swimsuit, swim goggles, gym pass, wallet, and keys. I take a bus over to North Park and hop off a block from the gym. It's a crisp October day but not so cold I need anything more than a sweatshirt. The weather has been amazing. I love fall. I think it's my favorite season with the changing leaves and a shift to clothing with more coverage. It always reminds me of my college years. Those were the days! My friends were awesome, even though I've lost track of most of them now. There was always something to do back then. Every night was filled with possibilities. Now, I go from home to work and home again. Boring.

When I walk into North Park Nutrition and Fitness Center, I see the perky woman who signed me up. When they saw me walk in, they were on me like flies on stink. They wanted me to sign up with their nutritionist on staff. They were sure I needed help in that area. But I don't have terrible eating habits, I swear. What I do have are portion control issues. I mean, who can stick to one slice of Chicago-style deep-dish pizza? Yeah, no one! It's my metabolism's fault and heredity. My dad's side of our family is all built like me. Thanks, Dad.

I make my way into the women's locker room and head into a toilet stall. I hate changing in front of people, but especially gym rats. Whenever I'm forced to change in the open, I get some different looks. There's the disapproving sneer, the pity-filled smile, and my favorite, the person who pretends I'm not there. So, to the stall I go. I strip out of my clothes, being careful not to let anything touch the ground. Gym floors are nasty. I pull out my Speedo swimsuit and pray it still fits. Speedo brand suits are supposed to be tight on your body, so you can swim faster. Speed is not my issue. I slide the black suit up my legs and then have to shimmy and wiggle until I have it up around my waist. The tough part is getting it to go over my chest. I slide my arms into one hole at a time and then stretch it out as far as I can, up and over the ladies. It's tight. My boobs are so smashed together they're pressing out the top. The racer back is twisted, but I get that straightened out in no time. I wrap my towel around me, put my things in a locker, and walk into the pool area.

I'm shocked. There's no one in the pool. Maybe I have the time wrong for lap swimming. The one other time I was here, the place was so busy I had to share a lane. That's not the case today. No, today I have complete privacy. It's awesome.

I drop the towel without a second thought and throw it on a nearby chair. I place the goggles over my eyes and put in my earplugs to help avoid water in the ears. Gingerly, I step into the pool. It has a ramp that leads down to the water for those people who need a handicap accessible pool. When my feet hit the water, I shiver. Damn, it's cold. I know I need time to acclimate, but it's not easy. I walk down at a faster pace, wanting to get it over with. As soon as I'm hip deep, I dive into the water. I move over into the farthest lane so I'm near the wall. It's more obscured than the other lanes. Even though no one is here, I still like having one side of me hidden away. I vary my strokes from freestyle to backstroke to butterfly, and I even do the breast-stroke. On my way back to the starting point of my lane, I'm doing the backstroke. I'm in the zone, eyes closed, relaxed, and just enjoying the feel of the water. When I open my eyes, I see a man standing on the side of the pool next to my lane. He's staring down at me.

Startled, I stop swimming and reach for the wall. The man is talking to me, but I can't hear him. I stand up since the water is only three feet deep there and pull out my earplugs. Oh, shit. "Mick? What are you doing here?" He's wearing board shorts and no shirt. Holy smokes. Mick Flynn without a shirt is awe-inspiring. He's holding a towel in his left hand and goggles in his right. He's not going to swim, is he?

"I thought that was you. This is my gym. What are you doing here?"

"This is my gym too." Okay, so I've probably been here three times since joining last year, but it's still my gym.

He shifts his feet and scratches his beard. "I've never seen you here before."

"Well, I've never seen you here before either. We have different schedules. It's not that big a mystery." Seriously. What's he insinuating? Jeez, I'm not a stalker, and I so work out. All the time. Yeah. That's it.

"True, but I'm here a lot. Odds are I'd have seen you here before. You like to swim?"

"Nope. Hate it. You?"

He chuckles. "Yeah, hate it."

"Okay. Good talk. I need to get back to my laps. See ya, Michael Flynn."

He laughs. "Yeah, okay."

I slide my goggles back on and put in my earplugs. I make it down to the other end when I see arms and a long body glide through the water in the lane next to mine. He's almost beaten me to the end. He's fast.

I pause at the end, hoping he keeps going, but I'm not that lucky.

"Wanna race?" he asks.

I point to my earplugs in the hopes he'll realize I can't hear him and keep moving. Instead, he dives under the rope that separates our lanes and swims toward me. I'm standing on an underwater ledge while holding on to the side. I see him coming my way, and I back up until I'm in the corner. He reaches out and plucks out one of my earplugs.

"I said, do you want to race?"

I giggle. I'm not a natural giggler, but that made me giggle. "No. I don't think so. In the time it took me to swim from there to here"—I point to the other end of the pool—"you walked around the pool, down the ramp, swam across the pool to the lane, and then lapped to this end. So, no, I'm not going to race you."

"So, you were watching me?" he asks with a cocky smirk.

"No." I roll my eyes. "I just assumed that's how you got into the pool."

He moves closer to me, so I'm truly cornered. I feel that telltale shiver run down my spine. When the chill reaches my chest, my nipples harden, which is extremely embarrassing in a swimsuit. I discreetly cover the front of my suit with my arm. It's not convincing. Mick places a hand beside the left side of my head, resting it on the edge of the pool. He does the same thing with his right hand, so now I'm between his arms.

"So, this is seriously your gym?" he asks again.

I sigh, exasperated. "Yes! Okay. I'll admit that I never come, but I've been a member for a long time. Happy?"

"Yeah, I'm happy. Now that I know you're a member, we can meet up and work out together."

I literally snort like a pig. Attractive. "Yeah, no. That's not going to happen. I'm not in your fitness realm." I point to his amazing six-pack abs. I look again and add two more to that sum. "It would be humiliating."

"Nah, it'd be fun. I'd love to have a workout buddy."

"Well, like I said, our schedules are vastly different and—"

"Do I intimidate you, Veronica?" he says as he moves infinitesimally closer to me.

"No, you don't intimidate me, Mick." Yeah. He's making me a tad nervous. Him and his stupid abs. I give him my most confident smile. I get it. He's just screwing with me, and I don't appreciate it. Not only that, he's looking down at my swimsuit. Yeah, my boobs are pushed together. It looks like I'm smuggling two basketballs in there. I guess I can't blame him for looking. They're hard to miss.

"Damn, woman, you look great in a swim suit. Who would have thought?"

I feel the smile fall from my face. *Why?* Why did he have to go there? He just assumed I'd look terrible in my swimsuit? And to think... I was having a perfectly good morning. Now, I'll have to work through thinking negatively about myself. It'll take all day to stop hating myself. But I can do it! I do it daily, though for some reason it hurts worse coming from him. Without a word, I dive under his arms and swim away from him as fast as I can across the pool. He's still holding my earplug, but I can get more later, because the faster I get to the ramp, the better.

As I swim, I hear him. "Veronica? What's wrong? What'd I say?"

Thankfully my face is wet, so he can't tell I've got tears running down my cheeks. I walk as fast as I can up the ramp, knowing he can now see my entire body. Great! I'm squeezed into the Speedo like it's a sausage casing.

I hear his voice closer now. "Roni. Wait up. What did I say?"

I ignore him, grabbing my towel. I speed walk into the women's locker room, grab my clothes, and change right there in front of three other women. One of them is my age, the second looks to be in her late thirties, and the third looks a lot like my mom. They're all very fit and completely nude. I smile weakly in their direction, and that's when I see it... all three looks: pity from the oldest of the three, disgust from the middle-aged lady, and my personal favorite, the "pretend the fat lady isn't here" look from my peer. Great. Just great.

I sniffle and dress quickly, throwing everything in my bag. I'm out of the locker room in less than five minutes. Hopefully, I was fast enough to beat him out. Yeah, like he would chase me. I turn the corner toward the gym entrance and stop. Crap! He chased me.

He holds his hands up to stop me from passing him. "Look, I realize what I said, and I didn't mean it like it sounded. All I meant was—"

"It's okay. I'm fine. I just realized I was late for an appointment."

"Roni, I know that's not true."

"You know it's not true? How the frack would you know that? You don't know anything about me."

He arches his handsome brow and crosses his muscled arms across his chest. I'm not intimidated or turned on. I'm not. Honest.

"You don't, Mick. We've met three times. You know nothing."

He uncrosses his arms, placing them on my thick upper arms. He's ignoring my rant. "Roni, what I meant was, I was just surprised you were so, uh, well endowed. On top. That's all. I mean, I noticed you had a nice rack, babe, but seriously, that's award-winning tittage right there." Pointing to my chest, he asks, "They real?"

Startled by his candor, I snort out a loud laugh. "Jesus, you're a tool, Mick. Tittage? And, yes, of course, they're real!" He's successfully distracted me from my hurt feelings. I'm so used to people saying things about my weight, my face, my everything, that my first reaction is to take offense—to flee.

He laughs. "I made that word up."

"No shit, Sherlock." I sigh. "Please promise me that you'll never say 'tittage' again."

"I'll make no such promise. I'm a breast man, and I've got to be able to express myself freely."

I laugh loudly at him, and people have started to stare. Mick has his head thrown back laughing too.

We've both gotten a grip when Mick asks, "So, does that mean you forgive me?"

I stare at him, thinking about his question. "Yeah, I forgive you."

"Great. I'm glad. But I gotta go. Got shit to do before work. I'll text you," he says, walking backward toward the men's locker room.

I wave and walk out the front door. So much for my workout. I think I only got in about ten laps. Shrugging, I throw the strap of my gym bag over my shoulder. "Better than nothing, I suppose."

7

———

MICK

Wow, I almost fucked up big-time with Veronica. I was seriously in awe of her chest. Jesus, I don't think I've ever been that close to such an impressive set of—well, you get the idea. Another surprising tidbit is the fact that she likes to swim. I love the pool. It's my go-to workout when I'm short on time, and today I was very short on time. I actually got no workout thanks to my stupid comment. How much would I have gotten done anyway? As soon as I got close to her and saw what she was packin' in her Speedo, my dick became uncomfortably stiff. Fact: swimming with a hard-on isn't fun. Trust me.

After jumping in the gym shower, I dress in my usual work uniform: jeans and a T-shirt. I throw my bag in the locker I rent and head out. I want to run over and see Katie, my brother Hank's kid, before my shift. She's the coolest kid—or should I say baby—I've ever met.

I stomp up Hank and Sophie's new back steps. They're fixing up Sophie's old Victorian that her grandmother left her. It's a cool house, but they still have a lot of work to do. It's certainly roomy enough for them to raise a family.

I never thought I'd see the day my big brother Hank settled

down. Even more surprising is who he ended up with. Don't get me wrong, Sophie is cool as shit. She's just, well, not the body type my brother usually dated. I snort. Dated? I mean fucked. He didn't date. Not until Sophie. For her, he worked his ass off to lock her down. She was a tough nut to crack, so to speak.

Giving the new back door a tap, I wait. I learned my lesson a few weeks ago when I walked into their kitchen without knocking and caught Hank and Sophie fucking like bunnies on the kitchen table. Seeing my brother bare-assed doing the nasty—well, it's an image I'll never be able to unsee. So, now I knock.

After knocking a second time, the door opens to my oldest brother holding my biggest fan, Katie Flynn.

"Katie-Did! It's me, Unkee Mick!" I say in a voice that could rival Mickie Mouse's.

Her face lights up.

What is it about having a girl's face light up when she sees you that makes your heart grow two sizes? Katie just did that for me.

"Gimme," I say to my bro with my arms extended.

Hank hands over his sweet daughter. She's such a beautiful baby with blonde hair, brown eyes, and an adorable turned-up nose. She looks like both of her parents, that's for sure.

"Where's Soph?"

"Upstairs. She wasn't feeling very well today. She's takin' a nap," grumbles Hank.

"Uh-oh. You knock her up again?" I ask with a smirk.

"I hope so." Henry beams. "I want a house full."

"I know you do, man." That's another change in my big brother. He was dead-set against a family. But I guess the right woman changes that.

I smile at Hank and walk into their kitchen. "Does Kate need to be fed? Changed? Anything?"

"Nah, she's all good. But if you'll hang here, I'll run up and check on my wife."

"Sure thing. Katie and I will have a chat while you're gone." Yeah, I tell Katie stuff. I tell her all my little secrets. I do it with as many weird voices as I can conjure up to make it more fun for her. I head into their living room and plop my ass in their big rocking chair.

There's a colorful baby toy on the side table that makes various sounds like crinkled paper and bells, and it even squeaks. I hold it up in front of her and manipulate it to make all of the noises one at a time. She gives me a gummy-mouthed smile.

"So, beautiful Katie, how has your day been so far? Good?" We rock back and forth, and I listen as she makes cute baby noises. There are gurgles, raspberries, and coos. All of them are equally adorable. "Let me see. I haven't talked to you in a while. So, I guess my big news is I made a new friend. Her name is Veronica," I say in a squeaky voice.

Katie's eyes usually get huge when I do that voice, and she doesn't disappoint today.

"That's right. But she's got a very funny last name. It's McGonigall," I say, tickling her tummy. "You don't know about Harry Potter yet, but there's a character in those books named Minerva McGonigall. Veronica doesn't look anything like a Minerva. No, she's almost as pretty as you are. Almost." I lean down and kiss her plump cheek. "No one is as pretty as you are, Katie-Did."

I pick up the toy and squeeze it so it squeaks. Katie's eyes get huge. I can't wait until this girl can talk. It's going to be a blast. "Anyway, Veronica's very pretty. She's got long blonde hair, slightly darker than yours. She's got freckles on her nose like your mama. Oh, and green eyes. Her mouth is pretty, and she's got a wicked good sense of humor. I bet you'd like her, little one."

We rock for a few minutes as I hum some random musical notes to her. She likes when I sing to her. "So, Katie, are you going out later?"

"Yes, she is. She's got a play date with cousin Abby."

"Oh, hey, Sophie. How are you feeling? Hank said you were under the weather."

"I'm fine. Just tired. And before you say it, there's no word about a pregnancy. Hank is picking up a pregnancy test for me later today. Please don't say anything to anyone, okay?"

She knows what a gossip-mill my family can be. "No problem. My lips are sealed." It's nobody's business anyway. "So, have you two figured out your Halloween costumes yet? Tick-tock. My party's only a couple weeks awaaayyy," I sing-song the last sentence, so Katie is entertained.

"We have a couple ideas, but you'll have to wait and see," Sophie says, smiling. "Here, let me take Katie. I want to give her a bath and change her before we head over to Keith and Beth's."

Keith is my older brother, and Beth is his wife. Their baby girl, Abigail, was born a month before Katie. She's a beauty too, and I don't mean to play favorites, but there's just an inexplic-able connection I have with Katie. Honestly, I think it happened the first day I met her. She was crying—no, wailing is more like it. Sophie tried to calm her down; then Hank tried. My mom, Sarah, stepped in, then my dad, Declan. Nothing they were doing would calm her. I decided to give it a try. What the hell, right?

Dad handed her over, and I looked in her eyes, and she looked into mine, and I whispered, "Hey there, Katie-Did, what's the problem?" She stopped crying right then and there and just blinked her beautiful eyes at me. I smiled at her and kissed her tiny nose and told her how pretty she was and how much fun we were going to have together. My family was stunned, to say the least. But that's the way it's been with us ever since. She's my Katie-Did.

"Aw, okay." I turn and kiss baby Kate on the cheek. "I love you, Katie. I'll see you soon." I step over and gently hand my girl over to her mama. "Well, I'm heading out. Nice seeing you, Soph. I hope you feel better." I wink.

As I'm stepping out the door, my phone chimes. I pull my phone out and read the text. I can't help but throw my head back and laugh. Veronica. Damn that woman is fun.

"Mick?" Sophie says, stopping me from exiting the house.

"Yeah?" I turn to look.

"What's up with you?"

"What do you mean?"

"You just laughed at something other than Katie." She gives me a small smile. "You seem different. Happy. Don't get me wrong; I'm glad. But what's going on to cause such a shift?"

"Nothing. I'm just in a better mood. I can't attribute it to anything in particular. But, Jesus, if you think I'm happier now, I must have been a real ass."

"Not an ass. Just a tad sullen."

"Sullen?" That's what Emily called me. "Well, I'll try to do better, okay?"

"No. That's not what I meant. I just noticed a change. That's all. If you don't mind me asking... are you seeing anyone?"

"You bein' nosey, Soph? You aren't going to run to my mom and sisters with the news flash that 'Hey, Mick isn't a dick anymore'?"

"No. I wouldn't."

"Well, I made a new friend, but that's all it is. She's funny but no one I'd ever date, which is perfect because I'm not dating material. She's just a friend."

"Friends are good. We all need them. Good for you, Mick," she says, smiling. "I'll see you later?"

"Yep. See ya. Tell Hank I'll catch him later."

I head out the back door. I'd like to see if Emily is home, but I don't have time now. She lives in the garage-turned-carriage house behind Sophie and Hank's place. Next time.

I glance at my phone again, wanting to read her text again.

Veronica: I've got bad news. You didn't invent the word "tittage." Poor, delusional Mick.

ME: On the one hand, I'm saddened that I wasn't the one to invent the term. On the other, I'm positively giddy that you looked up "tittage" on the interweb.

Veronica: You did not just type "positively giddy" and "interweb"?

Me: Yeah, what of it?

Veronica: Nothing. Nothing at all. You're a very strange man, Mick Flynn.

Me: Strange but hot, right?

Veronica: No comment.

Me: It's okay. You don't need to say it. I know I'm hot.

Veronica: Aren't you supposed to be working?

Me: You started it. And yeah, I'm late. Talk to ya later, babe.

8

———

RONI

Babe? I get a little chill whenever he uses that term of endearment. I know he just throws that word around like it's nothing, but it puts ideas in my head, and I've got no business hoping for anything with Mick Flynn. I might as well enjoy our budding friendship—accepting that friendship is all it is—and focus on Chris.

The rest of my Saturday is uneventful. I run errands, do laundry, clean my apartment, call Mom and Dad, and FaceTime with my sisters and their kids. I miss my nieces and my folks so much, but I chose the big city. The drive to visit them takes only a few hours, but I'd have to get a rental since I don't have a car here in the city. Car insurance is astronomical, and on top of that, parking is impossible unless you rent a space, which is also very pricey.

As I get ready for bed, I grab the book I've been trying to finish for the last few weeks. It's one of those great romances with a super alpha male and a woman in distress. I love those. Would I actually like a guy who was super bossy in bed? Who knows? I've had so few boyfriends or even brief encounters in my twenty-six years, I have no idea what I'd actually like. But I could give it a try. I open the book at my bookmark and hear my phone ding. A text. My heart jumps in my chest. I grab my phone and peer down.

Mick: Got a joke for you. What's the difference between a tire and 365 used condoms?

Veronica: **eye roll** Shouldn't you be working?

Mick: Answer the question, babe.

Veronica: Okay, but please note I'm doing this under duress... What's the difference?

Mick: One's a Goodyear. The other's a great year.

Veronica: No. Just no, Mick. That's so very wrong.

I'm giggling to myself, but since we're texting, he has no idea. I'll just pretend I'm offended.

Mick: If it's wrong, I don't wanna be right. ;)

I decide two can play at this game.

Veronica: What's the difference between a G-spot and a golf ball?

I wait for several minutes. Probably busy.

Mick: A G-spot is...? Hmm. Damn, that's a hard one.

Veronica: That's what she said.

Mick: LMAO

Veronica: Give up?

Mick: Yeah. I give.

Veronica: A guy will actually search for a golf ball.

Mick: You wouldn't say that to me if I were in your bed. I know the difference.

Veronica: **eye roll x 2** Whatever! Get to work!

Mick: It's dead tonight. Cubs are on. Playoffs. They're all up on three.

Veronica: So, you want me to entertain you?

Mick: Fuck yeah!

Veronica: Okay, here's a test for you. How fast can you guess these words? I'll time your responses.
1. B O O _ S
2. _ _ N D O M
3. F _ _ K
4. P _ N _ S
5. P U _ S _
6. S _ X
Go!

I can't wait to see what comes in. I already know what he'll say.

Mick: BOOBS (tittage), CONDOM, FUCK, PENIS, PUSSY, SEX. That was too easy. Next!

Yep. That's what I thought he'd say.

Veronica: You are such a pervert. The answers are BOOKS, RANDOM, FORK, PANTS, PULSE, and SIX.

Mick: What the hell? You tricked me. No one would come up with BOOKS for number one. No guy, anyway. Oh, damn. Hang on, customers. Back later.

Wow, that was fun. The guy cracks me up. I don't remember being this comfortable with a man—ever. I'm usually a nervous wreck when it comes to guys. Maybe I feel comfortable because in my heart I know he's unattainable and I'm just his buddy. Sure, we've kissed twice, but that was for Chris's benefit. Yes, he said some things about my boobs, but he hasn't made any other moves. Yep. Just friends.

I try to read my book for the next hour but can't concentrate. I'm too busy looking at my phone, hoping I'll get another text. *Chill out, Roni.* I decide to save myself from further torture and turn off the phone and my light and lay down to sleep. Just chill.

9

MICK

The crowd at Chrome tonight is spotty at best. People are trickling down from the third floor to dance and hang out with friends. Since there's a lull, I decide to restock the bar and clean. It's a never-ending part of bartending: clean, restock, repeat.

Lugging a case of Guinness from the basement, I turn the corner and see two familiar faces at the bar. "Hank? Keith? What are you guys doing here?"

"I didn't get a chance to talk to you when you stopped by today," says Hank.

"And I haven't talked to you in over a week," adds Keith.

Hank and Keith are two of my three older brothers, and they are best friends like me and Em. They're about four years apart. Hank is thirty-six while Keith just turned thirty-two, I think. It's hard to keep track of everyone's ages these days. That leaves David and Sandy who used to be close until Dave decided to marry Jen. Since Jen's a bitch, Dave and Sandy aren't as close. It's too bad. Blood before hoes, I always say.

"Been busy. What's new with you two besides raising the two prettiest girls in the world?"

That comment makes both of my brothers smile. They're proud papas. That's for sure. "What can I get you guys?"

"Beer," they say in unison.

I grab a couple imports I know they like and pop the caps, sliding them down the bar into their waiting hands. "So, why are you really here?" The truth is, they rarely come to Chrome—especially on a Saturday night.

"What's this I hear about you being a goddamn joy to be around?" asks Hank.

Here we go. I knew Sophie couldn't keep her mouth shut. "So, Sophie couldn't keep it to herself, huh? She's turning into Mom and our sisters. You'd better nip that in the bud," I say, nodding to Hank. I know that comment is going to piss him off. Sophie can do no wrong.

"Shut the fuck up, little bro. Sophie was just happy to see you more chipper. She cares. Get over it."

See? Told you. "Well, I must be a fuckin' nightmare if Sophie notices me smile and makes a big fuckin' deal out of it."

"Whatever. Tell us what's going on? You seeing someone?" It's Keith's turn to get his nose in my shit.

"No." *Jesus.* "I made a new friend who happens to be female. But we're just friends. She's not my type."

Hank chuckles. "So that means we'll like this one?"

"Fuck you, Henry." He hates it when anyone but Sophie or Mom calls him by his real name.

"You can't blame him. Lauren was a fucking nightmare. She was your last serious girl, right?" asks Keith.

"Don't mention her name. Not going to talk about her," I growl, walking away from them. I refuse to talk about Lauren Sly. Just *thinking* her name makes my skin crawl. I pull out the clean glassware from the dishwasher under the counter and turn to put them on the shelf behind the bar.

"Mick, what's going on? We're glad you're in a better mood. What's the deal with this new girl?" Keith's usually the voice of reason when Hank's around. Henry Flynn has a temper that he has a hard time keeping in check. He often regrets shit he says—he speaks first and repents later.

Turning back to face them, I say, "She's just a woman who came into the bar a few weeks ago. She's funny and smart, and she made me laugh my ass off. I don't remember the last time I laughed like that."

"She sounds awesome. What's wrong with her?"

"Shit, Hank. Nothing's wrong with her. She's pretty, it's just...."

"What?"

"She's not my usual type, like I said. She's, well, she's just not what I'm used to."

"Not what you're used to?" asks Hank. "You're being awfully vague."

"Honestly, Roni is beautiful. She's smart—"

"You already said that. What's really wrong? She flat chested?" asks Keith.

I spit out the swig of beer I just drank. "No. She's definitely *not* flat chested. As a matter of fact, her tits are spectacular."

"So, what's the problem?"

I blink at Keith. *What is the problem?* "She's got a thing for a guy at work, for one. And two, Veronica is a relationship kind of girl. The kind of girl Mom would love. The kind that wants a litter of kids, a dog, a cat, and...." The kind of girl who'd want commitment from me. "And I'm not getting into another relationship. The last one ended in disaster, and I can't go down that road again." There, that should shut them the fuck up.

"You cannot use that thing with Lauren you called a relationship as a Litmus test. She was a nutjob. You're lucky you got out of that when you did. Just imagine if you'd have married her." Keith shivers. "I'm just glad you figured things out before it got out of hand."

The thing is, neither of my brothers know what actually went down with Lauren. The only person I confided in was my baby sister, Emily, and she promised to keep my secret.

Hank pulls me from my negative thoughts. "You should invite her to a Sunday dinner at Mom and Dad's. We could vet her for you."

"She doesn't need to be vetted. She's cool. You'd like her, I'm sure. I'm just not ready to do that. It would confuse her, and I don't want to lead her on, man."

"I get it. So invite her to your annual Halloween bash. We could meet her then, and it'll be casual."

That's not a bad idea. If I want to keep Veronica around, as a friend, that's a perfect way for my siblings to meet her. There won't be any expectations—from anyone. "Keith, you're a fucking genius. I'll ask her to the party. Which reminds me, you got costumes yet?"

Both of the guys groan. Keith speaks. "The women are working on them. We don't get to find out until the day of. They're tired of us shooting down their ideas."

I laugh because I can just picture them in couple's costumes. "Oh, I know. You and Sophie could go as Raggedy Ann and Andy," I smirk. "Keith, you and Beth should go as Papa Smurf and Smurfette. Good luck getting that blue shit off after the party," I snicker.

"Shut up, asshole," grumbles Hank. "That could actually happen, and I don't want to think about it." The truth is, Hank would wear whatever Sophie wanted him to wear, and so would Keith. That's just how pussy whipped they both are now. They're an embarrassment to mankind.

When I look out into the club, I notice it's filling up. "Looks like my break is over. Hang if you guys want...."

"Nah, we need to skedaddle," says Keith.

Skedaddle? "Yeah, okay. Talk to you later." We give each other one-shoulder man hugs, and they're off. Time for me to get back to work.

10

———

RONI

Sunday afternoon I realize I hadn't turned my phone back on. I pull it from its charger and hit the power button. It dings awake, and I hold my breath, hoping there's a text for me from a certain bartender. Nothing. To say I'm disappointed is an understatement. I do my best to put it behind me, but all I accomplish all day is watching sad, romantic movies and eating junk food. I ended the night in tears thanks to the stupid movie *The Notebook*. Why do I torture myself? I should have watched something funny.

I wake up late on Monday and have to run around like a crazy person to get ready in time. Tossing and turning all night long makes you do that. I had a fitful night of sleep, including a short dream starring Mick. Chris was in it too, but his role was secondary. In this dream, Mick was serving me a cocktail naked. I couldn't see anything, sadly, because he was wearing an apron. Chris was nearby, but neither men spoke in the dream, which is odd, don't you think? The fact I didn't get any action in the dream wasn't a surprise. It's my reality. *Cue sad trombone.*

As I shower, I think about both men. They couldn't be more different. Mick is tall, broad, and muscular. Chris isn't. Mick has a full head of long, blond locks; Chris is losing his dark hair, starting on his forehead. Mick obviously knows how to work hard. Chris is a professional, but there are times I've noticed he lacks a little work ethic. He delegates a lot of his tasks to his assistant—and to me. Not that I mind helping. I don't. I'm sure he'll help me if and when I ever need it.

Chris and I are both market analysts for a large advertising company—and by large, I'm talking huge. We handle some major national campaigns. My job as an analyst is to perform research and provide insights regarding the market, trends, competitors, potential and existing customers, and current campaigns. After my research, I recommend changes and offer suggestions based on the market. It's an intense and challenging job and one I thoroughly enjoy.

By midafternoon, I'm sluggish. Monday seems to be dragging on and on and on. Hopefully, I'll sleep better tonight so Tuesday can be more productive. At five o'clock on the dot, I pack up my computer and head out the door. I usually put in extra time, especially when I'm working on something big, but I'm just too tired to work overtime tonight. I even grab a taxi instead of waiting for the bus. I can't handle the crowds or the extra time it'll take on the bus, so I splurged.

At home, I put on my favorite pajamas and throw a frozen pizza in the oven. Yeah, I live a very glamorous life. I turn on the television and see a Cubs game is on. Go Cubbies! After eating the entire pizza—don't say a word. I already know. Portion control, Roni—anyway, after eating, I straighten up my mess and head to bed. It's pathetic. I'm in bed before seven. I plug my phone into the charger and grab the book I can't seem to get into again. Five minutes later, I hear a ding. Peering at my phone, I smile. It's Mick. Yay!

Mick: Yo! What doing?

Me: I'm in bed.

Mick: It's seven o'clock. You're too young to be in bed before ten. Oh... unless I'm interrupting something.

Me: No, perv. I didn't sleep well last night, and I had a busy day at work. I'm tired.

Mick: What do you do for a living?

Me: Marketing. Market analyst, specifically.

Mick: And that means?

Me: I work with clients and their products to help get them on the market. I research other brands, demographics, and profitability, stuff like that.

Mick: Wow. That sounds super complex. I'm impressed. And I'm not easily impressed, babe.

Me: Gee, thanks, Mick.

Mick: Sarcasm. I can sense it even through a text.

Me: So, what are you doing tonight?

Mick: Babysitting my niece, Katie.

Me: Babysitting? Seriously?

Mick: Sure. I watch her every Monday night while her mom, Sophie, goes to class. My brother is a detective with the Chicago PD, and he's usually working, so I have a standing babysitting gig with my best girl.

Me: Oh, that's sweet.

Mick: Yeah, I'm a sweet guy. Oh, you pro'ly meant Katie. Yeah, she's my Katie-Did. Wait a sec... I'll send you a selfie of us.

I wait a couple of minutes until my phone chimes. When it appears, it takes my breath away. Mick is holding a baby that looks just like him. She's got white blonde hair and big brown eyes. I know Mick's are blue, but they have the same shape. She's beautiful, and seeing him with that baby makes my ovaries explode. Not good.

Me: OMG! She's so beautiful! How old is she?

Mick: She was born in June so almost five months.

Me: She's perfect.

Mick: She is indeed. Hey, it's time to put her down for the night. Can I call you after that? I want to ask you about something.

Me: Sure.

Mick: You sure you can stay awake for a few minutes more, old lady?

Me: Just call me asshat.

Mick: Sure thing, asshat.

Mick: Commas are important. ;)

Groan.

I busy myself with mindless tasks, like picking out my clothes for tomorrow, brushing my teeth and my hair, twice. I've started straightening my sock drawer when my phone rings. Finally. I was about to match socks.

"Hello?"

"Hey, it's me. Sorry it took so long. Katie wasn't very helpful in the sleep department. She wanted to talk instead."

"Talk? She's only five months old."

"Well, I talk. She listens. It's our deal."

I giggle. *God, he's so sweet.* "She listens to you? You do realize she has no idea what you're saying, right?"

He laughs. "Yeah, I know. She reacts to the tone of my voice though, so it's fun to watch her as I talk. Someday I'll be the one listening to her tell me things. I can't wait for that."

"That's so sweet, Mick," I say a tad breathlessly.

"What can I say? I'm hot and sweet."

I snort. "So, what did you want to ask me?" *Please say you want to take me on a date. Please say—*

"Well, there are two things. The first thing is, I want to invite you to my annual Halloween Party. It's on the 30th this year, and it'll be a blast."

Yes! "Is it a costume party? Would I have to wear a costume?" I dislike Halloween. For one, I eat too much candy, and second, I look terrible in costumes. But I did wear a halfway decent costume my senior year of college. I wonder where that is?

"Of course, you have to wear a costume. It's fucking Halloween, woman!"

"What are you wearing?"

"Oh, I'll never tell. You'll have to show up to see."

"I'll think about it. So, was there another thing you wanted to talk about?" The sooner we move on from Halloween party talk, the better. I'm sure I'll go because I'm a glutton for punishment. I won't be able to turn down any invite from Mick.

"Well, the second thing relates to your job."

"My job? How so?"

"I have an idea for a product, but I'm unsure where to start with it. Can I tell you what it is and get your feedback?"

"Sure."

"I'm what you call a mixologist."

"What's that?"

"It's a fancy name for a bartender," he says with a chuckle. "Actually, the term mixology is defined as the art and science of mixing drinks. Some mixologists even have degrees in chemistry. Some go to culinary school."

"Do you have a degree? How did you learn to be a mixologist?"

"No degree, just years of practice. Trial and error. I've created six original drinks that are on the menu here at Chrome."

"And do those recipes belong to the club now?"

"No. It's in my contract that any new drink recipes I develop are mine. I've researched patenting those, and it's possible."

"Yeah, you can patent almost anything. That's interesting. Does your product have a name?"

"Not yet. I know I want to bottle at least four of my recipes initially. But I'd like to have one primary brand name for them, so I can develop more recipes under that name."

"Okay, you have the drink names, you just need a brand name? Let me think for a second... forgive me if I talk out loud. I talk to myself when I work."

"No problem, I—"

"Okay, these are cocktails, right?"

"Right."

"You're a mixologist," I say absently then laugh. "It's funny. Your name is Mick, and you're a mixologist. You're a M-i-c-k apostrophe s-o-l-o-g-i-s-t."

There's silence on the other end of the phone.

"Hello? Mick? Are you still there?"

"Yeah, babe." He chuckles. "You're a damn genius."

"I am?"

"*Mick'sology?* Using my name instead of m-i-x? Fucking perfect. That took you five minutes to give me a brand name. I've been brainstorming for two years. I kid you not. Thank you so much! I'll pay you for this when I actually get going, okay?"

"Mick. No. It was nothing."

"It was *everything*. You're incredible, Roni," Mick says with sincerity. "God. Thanks so much." He sighs in the phone. "I can't wait to tell my sibs. They're totally sick of me asking for ideas." Mick laughs.

"I'm glad I could help." Right after I say that, I hear the cry of a baby. "Uh-oh, is little Katie up?"

"Yeah, that was her baby monitor. I guess I didn't get her to sleep. I should check on her. I'll talk to you soon, okay?"

"Night, Mick."

"Night, babe."

Babe? Again? I may never tire of him calling me things like babe and sweetheart. What would it be like to have a guy like Mick saying it and actually meaning it? I sigh, imagining a life with Mick Flynn. "No, shake it off, Roni. Mick is not for you. Focus on Chris."

11

___

MICK

Rocking Katie to sleep, I think about Roni and my new brand name for my drinks. "It was unbelievable, Kate. It took her five minutes to think of a name, and it's a genius idea. Mick'sology. Isn't it perfect?" I coo at the little beauty in my arms. "I should do something nice for her, right, Katie-Did? Someday, I'll be rich, and I'll buy you a pony," I whisper. "We just won't tell your daddy. He probably won't let you do anything he thinks is dangerous. I suspect he'll carry you to school every day himself. Oh, and good luck getting a boyfriend. That's never going to happen."

"Damn straight it's never going to happen!" grumbles my big brother.

"Honey? You're home early," I say sarcastically.

"Can't do anything else tonight on my latest case. It's cold as a dead hooker."

"Gross, dude. Now that's all I see in my head. Asshole."

He laughs at me. He's used to sick cop humor. "Has my girl been good?" He reaches out to take her from my arms.

I'm always a little sad to let her go, but she is his daughter. I stand from the rocker and gently put her in his arms. She gurgles at her daddy. "She's been perfect. She just doesn't want to go to sleep."

"She's been doing that lately. She wants to stay up, or she wakes up in the middle of the night and wants to party, unfortunately. Soph and I are exhausted."

"I bet. Hey, listen to this..." I tell him about Roni's idea for my brand name.

"That's fucking genius," Hank says, laughing.

"I know! Why didn't we think of that?"

"Because we're not creative. At all."

We both laugh. I pat him on the back and head out. Done early, I head out to my car. "What do I do now? It's only eight thirty?" I say aloud. My first thought is of Roni. I wish we could hang out. I could call her. Nah, I'd better not. She was tired tonight. Plus, she'll get the wrong idea.

Maybe the Cubs are on television. Decision made; I head to my shome away from shome. I like my apartment. I call it a shome because it's actually right above the shop used for the family business, Flynn Construction. My dad, uncle, brother Keith, and cousin Ed own a construction company together. When they needed a building to house their equipment and for custom carpentry work, they purchased a building that came with an apartment on the second level. So, shop plus home equals shome. Clever, huh? Anyway, I moved in right after my relationship with Lauren came to a screeching halt. Shit hit the fan with that bitch, and I had to get as far away from her as I could.

My place isn't far from Hank's house in Edgewater. It's pretty big with an open loft vibe. The only walls in the place are around the bedroom and bathroom. Otherwise, the two thousand square feet are taken up by a small galley-style kitchen and an area I call Manland, which houses my television and a huge leather sectional that used to belong to my brother David. It was in his bachelor pad. His girlfriend, now wife, Jennifer, hated it, so his loss is my gain because it's a kick-ass couch.

You can't beat the rent either. I only have to pay utilities on the place, which aren't cheap. But it's cheaper than paying rent somewhere else. My dad and Keith think free rent is the price you pay for having live-in security. The tools they have in the shop are worth a fortune, and thieves love to steal tools, so this arrangement works for all of us.

When I get to my place, I strip down and throw on a pair of athletic shorts and an old Blackhawks T-shirt. Grabbing a beer and some leftover takeout, I launch myself onto my couch and tune into the Cubs in the bottom of the seventh. I made it just in time.

I eat, drink, and watch the game. I think about my day and evening. Before long I start to doze off thinking about my new brand name, Mick'sology. Sleep soon turns into a dream about Veronica. A sexy-as-fuck dream.

Roni and I are in the pool at the gym. It's just the two of us. The ceiling lights are off, but the lights underneath the water are on and the place glows. She's shining like a beautiful sea nymph as she does the backstroke in her lane. My eyes follow the line of her body, starting at her feet and moving up to her face. Her eyes are closed, and she has a smile on her face like she's enjoying herself in the water. My eyes make their way back down her body, stopping at her chest. Fuck. The woman is built. I stalk toward her through the water. I need to get to her faster, so I dive under the water and swim toward her. She's startled when my head breaks the water's surface only a foot from her.

"Mick? What are you doing here," she says in a husky whisper.

"I saw you swimming and thought I'd join you."

She backs away from me, but I keep moving closer to her.

She stops by the edge of the pool, having backed herself into the corner.

I move in front of her and cage her in with my arms. "Veronica, what are you doing here? This is my gym. Are you following me?" I ask, hoping the answer is yes.

"No. This is my gym too. Are you following me?"

"Yes."

She gasps.

I move in closer, so I can feel her body against mine. We're chest to chest, close enough to feel hearts beating fast and furiously. Her breathing speeds up as she's looks away. I reach out and take her chin in my fingers, turning her to me. "Look at me, Roni."

"No." She pulls away again.

"I said look at me."

She turns her head and looks up. Our eyes meet. "Baby, you're fucking beautiful," I say, leaning down.

The kiss is hotter than the one in the Uber. Her arms move around my neck, pulling herself closer. I feel her legs wrap around my waist. Now she knows what she does to me. I'm rock-hard. I deepen the kiss until it's all tongue. Fuck, this girl is hot. I move forward in the water, so she's pinned between the wall and me. I shift myself so my dick is pressing against her center and thrust upward. Goddamn, that feels good.

I pull away from the kiss. "Take the swimsuit off. Now."

She nods and reaches toward the straps on her Speedo. The thing is damn tight. I help her pull it down past her breasts, and as they pop from the confines of her suit, it's my turn to gasp.

"Magnificent," I groan. I've got big hands, but they're no match for her tits. As I slide my thumbs over her nipples, she arches into my hands, and I'm done for.

I lean down taking her left nipple into my mouth. I suck and lick and suck again. I pull her areola into my mouth and use my tongue to tickle her nipple. She's writhing in my arms. I need more. I move to her right breast while using my hands to push down the suit the rest of the way. Once it's past her hips, it slides off easily and floats to the bottom of the pool.

She slides her soft hand into my board shorts, pulling them down until my cock is finally free. Fucking finally. When her hand meets my cock, she grips it with just enough tension that all hell breaks loose.

"Baby, I want to fuck you. Now."

"I need you too. Now, Mick. I need you so bad."

Damn, I love it. I love how she says my name. I love that she told me she needs me. "Wrap your legs around me."

She wraps her thick, soft thighs around my waist, and it feels like heaven. I grasp her hips and thrust up into her tight pussy. We moan in unison.

"Tight, babe. Fuck."

"Don't stop, Mick. Please."

"I won't."

I fuck her hard. She's taking my thick cock like a champ. Her softness feels so good against me. I'm pumping into her so fast I come like a rocket inside her. She's screaming my name as she comes all over my cock. Her walls are squeezing so hard I may black out.

"Fuck, that was good!" I say, taking in big gulps of air.

She sighs. "It was perfect. God, Mick, we're going to make such beautiful babies together."

What the fuck? I jerk awake, pun intended, and launch myself off my couch. I've got come all over my hand and stomach as I sprint to my bathroom. Fucking *babies*? I ruined the best wet dream I've ever had with fucking baby bullshit. God, I'm such an idiot.

12

RONI

So far, Tuesday at the office is much better than Monday. At ten o'clock, my meeting with my boss and Chris is interrupted by a call from the security desk in the lobby of our building.

My boss hits the speakerphone button. "Yes?" he says gruffly.

"Delivery for Veronica McGonigall, sir."

For me? It must be something from one of our clients. I turn to Bill, who looks perturbed.

"Send whatever it is up and leave it in her office."

"Yes, sir." The receptionist hangs up quickly. It's no wonder, the boss sounded irritated. He gives me a look that I read as anger.

"I'm sorry, Bill. I have no idea what that could be."

Bill grumbles, then looks at me and asks, "What the hell's going on with EnerSport?"

EnerSport is a new, huge client for us. Bill's been stressing out big-time about them. I get why he's surlier than usual. "Well—"

I don't get to finish my thought because Chris has decided to interrupt me. Again. He's done it several times today. "Things are great. I've been handling everything."

"Excuse me? I—"

Chris ignores me as Bill turns his chair to face him. "I've been working closely with Owen's admin on this."

"I thought Roni was working this one." Bill looks at me, then back at Chris.

"Well, Owen wants the best." Chris shrugs.

What the hell is happening?

"Good. Great. Whatever it takes. Thanks for taking charge, Chris. Good man."

A few minutes later, we're dismissed, and I'm still speechless. Chris follows me to my office, chatting about the research and plans for EnerSport. Doing my best to ignore the backstabbing twit, I step into my office and see the most beautiful bouquet of flowers I've ever seen. It's a mixed bouquet of pink and yellow roses, lilies, carnations, baby's breath, and a tall, purple, cone-shaped flower I've never seen before. It's gorgeous. I pluck the card from its plastic holder, gingerly opening the flap of the small white envelope and read:

Thank you for last night. You're amazing, Veronica!

P.S. I had to search, but I finally found a florist that carried the flower called Veronica. They're the purple ones in your bouquet.

I hope you like them. Talk to you soon. M

"OH MY GOSH! That's so sweet," I mumble. There's a flower called Veronica? I had no idea. But what did I do last night that was deserving of such a gift?

Chris interrupts my thoughts. "Wow, who sent you flowers? A client?"

Why would he assume they're from a client? That's a douche thing to say. "No, they're from Mick."

"Who is Mick?" He stares at me for a second. "Oh, wait. The *bartender?*" he asks, sounding smug.

"If you mean *hot* bartender from Chrome, then yes. They're from him," I say, looking smug. See, I can do it too.

"What does the card say?"

"That's none of your business, Chris. It's personal."

"You're right; I'm sorry. I've no idea what got into me. Say, Veronica? Would you like to have lunch with me today? I meant to ask you but, well, we've been so busy with this product launch."

I shouldn't, not after that meeting today, but this is what I wanted, right? I wanted his attention, and this beautiful bouquet of flowers did exactly as Mick intended. Chris has finally asked me out. "Okay. That sounds good. Noon?" Why do I feel like this is a terrible idea?

"I'll pick you up." He makes a snorting sound, laughing at his own joke.

"I'll be here. See you then."

As soon as I see Chris's back disappear down the hall, I pick up my phone.

Me: OMG! The flowers are beautiful! Thank you, Mick! You didn't need to do that. But I have to say, it worked!

He responds several minutes later.

Mick: What worked?

Me: Chris saw them and immediately asked me out.

Mick: Oh, well, that's terrific. I'm glad it made him get off his ass.

Me: You're a genius.

Mick: Well, actually, I sent them to thank you for coming up with my brand name. But if you think I'm a genius, then it's a win-win.

What? He didn't send them to make Chris jealous? I lay my head back in my chair, sighing. "God, I'm so confused."

13

MICK

Well, fuck. I sent Roni flowers to thank her for helping me with my brand and because I couldn't stop thinking about her after that fucking dream in the pool. One thing's for sure, its intention wasn't to make that idiot Chris jealous. I guess I should be thankful, though. I was getting a bit too cozy with her, and it's best if she gets herself a man—another man—so she doesn't fall in love with me. That would suck. Not for me. For her.

On Thursday, I wake up bright and early at ten o'clock with a plan. I know that sounds like late, but I worked, again, on what was supposed to be my night off. My Wednesday bartender calls in more than he works. It's time I let him go. There are other people who want the gig, and I'm sick of having to cover his ass. I dress in my best pair of jeans. They're dark and aren't torn or ripped. I also don a shirt that has sleeves and buttons. Yeah, fancy, I know. I slip on my best Vans, grab my wallet and keys, and head out so I can get there by eleven.

As I enter the impressive building, I can't help thinking the huge vaulted ceilings in the lobby make me feel insignificant. Its walls are paneled with warm, dark wood. The shiny, marble floor has veins of grays and brown running throughout. The October light illuminates the entire space thanks to the floor-to-ceiling windows. It's a beautiful space—inviting and warm. I make my way to the reception desk and stand, waiting for the attractive young woman answering calls to help me.

As soon as she finishes with the call, she looks up and smiles. "Well, hello. What can I do for you?"

I should be interested in *this* girl, but I see her every night at Chrome—not her specifically, but it's the same girl. Sure, she's dressed more demurely for work, but I recognize a party girl when I see one. She's got on too much makeup, her auburn hair is sleek and shiny, and her dark red dress is too tight. She's a petite thing, and on any other day, I'd have her in my bed before nightfall, but not today.

"I'm here to see Veronica McGonigall?"

"Roni? Really? Oh, you must be a client; let me buzz her office." She taps away at her keyboard, picks up the receiver, and says, "Roni? This is Tracy in reception. You have a visitor. A client."

I'm not a fucking client. The girl didn't give me a chance to correct her. I lean over and whisper, "Tell her it's Mick. And I'm not a client. I'm her boyfriend."

The receptionist sputters, "Oh, I'm sorry, Roni. He says he's your boyfriend, Nick."

"Mick," I correct her. "With an M."

"Mick," she repeats. "Uh-huh... Oh, okay. I'll tell him." She looks up at me and says, "She'll be right down. You can have a seat over there until then." Stacy—or is it Tracy?—turns to answer another call.

I guess I just got the brush off. I sit in the area with a group of chairs and pick up a magazine to leaf through. I don't have to wait long.

"Mick?" Roni squeaks. "What are you doing here? Is everything okay?"

When I look up, my breath catches. Holy shit. Veronica in a dress is fucking mind-boggling. It's a dark purple color that looks perfect with her wavy blonde hair flowing down and around her neck, resting over one shoulder and down to her left breast. The dress is tight in all the right places. It's got a V-neck that shows just a hint of cleavage—not enough, if you ask me. It's snug around her breasts, and then it ties at the side of her waist, cinching that in perfectly. From there, it flows outward to a skirt that floats and moves around her. My eyes follow farther down her shapely legs to a pair of black stilettos with thin straps that cross over the top of her foot. Jesus, it's sexy as hell.

I look up again and notice she doesn't seem happy to see me. I'll be damned. It's not often I stop in to have lunch with a woman, but the times I have, they've been thrilled. So much so I was rewarded with a little action in an office or stairwell, and there was that one time—

"Mick?"

I walk toward her and say loud enough for the receptionist to hear, "Oh, hey, baby. I thought I'd come surprise my girl at work." I lean over and kiss her softly on the lips.

Roni's face turns a bright red hue.

It's adorable. I lean in and whisper in her ear, "I came to make your boyfriend jealous. Is that okay? I also thought I'd take you to lunch. If you have time, that is."

Her shoulders seem to relax, like she was relieved. "Of course, come on up. I'll show you where the magic happens," she says, giggling.

I reach for her hand and hold it all the way to the elevator, on the ride up to the sixth floor, and even as we walk down the hall. Might as well show everyone we're together, right? Word will get back to Chris *the Douche* soon enough.

"Here's my office," she says as she leads me into a tiny space at the end of the hall. Her office has a dim overhead light, a desk lamp, and a tall floor lamp in the corner, but it's still dark. I wonder if she likes it like that. I see the bouquet of flowers I sent her sitting on her filing cabinet. They look as good as I hoped they would when I ordered them over the phone.

"Do you want to sit down?" she asks nervously.

"I thought you'd show me around, you know, let Chris know I'm here."

"Oh, right. Great idea. Yes. Let me show you around," she says stiffly.

She seems nervous. Maybe I made the wrong call here. I should have asked her about her work environment or something before I just surprised her. What if they don't like visitors up here? Damn it. I'm second-guessing myself, and that's not me. Time to take back some of my resolve. As we leave her dinky office, I attempt to grasp her hand again, but she avoids it by running her fingers through her hair. It's okay, I'll get her hand again soon enough.

We stop by several offices, and she introduces me as "my friend, Mick" one too many times for my taste. Jesus, we've kissed more than once. I danced so close to her she could feel how hard I was. We aren't *just* friends. Christ. Besides, aren't we trying to make Chris jealous? I'm so fucking confused right now.

At one of the million cubicles on her floor, Roni stops. Then, stepping into the opening, says, "Trisha? You remember Mick from Chrome? He stopped by to say hello."

I stopped by to say hello? Why do I feel like she's trying to make Trisha think I'm there to see her? I sure as fuck hope not. I grab Roni's hand and bring it to my lips. "I decided to surprise my girl with a lunch date."

Trisha stands up, ignoring Roni's hand in mine and wraps

her arms around my neck for a hug. "That's so sweet. I'm so glad to see you again. Did you mention lunch?"

What the ever-loving fuck? "Yeah, I'm taking Roni to lunch. Alone."

"Oh, right," she titters. "I just assumed—"

"I know what you assumed," I growl. "Roni, let's keep moving. I came to spend time with you." Yeah, I know I sound like an asshole, but it had to be done.

When we leave Trisha's gray cube, Roni leans in and mutters, "Mick! Don't be such a jerk. I have to work with these people."

"Right. Sorry. I just didn't want Trisha to get attached."

Roni's irritated expression turns into a smile. When she giggles, I smile down at her. Damn, I love the sound of her laugh, even though I know it's from nerves. "Here's Chris's office. Let me knock first." She taps lightly on the door three times.

We hear a voice call out, "Enter."

She turns the knob and opens the door to a huge office with views of Chicago that would rival the best hotel in town.

"Damn. Nice office," I let slip out.

"Chris? You remember Mick? He came to visit us today."

Us? What is she doing? "I came to take you to lunch, babe." I turn to Chris. "She was anxious for me to see where she works, meet her colleagues, you know the drill."

"Right," Chris says, sounding irritated. He gets up from his huge glass-top desk and walks over to Veronica. Placing his hand on her arm, he says, "Roni? I thought you and I would go to lunch today?"

Is he for real? I watch as she takes a small step backward, just enough distance that Chris's hand falls away from her arm. Interesting.

"Oh, I had no idea."

"Sure, don't you remember? We were going to talk about the launch party."

"Party?" I say, maybe a bit too happily. "What party, baby?"

"Oh, the company is throwing a big party to celebrate a new client. An athletic wear company. It's no big deal."

Just then, Trisha walks into Chris's office. "What's no big deal?"

"The big party," I reply.

"The launch party? Oh, that's a huge deal—black tie and everything. Are you coming, Mick? Did Roni invite you? Because if she didn't, I need a date."

"I was going to invite him at lunch. I just hadn't had the chance." She turns to face me. "Besides, it's Saturday, so you probably have to work anyway, right?" Roni says, looking at me expectantly.

If I didn't know any better, I'd say she doesn't want me to go to this party. Nah, she's just nervous right now. I'm sure she wants me along. I'm fun. "I'm free. I can easily switch with someone. I run the place, remember? I wouldn't miss this for the world, angel." I lean down and kiss her cheek.

"Great," she mutters. "Just great."

Shit. I think she really doesn't want me there. I feel an unfamiliar thud in my chest. I'm hurt and, I've got to confess, surprised. My girl doesn't want me to go to her party.

14
———

RONI

I really don't want him at this launch party. I'm nervous
enough as it is without having to worry about whether or not
Mick is having a good time or if someone is trying to hit on him
—namely Trisha.

I'm organizing the entire thing, a task that landed in my lap
because no one else wanted to do it. Yeah, I'm *that* person at
work. The one people assume will never say no to shit like this.
It's okay. I enjoy this kind of stuff. I'm creative even though my
job is a bit structured. Maybe it'll mean more money for me
down the road. Who knows? So, instead of making sure Mick is
having a good time, I'll be busy checking on the catering, the
booze, the music, the keynote speakers, and other stuff like that.
But, heck, if Mick wants to dress up in a tuxedo for the night,
I'm not going to stop him. I suspect Mick in a tuxedo would be
worth the price of admission.

Mick follows me out of Chris's office and back to mine. "So,
is Chris your boss or something?"

"No, we're both market analysts."

"Has he been here longer than you?" he asks, pressing his
brows together.

"No. I've been here about four years, and he's been here about a year and a half."

"Seriously?"

"Yes, seriously. Why do you ask?" *Seriously, why is he asking?*

"How did he get the huge office with floor-to-ceiling windows and you got this tiny dark dungeon." He points to my office door as we get closer.

"I've never really thought about it, I guess. This has always been my office. I'm used to it. It's far enough away from all of the cubicles and work drama. I'm secluded. I like it."

"But his office is like three times the size of yours. His furniture is even nicer. He's got a couch in there!"

I laugh at him. This is a penis-size issue, not a furniture issue. "Did you ever build a fort out of a blanket and chairs when you were young?"

"Of course. Why do you ask?"

"I did it all the time. I loved feeling cocooned and cozy. This office makes me feel like that. It's cool and quiet. It's perfect for me. Chris always has people in his office. What they talk about in there is a mystery. I guess he's just more social than I am. I like my privacy."

"I guess. It still doesn't seem fair."

I smile at Mick to disguise some of my true feelings, because it isn't fair. I wasn't given a chance to have that larger office. Hell, I didn't know it was going to be available. Chris grabbed it before anyone else had the opportunity. But I reassure Mick, saying, "I probably could have had that office if I'd asked for it, but I didn't want it." I didn't. Honest. I love my tiny office.

Mick sits in my one and only chair. I don't need a couch because I have that chair. It was my parents' chair once. It sat in their living room. I don't think anyone ever actually sat in it back then—no one used the living room—so it's like new. It's over-stuffed and cozy, like my office.

Mick leans back and smiles. "This is a great chair. I'm glad you have this, at least."

Ignoring his little dig about my office, I sit behind my desk. "Well, let me do a few things, and we'll go to lunch. How does that sound?"

"Sounds good. You do your thing, babe. I'll just observe."

Observe? Crap. I've got no choice, though. I have several calls to make related to the launch party before I can leave, so I let him observe. At twelve thirty, I'm ready to go.

"I'm impressed, Veronica."

"Oh, yeah? What impresses you?"

"You do. You're smart, professional, funny, and beautiful," he says, leaning over to kiss the top of my head. His arm is wrapped around my neck as we walk out of my building. He ruins it by adding, "I'm glad we're friends."

"Me too." I am glad we're friends. Really. I am.

It's just my feelings about him and about Chris are sort of confusing right now. Chris has lost some luster ever since the meeting in Bill's office. I no longer feel like we're a good team at work, so picturing us as a team at home is not possible anymore. Hell, I don't even trust him anymore. He's up to something.

As for Mick Flynn? He's the most confusing man I've ever met. One minute he wants to kiss me, the next he wants to friend-zone me so hard it hurts. My feelings for him have evolved, and I need for that evolution to stop. Lusting after or even thinking about Mick Flynn is a terrible idea. It won't end well. I'll be hurt like I've been hurt in the past, only this time it'll be worse because I've gone and done the unthinkable. I've pictured what our kids would look like. They'd be beautiful, in case you were wondering. And thinking like that, hoping like that, is like putting a nail in my own coffin.

15

———

MICK

I take Roni to lunch at one of my favorite burger joints in the city. M Burger is a fast food place, and while I know I should take her somewhere fancier, the food is really delicious, and neither of us has the time to do something more formal. There are five or six locations of M Burgers around the city, and this one is close to her office.

"You've probably been here before...."

"No, I haven't. I've heard they have good burgers, though."

"It's great. Get anything you want. My treat."

"No, Mick. It's okay. I can pay my own way."

"I invited you; my treat. No arguments," I scowl at her, then laugh. I'm messing with her, but I'm still buying.

"What's good here?" she asks timidly.

"I like the Hurt Burger or the Old-Fashioned Cheeseburger. Considering you drink Old Fashioneds, I think you might want the latter."

She smiles and giggles. "That's true. Okay. I'll get that but no onion, please."

"You want regular fries or cheese fries?" *Say cheese fries. Say cheese fries. I love those damn things.*

"Oh, no fries. I'm already eating so many calories I'll have to skip dinner."

"No fucking way, Veronica," I snap. "We've got to try the cheese fries. They're so good."

"I'm sure they are, it's just—"

"Please? I'm trying to thank you here for helping me with Mick'sology."

"You already sent me beautiful flowers, Mick."

"That wasn't enough. So, please? Get the cheese fries? I'm sure I'll help you out with those since one order isn't enough for me." I give her my version of a cheeky grin. "Pretty please?"

She smiles nervously at me. "All right. Sure. Sounds good."

"Chocolate or vanilla?" I ask next.

"Chocolate or vanilla what?"

"Malt. Chocolate or vanilla."

She's shaking her head already.

"And don't say no. Pick or I will." I smirk at her because we both know she won't win that argument.

Sighing, she says, "Chocolate. What else is there?"

My sentiment exactly. I add two chocolate malts to our order, and we make our way to the table. Once our number is called, I jog up and grab our tray. I pick up extra napkins and plastic silverware on my way back to the seat. I set all the food on the table and put the tray in an empty booth. "Are you ready for the best burger in the city?"

Roni laughs and nods. When she takes a bite, she moans.

Jesus. It's a deep, raspy moan that makes my dick twitch. Thank God I didn't get her an ice cream cone. If she were licking a cone, I don't think I could have made it through lunch without jerking off in the men's room.

Taking my mind off my poor dick, I ask, "So, you were supposed to have lunch with Chris?"

She shakes her head because her mouth is full, then swallows and takes a drink of her malt. "No. He never mentioned lunch today. He was just acting macho or something."

"Macho? Is this the 70s?" I chuckle.

"We had lunch on Tuesday. It was fine."

"Fine? Wow, high praise indeed. What was 'fine' about it?"

"No, it was good. We went to a deli across the street from the office. It's a very busy place, so we couldn't really talk. We had to stand at one of those long, skinny tables by the window, and he spent the entire time asking me about the launch party plans, about the new client, and quizzing me about some other work stuff. It wasn't a date kind of lunch. It was a work-lunch. He probably expensed it," she grumbled on the last sentence.

"Well, that sucks. What a dick."

That makes her laugh. Hard. She throws her head back and nearly chokes on the fry she just put in her mouth. Coughing, she calms down and says, "Yeah, he's a dick. I'm unsure how I feel about him now. I should let it play out, though, right?"

"Right. You need to let it play out." She needs to let it play out. She shouldn't set any hopes on me, on us, no matter how much I like the girl. I'm not good enough for her. She deserves someone who isn't broken and bitter. She deserves someone who deserves her.

16

RONI

"That really was the best burger I've ever had, Mick. Thanks for taking me."

I'll never go again. I'm pretty sure I consumed twenty thousand calories during lunch. Calories I'll never be able to burn off, ever. At least Mick didn't give me crap about eating junk food. I've been on dates before where the guy tried to order for me. "She'll have the vegetable salad, no dressing." Yeah, so this was much better. Mick was encouraging me to eat. It was a nice change.

"I'm glad you liked it. Well, I'd better go. Duty calls. I'll talk to you, okay?"

"Okay. Thanks again." I pat him on the arm.

He captures my hand and raises it up to his mouth. "I had a great time. Thanks for playing along."

Why did he have to say that? I'm sure he can see the disappointment on my face, but I pull myself together and smile. "Sure thing. Thanks for helping me with Chris. I appreciate it." But, honestly, I don't want Chris anymore. Now I want something more, something better.

Back at my office, I open the door in time to see Chris sitting at my desk, looking through my papers. *What the hell?* "Chris? Can I help you find anything?" *What the hell is he doing in my office? Didn't I lock my door?* My body stiffens, as does the hair on the back of my neck. There's something rotten in Denmark. I pretend to smile as I scan my office. *What is he up to?*

"I was looking for a pen. I wanted to leave you a note," he says quickly.

I reach over and pull a pen out of the holder near my computer. There's also a pad of scratch paper next to it. I tear off a piece and hand it to him.

"Oh, heck, I didn't see those."

Why is he acting so nervous? "Since I'm here, what is it you wanted to tell me?"

"I wanted to ask you out. On a date," he smirks.

"Oh, well. That sounds good, but we've got the launch this weekend, and I've got a Halloween party the following Saturday. What if we do it in November? We can talk about it later. Sound good?" I'm rushing the words, wanting him out of my office.

"Of course. That makes sense." He stands, stepping away from my desk. "We'll plan it after all of this event stuff is over."

I see sweat at his receding hairline. He's lying but doing a convincing job of hiding his true intent. "Sounds good, Chris. Okay, well, I've got to get back to it. Lots still to plan for Saturday."

"Right. Let me know if you need any help."

"I will. Thank you, Chris," I try to say as sincerely as possible. But the truth is that I won't be asking for any help from Chris. Ever. Sighing, I sit down at my desk and stare. One good thing that came out of me catching him in my office? I no longer have romantic feelings about Chris. I'm not sure I have *any* feelings for him except for feeling wary. Chris isn't who I thought he was, and I guess neither am I.

I look around. "What was he looking for?" It's so bizarre because I usually lock my office when I leave. I do have sensitive materials in here about our clients that, if they were leaked to the public, could be damaging. "I'm always so careful." I scan my desk again. I'm not a tidy worker. When I'm knee-deep in a project, everything is out and spread across my desk, but before I leave each day, I straighten up. I lift papers and check the tabs of the file folders on my desk. There's a large folder related to the new client and one for the plans of the party. Maybe he looked at my notes. But why?

I decide to shut off my suspicious nature and get back to work. This party is going to be the death of me. Shit! I invited Mick to the party. What if he doesn't fit in? Does he even know what black tie is? I know that makes me sound like a snob, but the guy is a bartender. I pick up my phone. I'm going to give him the chance to back out, let him off the hook. I know he thinks he's doing this to help me get Chris, so if I tell him I'm no longer interested, he won't feel obliged.

Me: You really don't need to come to the party with me Saturday. Thanks for playing along, though.

See how I used *his* words just then?

Mick: I wasn't playing along. I'm looking forward to it.

Me: Are you sure? Because I no longer need any help with Chris.

Shit!

Mick: Oh? Why not? Did he finally ask you out?

Me: No. He's not for me.

Mick: Why not?

Me: Long story. I'll tell you about it another time. But it means you're off the hook for the party.

Mick: Tell me about it at the party. Send me all the details like... when should I pick you up?

Me: Okay. I'll forward the details to you, but just meet me there. I've got to be there early in the day for setup. I'll change at the hotel.

Mick: Gotcha. I'll meet you there. Hey, before you go, listen to this one... Three guys go to a ski lodge, but there aren't enough rooms, so they have to share a bed. In the middle of the night, the guy on the right wakes up and says, "I had this wild, vivid dream of getting a hand job!" The guy on the left wakes up, and unbelievably, he's had the same dream too.

Me: **groan** Yeah? What does the third guy say?

Mick: Then the guy in the middle wakes up and says, "That's funny, I dreamed I was skiing!"

Me: LOL. Seriously. LOL. That was a good one.

Me: Okay, my turn. Here's a good one: A man goes to a $10 hooker and contracts crabs. When he goes back to complain...

Mick: This ought to be good.

Me: ...the hooker laughs and says, "What do you expect for $10? Lobster?"

I wait. I set my phone down and jump back to work on the party planning.

Mick: Oh my God, Roni. That was awesome. I had to stop typing to laugh. You win that round.

Me: I'm glad you liked it. Thanks for lunch today, BTW.

Mick: You're welcome, beautiful. Get back to work.

Beautiful? I wish I didn't love it when he called me that. I'm going to hate it when this is over.

Me: Okay. I'll send you the party deets. Have a good day.

Mick: ;)

The rest of the day is filled with phone calls, emails, and meetings. Before I leave, I send Mick the information about the launch party and, for the first time in a long time, I'm excited. I've got a date, and it's with Mick Flynn.

17

___

MICK

When I arrive at the hotel where the party is being held, I stop in front of a mirror in the lobby to make sure my tie is straight and my hair isn't crazy. I rented a penguin suit at a tux shop near my shome. I went with a classic black tux, white shirt, and black bow tie. I used some product in my hair to make it stay put. It's in a knot at the back of my head right above the collar of my shirt. I considered getting my hair cut off for this but decided that was too drastic.

I'm early to this little showdown so I can help Veronica if she needs it. I know about planning parties like this thanks to my time at Chrome. Stepping into the ballroom, I'm taken aback. The place is sparkling. Now, generally, I wouldn't have noticed—or cared—but since I know Roni planned this, I make a point to see all she's done. The room is huge with at least fifteen enormous chandeliers hanging from the ceiling. There are thirty-five or forty tables all covered in white cloth with accents of black and silver. I recall EnerSport's logo is black, white, and silver. Clever girl.

I scan the room looking for her. I'm sure she's running

around making sure everything is perfect. I stride toward the bar and buffet tables to see if she's there. I see waiters, a bartender, kitchen staff, and there... I spot the back of a woman in a long black dress. Her hair is up in a soft twisted bun intertwined with braids on the back of her head. I see tendrils of hair down her back and on the side of her face.

When she turns around, I see a look of concentration on her face. She doesn't see me yet, but holy shit! That dress is... amazing on her. It's classy and sexy at the same time. The top half is lace. It looks see-through, but as I get closer, I can tell it's not skin but some kind of flesh-colored fabric. The sleeves go to her elbows, but the part that takes my breath way is the neckline. It's a deep V-neck. Her breasts. Jesus. They're perfect.

The skirt is solid black and starts right below her breasts. There's an opening sliced up the left side of the dress so when she starts to walk, I get a glimpse of creamy white leg. She's wearing red fuck-me heels that match her lips and make me salivate. She looks amazing. I lift my hand, giving a small wave to get her attention. At first, she looks right past me, but her eyes move back and her jaw drops open. Yeah, I look good too.

Walking toward me, she gives me a million-watt smile. "Mick? Is that you?" She giggles.

"In the flesh. You look amazing, Roni," I say, sliding my right hand to her waist. I move my left to her opposite hip and pull her toward me, then lean down and kiss her lightly on her ruby red lips. "Fucking stunning, baby," I whisper in her ear right before I place a soft kiss there. Jesus, she even smells amazing.

She blushes. I watch the flush run from between her breasts, up her neck, and into her cheeks. She's taken my breath away. I feel things I've never felt before. Sure, my dick likes what he sees—who wouldn't?—but the part that's new is the fucking drum corps in my chest beating so hard I feel like I need to lean on something for support. Even though I've never felt it before, I think I know what it is. It's *feelings*. I'm getting feelings for this girl, and that's a fucking terrible idea.

"You look really good," she says breathlessly. "You clean up really well, Michael Flynn."

"Yeah, well, I'm not a complete Neanderthal. I can get myself dressed up from time to time."

"And you're here early."

"I thought I'd see if you needed any help."

"Aww, thank you so much. I could use your help. Since it's your area of expertise, could you go over and check on the bar setup. They've got a new banquet manager here, and I'm not confident she knows what she's doing. This party is a big deal to my company. I need it to go off without a hitch."

"On it," I say, then stride over to the main bar.

There are several smaller bars set up in the other corners of the large space, but this one is the one that'll get the most traffic. As I'm looking at the wine selection, liquors, mixers, and glassware, a young woman moves into the bar area. "Can I help you? We're not actually open yet, but I can get you something." She winks.

"Nah, my girl over there asked me to come over and make sure you've got everything set up over here," I say, pointing to Roni.

She looks at me, then at Roni, and back to me. "Really? She's *your* girl?" She shakes her head and mutters, "I'll be damned."

I ignore the comment because I don't get it. "I noticed you don't have any garnishes out. You going to get limes, olives—"

"Oh, shit. I forgot!"

Before she runs off, I add, "What about your top-shelf liquors. This group is going to ask for those."

"Fuck! Oops, sorry." She blushes. "I didn't mean to cuss, but I had those on my list for the new manager. I've been so busy setting up, I didn't notice. Thanks, I've got this now," she says, stomping off toward the door that will take her behind the scenes.

I saunter off toward the other three bar areas and check them out as well. Those don't need top-shelf liquors. People who drink those will know to go to the main bar, but the three smaller bar stations don't have garnishes either. After I remind them, they scramble around getting what they need before the party starts.

I make my way over to Roni and see her with a small group of people. I see the thin brunette from her office standing next to the douchebag, Chris, and the other woman I met at Chrome. Brenda? I don't remember her name. I move up beside Veronica and place my arm around her waist.

She jumps at my touch. "Mick. You remember Trisha and Chris, and you met Barb at Chrome a few weeks ago."

"Sorry I missed your surprise visit on Thursday. I had an appointment." She winks.

"Yeah, me too," I mutter. What is it with these chicks? Can't they see I'm with Roni?

"My, my, my, Mick, you look amaaazing," coos Trisha. She steps close to me and runs her hands up my chest, grasping my jacket lapels as she looks up at me and flutters her big, fake eye lashes.

Those look stupid. I pull her hands from my jacket. "Thanks, you too." I'm lying. Sure, she's dressed up in a brown dress that sort of reminds me of burlap, except that it's sparkly. Truth is, none of these women can hold a candle to Veronica. She's the star tonight.

I look over at the other chick, Barb. She looks marginally better than Trisha in a dark red dress. It's fitted around her waist and shows off a decent amount of tittage. So, that's good. But Chris? Oh, my man Chris looks like a complete douche. He's wearing a tux just like I had to wear to my brother David's wedding. The jacket is blue and black plaid, the vest is blue, and the pants are black. He's wearing a plaid bowtie, but it's red. Not a good look, dude. He's got gel shit in what's left of his hair, and it's slicked back. I think he's trying to pull off a Don Draper look from Madmen, but it's a fail.

"Don't you think Veronica did a fantastic job with this party?" I ask the group, running my hand up and down her back as I praise her.

She blushes.

Chris scoffs, Trisha scowls, and Barb nods in agreement.

"She has! You have, Roni. It's beautiful," Barb says. "It's so clever the way you used the company logo throughout."

I hadn't really noticed the logo; it's subtle. But now I see it projected with hidden lights throughout the room. It's on the floor, on the wall behind the buffet setup, and there are logo cutouts on each table. Nice touch. I lean over and kiss her cheek. "This place looks stellar, babe."

She smiles at me and then at the group. Trisha's still scowling, go figure, but Chris is preoccupied. I turn to see what he's looking at and whisper in Roni's ear, "Who's that?"

She turns too and sees three men and one woman walk into the ballroom. "That's the owner of my company, Bill Phillips, and his wife Janice. The other man next to her is Owen McCormick, CEO of EnerSport, the shoe company and new client we're honoring tonight. I don't recognize the third guy," she whispers.

Chris had already made a beeline for them and is shaking hands with each of them. I remember his handshake; it's moist, weak, and there are too many pumps. They're smiling at him, but I can tell they aren't impressed.

"You should go over there and welcome them." I place pressure on her lower back to propel her forward.

"I hate doing that stuff. It makes my palms sweat." She laughs.

"I'll go with you. Introduce me as Michael." I take her hand in mine and lead her over to the people she hopes to impress.

We stop in front of the group and wait for Chris to stop pandering. When he finally stops talking, the three men turn to Veronica. I can see appreciation in their eyes when they see her dress. They're subtle about it, but they're checking her out. Janice, who I'd guess is about fifty years old, has her eyes on me. I've seen that look before. She's eyeing me like I'm dinner.

Before Roni has a chance to speak, the owner of her company raises his hand to shake hers. "Roni, it's so nice to see you. Chris was just telling me how hard you two have worked to get this going."

"The two of us?" she says, dazed. I feel her back stiffen beneath my palm.

"He told me how he renegotiated the price of the space. Saved me twenty-five percent off the top, didn't you, Christopher?"

I turn to Chris. He's smiling like a fucking idiot. When the three men and the woman turn back to Roni, I see Chris smirk. He's lying.

"Now, sweetheart, he did tell us what a good job you did with the decorations," Owen McCormick from the shoe company says condescendingly.

Sweetheart?

"I think the lights you designed are the best part of this whole room," Janice says, turning to Chris.

He smiles proudly. "What can I say, I'm a genius."

The group laughs at his stupid joke. I look down and see

Roni's hands twisting into her black skirt. She's tugging on it so hard I think it might tear.

"And who do we have here?" asks the boss's wife, leering at me now.

Roni's not ready to speak, I guess. I raise my hand to take hers. "I'm Veronica's boyfriend, Michael."

"Boyfriend? How lucky for you," she says, looking at Roni. "How in the world did you make that happen?"

Roni clears her throat and looks at the woman. "I keep wondering that myself. Can you excuse me?" she says, turning and moving quickly toward the lobby.

"It was nice meeting you all," I say, then turn to follow Roni.

She's stomping toward the entrance at a fast clip, but I catch up. I reach out and take her hand in mine. She jerks it away, then looks up at me. Her face is red, and there are tears at the corners of her eyes. "I'm sorry. I didn't realize it was you."

I take her hand again and lead her over to a semi-secluded corner. "What's wrong? What happened?"

She wipes away a tear. "Chris. It's... he did none of this." She lifts her hand, letting me know she means this whole party.

"What?"

"When we got back from lunch on Thursday, I caught him in my office rifling through my papers. When I asked him what he was doing, he said he wanted to leave me a note. He wanted to ask me out."

I pull her closer to me, so I can wrap my arms around her waist. "And? You don't think that's why he was there?"

"I was suspicious at the time, but I couldn't figure out what he was looking for. Now I know."

"What was it?"

"The cost—numbers and information about this party. I had a lot of notes, notes that outlined everything from the rental of all of the crystal vases from the partner of our human resources director as well as those overhead projectors. The main thing was the notations of the renegotiated price of the venue and food. He also must have seen my sketch for the graphic designer who made the transparencies for me for these light graphics on the walls and on the tables."

"So, he did nothing?"

"Nothing," she mumbles.

"That fucker! I should kick his ass. That's complete bullshit. Why didn't you say anything?"

"I froze up. I was shocked. Besides, they'd just think I was trying to take away his thunder. I'm not like that."

"Roni, babe, it's not right—Chris, taking credit for this." I use my finger to lift her chin, so I can see her green eyes. There are tears in her lashes.

"I know it's not right, but there's nothing I can do about it now. I'll deal with it on Monday. To be honest, I just want to go home, but there's a ton of stuff to do after the party."

"Like what? I can help."

She smiles at me. "Like take down the projectors around the room. There are three of them. I was here at eight in the morning today climbing up a huge ladder, getting them set up.

"Why didn't you call me? I would have helped you. You shouldn't be up on a ladder like that, anyway."

"Don't you start. I can do anything you can do, Mick Flynn. God, I can't believe he only gave me credit for the decorations. What a flucking tool."

"Flucking?"

"Yeah, flucking." She laughs.

God, she's so beautiful. Without thinking, I lean down and kiss her lips. They're still cherry red and glossy. She's got a great mouth. When my lips meet hers, I feel it down my spine. This woman drives me crazy. I turn my head and slide my tongue inside her mouth. It's probably inappropriate to have my tongue down her throat at this fancy party, but who the fuck cares?

She moans as I reach around and pull her into me. My dick is getting harder by the second, and I'm sure she can feel it against her. I'd love to grab her ass and lift her up, her legs wrapping around me, but that's not going to happen here. Not tonight, anyway.

18

―――

RONI

I know it's probably unprofessional to be kissing Mick like this in plain sight, but I don't care. He kisses like it's his job. I wrap my arms around his neck, so I can press closer to him. He moans when my breasts press against his chest. He's definitely a guy who likes boobs. Lucky for me, I've got that in spades.

A throat clears behind me. The sound pulls me from the private moment Mick and I were having. I turn and see Barb. I remove my arms from around his neck and slide back from my tiptoes. Even in heels, I had to step up for the kiss. "Hey, Barb."

"I just heard what he did, Roni. That was a total dick move."

"I couldn't agree more," interrupts Mick.

"Trisha knew he was going to do it too. She looked like the cat that ate the canary when you were all over there talking. She told me what Chris was doing."

"She say why?" asks Mick.

"Chris is just super ambitious."

"I'm ambitious too, but I wouldn't take credit for someone else's work," I snap.

"Normal people don't do things like that, Roni. But Chris isn't normal," says Barb.

"What did I ever see in him?"

"No idea," Barb and Mick say in unison.

I laugh at that. They're right, of course. "Well, the show must go on. Time to check with the caterers to see if they're restocking food."

"Let Chris do that," suggests Mick.

"I can't. He doesn't know what's going on, the timing of things. I won't let this night get ruined over all of this personal drama. I'd feel terrible."

Mick takes my hand and leads me back to the party. The food is well stocked, and people are eating. I look over and see Chris sitting at the main table with Bill and Janice and the shoe company executives. Hells bells, he really is mercenary. He must have switched nametags because the VP of sales, Deborah Adams, and her husband were supposed to be at that table.

I look around the space and see Deb sitting at table number eleven, in the back. I make eye contact with her and her expression lets me know that she's not pleased. I mouth, "I'm sorry." But it doesn't seem to appease her. I let go of Mick's hand. "I'll be right back. Will you get me a glass of wine or something? I need a drink."

I weave through the sea of tables toward Deb. She and I have lunch together once a month. We've talked. She knows the kind of person I am. She has to know I'd never diss her like that. "Deb, I'm sorry. I had you at the head table. There must have been a glitch."

"Does the glitch have a name?"

"Chris Smith," I deadpan.

"I thought so. That fucking asswipe," she mutters. "I can't stand that guy. He's worthless. I'll get him back, my pretty. Just you wait and see," she says, still scowling.

I believe her. "He must have done it when he first arrived. I didn't see the switch. And that's not all."

"Oh, hell. What'd he do?" she groans.

"He just took credit for this party: the planning, budget, graphics on the walls—everything. Oh, well, he told Bill and Janice that I decorated the place. Like a good little woman."

"That fucker!" Deborah is a card-carrying member of NOW, the National Organization for Women, and has been since 1973. Seriously, she literally has a card with her name on it.

"I know. The sad part is he gets the credit, and I still have so much to do tonight. I'll be here until morning."

"Why? What do you need to do?"

I explain about taking down the projectors, closing out the bill, taking the centerpieces back to the office, things like that.

Deborah's face lights up. "Oh my God, I know what you should do."

After hearing her plan, I grimace. "I can't do that. It would be wrong. He'll screw it up, anyway."

"So. If he wants credit for this spectacular party, he should get the blame if something goes wrong."

I sigh. "I'll think about it."

"By the way, dearie. Who's the arm candy?"

"His name is Mick. We're just friends."

"It looked like more than friends over there in the corner." She points to the spot near the entrance where Mick kissed me.

I blush and roll my eyes. "I'm sorry. I don't know what's going on with him. It's confusing. One minute he wants to be best friends, the next he's kissing me."

"Enjoy the ride, Roni. Enjoy the ride," she says, patting my arm. "Then, give me all the details. You know how I love good porn." She cackles.

I laugh too and look up to see Mick staring at me. He lifts up a short glass. My man got me an Old Fashioned. *My man? Uh-oh.*

I walk toward him. "Is that what I think it is?" I say, smiling at Mick.

"You deserved a drink. So, I made you your favorite. Plus, we should eat? I'm starving, and the food looks good."

"Sure."

At the buffet table, we grab our plates and make our way through the line. I tried to choose a wide variety of menu options. With this many people from P&P Inc. and from our client's company, I'm sure there are a few vegetarians and others with dietary restrictions. I created labels to place next to each dish with ingredients, nutrition information, and a special designation for anything that was purely vegetarian. Our client is a sporting goods company, after all.

Sitting at the table farthest from the main table, we eat. "Damn, this is good, Roni. Did you choose everything?"

"I did. I'm glad you like it."

"So, what's the matter? You don't like it? Because you're not eating; you're just moving things around your plate with your fork."

"My dress is tight. If I eat, it'll be more uncomfortable." Plus, I'm wearing the most uncomfortable pair of Spanks known to man.

"What's really on your mind?" he asks between bites of mashed potatoes.

"Deborah thought I should stick Chris with all of the work after the party tonight."

"Seems fair," he agrees. "He did take credit for shit he didn't do. He should pay for that."

"I guess," I say absently.

"Want to dance?" Mick asks, wiping off his face as he stands.

I'm surprised, to say the least. The dance floor is in the center of the room. I've watched couples take a turn on it through the evening, but I didn't figure Mick for a dancing kind of guy. I'm not going to pass up the chance. "I'd love to."

He takes me by the hand to the center of the small dance floor. We don't have a live band, but the DJ is pretty good. Most of the music is slow and mellow. Mick wraps his left arm around my waist, pulling me into him. He takes my left hand in his right and raises it up, taking a step, then leading me around the room.

A laugh escapes me. "You know how to dance?"

"Of course. Two years of ballroom dance lessons when I was young."

"Seriously?"

"Yep. We all had to do it. My mom is a firm believer that we should know how to dance properly."

"I think I love your mom." I giggle as I rest my cheek against his chest.

"She's somethin', that's for sure," he says with a chuckle.

We dance the night away, and it's fantastic. As the party starts to wind down, I turn to Mick. "Ready to do this thing?"

"Hell yeah, I'm ready." He takes my hand and leads me to the head table.

Chris is still there talking to Mr. Phillips. In addition to Chris and Bill are Janice, Deborah, Trisha, and Owen. We walk up to stand between Chris and Bill.

I place my hand on Bill's chair and lean down. "I'm sorry to interrupt...," I say smiling. "I just wanted to tell you that we're leaving now."

There are weak mutterings around the table like, "Oh no, don't go." I ignore it and turn to Chris, then say loud enough for everyone to hear, "Chris, thank you so much for letting me help you with this party." I smile brightly. "I learned so, so much."

I reach into my purse and speak right to Bill. "Chris was so smart. He thought we should separate the duties. I'd set up, and he'd stay and tear down. He even made us both this checkoff list." I pull out two sheets of paper with a single-spaced list I'd typed for myself, so I could remember everything I needed to do after the party. "I hope you all enjoyed the evening. I'll see you at work on Monday." When I finally look up at the others at the table, Deborah is laughing so hard she's crying. Both Chris and Trisha look like they want to kill me, and Janice can't take her eyes off Mick.

She stands up and, with hips swaying, makes her way to him. "I'm sorry you're leaving, Michael. I didn't get a chance to talk to you. Alone."

"Maybe next time," he says, looking at me. "It was nice meeting you, ma'am."

Oh no he didn't! Ma'am? That's like calling her grandma. She isn't pleased. I give Mick a panicked look. He sighs and leans down and whispers in her ear. Her face lights up. She squeezes his arm with her hand and returns to her seat.

I walk over and grab his hand. "Let's go, dear." We get far away from the head table when I ask, "What the hell did you say to her?"

Mick chuckles. "I may have mentioned that her ass looked great in that dress."

I gasp. "You did not!"

"I did too. I knew I had to salvage the 'ma'am' comment. Besides, her ass was all right."

"All right?"

"Just all right, baby. Nothing like yours, though," he says, reaching around to run a hand over my ass.

I squeak when I feel his hand. "God, Mick, you're such a tease." I giggle.

"Who's teasing?"

Surprised, I look up at him, and he starts to laugh, hard.

It wasn't that funny. God, this thing with him is so confusing.

19

———

MICK

I wake up early Sunday morning to get ready for my double shift to make up for Saturday night, but before I leave for work, I straighten up my place and throw in a load of laundry. I want to take the tux back on my way to work, so I don't forget to. As I'm walking out the door, I see a text from Veronica.

Roni: Thanks for going to the party with me last night, Mick.

Me: I'm glad to help. I had a great time. Any word on the clean-up from last night?

Roni: I had fun too. Thanks for being my date. Well, not date. You know what I mean.

And no, I haven't heard anything about Chris.

Roni: I still feel bad about leaving everything for him to do. Not about him, but I am responsible for a lot of the equipment and centerpieces. What if he screws that up?

Me: I *was* your date. For the night, anyway.

Ignoring his last sentence, I change the subject.

Roni: How's your day going?

Me: It's just getting started, so shitty. LOL. I've got to work a double today. At least the first shift will be mostly office/paper work.

Roni: Okay, maybe this will turn your day around. I just did an interweb search for bartender jokes.

A guy walks into a bar, orders 12 shots, and starts drinking them as fast as he can.

The bartender asks, "Dang, why are you drinking so fast?"

The guy says, "You would be drinking fast too if you had what I have."

The bartender asks, "What do you have?"

The guy says, "75 cents."

I start laughing, and I can't stop.

Me: Roni, Roni, Roni. I definitely needed that. That's actually happened to me before. It's still funny, though.

Roni: Okay, well, I'll talk to you later. Hope your day runs smoothly, I do.

Me: Did you just say that last part in Yoda speak?

Roni: Never tell, I won't.

Me: Goddamn, you make me laugh.

Damn, this girl makes me feel better every time I talk to her. When I'm with her, I feel... more alive and optimistic. Maybe I should dive into something with Roni. I shake my head, talking to myself. "No, Mick. She's too good for you."

Me: Before I forget, what are you doing tomorrow night?

I wait for a few minutes for a response.

Roni: Working, then nothing.

Me: Wanna babysit the most awesome baby in the world?

Roni: Oh, you can't? You need someone to fill in? I can do that.

Me: No, babe. I thought we'd babysit together. It'll be fun. We could watch a movie and chill.

Roni: I'd love to. Where and when?

I text her the time and the address. Shit, I just invited her into the other part of my life. That was probably a mistake. I've just invited her to meet the most important person in my life. I'm letting her in. All I need to do is keep telling myself that we're just friends. I'm pretty sure it's what she wants too. Otherwise, wouldn't she say something? Shit, I've kissed her repeatedly. If she wanted more from me, wouldn't she do or say something? She must not want me, and that's probably for the best. Probably. Maybe.

20

———

RONI

At work on Monday, things on our floor are quiet. Too quiet. I had already scheduled a half-day off because I thought I'd be wiped out from the party. Since I got a full night's sleep Saturday night, it was just a bonus. The vibe on my floor is uncomfortable. Something is stirring, and I don't think I like it. I walk into my office and see my phone blinking. I hit the message button and wait.

"Roni, it's Bill Phillips. Please meet me in conference room B as soon as you get in today. Thanks." Click.

Oh, shit.

I set my purse and coat down and walk out the door with only my computer case. I may need it for notetaking or perhaps for distraction at this meeting. I slowly walk down to the conference room, dread pooling in my belly. This is going to suck. I'm about to pull the door open when I hear voices from within. More than one person? I open the door and step in. At the table are Bill Phillips, Chris, Trisha, Deborah, Martha from Human Resources, and Bill's administrative assistant, Gloria, who's taking notes. Fuck!

"Hi, everyone. What's going on?"

Bill clears his throat. "Ms. McGonigall, nice of you to join us today."

"I took the morning off. It's been on the schedule for weeks. Someone could have called...."

"Is it true that you planned the entire party on your own?"

I look around the room, hoping for a clue about this meeting. "Yes. I planned and organized the party. Alone."

"So, when Mr. Smith here"—he points to Chris—"decided to take credit for your hard work, you just let him do it? You didn't want to speak up, defend yourself?"

"I didn't think causing a scene in front of our new client was appropriate. I'd planned to talk to you today."

"Okay, I agree with that. That was the right move. But, you could have pulled me aside during the night and told me."

"Would you have believed me? You seemed eager to believe that Chris was the star of the evening," I snap.

"We'll never know, Roni. You never gave me a chance."

"I'm sorry. That's true," I say, lowering my head.

"So, at the end of the night, when you came to the table with the list of things to do after the party ended, you knew Chris had no idea what needed to be done," Bill asks, already knowing the answer.

"Yes, but my list was incredibly detailed."

"Unfortunately, Roni, we don't have a copy of that list, so I can't verify it was as you say," Bill says as his face flushes. I reach down into my bag and pull out a copy and hand it to Bill. "You just happened to have a copy of this on you?"

"I made several copies in case I misplaced one. The list had everything he needed down to the location of the boxes for the crystal vases and the ladder to take down the three projectors."

"Hmm, I see that." He turns to Chris. "So, you didn't see on here that she'd listed where the boxes and the ladder were?"

"That must not have been on my copy."

Bullshit! "It was. That's a copy of my notes. You had the original." I turn to Bill. "What's this about? Did something happen?"

Deborah says, "Uh, yeah, Chris and Trisha happened."

"Not now, Deb," warns Bill.

"Sorry," she grumbles.

"Yes, something happened. The projectors are missing, which means we'll have to pay the equipment rental company three thousand dollars each for replacement costs. Ten of the crystal vases were destroyed, and we cannot locate the other thirty."

"What? How can the projectors be missing?" I turn to Chris. "What'd you do with them after you took them down?"

"I—" Chris starts.

Bill says, "He didn't take them down. He claims he didn't have help or have a ladder and didn't know how to do it. He called the hotel this morning to ask about them, but they said they have no knowledge of the projectors or the remaining vases."

I just bet they didn't. "I put them up all by myself! There were directions with the projector cases in the closet behind the main bar. Those sat next to the ladder that was in the same closet with forty boxes and protective wrapping for the vases. See number five on the list?"

I turn to Deb and Martha. "What happened to Martha's vases?" I can't look at her. She'll probably hate me forever.

Trisha interjects, "We had no idea there were boxes. Do you know what a hassle it was to get those over here in a taxi? You're lucky we got ten here."

I turn to her and stare. "Of course I know, Trisha. Because I'm the one who transported forty boxes, three projectors, and all of the other items that decorated the tables. In. A. Taxi. I had no help." I look at both Chris and Trisha. "I paid seventy-five dollars out of my own pocket to have the cab driver wait while I made seven or eight trips into the hotel. So, yeah, I know what that was about. Where are the other thirty vases?"

"We. Don't. Know!" shouts Trisha.

"Enough!" barks Bill. "Trisha, not another word."

"But...," she whimpers.

"That's enough from you too, Roni."

I close my mouth and let my hands roll into fists against my legs. I'm so angry I could spit right now.

"Bill?" Deborah says. "Don't be so hard on Roni. She worked her ass off for us on this deal, and then Chris swooped in there and claimed victory. I commend her for holding her tongue. She took the high road."

"Until she played this stupid game with Chris," Bills says, turning back to me. "Do you want to know how much this deal is costing me?"

I already know but remain silent.

"Nine grand for the projectors plus ten grand for the crystal vases. Replacement costs for those are $250 each. That's cost."

"Bill?" I attempt to speak.

"No. No talking. Here's what's going to happen, Roni. You're going to pay for that entire loss. We'll start with your bonus for this year. If there is any remaining balance, you'll need to sit down with the business office to work out the difference."

"What?" I screech just as Martha and Deborah jump in to defend me.

"Not only that, but you're suspended without pay for two weeks."

"You cannot be serious?" I look at him dumbfounded.

"Oh, I'm deadly serious."

"What about Chris and Trisha?" asks Deborah. "They're the ones who broke the ten vases and left them in the lobby."

"Fine. Chris can pay for those. But you're still suspended, Roni."

I grab my bag and turn to leave.

"You haven't been dismissed, Ms. McGonigall." Bill's now standing, vibrating with anger.

I turn to look first at Bill, then at the smirking Chris and Trisha. "Oh, on the contrary, I think I'm done here."

"What?" Bill shouts. "Roni! Don't you dare walk out of here." Bill's spitting and sputtering now.

It's too bad. He's going to miss me. I did a lot of shit around here that he doesn't know about—a lot of Chris's work for one. I open the door, step out, and slam it shut behind me. Fuck those assholes. I stomp to my office and grab everything that's mine. I have family photos on my wall and desk and a drawer full of snacks and beauty products. I empty the contents of the drawers into my bag and grab every flash drive in there as well. I save all of my work on flash drives, not on my computer. I've always been afraid of losing important documents.

Another precaution I've always taken was keeping duplicate copies of all of my personal notes and ideas. Those are at home in my filing cabinet. I keep the originals here and separate from the confidential work forms and contracts, etc.

I open the drawers that hold my notes and take my first handful and place them on my rolling desk chair. I move through the other three drawers and do the same. I roll my chair out the door of my office and see Barb standing there.

"Roni, I—"

"Not now, Barb. I've got to shred some shit." I roll the chair two doors down to the copy room where we have a massive shredder. I start with a handful of folders and shove them through. It chews the papers up fast. "This is fucking therapeutic," I mutter to myself.

"Roni, you shouldn't be doing that. It's company—"

"These are *my* notes. Nothing more. All of the work documents are in another filing cabinet. These are my sketches, my ideas, and my brainstorming sheets. There's nothing in these folders that means anything to anyone but me. Anything important that was used for an actual account is with the original file. Besides, I'm not taking them out of here. I'm just getting rid of excess junk from my office." That shuts her up. I know she's looking out for me, but she needs to step away. I turn and shove more files into the mouth of the beast. It takes me only ten minutes to shred it all. I roll my chair back to my office, to the spot behind my desk, and turn to my mom and dad's old chair. I sigh. I'm not leaving here without that chair.

I load the seat of the chair with a box holding my personal items, my purse, and my computer bag. I add my desk lamp and find a spot for the floor lamp. The thing isn't on wheels, but it's not very heavy, so I drag it out of my office. It barely fits through the door, but I get it done. I get the chair out the door and see a crowd has gathered. Chris has a fucking smirk on his face while Trisha looks pissed. I push the chair with one hand and my hip while hanging onto my lamp in the other. It's awkward, and I'm sure I'll lose some things, but I make it to the elevator, at least.

"I sure hope you're not stealing anything, Roni," simpers Trisha.

"Shut up, Trisha," mutters Martha.

I turn to see Martha watching me go. She follows me closely as I walk to the elevator. Whispering, she says, "Roni? Please call me this afternoon. Will you? Let's talk about this. I'll talk to Bill."

I give her a nod, then a chin lift since I can't wave. The elevator finally arrives. I force my shit on board and push the Lobby button. I'm lucky no one else jumped on with me. Once the elevator begins its descent, I realize what just happened. I just quit my job. I loved my job. I really did. I gasp, trying to catch my breath so I don't hyperventilate. "I just quit my job. Now what the hell am I going to do?"

I make it to the taxi stand out front and let a veteran who hangs outside of the building help me load the chair in the trunk. The cabbie has to use a rope to secure the trunk, and he's not the least bit happy about it. I put the box and bags into the back seat. I hand the vet ten bucks and slide into the cab. "Home, James," I say with a British accent. I state my address and sit listlessly the entire way home.

Once my office stuff is thrown into my living room, I drag the chair to a prominent place near my television. I run into my bedroom to change into jeans, a sweatshirt, and tennis shoes, then grab my purse, and I'm back out the door. I jump in a cab and head to the hotel where the event took place on Saturday.

I jog in the entrance and straight to the banquet manager's office. She's inside searching through piles of paper. "Hello?" I mutter, not wanting to startle her.

"Oh, hey. It's you, from Saturday night."

"Yep. It's me. Listen, I need your help."

"You do?" she looks nervous. She knows what this is about.

"Do you remember the three projectors we had hanging from the ceiling?"

"Yeah."

"What about the large crystal vases I had on each table?"

"I think so."

"Good. Now, can you tell me where they are?"

"Someone already called about it," she says way too quickly.

"Look, I just quit my job over all of this. I was suspended, and I'm going to have to pay for each of those items out of my own pocket because—"

"What? Why would you have to pay? That jerk and the girl should pay. It's their fault the things are missing."

"Chris and Trisha? Yeah. No. They don't have to pay. I do. I was suspended for two weeks over it all, but I quit instead."

"Good for you!"

She seems to be taking an interest in my plight. "That's where you come in."

"Me?"

"I know you're new here, but can you think of any place the banquet staff could have put that stuff? I know there were like fifty people in here putting things away. There's no way you could have known if they grabbed anything on accident. Right?" I know she knows where everything is. I just gave her an out.

"Oh, yeah, maybe." She's getting it. "Let me think. Maybe they put some of it in one of the thousand storage closets we have here," she says, exaggerating the word "thousand."

"Oh, God, I hope so. If I can get it back, I can return the projectors to the rental company and get the vases to the party planner."

"Wait here," she says, standing.

I'll wait forever if it means I'll get everything back.

It's not long, though, and she's back. "You're in luck! I found everything."

I jump up and screech, "You're kidding?" I hug her and repeatedly say, "Thank you, thank you, thank you! Can you show me where it is? Then, I'll put them in a taxi and be out of your hair."

She touches my arm. "I'm sorry about your job. That guy and the woman? They were really mean. They made one of my servers cry."

"I'm sorry they did that. Just remember karma's a bitch," I say with a giggle. "Now, can you direct me to my things?"

She takes me to the closet housing the ladder and the boxes. Everything is there. It's even packaged up, ready to go. It was all there for him to find. So, why didn't he? Did he do anything that night? I guess it's a good thing I quit my job today and came back here. If I'd waited any longer, the equipment and vases could have been gone.

I grab a luggage trolley and move everything to the valet. My first stop is to the equipment rental place. There, I get a receipt to show that it was all returned in good working order. My next stop is the party-planning place owned by Martha's partner. She let us use them for free because of her relationship with Martha. I open up her shop door and see Kim, Martha's partner, sitting on a stool, typing on her computer. "Kim?"

She turns to look at me. I thought she'd be angry with me, but instead, she stands up and opens her arms to me. "Oh, baby doll. Martha told me everything. I'm so sorry."

"Thanks, Kim. I'm okay, and I've got some good news."

"What's that?" she asks, smiling.

"I've got thirty of your crystal vases."

"What? How?"

"They were still at the hotel, in the boxes. The banquet staff must have packaged them all up."

"But Bill said they were gone."

"Apparently Chris and Trisha were real assholes to everyone, so I think they may have hidden them out of spite. Once I explained everything to the banquet manager, they miraculously reappeared. So, wait here, and I'll get them out of the taxi."

"I'll help."

We bring in all thirty boxes, opening a few just to check on the glass. I ask her for a receipt to take to Bill and Martha, so my pay won't be reduced on my final paycheck. I'm going to need that money. Jumping back into the cab, I head to the office. The security desk is shocked to see me. I hope they don't think I came back to cause trouble.

"Can we help you?"

"Yeah, can you please call Martha in Human Resources and ask her to come down? I have some documents she needs."

"You can just leave them here. I'll make sure she gets them," snaps the crotchety old security guard.

"No. These are confidential documents. For her eyes only." *Come on. Call her.*

She lets out a heavy sigh. "Fine."

In minutes, Martha is hopping out of an elevator and making her way toward me. "Kim called. I've been expecting you. What've you got?"

I hand her both receipts and ask her to make me copies for my records. She says she'll do that and mail them to me today. I hug her and thank her for understanding and not being upset with me.

"Never. I'm so sorry about everything. Deb feels terrible. It was her idea, and you didn't tell Bill. You could have thrown her under the bus, but you didn't."

"I don't do that to my friends, Martha."

"I know, sweetie. I know. Now, if you need anything—a recommendation, anything—call me. Okay?"

"I'll do that. Thanks!"

We hug again, and I'm out the door. I decide to walk for a while. Clear my head. That's when I remember my babysitting gig tonight. A chill of excitement runs down my back. I get to see Mick tonight. It's something to look forward to after a shitstorm of a day.

21

MICK

I watch as Katie lies on her back kicking at the noisy objects hanging from her floor gym toy. This one has a monkey, an elephant, a giraffe, and a parrot hanging down from the padded cross bars above her. I press a flower on the mat that plays music, and we're happy as a clam. Wait... are clams really that happy?

As I contemplate one of life's many mysteries—clams and their ability or inability to be happy—I hear a tapping on the front door. I quickly place pillows around Katie's area and jog to the front door. When I pull it open, I smile at the sight before me. "Hi, honey. How was your day?" I chuckle. I answered the door like a 50s sitcom to be funny, but why did it feel natural to say it to Roni?

"Oh, you know. Same old, same old." She steps into the front room and looks around quickly. She's nervous. She shouldn't be, but this is someone else's home, and this situation is a bit more personal than we're used to. "Come on in and meet Miss Katie."

She walks in farther and looks down. "Oh my goodness. She's even prettier in person than she is in the picture you sent to me." She kneels down on the floor to coo at the baby. "Hi, Katie. I'm Roni," she whispers. "My goodness, what a neat toy you have here. My nieces had something like this too. I bet it makes some fun noises."

She looks up and smiles at me. What is it about seeing women with babies that make men 1) nervous as fuck and 2) happy? I use this time to really look at Roni. I take a moment to check her out—because I'm a guy.

She's wearing black yoga pants and one of those big, slouchy gray sweatshirts. One side has slipped off her shoulder, revealing a lot of smooth, porcelain skin. She's got on a black bra or a tank top underneath because I can see a strap. She's wearing white Keds and no socks. In summary, she looks good. Hot.

"Will you stay with her while I get her bottle?" I ask Roni.

"Sure," she says, smiling.

She lays down, resting on her side next to the mat. As she reaches for one of the swinging toys on the gym, her shirt slides up from her hip to her waist. She's got a curvy body, and this only reinforces my need to get my dick in check.

Jesus, what is wrong with me? Friends. We're just friends.

I grab a bottle from the fridge and set it in the bottle warmer. It only takes ten minutes to warm, so I yell out to Roni to see if she wants something to drink.

"Just water," she replies.

I pull out two bottles of water and a plate of cheese and crackers I made while Kate was napping earlier. I bring it all out and set it on the coffee table. "I'll be back. The bottle just needed to warm up a bit."

I walk back out to the kitchen and stand near the door so I can eavesdrop on Roni and Katie.

"You really are just as lovely as Uncle Mick said you were.

You look a lot like your uncle. You've been blessed with some great genes."

I peek around the corner just as Roni reaches out and touches Kate's tiny hand. Katie grabs her finger and squeezes. "My goodness, you've got quite a grip on you, sweet Katie. I bet that means you'll be a strong, confident young lady when you grow up."

The bottle warmer beeps, letting me know it's ready. I grab it, check the temp on my wrist, and take it out to my girls. "Do you want to feed her?" I ask Roni.

"Yeah, I'd love to."

Roni stands as I pick up Katie. She steps over to the rocker and sits down. I hand her Katie first, then the bottle. I don't need to tell her what to do. I'm sure she's fed her nieces before. Katie immediately starts to suckle the bottle voraciously.

Veronica looks up and smiles. "She was hungry."

I'm trying not to look at Roni and Katie as anything more than my friend and my niece, but it's hard. They look similar. They both have blonde hair and beautiful faces. They've both got plump lips and turned-up noses. It's uncanny, really. I could picture Roni with my baby. Oh, God, I mean a child. Not my baby.

I clear my throat just as Katie finishes her snack. She's getting fussy, so she either needs to burp or wants more food. I take her from Roni and pat her back until a loud burp escapes. "Jeez, girl, you belch like a sailor," I say, laughing at Katie-Did.

Roni laughs too. Patting Katie's back, she adds, "She did. That was a good one. I bet you feel better, don't you, sweetie?"

"Okay. I'll be right back. I'm gonna give her a quick bath and get her in her jammies. Unless... do you want to help?"

"Sure. That sounds fun."

The three of us walk upstairs and stop first in Katie's room. Sophie and Hank have it decorated in bright pink, yellow, and green. Her furniture is white, and the theme of the animals continues up here. A mobile above her crib has creatures like a monkey, a lion, an elephant, and a bear. The rug is green in the center of the room and has an abstract design like a forest floor. There are wall stickers of happy cartoon animals frolicking around the space, and the rocker is covered in an abstract pattern of the same colors as the rest of the room.

"Her room is adorable. They did an excellent job." Roni walks around looking at the books and the knickknacks. There are photos on the wall of each of her aunts, uncles, and grandparents holding her. "I'm going to guess that these are your brothers and sisters. Oh, and your parents. You all look a lot alike. But where are Sophie's parents?"

"Dead. She doesn't have any living relatives."

"Oh, that's so sad. At least she has you." She looks at me, and I think she actually means just me.

"Yeah, we all like Sophie a lot. She felt like part of the family the first time we met her."

"Good. I'm glad," she says as she pats Katie's back. "Ready for a bath, little lady?"

I hand Katie to Roni as I grab her baby bathtub and towel. "Let's do this thing."

Bath time has never been this much fun. Roni giggles the whole time, using toys to entertain the baby while I wash her. In no time, she's clean and dressed in warm pajamas. "After I give her another bottle and put her to bed, let's order a pizza and watch a movie."

"Sounds good. But are we ever going to agree on a movie? Something tells me you like bloody, action flicks."

"Of course I do." I really don't. "I've got something in mind, but we'll find something on Netflix that we both want to see."

After I put Katie to bed, we make our way back downstairs.

"Okay, if you want to make the microwave popcorn, I'll get us set up in the living room."

"Sounds great," she smiles.

"The popcorn and a bowl are on the counter."

As Roni walks into the kitchen, I turn to the living room. It's a cozy space, but the furniture is old. I think it belonged to Sophie's grandmother. It's stiff and uncomfortable. Why they didn't bring over Hank's furniture from his old place is a mystery to me. Not to mention the super high-definition television he had there.

As I look around the small space, I realize that none of his things would have fit in this room. They're too big, and they'd clash with the house. The good news is, what Sophie lacks in comfortable furniture, she makes up with pillows—lots and lots of pillows. I quickly grab two dining room chairs and bring them to sit back to back in front of the sofa. I place them about five feet apart. In no time, I have everything arranged and just in time.

Roni rounds the corner and gasps, "Oh my gosh, Mick. Is that a blanket fort?" she giggles. "I used to love those."

"I know. You mentioned it when I visited your office."

"Oh, I did, didn't I?" She giggles again. "That's so cool." Roni bends over to peek inside. There are pillows to sit on, and I've placed a small table just outside our tent for our drinks and the laptop so we can stream Netflix.

"Come on in." I gesture to the seat next to me in the cave.

She hands me the bowl of popcorn as she lowers herself to her knees. She bends over and starts to crawl inside. I don't mean to, but I moan. First, she's bent over crawling toward me. Envisioning her crawling to me because I told her to makes my dick come to life. Second, I can see down her oversized sweatshirt. She's wearing a lacy black bra that I want to tear from her body. Why did I say I wanted to be just friends again? Seeing her like this is blurring my self-imposed lines.

Inside my makeshift tent, she gets comfortable right next to me. "Okay, let the negotiations begin. What do you want to watch? But let me just say this, Halloween is this weekend. I recommend we choose a horror movie. Thoughts?"

"I suppose. But I don't usually watch scary movies. You're going to have to recommend one."

"What have you seen?"

"Hmm, let's see. I saw *Psycho*. The old one. *Frankenstein*. The old one. *Dracula*. The—"

"Don't tell me, the old one?"

"Yeah. Sorry. I get weirded out by scary movies. But I'm game to watch something as long as it's not too bloody."

"What about *Blair Witch Project*? The old one," I suggest with a chuckle.

"What's it about?"

"Well, it's about some college students who hear about some witch that lives in the woods near their school. They decide to hike into the forest to see if they can film the witch."

"And?"

"And you'll have to watch the rest to find out."

She groans. "Okay. If you want to watch it, I'm game."

The pizza arrives just as we start the movie, so we eat and watch. Roni is riveted to her spot. We're sitting next to each other—so close our thighs are touching. I know I should move, but I don't want to.

"Why I ever let you talk me into this movie, Mick, I'll never know. I don't like scary movies, and this one is creeeeeepy." Something jumps out at us on the screen, and Roni screams as she clutches my upper arm. "I hate you, Mick," she squeaks.

I slide my hand over her upper thigh and squeeze it before

leaning over and whispering in her ear, "Ahh, baby, it's gonna be okay. I'll protect you."

Roni slowly turns her head toward me, and I freeze. This is the moment of truth. I want this girl. I can't deny myself any longer. I want her bad. I lean down and touch my lips to hers. She lets out the tiniest whimper. It's barely audible, but I hear it. I slide my mouth over hers, back and forth, teasing her. Leaving my hand on her upper thigh, I twist toward her and place my free hand on the back of her neck. "Come here, baby."

I pull her, urging her my way. I want her on me. I want her pressed against me. She doesn't disappoint. Getting up to her knees, she turns her body toward me as her arms slide around my neck. My hand moves to her round ass as I bring her closer to me. I lean my back on the base of the sofa.

"Mick, I'm too heavy."

"Shut up and kiss me, woman."

Scooting closer until her soft breasts are pressed against my hard chest, she leans down and kisses me, and it's the best kiss yet. She's in control like our first kiss in the taxi, but that only lasts a few seconds, and I've got to have more. My tongue slides into her mouth, seeking its counterpart. She moans, and it breaks me apart.

I grab her ponytail and pull, so I can see her face. Damn, I love some hair pulling. "Fuck, Roni. You drive me crazy."

She's not fighting me as I pull her hair. She breathes, "I feel the same about you."

I sit up and look in her eyes. While she stares back, I slide my hands under her sweatshirt and lift. Her arms move up without having to ask. Underneath, she's wearing the sexiest fucking bra I've ever seen. It's black lace and almost transparent. I gaze at her breasts then at her face just as she smirks. Damn, this girl is surreal. Leaning down, I take one of her hard nipples into my mouth. I lick the lacy fabric of her bra and then suck again. I'd love to bite right through the bra, but I'll be patient.

Roni arches into my mouth as she uses her hand to hold my head in place. I look up at her as she gazes down at me. Her pupils are dilated. She's as turned on as I am. I move to the other breast, repeating my steps. Like in my dream, I use my tongue to tickle her nipple. She squirms and moans. I'm so focused on her breasts, I didn't feel her hand move down, but as soon as her fingers make contact with my hard length straining to get out of my sweatpants, I take notice. I move my hand down over hers and pull it away. I'm going to come in my pants if she touches me. I wrap my hands around her waist to coax her down onto the ground. There, I raise myself above her. I lift her arm up and say, "Oh, no, Roni. Did I say you could touch me? You naughty girl."

"But—"

"Shh, I'm in charge here."

She scoffs at me, so I quiet her annoyance by moving my hand over her left breast. I pull the thin fabric down just enough to see her nipple. It's perfect. The rose-colored areola is the perfect half-dollar size, and her nipple is hard and puckered. I lean down and swipe my tongue over the hard nub, and my girl moans like a porn star. Jesus, she's sexy as hell.

As I move to take the other nipple into my mouth, she asks, "Mick? What if Sophie or your brother comes home? What if Katie wakes up?"

I look up at her. "They'll come through the kitchen. We'll have time to regroup." Now she's distracted. "Roni, take the bra off."

"Oh, okay." She reaches back and unclips her bra and slides it off and drops it on the floor.

"Holy... sweet Jesus. I never...." In my whole life, I've never seen breasts this beautiful. They're big, more than a handful for sure, but the amazing thing is the shape. They're like teardrops with the nipples pointing up at me. It's like they're calling to me. "Veronica, you are without a doubt, the most stunning woman I've ever seen."

"Oh, you're just saying that because you like my boobs, Mick." She laughs.

"I'm not just saying that, Roni. You're the most beautiful woman I've ever seen."

She reaches out and strokes my cock. "You're beautiful too, Mick. I can't believe you're even real."

I know I should pull her hand away again, but I don't want to. "Can't you feel how real this is? I'm going to burst if you don't stop, little one."

22

___

RONI

ittle one? "Little one?"

"You are little. I'm twice your size."

I ignore his words and wrap my free arm around his neck to encourage a kiss. "Time to stop talking." He pulls my ponytail back again, and I moan in his mouth.

"You like that, babe? You like getting your hair pulled?"

I've never thought about it before. In my rather minimal sexual encounters, it's always been missionary with no extras thrown in. All I know is I like it when Mick does it. "I like it when you do it," I say huskily.

"Fuck, Roni." He attacks my mouth with a passion I've never experienced before. His hands are everywhere, but when he slides his hand down into my leggings, I freeze. "Is this okay, Veronica?"

"Yeah, it's just been a while since someone had their hands on me. I don't want to stop, though."

His hand moves farther down underneath the elastic of my panties as he whispers in my ear, "Are you as turned on as I am, Roni? Are you wet, baby?" He cups my mound and slides one long finger through my heat. "You're fucking drenched. I love that," he says in my ear right before he bites my earlobe.

I moan again. Everything this guy does turns me on. He removes his hand and slides his body between my legs before pulling my hands above my head again while I'm beneath him. His cock is centered perfectly over me, and I want more. I want all of him. I shift my pelvis upward to let him know.

He leans down and kisses me with so much lust and passion it makes me breathless. I slide my tongue over his bottom lip to urge him on. He shifts his hard length upward to meet my thrusts. We're both still completely clothed—well, he is. I'm topless, but it still feels amazing. I pull my hand free from his grip and slide it down to his shaft. I want him—I slide my hand up and down his cock on the outside of his pants. Damn, the guy feels huge. As I'm about to slide my hand inside, the baby monitor squeaks to life with the cries of Katie.

"Fuck!" Mick exclaims.

We're both breathing heavily. His eyes are pinched shut, and mine are wide open. When he opens his eyes, we smile at each other.

"Let me go see what she needs," Mick whispers.

"Okay." Shit, I'm buzzing. I wanted to come, and I know he did too. I hear his footsteps as he jogs upstairs.

"Roni?" Mick yells from upstairs. "Can you come here?"

I quickly put my shirt back on and head upstairs and see Mick in the hallway holding Katie. "She's hot. I think she's got a fever."

"Okay. Is she teething?"

"I don't know." He looks worried.

"Do you know if they have a thermometer around somewhere?"

"Try the bathroom cupboard." He nods toward the hall bathroom.

I run into the bathroom and see a cloth basket filled with baby medical supplies. There's a thermometer that I'm sure is rectal. I grab the basket and head back into Katie's bedroom. "I found a rectal thermometer. We'll need to take her diaper off so we can—"

"Rectal thermometer? Won't that hurt her?"

"No. It won't be comfortable, but it's the most accurate way to take her temp."

"Are you sure?" He's hugging Katie closer to his chest like I'm going to steal her away and hurt her.

"I'm pretty sure, Mick." I'm sure.

"Let's see if I can get ahold of Hank or Sophie." He hands me the baby as he pulls his phone from his back pocket.

When Sophie's phone goes to voice mail, he leaves a quick message for her to call him when she has a chance. "I don't want to freak her out," he explains. Next, he tries Hank whose does the same. "Damn it." He starts pacing the bedroom.

"Mick, it's going to be—"

"No. Let me call my sister. She's a med student. She'll know."

I roll my eyes and look at the baby. She's flushed and warm to the touch. We need to know what her temperature is before we decide what to do.

"Em? It's me, Mick." He pauses, listening to Emily. "I know, shut up. Listen. I think Katie has a fever. No, we haven't taken her temp yet. What? Me and Roni. ... No, she's a girl. Roni is short for Veronica." He starts pacing again, then lets out a frustrated sigh. "Can we talk about this later? We need advice. We have a thermometer, but it's rectal, and I thought... What? Seriously? ... God, I can't do it, Em." He turns to me. "Will you do it? Will you take her temp, rect—you know?" he adds hesitantly.

I nod.

"She said she'd do it. Okay, bye." He starts to hang up when he hears her yelling on the phone. I can hear it from here.

"What?" he asks impatiently.

"103 degrees?" He turns back to me and states, "We want it below 103 degrees, Roni."

I nod again as I set the baby on her changing table. I unfasten her onesie, then her diaper. She's warm. I hope she's not over 103 degrees. I turn her so she's on her side facing away from me, pull the thermometer from the case and wipe it clean with a baby wipe, then turn on the power button. I look at Mick and ask, "Will you put your hand here, Mick?" With one of his big hands on her tiny shoulder, I slide the wand into her bottom. She wiggles around and whimpers. I'm sure it's uncomfortable. I wait until I hear it beep and slowly pull it out.

"It's 101.7. That's high but not in the danger range. I think we should—"

I don't get the words out before Mick is on his phone again, "Em? It's me, Mick."

I giggle when I hear him say "It's me, Mick." God, he's so cute when he's worried. But he doesn't see it that way. He thinks I'm laughing at him, so I get a dirty look from him.

"It's 101.7. Yeah, okay." He pauses, listening. "All right, we'll do that." He hangs up the phone and turns to me.

I hold my free hand up to stop him. "Before you speak, can I tell you what I think Emily recommended?" It's important I show him I'm not completely incompetent right now.

"Okay."

"I think we should get her a bottle. We need to keep her hydrated."

He nods.

"We can give her a dose of her acetaminophen that they have here." I hold up the bottle.

He nods again.

"And we can give her a bath in tepid water."

He nods a third time. "How did you know all of that?"

"I have three nieces, but I used to babysit a lot of the neighborhood kids when I was in middle school and high school. It's how I made my spending money."

He walks over to me and runs his thumb across my cheek. "I'm sorry. I panicked. It's not that I don't trust you. I don't trust myself. I was scared."

I set Katie in her crib and turn to hug Mick. "You're such a good guy, Mick. It's okay to be scared, and you did the right thing calling your sister, the doctor."

"Future doctor."

"Okay. Future doctor."

"Why don't I get the bath ready while you get a bottle. We can both do the medicine. Sound all right?"

He leans down and kisses my lips softly. "Yeah. Thanks, Roni. If you hadn't been here, I'd have run screaming into the streets," he says, chuckling.

"I doubt that. You would have done what you did tonight— called for help."

By the time Katie is tucked back into bed, it's after ten. "I'd better get going. Big day tomorrow." Not. Mick doesn't know about my job situation. I should probably tell him, but I don't want to talk about it yet. Even though we've just met, I know enough about Mick to know he'd probably find Chris and punch his lights out over the reason for my quitting. I'll tell him another time. In the meantime, I need to get started with a job hunt. Might as well start tomorrow.

"Sophie should be home by ten thirty. Wait here, and I'll drive you home."

"No, that's okay. She'll want to get updated on Katie's fever."

"But I want you to meet her."

"And I will. On Saturday. At the Halloween party." I smile up at him.

"Oh, yeah. Okay. That's true."

He walks me to the front door and kisses my forehead. "See you on Saturday."

"Yep. See you on Saturday."

Isn't he going to kiss me goodbye? Will he call me or text me before then? Shit, let the crazy, irrational thoughts begin. I'm not that experienced with guys or relationships. The small amount of knowledge I do have is stressful and full of heartache. Can I handle this? What are we doing? Are we a couple now? No. Not a couple. I'm sure he won't give tonight a second thought. We were just fooling around. Nothing serious. *Friends with benefits*. That's all we are.

23

MICK

I stand at the front window and watch Roni leave. Now that I'm no longer worried about Katie, I can reflect on our time in the tent.

"Fuck." Roni is hands down the sexiest woman I've ever been with. Her damn curves make me want to follow her home, so we can finish what we started. As I stare at Roni's ass, my phone rings.

"Hello?"

"Hey, Mick. It's Sophie. Did you call?"

"Yeah, Katie woke up fussy. She had a fever." I explain what happened and what we did to bring the temperature down. "She's asleep now, and the fever is down. I talked to Emily, and Roni helped out a lot, so no need to worry."

"She's teething already," Sophie explains. "It seems early, but the pediatrician said it happens. I should have told you about that. It makes her fussy and can cause a slight fever. I'm sorry I didn't warn you."

"Don't worry. She's fine. I'm fine. We're all fine."

Sophie lets out a relieved laugh. "I'm glad. I'll be home in about fifteen minutes. I left the library as soon as I saw the missed call."

"Sounds good. See you then."

Not fifteen minutes later, the back door is thrown open with a bang. "Sophie called, said Katie was sick. Where is she? Is she okay?"

"Hank, calm down. She's fine. Sophie says she's teething. Emily and Roni both helped me out, so she's sleeping and her temp is down."

"Thank God. Jesus, man. Next time just leave me a message. I left right in the middle of my prelim on a John Doe to get here."

"Sorry, Hank. I was freaked too."

Hank slaps my back hard. "Ouch, dude. That hurt."

He chuckles. As the oldest in the family, he was always the strongest and most domineering sibling. That hasn't changed; although, I could take him in a fight. "I'm out. I've got shit to do for the party on Saturday, and I've got to work every day this week, a couple doubles."

"Sorry to hear that, Mick. Thanks for watching my baby girl."

We do that one-arm man-hug thing and turn. Before I'm out the door, I ask, "Hey, you gonna be a daddy again?"

Hank smirks and then winks at me. He's not going to say it out loud, but I guess it's a done deal. "Congrats, man," I say, smiling. "I'm happy for you."

"And, Mick? Don't say a damn word to anyone. Not even Emily. We want to wait to make sure the baby is out of the woods. Got it?" he says seriously.

"Got it. My lips are sealed."

24

RONI

I slept late again today. I always like to sleep in on Saturdays, but I've been sleeping in all week. Actually, each day I've progressively slept longer, so today I woke up at eleven. Pathetic. I've got to get a life. Something that is not helping with this effort? It's been four days since I've heard from Mick. The absence of any text messages makes me wonder if I should even go to his party tonight. Maybe he regrets the night babysitting Katie. He regrets messing around on the living room floor. Well, I don't regret it. I didn't, anyway. Mick is hot and sexy, and he knows what he's doing. I can only imagine what sex with him would be like. He made me feel like I was the most beautiful thing he'd ever seen. I got a taste of his dirty talk too. And oh, God... the hair pulling. Just thinking about it turns me on. That guy is sex on a damn stick.

It doesn't help that I had absolutely nothing to do this week except apply for jobs. I haven't talked to anyone from P&P either. Martha sent me the receipts for the equipment with a note telling me to "Hang in there" and "I'll be in touch." I hope she isn't trying to get my job back. I don't want it, so that would be a waste of time. I'm so determined to find work elsewhere,

I've sent out nine resumes and updated my LinkedIn account—twice. Maybe someone will see it, hire me without even talking to me, and pay me a gazillion dollars to work for them. I snort out a laugh. Unless I'm willing to move, it's going to take me a while to find a job like the one I just left at P&P Advertising.

Okay, no more worrying about work. I need to focus on tonight. Now I want to go to the party to see if what happened to us on Monday was a one-off, a fluke, or the start of something. I drag out the plastic bin in my closet and pull off the lid. "I know it's in here somewhere," I say to myself while digging through old clothes from my college alma mater and reminiscing about the good ole days. College was so much fun. I loved my roommates and the friends I made. I should actually catch up with them. I pull out my big college sweatshirt and hug it to my chest, then slip it over my pajama top and continue my search. I dig to the bottom, and there it is. "Ah-ha! Found it!" It's my costume from a Halloween party my roomies and I attended senior year.

It was an awesome costume. We all giggled getting ready for the shindig. Having a theater major as a roommate and best friend certainly had its perks. She was able to score me this outfit from the costume closet at school. I'm pretty sure I was supposed to return it, but it fit me so well—at least it did at the time. Let's hope I can still squeeze into the thing.

I lay the costume on the bed, and as I'm walking back to the tub to dig out the rest of the outfit, my phone dings. I pick it up and feel flutters in my stomach.

Mick: Roni? You around?

I know I should wait a few minutes to reply, so it doesn't appear that I was just doing nothing, but...

Me: Yep. What's up?

That sounded cool, right?

Mick: Just pulling my hair out trying to get the party ready.

Me: Been busy?

Mick: Fuck, yeah. Worked three doubles this week.

Me: Sorry to hear that. Are you still having the party?

Mick: Of course. It's a tradition!

I wait for more from him.

Mick: I need help. Can you come early?

Me: I think so.

Of course, I can.

Me: What time?

I know the party starts at eight.

Mick: 6 or 6:30?

Me: Sure. Should I bring anything?

Mick: Nothing but your superior party-planning *skeeeels*.

Me: LOL. Okay. I'll see you.

Me: Oh… what's the address?

Mick sends me his address, and I plug it into Google maps. It's not far from here, in North Park. Now it makes sense that he has the gym membership in that neighborhood.

I look around my room. It's two o'clock, and I've got a ton of stuff to do before the party. "Time to get busy," I murmur.

At precisely 6:10 p.m., I step out of the Uber in front of a nondescript brick building located in an industrial neighborhood in North Park. "Is this the right address?" I mutter, double-checking my phone and the number on the building. "Yep. It's right." I look up and see lights coming from the two front windows on the second floor.

I walk to the side of the building and see a long set of metal steps that lead up to a door. I'm going to take a guess and assume that's the entrance. "God, I sure as heck hope he lives here. If not, I could be knocking on the door of a serial killer." I snort at my nervous jabber. At least I hope it's a joke.

I start up the steps and look to my right. On the brick wall is a sign that I can just make out. "Flynn Construction." Mick's last name is Flynn. I'm in the right place. I make it to the top and take a second to catch my breath. "Jeez, I need to work out." At 6:15 p.m., I knock on his door. Yeah, I know. I timed it so I wouldn't be too early or too late.

When I hear nothing, I knock again and hear, "Coming."

I busy myself by looking in my cinched purse for a mint or something until the industrial-size door squeaks open. I lift my head and see the most breathtaking sight ever. In the world. No! In the universe! Mick Flynn in a kilt. And nothing else. "Sweet baby Jesus," I murmur under my breath and then giggle. I've no clue why my first reaction was to giggle, but it's better than exclaiming, "Holy shit, Mick. You're a God!" So, I went with the giggle.

My eyes start at his leather flip-flop-clad feet, then up to his lean legs, to a glimpse of a muscular thigh. The kilt starts just above his knees. I've never considered knees to be particularly sexy, but Mick has changed my mind about that. My eyes take in the fabric of the kilt. It's plaid, of course, in browns, oranges, blues, and white. My eyes follow the kilt up to his... to his man-bits region. There's a leather pouch that hangs loosely from his hips with a string. I've seen those in movies. I can't recall the name, but his pouch looks authentic. Even the kilt looks real—not a cheesy costume.

I let my eyes roam up his tight abs to a chest that was designed by the angels. His hair is down. Holy shit, his hair is down! It's the first time it hasn't been in a man-bun since we met. It's long. It probably hits the middle of his back.

When my eyes finally make it up to his handsome face, I see he's clean-shaven. His beard is gone. Plus, his face is painted with blue makeup. The entire right side of his face is blue, and a stripe of blue is on the left. I've seen that before.

"What...?"

"Braveheart," he says, smirking.

"Oh, right! Well, uh, you look good, Mick." *Really good! Damn, son!* "Your costume looks real."

"It is. The kilt was my grandfather's, from the old country," he explains. I hadn't noticed at first because I was ogling, but I catch Mick checking me out too. "So what are you? A sexy witch?"

Ooh, he called me sexy. That's a win. I can see why he got that right away. I'm wearing a black coatdress that hangs to my midcalf. I'm holding a broom, a witch's hat, and a stuffed black cat. "No, I'm Minerva McGonigall. You know from—"

"Harry Potter?" he asks, chuckling.

He must really think it's funny because his chuckle turns into a full-blown laugh, one of those that makes him throw his head back. He clutches his abs. Damn, those abs.

"What's so funny?" I say, punching my only free fist onto my hips.

He calms down a bit. "Jesus, Roni. Nothing. It's just... you're hilarious. You surprised me. Of all the costumes you could have picked, that one is the goddamn best."

"I'd like to say I came up with the idea myself, but it was all my college roommate's. She thought it was funny too."

"I've got to say, though, Minerva McGonigall never looked like that." He points at my cleavage.

Yeah, the costume is kind of sexy. It's a dress that the theater must have used for an Old West production. It has buttons all the way up in the front like a coat. The top half is dark green, and the bottom half is black. I think the part he's fixated on is the opening at the top. It's rather low-cut, and because the thing is much tighter than it was in college, I'm practically falling out of the top.

Mick looks me up and down again and smiles. "You look hot, babe."

Oh, dang. First sexy, now hot? Honestly, I almost gave up on this outfit. I didn't think I'd get it buttoned, but I pulled out a girdle-like corset thing that I wore to a wedding once. It pulls me in so much that I was able to button the dress at the cost of my overflowing décolletage. My long hair is in one braid down my back. I've got a witch hat that I bought at a local costume shop, and I tied the entire thing together with some heeled black booties.

Actually, I do look hot. I smile confidently at Mick. "Thanks!" I push past him and into his place. "So, what do you want me to do?"

He walks up behind me and puts his hands on my waist. "Damn, Roni. I kinda wish no one was coming over now." He leans down, kisses my neck below my ear, and whispers, "Maybe next year I should dress up as Harry Potter. Or better yet, you should dress up as a naughty Scottish lass."

Next year? He's talking about next year? Like I'm still going to be in his life. With a shaky breath, I pull away. "Well, they are coming, so we'd better get this thing set up." You have no idea how hard it was to pull away.

Mick chuckles. "You're right. Let's head to the kitchen, and I'll tell you what I have left to do."

He leads me through a huge, open loft-like space that holds a large television and a big sectional couch. It definitely has that single-man vibe. I follow him into his galley kitchen. It's open to the big room, which is conducive to hosting parties. The place is big. Maybe a couple thousand square feet. That's a coup in Chicago. I bet my place isn't more than five hundred square feet. The entire space is concrete and brick. The only real walls are those around what I presume are the bathroom and bedroom. Both of those rooms have doors as well. I'm still looking at his place when Mick clears his throat. I guess I was distracted.

"So, what can I do?"

"First up, can you make the punch?"

"Punch?"

"Yeah, some of my guests don't drink, so I like to serve punch." He hands me a recipe card. "Use this. Everything is in the freezer, fridge, or over there on the table." He points to his small, round dining table filled with cloth grocery bags.

"I'll be setting up the beer area, so yell if you need anything." He moves toward the makeshift bar he's set up but turns back quickly. "I almost forgot." He walks over to his large pantry cupboard and opens the right side. "Come here," he says, beckoning me with his finger.

I come to him. He opens the door as he pulls my arm closer. "I bought everything to make you Old Fashioneds, and because I'm only serving beer and wine, I put the stuff in here. Do you want one now?"

"Sure. That sounds good." Oh, my gosh. That was so sweet.

He sets to work making my drink, and I move back to the punch area. I pick up his recipe:

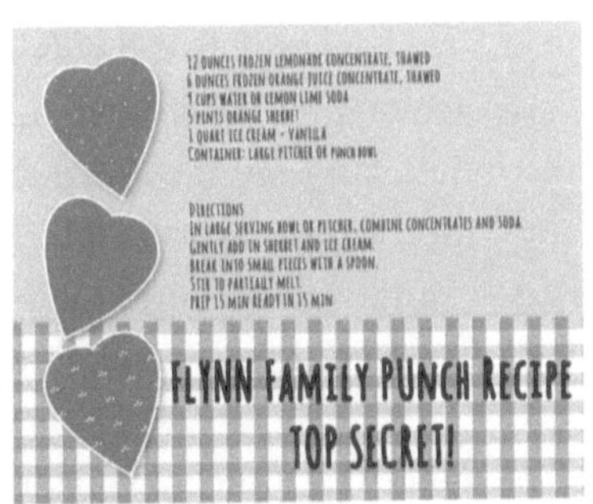

"MICK? Got any music? I love to work with music."

He reaches over to something on the counter and hands me an iPod. "Here. It's Bluetooth. Pick whatever you want; knock yourself out. You can control the volume with that thing too."

I take the device from his hand and start scrolling through. He has a great mix of music. Some classic rock, bluegrass, jazz, blues, punk, and ooh, dance music! "Oh, you've got some great music." I click on Rihanna and Calvin Harris's "This is What You Came For" and hit play. This song starts off slowly, but it builds. It's emotional but still fun to dance to at the same time. It's going to be hard to hold back. I love to dance to this song.

"I'm going to run down to my car to get the rest of the party stuff," Mick says, stepping past me.

"Okay. Sounds good." I'm distracted by the song. I watch him as he exits his apartment, and I turn the song way up. I can't help myself. I've got to move to this song. "It's my jam," I giggle to myself. I sing along to the lyrics, knowing Mick is outside and can't hear me. Or see me as I move my hips to the beat. I'd love to go out to his big open plan space and really dance, but no. Not when it's just the two of us here. So, I appease myself by dancing in the kitchen as I work on the punch recipe. He's already thawed out the lemonade and orange juice. I dance my way over to the freezer to grab the ice cream and sherbet. I'm rolling my hips to the beat when I feel hands slide around me from the back. I stop moving, but the hands urge me on. He's moving behind me, mimicking my moves to the tempo of the song. His big hands slide up and down my sides, feeling my body as it moves. One hand slides around the front of my stomach, pulling me back into him. I feel warm air on my neck next to my ear.

"Jesus, Roni. You dance like a fucking goddess."

I turn my head to smile at him, and it's the invitation he needs to slam his mouth down onto mine. He's turned on. I know this because I can feel him behind me. Well, his penis. I can definitely feel that. I slide around in his arms and wrap my arms around his body. We're still moving to the music but not like we were. We've slowed down, and now it's just about our bodies together.

Mick pulls away slowly. His eyes are dark and hooded. He licks his lips as he looks at my mouth. "I want to fuck you so bad, Roni."

I gasp, but it's only because he said exactly what I wanted to hear. "I want that too," I whisper.

He grabs my hand and pulls me out of the kitchen toward what I assume is his bedroom. He pushes the door open and yanks me inside. Not hard enough to hurt but enough to show me his urgency. He reaches out and starts to unbutton my dress.

"I'll do it," I say with shaking hands. I start to unbutton, but he moves my hands out of the way.

"I'm doing it," he growls.

I stop but slide my hands over his biceps. His breathing is erratic, and it's a turn on to know he's this excited about getting me undressed. I look down and see his kilt is tented. I want to see him undressed too. I reach for his kilt, but he moves my hands away.

"Not yet," he growls again. Once my dress is unbuttoned, he opens it up and slides it over my shoulders. "Jesus. Fuck, baby. What're you wearing?"

"A black corset."

"I think I could come just looking at you." He's dead serious. As soon as the coat falls to the floor, he uses his hands to move me back. When the back of my legs hit the bed, I lose balance and sit. "Scoot up onto the bed and lie back."

"Bossy, much?" I chuckle.

"Hm-mmm. Get used to it."

Get used to it? Holy crud. I could *so* get used to this.

"Lie back."

I scoot my bottom to the middle of his king-size bed and lie back with my head on his pillows. He's moved to the end of the bed. "Show me."

I blink at him. What does he want to see? I reach up to pull the cups of my corset down, but he stops me. "No. Show me that sweet pussy. Are you wet, Roni?" He's got his knee up on the end of the bed now. He could be face to face—I mean, face to crotch with me any second.

Nervously, I flatten my hand and slide it down my stomach over my lace panties until it's between my legs. Unsure what he wants exactly, I slide my fingers into the edge of my underwear and pull it back, so he can see.

He makes the most intense, guttural noise I've ever heard. It's half angry and half sexy. "You're so wet, Roni. Your pussy is practically shimmering."

My breathing picks up as he moves closer to me. His face is inches from my center. No one has ever done this to me. I've never had a man go down on me. He pushes my hand away and reaches up to the waistband of my underwear, then slowly slides them down. "Lift your hips." I rise up so he can slide them down my legs. Once off, he tosses them on the floor.

He moves back, but this time he doesn't stop. Using his hands, he opens me up even farther, pressing my inner thighs outward. It's painful, but I can't think about that now. I feel a warm sensation and peer down just as his tongue swipes over my clit. My hips jerk upward.

"Mick!"

"You have the sweetest pussy, Veronica. It's smooth and pink, and you taste fucking delicious."

"I do?"

"You do, baby." He stops talking and crawls the rest of the way up my body. He stops at my chest. My breasts have fallen out of the top of the corset, and he's licking each one back and forth now. I arch off the bed again as his hand slides down through my wetness.

His long middle finger glides into me, pumping in and out as he suckles and nips at my breasts.

"Mick?"

He looks up. "What do you need? Tell me."

Panting, I confess, "I need you."

"You have me."

"No. I... uh, need you inside of me."

"You sure?"

I'm so fucking sure I can hardly say, "I'm sure."

He reaches into the pouch around his waist and pulls out a condom.

I giggle. "You keep condoms in your pouch?"

"It's called a sporran, and yes, I do." He chuckles. "I've also got lip balm, cash, a pen, and some other stuff," he says quickly.

"Were you expecting to get lucky tonight?" I'm trying to seem upbeat. I mean, am I just the lucky one right now or was he hoping it would be me? I can't think about it because I want him—want to feel him.

"What can I say? I'm an optimist, Roni. Anyway, these have been there a while. I keep condoms in here every year. You know, like a party favor."

"Every year?"

"Yeah, babe. I wear this costume every year. It's a running joke with my family, so why change things up?"

So, he gets lucky at his Halloween party every year? No wonder he has one every year. Not like a guy like Mick can't just wink and get laid. I'm sure he can. It's just strange.

He continues, "Plus, I'm a firm believer in safe sex, so I hand them out at the party."

"Oh, I see," I say as I run my hands up over his pecs and then down his abdominals. The guy is cut like a pro athlete. I want to explore farther down, but he stopped me last time. He watches my hands, so I keep moving down. His kilt is still tented. Is he commando underneath? I slide my hand to the front and move the pouch over. "Can I touch you?"

He nods.

I sit up and glide my hand up his thigh to the junction of his legs. Yep. Commando. I let my fingernails skim his inner thigh. He groans. Then I move up his length, making sure to grasp the head. I can feel wetness—precum.

"Roni?" he hisses.

Damn, I feel powerful. I grasp him. My fingers don't make it completely round him, so I take what I can and move my hand back down.

"Stop. I'm going to lose it if you don't stop, Roni."

He pulls off the pouch, and his kilt starts to fall off. Is that the only thing holding the kilt up? He unwraps it quickly until he's naked—completely and utterly naked. I take him in in his entirety, and let me tell you, I could die a happy woman right now. I've now seen Mick Flynn naked. Not just naked, but naked and wanting. He wants *me*. Veronica McGonigall is about to get sexy with Michael Flynn.

"I'd love to take this corset off you, but I like it, so it stays."

I nod and wait. He's looking down as he reaches behind me. Before I know it, I've been flipped over onto my stomach. How did he do that? He pulls at my hips so I'm on my knees. I place my palms on the bed and lift my upper body. Doggy style. I've never done it like this before. I read about it in my steamy romances, and it always sounds amazing. I'm game.

He slides his hand over my round bottom. "Beautiful ass too. Tits and ass. You've got it all, Roni."

I know I've got plenty of ass and breasts. He's not telling me anything new. He runs his hand through my core, and we both groan. Mick slides his finger into me and pumps it in and out. I squirm and attempt to move back into him to get him deeper.

"Patience, baby," he coos.

"No. I need it. I need you," I whine.

I hear the tear of a wrapper and wait. Then his big, warm hands slide over my hips as he presses his cock through my wetness. When is he going to get going? Jesus! It's then that I feel him start to push inside. It's been a long, long time, so it burns a little. I take panting breaths until he's fully seated inside.

"Fuck! Roni." He's leaning over my back so he can speak into my ear. He sits back up and slowly pulls himself out. Without giving me a chance to prepare, he thrusts back in, making me squeal.

"Did I hurt you?" He sounds apologetic.

"No! Don't stop. Do it again," I exclaim.

Without any words, he does it again, and again, and again. Sex has never felt this good. Never, ever, ever. I get into the rhythm with him and push back as he pushes forward. I spread my legs farther apart to see if he can get deeper. It works.

"Oh, God... Mick!"

"I know. Goddamn it, are you close, Roni?" he says urgently.

"I am. Don't stop. Please, don't stop."

He's pumping into me so fast I nearly fall onto my face. I breathe deep and concentrate on that spot inside of me that he keeps hitting. Two more times, and I'm hurling over the abyss. I moan his name over and over.

He comes soon after, whispering dirty things in my ear. Things like "best pussy ever." God, I love the dirty talk. It always turns me on when I read about it, but now I get to experience it for myself. It only adds a layer to the best sex I've ever had. Not even BOB (my Battery-Operated Boyfriend) could give me that orgasm. I should know.

"I want you to stay tonight, Roni. After the party. I want you in my bed. Yeah?"

"Yeah," I say, catching my breath. *An entire night with Mick Flynn? Hells yeah!*

I just had the best sex of my life. Who'd have thought? Roni's a conundrum. On the outside, she seems insecure and some-what self-deprecating. But put some dance music on and get her naked and she's confident, fiery, and so fucking sexy.

While Roni puts her costume back on, I wrap myself in the kilt again. I search for my sporran—the small leather pouch that keeps my kilt secure. I find it behind the wastebasket. When I pull it free, the contents spill out. I find my lip balm, the twenty I had stuffed into the pouch, my pen, and, oh, a bottle opener. I chuckle. I'd been looking for that thing for a year. I spot several condoms of all different brands and types to the left of the can. Some ribbed for her pleasure from last year, and there's a flavored condom from a few years back. It probably tastes nasty by now. I bend over to grab a couple neon condoms from, Jesus, a long-ass time ago. Nevertheless, I grab those along with a few stragglers and stuff them back into my pouch.

I turn to see Roni rebraiding her hair and adjusting her costume. "Come out when you're ready, okay?" I lean in and kiss her temple. She smiles sweetly in the mirror. I could get used to Roni McGonigall. When I open the bedroom door, I stop in my tracks. Fuck. My sisters are here. "Oh, hey, Em. Sandy."

They both turn to me and smile brightly. They heard us. Emily speaks first, "Whatcha doing in there, Mick? Huh?"

Sandy snickers. "I think we both know what he was doing in there. The question is, who's the girl?" Before she can say more, Roni steps out of the bedroom, takes one look at the two women in my kitchen, then at me, and immediately turns the most intense shade of red I've ever seen.

"Um, oh...," she stutters.

"Roni, meet my sisters." I point to Emily first. "Emily and Sandy."

Emily hops off the stool at my kitchen island. Sandy was working on the punch recipe but stops and comes around the island and heads straight to Roni.

Emily wraps her arms around her. "It is good to finally meet you."

"You too," says Roni nervously.

"So you're the one who has Mick in a good mood for once," Sandy says, glaring at me.

"Hey, I'm always in a good mood."

Both sisters start speaking at the same time, letting me know that my statement is false. Yeah, I'm an asshole. I've always been moody, but after the deal with my ex... well, it's taking me extra time to get happy.

I look up as Emily whispers something in Roni's ear. They both look down at the skin above her dress. Oops, blue face paint. Roni races into the bathroom. No doubt to remove the blue evidence. When Emily turns to look at me, I smirk and shrug my shoulders. I'm not going to apologize. This is my house, and Roni's my girl. Uh... wait. Not what I meant.

Sandy interrupts my thoughts. "So, little brother, Roni seems nice. Not your usual type, so that's refreshing."

"Yeah, not your type at all. I love it. I can tell she's cool already. So what is she supposed to be tonight?"

"Minerva McGonigall."

"From Harry Potter," squeaks Emily. Those books have always been her favorite.

"Yeah, her last name is McGonigall. Veronica McGonigall."

Both sisters laugh at that. "That costume is fucking genius," says Sandy with awe.

"I thought so too." Plus, she's sexy as hell.

"So what the hell are you two supposed to be?" They're both wearing old, torn-up dresses that look like something someone threw away. They have dirt and red splattered all over them. They're both barefoot.

"That's why we stopped by early, big brah. We wanted to finish our costumes."

Just as Roni steps out of the bathroom, I ask, "And they are?"

"We're going as zombies, and we need to use your bathroom to do our makeup. Can we use it now?" asks Sandy, smiling at Roni.

"Sure. Of course. Sorry."

"You don't need to apologize, Roni. They're imposing on me."

Sandy turns to me. "Yo, Mick. If you're mad, we can leave. It's just—"

"Nah, just fucking with you. Hurry up so you can help Roni and me set up."

They both salute me as they skip—yeah, skip—into my bathroom.

"Sorry it took me so long. There was blue makeup all over me," she says, turning pink again.

"Damn, I wish I could have seen it."

"You probably should touch yours up too. It's a little smeared," Roni adds.

"Maybe later. Let's finish what we started." I look at her and wink.

By nine o'clock, the party is in full swing. Nearly everyone I invited showed up, and the costumes are great. My brother Keith showed up with a giant cardboard magnet painted red and silver around his neck with stuffed cats glued to it. When I asked him what it was, I nearly fell over.

"A pussy magnet? Jesus, that's crass." I laughed.

"It was Beth's idea. She even dressed up as a cat."

I turn to Beth, who has a smirk on her lips. "You're a dirty girl, Beth Flynn. You know that?"

"She knows," Keith says proudly.

When Hank and Sophie show up, I'm not sure what they are but Roni figures it out pretty quickly. "They're Daisy Buchanan and Jay Gatsby, from the Great Gatsby," she says.

"How in the hell did you figure that out?" I ask, astounded.

She looks sheepish as she says, "The flapper costume?"

"It makes sense. Sophie found a rare first edition of that book and auctioned it off."

"Really? Wow, that's cool. Is it okay if I ask her about it?"

"Yeah, let me introduce you."

I hold Roni's hand as we move around the party. I introduce her to everyone as "my friend, Roni." What else should I call her? We haven't really talked about this thing between us. Why would we? We're not dating, but maybe I should explain that to her—that I'll never date again. I don't really want anyone to get any ideas about us. We're just friends—friends with benefits. The only glitch happened when I introduced her to my brother David and his bitch wife, Jennifer. She's a fucking snob; I can't stand her. But she's married to my brother, so I've got to at least pretend to tolerate her. I'm not the only one who despises her, though. I'm pretty sure Hank would rather not see her at family functions, but that's never going to happen. I look at her from my spot in the room and sneer to myself. She's dressed up in one of her typical sexy something or other costumes. I think it's a sexy nurse this year. Last year she was a sexy pirate or sailor or some shit. It's the same thing every year. I honestly don't know what my brother sees in her. When I finally get the balls to introduce her, it goes like this.

"Roni, I want to introduce you to my brother Dave and his wife, Jen."

Roni gives them both the most beaming smile I've ever seen. She's having fun, I think. I hope. "Hi," she says, raising her hand to shake theirs. "It's nice to meet you. Your costumes are great."

Dave reaches out and shakes her hand. When Roni turns to Jen, she raises a limp hand and barely touches my girl. Fucking weak, limp handshakes.

"You look beautiful," Roni adds, giving Jennifer a compliment that she doesn't need or deserve.

Jennifer looks over Roni from head to toe. Her nose is all bunched up on her face like she's smelling dog shit. God, she's such a cunt.

"Yeah, thanks. You look... interesting."

Fucking Jen. I growl at her, "If you can't be nice, you can fucking leave my party." I turn to my brother. "I mean it, Dave."

"I know," he says glumly. "Jen, knock it off."

She glares at him. "What did I do now? Jesus, David. I can't do anything right," she says as she storms off toward the kitchen.

"I'm sorry about her, Roni. She's just had a bad week," my brother tries to explain.

"Bullshit, Dave. She's like that every time I see her."

"You should talk, asshat. You're no picnic either."

I turn and grab Veronica's hand as I march toward a new group of guests.

26
———

RONI

This party is really great. It's kind of huge too. There have to be at least seventy-five people here. It's a good thing his apartment is big and private. It's loud too. The music is blaring, people are yelling and laughing. It's a great atmosphere. I'm not surprised the party is so well-attended. Mick seems to be the kind of guy people gravitate toward. I know I did.

Mick is talking to one of his brothers, so I decide to start the trek to the bar area for another drink. "Hey, Mick, I think I'll go get a drink. Want anything?"

"Yeah, grab me a beer, would ya?"

"Sure thing." I weave my way through the crowd to the bar area. It's three deep at the counter with people pouring wine and grabbing beers. I decide to use the restroom before I try to fight the crowd. As I walk to the back of the building, I notice family photos hanging on the outside of his bedroom. Just as I'm about to turn the corner into a small alcove, I hear a woman's voice.

"You'd better get your ass over here."

Silence. She must be listening to someone on the phone.

"He has someone here. Some fat chick with a guy's name."

Oh, I think she's talking about me. Great.

"No, she's not near as pretty as you are, so you don't need to worry about that. Besides, you and I both know how much he likes his women on top. She'd crush him. He'll have to stick to doing her from behind, so he doesn't have to see her fat jiggle around," the terrible woman cackles. "Yeah, just hurry, okay?"

She stops talking, so I quickly decide to hide. I don't want her to know I overheard her, whoever she is. I'll wait until she walks out to see who it is, and maybe I'll say something. When she walks out, I'm not surprised to see it is Jennifer Flynn—a typical tall, thin, beautiful, mean girl. And Mick's family. I'd better keep my mouth shut.

I skip the bathroom and make my way over to the bar. I need whiskey, straight up. I open the pantry cupboard to grab some when Jennifer places a hand on the door. "Making yourself a bit too comfortable, aren't you?" she sneers. Peering into the pantry cupboard she rolls her eyes. "Oh, I get it. You're hungry. Well, the food is over there." She points to the dining table. "Mick won't appreciate you eating him out of house and home, Robbie."

"Roni. My name is Roni. And I'm getting a drink."

"Sweetie, the drinks are over there too. You don't have to lie to me. I get it. You can't go more than an hour without a meal, huh?"

What a fucking bitch. I turn and make my way back to Mick, empty-handed. I stand next to him as he reaches over and takes my hand in his. He kisses the inside of my wrist.

"Where's my beer, babe?"

I feel tears burning the back of my retinas, but I won't let them out. "Too many people. I'll go back in a bit."

"I'll get them. Come with me," he says, pulling me along by the hand.

We're making real progress until Mick stops abruptly. So

suddenly, in fact, I almost run into his back. I step around him, looking up at his face. His focus is in front of him and down. I follow his line of sight and see a tiny blonde in a sexy Scottish lass costume. There's not much to the costume, really. She's wearing a tiny plaid skirt in browns and oranges just like Mick's and an even tinier white halter top. Her long legs are wrapped in white thigh-high tights, and the whole thing is topped off with a plaid beret. She's stunning, actually. Her hair is long and blonde, styled in two pigtails that rest right about her huge breasts. They don't look real, but they look impressive.

"Lauren, what the fuck are you doing here?" Mick asks, sounding angry.

"I was invited."

"Not by me."

"Does it matter? Who's that?" she says, pointing to me.

Mick drops my hand so fast I nearly slap myself with it. "Nobody. I'm just doing her a favor."

And... boom, there it is. The hammer's dropped right along with my stomach. I feel that telltale burning behind my eyes, but I squeeze them shut and focus on breathing.

"Obviously," the petite blonde sneers.

Without even looking back, Mick walks toward the woman. Not knowing what to do, I twist my hands in my skirt. People are staring first at me, then Mick, and then the woman. I see looks of pity on their faces when they look to me. I know the saying is fight or flight. I have no right to challenge. We're just friends. The burning behind my eyes starts all over again. Flight it is. I turn and make my way to the door as quickly and discreetly as possible. Just as I'm turning the knob to leave, Jennifer steps in my path.

"Yeah, it's best if you leave. Lauren wants him back, so you won't stand a chance now."

I wrench the door open, nearly knocking her down. Who

the hell is Lauren? I hit the stairs, taking them as fast as I can in my heeled boots. Luckily, I'm holding my small satchel; otherwise, I wouldn't have any money or a phone to call Uber.

I hit the ground and start to run—well, walk fast. "Roni!" I hear someone yell. "Roni! Wait up!" she shouts again. I turn to see Emily jogging toward me. "Roni, wait! Where are you going?"

"I'm heading home. Big day tomorrow." I know I sound pathetic. At least I'm not crying yet.

"Don't go. It's only ten thirty. The party is just getting started."

"It's a great party. I just.... I'm tired."

"Bullshit," she mutters. "You're fleeing. I don't blame you. Lauren is a fucking bitch."

Yeah, and so is Jen. "I don't know her so...."

"It's his ex."

"I figured."

"Listen, Roni. I like you, and I know my brother likes you a lot. He's been so much happier since he started hanging out with you. Don't let whatever that was upstairs bother you. He and Lauren were serious, but she screwed him over."

"She cheated on him? On Mick?" What kind of woman would cheat on Mick Flynn?

"No, she didn't cheat, or I don't think she did. She hurt him in other ways."

"How?"

"Not my story to tell. You'll have to talk to him. Don't go. Give him a chance to explain, will ya? Please?" Emily is full-on begging now.

I'd laugh at her with her pleading hands raised in front of her in prayer if this whole thing weren't an emotional clusterfuck. "I'll go back," I agree reluctantly. "I just need a few minutes. The fresh air feels good. I'll be up soon."

"Great. See you in a few." She reaches out and hugs me, then takes the metal steps two at a time.

I know I should leave. It was awkward up there, and I don't like it. I sit on the bottom stair until my butt hurts from the metal teeth on the stair tread pressing into my flesh. I stand and fix my dress and slowly walk back up to his place. At about the halfway point, I hear the door to Mick's apartment open. Light shines out onto the landing above me. I pay no attention since my focus is on getting up the narrow steps in my costume. That is until I hear the click-clack of heels descending the staircase and a voice. The same voice I heard a few minutes ago.

"Well, well, well, if it isn't Mick's new woman."

I look up and see Lauren in her Scottish lass costume. "Oh...." I don't know what to say to that, honestly. I do know this isn't going to go well for either of us. I grasp the railing as I take another step up. Before I can blink, the tiny woman is standing on the step above me, looking down. She'd be a pretty woman if she wasn't scowling at me. She leans down, forcing me to lean back on the railing. When she steps down onto my step, I feel a little more in control since now we're on the same level. But apparently Lauren doesn't agree.

"I don't know who you are, and I don't really care." She shrugs. "All I do know is that you"—she jabs a finger onto my chest with her long fingernail—"are not Mick's type. He prefers this." She points down to herself. "So, don't get your hopes up. You'll just be disappointed." She turns to step away but stops and leans in so far I feel like I'm going to fall over the rail. "But I suspect you're used to that. Aren't you, tubby?"

I should say something. I should jab my own finger into her chest. I should lean into her. But I don't. Instead, I watch her walk down the steps in her higher-than-necessary heels and disappear into the night.

"Why don't I ever stand up for myself?" God, I'm so frigging weak.

I still want to go home, but I promised Emily I wouldn't, so I won't. I take the remaining steps up to Mick's door. I open the door and see the party is back in full swing. The dramatic scene is over, and they're all drinking, laughing, dancing, and singing once again. I weave my way through the crowd, this time looking for the tall Scot in the kilt. He's no longer standing in the center as before. I look toward the couch and television area, but he's not there either. I work my way up to the bar area next but don't see him. Maybe he's taking a break from everything and escaped into his room. I break through the throng toward his bedroom.

Stepping into his personal space, I notice for the first time his room is pretty sparse with only one nightstand and a tall dresser on one wall. The time we spent in here earlier I was distracted, so it makes sense I'm seeing the long bar attached to the wall for his clothes. The guy doesn't need much apparently. My eye follows the length of his closet. When it reaches the end, I blink. There, huddled in the dark is Mick. He's sitting on the floor, back against the wall, head in his hands. A short glass, empty, sits on his right. A bottle with something inside sits on his left.

"Mick?"

"I thought you left," he says curtly.

"I was going to but—"

"You should leave."

"Mick. I—"

"This thing"—he throws his arm toward his bed—"is a bad idea."

From his gesture, I'm going to assume he's referring to the sex earlier.

"Mick—"

"Just go, Roni." He picks up the bottle, twists off the cap, and starts to pour some into his glass. He must have changed his mind because he skips the middle man and just brings the bottle to his lips and gulps.

I try again. "Listen—"

Dropping the bottle, he shouts, "No! You listen, Roni. This shit with us was never going to work out. I can't do it. You hear me? I. Can't. Do it. Just go home." He sighs and runs one hand through his hair. "Fuck."

I swallow down the anger and sadness that's crawling up my throat. I'm not going to stand here and let him talk to me like that, like I'm nothing, like I don't matter. Turning on my heel, I do a repeat of earlier and make my way back out through the crowd and out the door. This time, I let the tears fall.

27

———

MICK

"What the hell were you thinking?" Emily yells. She's in my face, literally. The majority of the people have left the party, and I'm lying motionless on the couch. With her hands on her hips, she yells again, "I asked you a question, dick-face. What were you thinking? She ran out of here so fast I couldn't stop her. She was crying, Mick. What'd you do?"

"Nothing," I mutter.

"Oh, you did something. What was it?" No, it's true. I did nothing. She saw me in my room hiding after I kicked Lauren out of the party. I needed space. Time to think. When she appeared at my door like a fucking beautiful angel, I knew I had to make a choice. I pushed her away because I'm an asshole. I'm not good enough for her. Lauren Sly broke me. But shit, the look on her face. It pains me so much to think about. "I did what I had to do. She deserves better than someone who'll never be able to commit. She's a commitment kind of woman, Emily. It's for the best."

"Bullshit, Mick. You're a good guy. You're just talking this bullshit because Lauren showed up. Besides, don't you deserve someone like Roni? She's awesome."

"Em, I'm not ready. I know Roni's cool. She's fucking beautiful, but what if…?" I can't finish the sentence, so I take another swig of bourbon instead. I know Roni wouldn't do the same thing Lauren did to me, but shit, I never thought Lauren would either. I'm just a clueless fucking idiot. I can't trust my own goddamn instincts anymore. I take another swig. I've almost gone through half the bottle and can feel the numbness down to my feet now. Finally. Shit, I started drinking as soon as I kicked Lauren's sorry ass out of my party. I should be numb.

"Who the hell invited Lauren, anyway?" asks Sandy, getting her nose into my business. Typical. My family has no boundaries.

"No idea." I shrug. "It's not like she didn't know about the party."

"No, someone had to have let her know what was going on tonight. Someone from the inside," adds Hank.

"Jesus, cop much?" mutters David.

"I am a cop, asswipe. I can't help it."

As I listen to my brothers and sisters bicker, I lay my head back on the sofa and wish for peace and quiet. I just need time to clear my head. Just as I'm about to close my eyes, I hear it. Jen. I look up and see Hank moving toward Jen. "You didn't learn your lesson with Angela?" Hank sneers.

"What?" Jen is doing her best to look shocked that we'd think she started this shit-show.

By now, the rest of my clan is getting involved. I look at Dave, and he's staring off into space. Is he drunk too? They're all yelling at Jen to hand over the phone.

Dave yells, "Shut the fuck up. Everyone. Shut your mouth." He turns to Jennifer and says in a disarmingly calm voice, "Did you invite her?" They stare at one another for too long. "You did. You invited her here. Why? Why would you do this? You know she hurt him."

"But, David, honey—" She sputters, attempting to come up with some excuse. "She loves him. She wants him back."

I let out a hateful laugh. "Yeah, right. She wants me back? Well, she can't have me back. She broke me, ruined me. I hate her fake fucking guts." I'm now standing in front of Jen, yelling in her face.

Only Emily knows what happened, but maybe it's time I enlighten everyone, so I turn to face my siblings. "Do you want to know what she did? Huh?" I look at my brothers and sisters. "She aborted my fucking baby. I didn't even know she was pregnant until after the fact. She didn't give me a chance."

My sibs all gasp. But strangely enough, Jennifer isn't surprised by the revelation. I turn to her again. "You knew?"

"Well, she is one of my best friends," she tries to explain.

"You knew she terminated her pregnancy and you still invited her to my fucking Halloween party?"

"She regrets it. She almost changed her mind at the clinic, but—"

"Wait? What? At the clinic? You were with her at the clinic?" This time it's David asking the questions.

"She's one of my best friends!" she shouts.

"That was my niece or nephew. Shit, Jen, it was *your* niece or nephew," he sputters.

"Oh, I didn't think of that," she whispers. "Well, I'm not related by blood."

We're all silent now. The few nonfamily people who were hanging around the party took the argument as their cue to leave. I look around and see Sophie, Beth, Sandy, and Emily staring at Jen. Sophie's crying, and Beth is barely holding it together. They're both mothers, so it makes sense they'd take the news hard. The thing is, I believe that a woman has a right to choose, but in this case, we were dating. We were serious. Hell, I was toying with the idea of popping the question, and we weren't too young to have kids. She was twenty-five, and I was a year older than that. It just didn't make sense that she didn't clue me in on the whole thing. Maybe I would have agreed with her that it wasn't the right time or that we weren't going to make it long term. What am I fucking saying? Of course, I would have wanted the baby. I would have raised our baby by myself. But she didn't give me a chance.

"I can't do this anymore," says David softly. "I want you out of my house by Monday. Get your shit and get out." He's shouting now.

"But... but... Davey, baby," she whines.

"Don't 'baby' me, Jen. Besides, I know you've been fucking your personal trainer. Got the video to prove it."

Her face turns fifty shades of green. "But... when...? How?"

"Does it matter? It's over. It's been over for a long time." He hands her the keys to the car. "Take these and get gone. I'll be back on Monday night, and you'd better be out of there. And don't even think about taking any of my shit, Jen. It won't end well for you."

She grabs the keys and runs out the door. It slams behind her, and we all stare at one another.

"Now, what are you going to do to get your girl back?" asks Keith. He's remained relatively quiet during this whole ordeal.

"Nothing. It's over. I fucked everything up. I'm just gonna get drunk now. You can all let yourselves out." I grab the bottle and head to my bedroom.

"Mick?"

It's Emily, but I'm going to ignore her too. "Night, everyone. Thanks for coming to my last Halloween bash." Okay, now I'm just pathetic.

I throw myself onto my bed, sloshing whiskey out of my glass. I don't need it anymore.

I don't need anyone.

28

RONI

Bang, bang, bang.

Bang, bang, bang.

"What the hell?" I say groggily.

Bang! Bang! Bang!

"Who...? What time is it?" I say as I look at the clock beside my bed. "Three o'clock in the freaking morning?" I stumble out of bed just as another *Bang!* sounds at my apartment door.

"Just a second!" I shout out. "Jeez." I reach the door and step on my tiptoes so I can see who the hell woke me up. "Fuck," I whisper-mutter.

"I heard that," says none other than Mick Flynn.

Speaking through the door, I say, "Mick, it's late. What do you want?"

"Can I talk to you?"

"Can't it wait?" *Until never?*

"No, it can't wait," he says, his voice getting softer. "Please, Roni. Let me in."

Shit! "Yeah, okay, but just for a minute." I take the chain off the door, then flip the deadbolt and turn the knob, which makes that lock pop open. I pull the door open to see a disheveled

Braveheart. His hair is a wild mane, and what's left of his makeup is smeared down his neck onto his chest. Hot mess comes to mind—emphasis on "hot," mind you. It is Mick Flynn we're talking about.

"Thanks, Roni," he says, stepping into my home.

"How did you know where I lived?"

"Oh, you know Sam, the Uber driver?"

Yeah, I know Sam. He drove me home that first night at Chrome. He helped me up to my place and gave me his card. I've called him anytime I needed a cab. Of course, he'd know where I lived.

"He's a buddy of mine. He remembered where you live. He even knew which apartment is yours."

Why is he here? He made it clear... Damn it. He looks terrible. "Uh-huh. What can I do for you, Mick?"

"I came to explain. To tell you about... some things. Explain."

Yeah, he said that already. "Okay. Explain," I say, crossing my arms in front of my braless chest. I should probably put on a robe. I'm only wearing a tank top and my underwear. I showered when I got home for obvious reasons and put on a fresh pair of white cotton bikinis. Cotton: the fabric of my life. Hell, I must still be asleep.

"Can we sit?"

"Sure." I point to my love seat and chair. My place is small, so I had to go with small furniture. He takes the love seat, and his big body makes it look like children's furniture. I sit in the chair across from him.

He leans forward with his elbows on his knees. With his head down, he runs his fingers through his long, messy hair. "I wanted to apologize, and tell you the whole story."

"So you said." The apology was new, but yeah. He looks up at me with bloodshot eyes. "Mick? Are you drunk?"

"No. I was well on my way, but I decided to sober up so I could come see you."

I remain silent. I want him to talk, then leave.

"Lauren is my ex-girlfriend."

"I know."

"She wasn't invited to the party. I told her to get the hell out of my house. She's stubborn." He sighs, then takes in a gulp of air before he continues. "Let me start at the beginning." He slides back onto the sofa and looks down at his lap. "Lauren and I dated for over a year. It was serious. I thought she was the one, you know?" He looks up at me sadly.

I nod.

"I was toying with the idea of proposing or at the very least moving in together. We both felt the same about each other, or I thought we did. But..." He squeezes his eyes shut, then leans forward again. His eyes meet mine. "She got pregnant."

I know I must look shocked because I am.

"But she didn't tell me. Instead, she terminated the pregnancy."

I gasp, "No!"

"Yes. She wasn't ready to be a mother, I guess."

"How did you find out?"

"I.... The papers from the clinic about her procedure were just sitting on her kitchen table. It was like she wanted me to see them." He shudders.

"Oh, Mick...."

"The thing is, I believe in a woman's choice. I do. But like I told my family tonight, she didn't give me a chance. I thought we were going to get married—have a family. But—"

"Wait? Your family didn't know about this before tonight?"

"Only Emily."

I nod. I know they're close.

He continues, "But the thing is, I can't get the idea out of my head that I'd have a kid by now. She would have been born in June."

I look him in the eyes. I know it's a look of pity, but I can't help it. This man... he makes me wish for more. "It makes sense."

"What does?"

"Your connection with Katie."

"What do you mean?"

"Well, she was born in June, right? And...." I stop midsentence because the sound that just came out of Mick was agonizing.

"Oh, God!" He stands up abruptly. "Oh, God, I never thought of that." He puts his hands over his face and bends at the waist. "Ah, fuck!" He's crying. Mick Flynn is crying. It's heart-wrenching. He's crying so hard his entire body is shaking. He speaks in jumbled words, but I understand him. "I never thought of that, Roni. I love that little girl so much!"

I stand and walk to him, then run my hand down his back. I have no words for him right now. Maybe he just needs to know I'm here. He may just need to let this out. I use my hands to soothe the best I can.

Still bent over, he shifts his big body around and wraps his arms around me. Nuzzling my neck, he weeps. "I would have taken care of my baby, Roni. I would have loved my baby. But she didn't give me a chance."

"I'm so sorry, Mick. I'm so sorry." I move us to the love seat so we can sit down, his arms still wrapped around me tightly. The feel of his body shaking with emotion is painful, but I'm his friend. This is what friends do. They provide comfort at times like this.

We sit like that, me wrapped up in his arms, for I don't know how long. My hands are touching him, soothing him. I run them up his arms, his back, through his hair. He takes gasping breaths when the crying stops. He's getting himself together. He pulls his head back and looks me in the eye. His eyes are bloodshot and swollen.

I slide my palm across his stubbled cheek and smile at him. "It's going to be okay, Mick."

Mick's hand glides up from my lower back and into my hair. His eyes turn a deep blue as he looks into my eyes. I see a sparkle from his tears on his lashes as he lowers his mouth to mine. His kiss is slow and sensual. His hand wraps around and around in the strands of my hair, getting a tight enough grip. He pulls my head back, causing me to open my mouth, and he uses the opportunity to slide his tongue deeply into my mouth, deepening the kiss and turning it from sensual to frantic. He moves from my mouth, kissing my face and chin, down to my throat. I feel myself getting wet, and he's barely gotten started. He swipes his tongue across my pulse point on my neck, then bites my earlobe. A moan escapes that I tried to keep inside. His left palm slides up to cup my breast. His fingers close over my nipple with a pinch.

"Mick," I whine.

"Shh, I need you, baby. Please?"

I need him too. I stand quickly. It startles him, but I reach my hand out for him to take. He places his hand in mine, letting me lead him to my bedroom. Backing him up, I push him down onto my bed. I place my knees on the edge of my queen-size bed and maneuver myself so I'm on my knees next to him. I slide my hands down his chest, over his amazing abdominals, to the pouch at his waist. I untie it and pull open his kilt to reveal his long, hard dick. Wrapping my fingers around him, I slide my palm up and down.

"Don't stop, Roni. That feels so good."

He adjusts himself so his weight is on one elbow and his forearm as he reaches up with his other to cup one of my breasts. Then he leans down and sucks one nipple into his mouth through my shirt. It makes me delirious. Exhausted and mentally drained, I think it may actually be heightening my arousal. He takes my hand, pulling it away from his cock.

"Hands and knees, babe," he demands.

I do as he asks and wait. His hands slide under my hips to encourage me to get up higher. He slides my panties down to my knees and then runs his fingers through my wet crease. "So wet for me, angel," he whispers. He pulls his hand away, and I wiggle my backside to get him back.

He leans over me and kisses the back of my neck and down my spine. His hands reach around to cup my breasts, and I feel his erection pressing against me. He's ready himself to enter me when I remember what Jennifer said on the phone at the party.

"Besides, you and I both know how much he likes his women on top. She'd crush him. He'll have to stick to doing her from behind so he doesn't have to see her fat jiggle around."

I stiffen at the thought, and Mick stops. "Are you okay? Do you want me to stop?"

"No. Do you...?" *Oh, shit. I can't say it. Courage, Roni.* "Do you like to do it any other way?"

"What do you mean?"

"We did it this way in your bedroom."

"From behind? No, I like it every way. What do you want to do?"

I don't want to be on top, that's for sure, but I feel I should test him. It's wrong. I know it is. "Can I be on top?"

"On top? You want to be on top?"

"Yeah," I say into the pillow. I'm still face-first, pressed into my bed. It's off-putting, to say the least.

"I guess. Let's try it."

Oh my God. Why did I even ask? I can never just enjoy myself. I have to mess with everything. "Okay."

He rolls over onto his back. He's no longer fully erect. I think I ruined the moment. I sit up on my knees at his side again and place my hands on my thighs. I hold my breath for a second, trying to conjure up some courage as I slip my sleep shirt off. He smiles up at me and runs his fingers over my nipple. When I arch my back to urge him on, he rolls toward me to take one nipple into his mouth and uses the flat of his tongue over the top of each, then flicks them fast with his finger.

It feels so good. I can tell he likes it too. He's getting excited again. Wanting to touch him, I lean forward, forcing him to lie on his back. I kiss his mouth and run my fingers through his hair. When I look into his eyes, I feel lost in them. They're still red from earlier, and he looks tired.

He reaches down to grab something from the floor. It's his pouch thing. He pulls out a condom, tears open the wrapper, and rolls it down his length. Mick places his hand on either side of my waist and helps me straddle him. He's a big guy with broad shoulders and chest, but his hips are slim, so it makes it possible to get my much shorter legs over him.

No one ever talks about these things in my romance books. It always sounds so easy. He keeps spreading his legs apart, which forces mine farther outward. It's a tad painful. I'm not the most limber person, but I refuse to give up just yet. I slide my palms over his chest and down his stomach. I'm trying to get my pelvis over him, and to do that, I have to put pressure on him. He lets out a guttural sound like I've pressed so hard I forced the air from him. I'm too heavy to be in this position. I don't have anything to hold onto. I can't use him; I'll break one of his Brunette or collapse a lung.

He gently rolls me over so I'm on my back and slides his body between my legs. "Maybe we'll try that again another time. We're both tired."

Tears sting the corners of my eyes. Those girls were right.

I'm too fat for Mick. He runs his hand down to my core and presses a finger into me. It feels good. I force myself to concentrate, so he'll bring me out of this funk. He runs his finger in circles around my clit. If he keeps it up, I'll come. I wriggle and moan as he uses his finger to bring me closer and closer to the brink. "Don't stop, Mick. I'm almost there."

Moving his first finger over my clit, he slides his middle finger into my core, in and out as he rubs around in the most wonderful circles. It only takes a few minutes before I'm coming hard at his fingertips.

Mick kisses me sweetly. "Are you ready for me, Roni?"

"Yeah."

He moves his body between my legs and slides into me. It feels so good I forget the other stuff. It's euphoric, this feeling of Mick and me together.

"You feel so good, Roni," he moans as he thrusts into me over and over. He's moving slowly in and out, saying dirty, dirty things.

"Fuck, Roni. You're wrapped around me like a fist. God, I could fuck this pussy all day every day."

I wish he would. I think he's even more excited than me because he's moving faster, thrusting harder. I like it. I do. I just keep going back to the humiliation of me being on top. I never should have tried it.

"Babe, are you there yet? I'm not going to make it much longer," he groans above me.

When I look up, his eyes are squeezed tightly together, and he almost looks like he's wincing. No matter, the man is still breathtaking.

"Yeah." I'm not. I already came hard with his hand. Now, I just want him to get his release. It'll make him feel better.

"You sure?"

"Yessss. Don't stop." He feels good, even if I don't feel another impending orgasm.

Before I know it, he's moaning out as he empties into his condom. I moan like I'm coming too. I just can't get there this time, but I don't want him to feel bad about it. I'm lost in thought when Mick leans down and whispers, "That was hot, babe." He kisses my forehead, then my nose, then he kisses me sweetly on the lips.

"Yeah, it was," I whisper.

He pulls out slowly, and I watch him walk to the bathroom. I quickly grab my top and panties and slip them on. A few minutes later, he slides back into bed and reaches for me. "Oh, you got dressed?" he asks, surprised.

"Yeah, I feel more comfortable sleeping with something on."

He pulls me closer to him, my back to his front so we're spooning. He slides his hand up so it rests beneath my breasts, then nuzzles my neck and hair and breathes in deeply. "Night, babe."

It's peaceful and cozy. I'm ready to go to sleep, but I've got to say something else to him. "Mick?"

"Yeah, babe?"

"It'll be okay. It'll happen for you."

His fingertips are making small circles on my belly, making me drowsy.

"What'll happen?" he asks tiredly.

"You'll have kids someday."

He jerks back. "No! No children." He pulls his hands away from me, rolls over to the other side of the bed, and stands up. "No kids, no relationships, no nothing!"

I roll over to look at him. "Mick? You can't know—"

"Oh, I know! That's why this thing with us can only be about fucking. No emotion. I can't do feelings."

Could have fooled me, but I remain silent. I'm not a fuck

buddy kind of girl. I'm a forever kind of girl. I'm his friend first, so I'll give him the benefit of the doubt. He's tired and upset from tonight. "Mick?"

He sighs heavily. "Roni, I'm tired. Tonight has been a fucking nightmare. I just need to sleep. Can we do that? Can we sleep now?"

Wow, that hurt. More than you could ever know. I sigh. "Yeah, fine. I need sleep too."

He doesn't say anything about talking later, which bothers me. He just wants this conversation to be over. That means I've got to accept the fact that I'm his fuck toy and that's all. I know I'm worth more than that. Can I be only that for him? No. I don't think so. Not even for Mick Flynn.

"Do you mind if I take a quick shower, Roni? I don't want to get blue makeup all over your sheets."

"Sure. Towels are under the sink. My shampoos and soaps are all in the shower. Let me know if you need anything."

When I hear the bathroom door click shut, I reach up and turn off my bedside lamp, casting the room and hallway into darkness. As the shower runs, I do my best not to picture him dripping wet. When the door to the bathroom opens, I squeeze my eyes shut. The bathroom light flips off, thrusting my room and the hallway into total darkness. I can tell he's feeling around on the walls in an attempt to get to the bed.

He bumps into my dresser and cusses. "Shit!"

"Did you hurt yourself, Mick?"

"No. Yes. I jammed my toe into a piece of furniture. What-ever the hell it is. Keep talking so I can figure out where you are."

"I'm here. Follow my voice."

My room is small, so in two strides, his knees hit my bed. He slides his big body over me to land next to me. Mick rolls back over to face me, sliding his hand over my body, resting it at my middle as his face meets my neck.

"Night, Roni."

"Night." I will do my best to forget about all of this. Forget Mick because he doesn't want a relationship and he doesn't want kids. But I do. I've always wanted a family. I want it all.

29

___

MICK

I lay in Roni's bed with one arm behind my head, the other at my side. I'm staring up at the ceiling, listening to her sleep. She's got a snore that's kind of cute. She must have been tired. Waking her up in the middle of the night wasn't my best move, but I wanted to see her. No, I needed to see her. I wanted her to know the truth about Lauren and about tonight.

It was a dick move demanding she leave the party. I was confused. Shit, I'm still confused. I meant what I said when I told Roni that I don't want kids or a relationship. I saw her expression after I said it. No doubt she had hopes for us, but I hope now she understands why this thing between us can't be more than this—sex. Friends with benefits. It pained me when her expression turned from sadness to anger when I told her all we could be was lovers. Well, I didn't use such sweet words. Fuck buddies. That's what I said. Jesus, I'm so screwed. I meant what I said, for the most part. It sucks because a part of me wants more with this girl, but I just can't. I just can't.

Fucking her tonight wasn't my smartest move either, but I can't help myself when I'm near her. I know she didn't come. After we had tried it with her on top, her confidence waned. I felt it. I saw it. She's like an open book. Her facial expressions give away everything. The truth is, having the woman on top isn't my favorite position. I don't have as much control that way, and I love being in charge during sex. Lauren always wanted to be on top. It was fucking annoying.

<hr>

MY EYES FLUTTER open to a bright light. *Where am I?* I look around the tiny space and see the culprit. Bright autumn light is pouring into a bedroom window. Roni's window. I roll over toward the center of the bed, hoping to see my girl. Goddamn it. Not my girl. She must already be up. I sit up, feeling the remains of a hangover that I, mostly, slept off. I run my fingers through my mop of hair and take a better look at her space. It's feminine. White walls, hardwood floors with one of those coiled rag rugs on the floor. There's a white dresser on my left and a matching armoire in the corner. Nightstands sit on either side of her queen-size bed. The bedding is soft and puffy. It's cozy and comfortable. I slept really well once I finally fell asleep.

I stand up, stretching, and my hands hit the ceiling. "Damn, this place is small," I say only to myself. I walk out into the short hallway to find her bathroom. "Maybe she's in the shower?" That'd be nice. I could join her.

Nope, the bathroom is empty. I finish up in there and make my way through to the main room. That's all there is to this place, one small bathroom, one small bedroom, and a room with a tiny kitchen and an even smaller sitting area. "This place can't be over 500 square feet," again, speaking to myself because Roni is nowhere to be seen. There's no coffee brewing, no eggs cooking, nothing. It's not like I expected her to fix me breakfast or anything. I'm not like that. I just assumed because Roni is *that* kind of girl, the kind of girl who makes breakfast for her man.

Even though I barely know her, I know Roni takes care of other people. She's a nurturer. Now, *she'd* be a great mother.

Fuck! I didn't mean for my mind to go there. I have no business thinking of Roni like that. But I'm sure she will be a great mom when she meets the right guy. That guy isn't me. I look into the kitchen once again to make sure she isn't just hiding. It's then that I see a key and a note:

Mick, I hope you're feeling better today. When you leave, please use this key to lock my deadbolt and slide it back under the door.

Thank you, Roni.

"THANK YOU, RONI?" *What the fuck?* "Thank you?" A chill runs down my spine because it's at that exact moment that I realize I've ruined everything.

30
———

MICK

I waited around Roni's apartment until I had to get ready for work, so about four hours. She never came home. I just sat on her tiny sofa and waited. I walked around her place looking at her photos, the stuff she had on her shelves, and her books. Surprisingly, I think I learned more about her by snooping than I have just by talking to her. I know she's the prettiest one in her family. Her sisters aren't bad looking; they just aren't beautiful like Roni. All three girls have blonde hair. The sisters look like their dad, but Roni looks just like her mom, stunning. I imagine Roni will be the same when she's older.

I learned she likes to collect odd things, like old skeleton keys, delicate teacups, and Pez dispensers. Ancient and new, they're all over her place. She has books everywhere too. From books about marketing to books by the classic authors like Jane Austen. She's got some new books too, primarily romances. I pull out one and check out the cover. It's a shirtless dude, and it's only showing his torso. It's obvious the guy is a gym rat, but beyond that, he's nothing special. I slam that book back on the shelf.

"She can do better than that," I mutter.

I peek in her nightstand and see a journal. While I'm tempted to look at it, it would be crossing the line. I won't invade her privacy like that. What I will do, though, is check out her bathroom medicine cabinet. You can learn a lot about someone that way. I pull open the mirrored panel above her sink and take inventory. Okay, there's standard stuff in here. Nothing that screams addict or psycho killer. There's aspirin, Midol, eye drops, nail file, nail clippers, and what the hell? Condoms? I pull open the box and count. There are supposed to be twelve condoms in the box, but I only count eight. What the fuck? I reach in and grab one and think. I flip it over and see a small date printed in black. I hold it closer to my face. "Expiration date?" I turn the box over in my hand, thinking. I spot a small printed date: EXP01-2015. "Well, at least I can assume she hasn't been with anyone recently. The damn things are expired," I mutter to myself. I blink. And then stare at my reflection in the mirror. I walk out into the living room and grab my sporran, pulling out the remaining condoms. I honestly didn't give thought to expiration dates. The ribbed for her pleasure condom expiration date isn't until 2020. I pull out the flavored rubber and note that it expires soon. I toss that one in her garbage and check out the neon condom. EXP05-2014.

Oh, holy fucking shit.

Which did I use with Roni? I squeeze my eyes shut, trying to think. I can't remember what we used at my place. I know it wasn't ribbed. I threw away the condom after our last time. I lean over and peer into her wastebasket. Just barely peeking out of a wrapped-up piece of tissue, I see the color green. Bright, neon green. Fuck! I toss all of the condoms from my pouch in the garbage. I knew condoms expired. Of course, I knew that. I just thought they lasted a lot longer. I run my fingers through my tangled hair. I need to get home, shower, and get to work. I'll think about all of this later.

I leave a note:

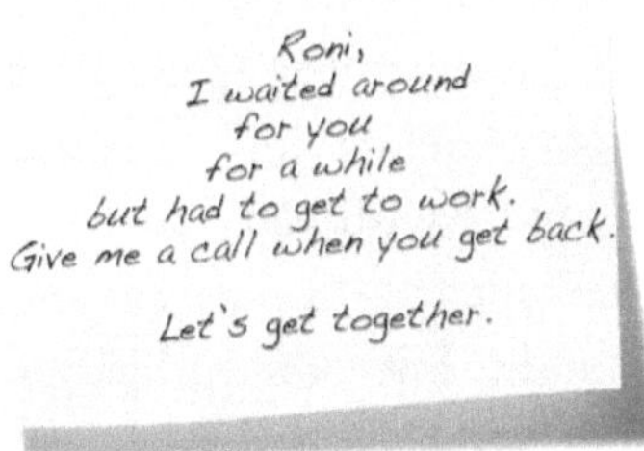

HOW SHOULD I SIGN IT? Yours? No, not "yours." Love? Oh, hell no. Best? No. I decide to just sign it, Mick. Simple. No need for anything else.

———

I RACE HOME, shower, and dress for work. Jogging down to my car, I feel my phone vibrate in my pocket. Maybe it's Roni. I pull it out of my pocket and peer at the screen.

I answer the phone, "Hey, Mom." When I hear her sniffle, I ask, "Mom? What's wrong? Is everyone okay? Is Dad okay?"

"Oh, Mick. Honey. Now I understand. I get it. Why you've been so sad this last year. I should have known it was something big. You aren't the type to stay down." She sniffles again.

I don't really want to talk about this with her, but I don't want her upset either. Besides, I knew it was just a matter of time until she found out. My family can't keep a secret to save their lives. And I didn't swear them to secrecy last night. It is time to get it off my chest. I should have done it sooner. My family would have carried some of this burden for me. It's what we do. We're good at taking care of each other.

"Mom, are you okay?"

"Oh, Michael. Yes, I'm okay. I'm just so sad for you, honey. And for us." Sarah Flynn's a nurturer too. Just like Roni. "I don't have words, baby boy. I really don't. I can only imagine how you've felt all this time. I wish you'd told us. Maybe we could have helped. But we know now, so we can move on from here." Sniffling again, she adds, "I never liked Lauren."

I chuckle. "Mom, you liked her when I was dating her. You just don't like her now."

"No, I never liked her. She was mean-spirited like Jennifer."

"So, I guess you heard about Jen and Dave?"

"He stayed at our house last night. He told us everything that happened at the party and afterward. Oh, Michael, I'm so worried about you and David."

"Mom, I'm really fine. Actually, I feel better today than I have since it happened. My friend R—"

"Roni?"

I laugh again. "Yeah, Roni. My friend. I talked to her last night and told her about it. She's a great listener, and she can hug almost as good as you can. Not quite, but almost."

"Hugging is an art form. It's nice to know a fellow artist," she smirks. "I can't wait to meet her. Why don't you bring her over for Sunday dinner? That is if you can ever get a Sunday night off."

"I do the schedule here, so I can make that happen. It just hasn't worked out the last few weeks. As for Roni at the family dinner? Maybe. I'm unsure about things with her."

"What aren't you sure about, Michael?"

"Mom, I just don't know how I feel about anything. I'm still pretty mixed up. That's all. She's not my type, anyway."

"She's not your 'type'?"

"No, she's not my type." *She deserves someone better, much better.*

"Well, your 'type' sucks, son."

I choke on my laugh. "What?"

"You heard me. Your type sucks. Just like Henry's used to suck, and Keith—well, Keith had a good eye. That's how he got Beth."

"What about David?" I ask to get her off me.

"Same thing. His type sucks."

"All right. I get it, Mom."

"Do you? Do you really? I don't have to look far for a great example. Take Sophie, for example. She wasn't Henry's type. But have you ever seen your brother so happy?"

"No. I know, Mom. Sophie's great."

"It's more than that, honey. Sophie takes care of Henry. She gives him balance, and part of that is because they're so different. She's soft to his hard. She's gentle to his rough. Does that make sense?"

I am listening to my mom, and it's like she's describing Roni and me to a tee.

"You boys that have chosen women similar to yourselves have been miserable. Look at David and Jennifer. She's razor sharp to his hard. She's rough to his coarse. Before yesterday, I'd never seen David so unhappy."

"What? He's happy today? He just kicked her out of his house. He wants a divorce. How can he be happy about that?"

"Because, Michael, she wasn't the right one for him. I think he sees Henry and Keith and wants what they have. Don't you want that?"

"Mom, honestly, I don't want any of that. No relationship, no kids... none of it."

"Michael Francis Flynn, now you listen to me! You have

always wanted a family. When you were a child, you used to tell me how much you wanted to have lots and lots of kids."

"Come on, Mom. I did not."

"Don't you talk back to me, young man. I can still paddle your bottom."

I groan. *Jesus, how emasculating is this gonna get?* "Mom, I did not talk about that shit with you."

"Language! Well, I see that this conversation is falling on deaf ears. Very well. I guess all I can do is let you get there on your own. I only hope it happens before I die." I hear her laugh softly. "Just think about what I said, Mick."

What? She never calls me Mick. What's up with that? "I will, Mom. I will. Okay, Mom, I've gotta get back to work."

"Fine. I hope to see you and your friend Roni at a Sunday dinner. Soon."

"Yeah. We'll see."

"I love you, Michael. No matter what, you'll always be my baby boy. Don't forget that."

"I won't."

31

———

MICK

On Monday, I wake up with a pounding headache. It's not a hangover. Maybe I'm coming down with something. It's getting cooler outside, so it's possible. Maybe I should check in with Roni—see what she thinks. She still hasn't contacted me since the other night. I'm starting to worry. We need to talk.

Me: Hey, are you busy?

I wait a few minutes. She usually responds right away.

Me: You must be. Text or call when you have time.

I hold my phone in my hand for a while, hoping she responds, but I get nothing. She must be busy at work. I get up and grab my towel and head to the shower. I've got some work to do early today, and then I babysit tonight. Ah, Katie. I know what Roni said was true. My subconscious probably had me thinking Katie was mine. I'm not crazy. I know she's not. But there is a special connection between us. We'll always be favorite uncle and favorite niece. I can live with that.

After my shower, I cook myself an egg white omelet and make a plan for the day. As I'm about to take my first bite, I hear my phone chime. "Text!" I hope its Roni. I grab the phone from on top of my bed and read.

Sophie: Hey, Mick. My class is canceled for tonight, so you don't need to babysit. Plan on next week, though. Okay?

Me: Sure thing. Thanks for letting me know.

Damn it. Now what do I do? "Ah-ha!"

Me: Roni? What are you doing tonight? My babysitting services aren't needed tonight, so do you want to get together? We could watch some Netflix and chill.

Yeah, I know what that means, and I know she knows what it means. I'm asking her to get naked with me tonight. Let's see what she says. I wait, peering down at my phone for longer than is cool. "Why isn't she answering me?" Maybe she's in some meetings. Yeah, that's probably it. Since I no longer have a strict schedule, I decide to head to the gym to work off some of this shit from the weekend. Plus, I've neglected my workout routine so much, I think I'm getting soft around the middle so much so my jeans were tight yesterday. I grab my duffle and head out the door.

Me: Do you think I've gained weight? My jeans were so tight yesterday I could barely button them. Am I getting a Dad-bod? **shudder** I guess that's what I get for drinking beer three out of four nights last week. Right? LOL

That'll make her laugh. I wait for a response from Veronica, but none comes.

———

IT'S BEEN three days and nothing from Roni. Not one text, voice mail, or even an email. I've counted. I've texted her nine times, left three voice mails, and I'm about to send her a lengthy email outlining my serious irritation with her lack of timely responses. Shit, I've even been to her place twice, and she's never home. Either that or she's playing possum. Could she be avoiding me? Why would she do that? What could I have done? I've rehashed the whole thing at her place, and I can't think of anything that happened that would have made her go complete radio silence on me. It couldn't be anything I said, could it? She seemed to get where I was coming from when we talked about kids and the rest. She must just be busy.

The only place I haven't tried to catch her is at P&P Advertising, so I decide to surprise her like I did before, right around lunchtime. When I walk up to the same receptionist, she gives me a shy smile. "What can *I* do for you?" Yeah, not shy.

"I'm here to see Roni McGonigall." She blinks at me as if she doesn't know who I'm talking about, so I repeat. "Veronica? Roni McGonigall?"

"I know who Roni is, sir. It's just... hang on, let me make a call. Can I get your name?"

What the fuck is going on? "Mick. It's Mick." I step away from the desk to let the next person in line get the runaround. I pace around the lobby for ten or fifteen minutes until I finally hear, "Mick?"

I turn, thinking I'll finally see Roni, but it's a different woman. One I met at the big party. "Yes?"

She walks up to me, hand extended. "Hi, I'm Deb. We met at the launch party?"

"I remember. It's good to see you, Deb, but I'm here to see Roni."

"So, you haven't talked to her lately? In the last couple of weeks?"

"I saw her Saturday night at my Halloween Party."

She looks surprised by that.

"What? Why?"

"I'm not supposed to say anything, but Roni doesn't work here anymore."

"Excuse me? Since when?"

"The day after the launch party. She quit." This Deb woman arches her brow at me.

"She quit? She didn't say anything. Why'd she quit?"

"I can't say. You'll need to ask Roni about that." She pats my arm. "I'm sure she'll tell you."

None of this makes any sense. Why would she have kept that from me? I look up at Deb. "I can't find her. She won't return my calls or texts. Do you know where she is?"

She shakes her head. "No. I haven't talked to her for a few days. She didn't mention anything to me."

Fuck! Looking down at my feet, I know I should say something. "All right. Thanks for your time. I'll check her apartment. Maybe I'll catch her at home."

"That's a good idea. Good luck, Mick."

"Thanks," I barely mutter.

When her apartment yields no results, I head into work. "God, I need time off. I haven't taken a real break from this place in over a year. Work is what I needed after everything went down with Lauren, but now I'm tired. Sleep will clear my head. I want to do nothing; I want to see no one. Except for Roni. I want to see Roni, damn it. I make one last-ditch effort with a text. After that, I'll leave her alone. That's obviously what she wants.

Me: Roni. Where are you? I'm worried. No one knows where you are.

I set my phone down, and shockingly, it dings.

Roni: I'm fine. Don't worry about me. Take care.

Take care?

Me: Take care? What's that supposed to mean, Veronica?

I stare at the illuminated screen on my phone and wait like Pavlov, salivating in the hopes that I hear another ding. Yeah, I remember that shit from school. I chuckle to myself. That's it! I'll send her a joke. It's *our* thing.

Me: Here's a good one... An atheist, a vegan, and a Crossfitter walk into a bar. I only know because they told everyone within the first three minutes. LOL. Good one, right?

Nothing. No reply. *What the hell?*

The next few days drag on and on and on. As each day passes, I get more and more depressed. I miss her. I guess it's true what they say. Absence makes the heart grow fonder. Or is it distance? All I've done when I'm not slinging drinks is think about my time spent with Roni. Then there's our text messages and phone conversations. Babysitting Katie. And the sex. Goddamn, the sex. I have to rub one out daily just to work through those memories. I almost can't take it anymore. I've got to do something. *Where are you, Veronica?*

32

———

RONI

A week at home has done me good. I needed to see my parents and sisters—to recharge. Being away from the drama, literally, helps put things into perspective. Talking everything related to Mick out with my sisters? Not so helpful.

I'm the middle daughter. Growing up, I was the ugly one. The fat one. Still am. I know I'm not ugly; it's just Frankie and Gloria are both gorgeous. They're tall and still slim even after having kids. Their hair is long and styled perfectly no matter what time of day it is. I could surprise them at two in the morning and they'd look runway ready. No joke.

Their children are the same—always wearing clean clothes, hair combed and neat. It's unnatural. My older sister, Frankie, has one girl, Lillian, age six. The baby of the family, Gloria, has two hellions, Polly and Maddy, five and three respectively. I love them all fiercely, but there are times when I don't really like my sisters. They're so obsessed with appearance, dress size, and weight that I have trouble talking at any length with them before they start to nitpick at my faults.

Maybe it's because they are both stay-at-home mothers. They spend their days surrounded by other moms and babies all day, comparing themselves to the others. I know that staying home to care for your family is a full-time job and hard as hell, but my sisters are different. How do I know this? Well, I've got a couple friends who stay at home, and they aren't like my sisters. No, instead of organizing playdates, cleaning, and grocery shopping like my friend Karen always grumbles about, my sisters worry about making sure they keep their bodies in check for their husbands for fear they'll leave them if they gain weight. I'm not making that part up. I've heard the two of them talking. They're more concerned about not looking the part than they are about anything else.

They spend extra time getting dressed and made up because if they leave home looking less than perfect, they may embarrass their men. I don't get it because my brothers-in-law are no Flynn brothers. Let me tell you. They are average at best. I'd definitely put my sisters into the trophy wife category. It doesn't matter what I think. My sisters are still going to worry.

The funny thing is, none of that vanity came from my parents. My mom was a real beauty, still is, but she was so busy raising us and working with my dad to keep a roof over our heads, she didn't have time to worry about her hair, her makeup, or the latest fashion. Take Mom's hair, for example. She's always kept it short. She said she never wanted to fuss with it in the morning, so keeping it short gave her that freedom. I sort of envy that. Maybe that's what inspired my recent change. I've threatened to chop off my hair many times, but my sisters have always talked me out of it, saying stuff like "It's the one good thing you've got going for you. Don't cut your hair." But I didn't listen this time.

No matter how annoying my sisters are, though, they're still my sisters. That's why we decided to celebrate tonight by going out to the one and only bar in our tiny town called Smitty's. We wanted to bond since it's my last night in good ole Goblesville,

Indiana. Population 1,928. Well, it dropped to 1,927 when I left, and I don't think anyone else has fled.

When they picked me up at Mom and Dad's, they were shocked to see the new me. I hadn't warned them I was going to chop off all my hair. I knew what they'd say. (See above) In typical fashion, my siblings were so upset by the new look that I think Frankie had tears in her eyes, and while I value their opinions to a certain extent, I'm not going to let their reaction get to me because I really like it. It's short and easy to style. It only took me twenty minutes to get ready, including a shower. Yay me.

My new cut is really cute. It falls to my chin in a layered, choppy bob with bangs. It's edgy. At least that's what Pearl called it, and Pearl knows where it's at when it comes to hairstyles. You may think Pearl is elderly, but she's actually my age. Her grandmother, Granny Pearl, left the salon to Pearl Junior in her will. I believe the look suits me. It's more professional than big, wavy hair. It makes my face look less round, and my eyes look huge.

Once my sisters get over the shock, we head to the bar. I'm not surprised to see it hasn't changed since the last time I was here. Smitty's is the most disgusting dive bar in the US. No! The world. There are peanut shells on the floor from the Johnson administration. I'm not kidding. It's one of their claims to fame.

Frankie wanted girl time, and I wanted to get sloshed. Girl time it is. Gloria plops down in the one and only corner booth. I slide in next, then Frankie. Now I'm sandwiched between the two of them, so I can't escape either side without one of them getting out. My ass has found its way into a large crevice in the bench. It's a section without padding and not much vinyl. I feel thick wires poking into my butt.

One of my old classmates, Chelsea, is our waitress. "What

can I get you, girls?" It's good to see her. She was always pretty nice to me.

Frankie speaks first. "Gloria and I will have a Cranberry Cosmo. Be sure they use Skinny Girl, please. Roni, you should try Skinny Girl. It's delish. They keep it here just for us," Frankie brags.

"I'll have an Old..." Should I be drinking? Maybe one of us should be responsible tonight. Although, being out with these two makes me want to drink. "I'll have a cola."

"Cola?" Gloria gasps. "First of all, I thought you wanted to get drunk tonight, and secondly, do you know how many calories are in regular cola? At least get diet," she huffs. "It's no wonder..."

I know what she's saying. It's no wonder I'm fat. Whatever.

Before I can speak, I see Frankie clicking away on her phone. Her gasp clues me into what's coming next. "Two hundred calories for one bottle of cola, Roni. That's too many calories."

"You shouldn't drink your calories," adds Gloria.

"I'll be okay. I'll walk home. Burn it off," I deadpan.

"You'd better," chides Gloria. "You do not need to gain any more weight, especially now that you've got that short hair." I swear she shivers at that.

I want to talk to them about Mick, but I've tried talking about boys before and it's always the same. They listen and pat my arm like I'm some poor sap who can't keep a man. We get our drinks, and it's time.

Frankie goes first. "Now, Roni, tell us what's going on. You've been home for five days now, and we want to know why."

"I told you. I just missed you guys."

Gloria snorts. "I can believe you missed your nieces, but beyond that, I say that's bull*pucky*."

Bullpucky? "Yeah, well... it's complicated."

"We love complicated," interjects Frankie.

"Yeah, our lives are boring as hell. Spill," demands Gloria. Gloria may be the youngest, but that doesn't preclude her from being the bossy one.

"I don't want Mom and Dad to worry, and I'm doing fine. I've got savings—"

"Oh shit," both sisters say simultaneously.

"No. It's not bad. I've got it under control."

"What? Did you get fired from your fancy city job?" says Gloria sarcastically.

"No. I quit!"

"You quit? Why? That was a great job for you. You were lucky to get it." That came from Frankie who has never, and I mean never, held a job. Not even in high school because of all of her activities. Her dance team, cheerleading squad, and drama club took up too much of her time. Then she married Matt right out of high school.

I'm sick and tired of the way they make me feel. "What would you know about it, Frankie? You've never worked a day in your life."

"I work! Being a mom is a tough job."

"Yeah," agrees Gloria.

Of course, she agrees. Except for a two-month stint at The Dairy Cone, (yeah, stupid name) she hasn't worked either. She claimed she was lactose intolerant and had to quit. She is not lactose intolerant. She eats cheese like it's air. Mind you, it's light cheese.

"Look, it's a long story, and I don't want to get into it tonight. It's my last night with you guys, and I want to spend it bonding." *And getting drunk.* I blink like I'm going to cry. I'm appealing to their emotional sister side.

"Awe, we do too, VeeVee."

I hate that nickname. I didn't mind it when I was five, but when I hit puberty, having the tag "VeeVee" was super embarrassing. Might as well call me Vagina, Vagina. So, I made them stop by telling them I'd send pictures of both of them to the Goblesville varsity football team without their hair and makeup done. "VeeVee" died a quick death.

"So," Frankie says cheerily, "met any guys lately?"

Should I talk to them about Mick? I know I shouldn't because I am aware I'll feel worse when it's over than I do right now. But fuck it. Maybe if they know about him, they'll let up on the harsh comments. "I have a friend."

"A friend?" asks Gloria.

"Yep. A hot friend." They're both looking at me pityingly, so I add, "With benefits."

That perks them right up. "With benefits? What does that mean in your world? Have you gone on any dates?" asks Frankie.

"Have you... done it?" Gloria whispers the last two words.

For two married women, they act like they've never had sex. I whisper back, "Yes." And then I smirk.

"So, what happened?"

"What do you mean?" I ask Frankie.

"Well, it must be over if you're here. If he were so hot, you'd be with him now. Right?" she asks, looking at Gloria.

"Yeah, I see what Frankie's saying. Poor VeeVee. Did he dump you?"

Jesus. See? I knew this would happen. "No, he didn't dump me. He's just... he's—" *standing in the fucking doorway of Smitty's Tavern looking like a goddamn wet dream in a pair of jeans that are not too baggy and not too tight.* He's got on a tight gray tee that says something on the front. A band tee? But that's not enough. He's also wearing a black leather jacket that looks old and worn. It's not fair he can look that good. When my eyes find his face, I notice his hair is pulled back into a ponytail and he's got a full beard. Shit, how long has it been since I've seen him? "What is he doing here?" I whisper-squeak.

Both sisters follow my line of sight. "Ooh, I don't know, but I'm glad," coos Gloria. "He's hot."

Frankie decides to join in the conversation. "Oh my God! That's the hottest guy I've ever seen. In. My. Life."

"Yeah." Mick Flynn is hot as hell. I watch as he saunters over to our table. "Ladies." He nods at my sisters.

"Well, hello there," says Gloria, wiggling her red-tipped fingers at him.

Then he says, "Roni? I've been looking for you for over a week. I've been worried about you." He puts his hands on his narrow hips and adds, "Should you be drinking?"

I blink up at him and wonder what that's supposed to mean. "Not that it's any of your business, but this is cola. I'm the designated driver tonight." *But, God, I could sure use a drink now.*

"Wait a second, Roni. You know him?" squeaks Frankie.

"No way," says Gloria.

While I too am surprised I know him, I roll my eyes. "Mick, meet my sisters." I point to Frankie first. "This is Frankie, and the other one is Gloria. Guys, this is Mick Flynn. The friend I was just telling you about."

"No way," says Gloria again. "There's no way you can get a guy like *that*." She points accusingly.

"Gloria! That's not nice," warns Frankie. "They're just friends. Remember?"

"Oh, yeah. Phew, for a second there I thought the sky was falling." She giggles. "Or it's the end of the world as we know it. Ooh, no wait—Hell froze over!" Gloria throws back the rest of her Skinny Girl cocktail. It only takes one or two drinks for her to start the descent into drunk since she probably skipped dinner tonight to make up for alcohol-related calories.

I'm listening to them but not really hearing what they're saying. I'm so used to these kinds of comments, I let it slide right off my back. Besides, I'm more interested in looking at Mick. God, he's beautiful. But it's apparent that he heard them. He's giving my sisters the stink eye. I should probably explain our sisterly dynamic, the one where they act superior in every way, talking down to me, criticizing me, and for some inexplicable reason, I let them; but I'll save that conversation for another day.

I'm pulled from my thoughts when he asks, "Roni. Can I talk to you? *Alone*."

"Oh," I hesitate. "Sure. Can you let me out, Gloria?"

She moves out of the booth and stands next to Mick. She's peering up at him, fluttering her eyelashes.

"Do you have something in your eye?" Mick asks her.

"No. Why do you ask?" Gloria giggles, still fluttering her false lashes. See? Drunk already.

"You're blinking a lot. It looks weird," he deadpans.

She stops immediately just as I step between them. Giggling, I grasp his firm, muscular arm and pull him toward the door. There's no way I'm having this conversation in front of sisters and the entire town bar.

It's chilly outside but not the common November cold I'm used to in Chicago where Lake Michigan brings in frigid temperatures. Since Goblesville is landlocked, it's only brisk. I move him to the side of the building that obscures any curious gawkers and blocks the chilly wind. I lean back on the wood-clad siding and look up into his clear blue eyes.

"Do you want my coat?" Mick asks as he starts to pull off his leather jacket.

"No, we won't be out here long. What are you doing here? How did you find me? This is creepy as hell, Mick."

He chuckles. "Yeah. It's got that stalker vibe all over it, doesn't it?"

"Uh, yeah."

"I was worried. I've tried calling and texting. I've been to your apartment at least six times. I even stopped by your work. You quit your job?"

"Yep."

"Why? And why didn't you tell me?" he says, sounding hurt.

"I guess I didn't want to talk about it. You know how that feels, right?" He does. He went a year without telling people about Lauren and the baby.

"I get that. I guess I thought we were closer. Close enough for you to be able to talk to me," he says, sounding sad again.

I sigh. We're not close, really. We're friends. "I'm not at the point in this *friendship* where I feel like I can confide in you about everything, Mick." I'd risk getting hurt, and I don't want that.

"I get that, but you just disappeared, baby," he whispers, moving closer to me. One of his hands now rests on my hip while the other moves up to the back of my neck. "You cut your hair off?"

I sigh. This isn't going to be good. "Yeah. I wanted a change."

He runs his fingers through the short strands. "I like it. You look hot, babe." He brings his other hand up to touch my hair. "So soft," he says distractedly. He puts his forehead against mine, smiling down at me. "It's still long enough for me to pull," he smirks.

Oh, hell. I decide to forget that entire exchange because he's turning me on. Instead, I explain my trip home. "I didn't just disappear. I was planning on heading back to my hometown first thing Sunday morning. I had my bags packed and the rental car parked right out in front of my apartment building. I woke up and grabbed my stuff and left. You were sound asleep. I didn't want to wake you up. You'd had a hard night. You needed sleep."

The truth is, I woke up at five thirty in the morning and tiptoed out of my place. I didn't want to wake him up because I wanted to escape. I knew he'd find a way to keep me in bed—either that or he'd want to talk about our "friendship."

"But you didn't return my calls, and you only replied to one text."

"I've had my phone off most of the time I've been home. My boss, I mean ex-boss, Bill Phillips, has been blowing up my phone this week. I was tired of hearing it ding. It gave me a headache."

"What does he want?" Mick is using his fingers to touch strands of my blunt haircut.

I could fall asleep to that. I love having my hair played with, but I press on. "Oh. He wants to talk to me. Why?" I murmur as I feel his hand move from my hair down to my waist, then up under my sweater. "Mick? What are you doing?"

"I've missed you, Roni." He leans down and covers my mouth with his, and I let him. His tongue sweeps inside my mouth, and when I hear his deep moan, I can't take it. I wrap my arms around him and kiss him like it's our last kiss. He slides his mouth from mine to kiss down my cheek to my neck. "I missed you so fucking much. I need you bad, angel."

I can tell. His hard-on is rubbing me right where I need it. He reaches down and grasps my ass and lifts me up. Out of fear of falling on my ass, I wrap my legs around his waist and hold on to his shoulders. I can't believe he lifted me up like I weigh nothing.

"All I could think about all week is fucking you again."

Really? That's all he thought about? I drop my legs and wiggle until he lets me down. "Mick? I thought you said you were worried about me. That you missed me."

He reaches for me to pull me back. "I *was* worried. I *did* miss you."

"You missed your fuck buddy? Is that it?"

"Well, yeah. We're friends with benefits. Right?"

I pull farther away from him. "No. We're not. You only see to your own needs. I don't want to just be a booty call, Mick. I'm not that girl. I'm the girl who wants to be in a real relationship and have a family someday. Since I know that's not what you want, I think we should just end this, part ways. It's for the best. Let's just nip this in the bud."

I turn and start back to the bar. I'm chilled through, and not all of it has to do with November in Indiana. I feel a large hand wrap around my arm.

"Roni. Wait. I'm sorry. I... I know I came on too strong there. You've got me coming and going."

"I'll help you figure this out. You're going," I pull my arm out of his hand and almost make it to the door when he slides in front, blocking my entrance.

"I know you're pissed, babe. I don't blame you."

"You don't know anything about me, Mick. If you did, you would have handled this differently. How the hell did you find me, anyway?"

"I googled you. You've got your hometown listed on your Facebook page, and I just searched from there and found only one McGonigall listed. I tried it, hoping it was your parents' phone number. I figured I'd call them to see if they knew where you were. When I mapped it, I saw you were only a few hours away, so I decided to drive here. When I got to their place, your mom said you were out with your sisters," he says, pointing to the bar.

"You still have my key?"

"I do. I was going to do as you instructed, but I thought it'd be better to give it to you in person. Safety first."

"You went back to my place? Six times?" *Shit. I hope he didn't read my journal.*

"I didn't read your journal, if that's what you're worried about."

"The fact that you know I have a journal is enough to give me chills. What the hell?" I yell. "Go home, Mick. I'm trying to be nice here. I don't want to hurt your feelings, but I just want to spend time with my family. My sisters are—"

"Bitches," he pronounces.

"You know what, asshat? You cannot call them that! You don't even know them. Only I can call them names. Me! Not you! How would you like it if I called your sisters bitches?"

He chuckles. "They have their moments, but they aren't bitches, Roni. You know that."

"You're missing the point here. You don't have any right to call my sisters names."

"No right? I love you." He stares at me and blinks. Thinking quickly, he adds, "Like a friend, Veronica. I hated hearing them talk about you like that." He nods to the door of Smitty's.

Why did that make me even angrier? "You love me? Like a friend?"

"Of course."

I flutter my eyelashes at him and bring my hands up like I'm in prayer. "You love me like a friend? Oh, thank you so much, Mick. I'm the luckiest girl in the world. I'll cherish that. I really will." Yeah, sarcasm is awesome. I place one fist on my hip and point toward the highway. "Now go home!"

"What? Jesus, Roni. You confuse the fuck out of me. I thought we were on the same page."

Okay, my anger has morphed in seconds. It's now something else entirely. I'm on the verge of tears, but I just can't let him see those. I'm resigned. That's it. He's trying to make me feel guilty.

He's blaming me and making it seem like I've changed on him. Or maybe he thinks he didn't have the real Veronica before.

One tear leaks out of my eye. I can't stop it. "I'm confused too. You confuse me too. One minute you want a friend who makes you laugh. The next, you want benefits. Sure, I'm both of those things, but I'm a whole lot more too. The problem is, you don't want the other parts of me. You want the funny friend who you can fuck."

"That's not true. I need to tell you—"

"I'm not built that way, Mick. Since you only want part of me, I've got to say no—you get none of me. My heart can't take it. I have feelings for you. Feelings I know you can't or won't reciprocate. That's your choice." I back away from him. "My choice is to salvage what's left of my heart and go back to the way things used to be." *Being alone, like I used to be.*

"Baby. Don't. I care about all of you."

"No, you don't." I pause. "It's okay. I can't ask you to give me more than you're willing to give. That wouldn't be fair of me. Like it's not fair of you to ask me to give less of me. I can't. When I'm in, I'm all in. I take care of the ones I love, and I need the same in return."

I reach for the door handle, but I turn and walk up to him. I place my hands on his upper arms and lift up onto my toes. I give him a gentle kiss on his lips. "You're an amazing guy, and you were actually a good friend. While it's not fair of me to ask it of you, I just need more than that from you. So, go home. Go back to Chicago and live your life as you want. I want you to be happy." I kiss him one more time and head back into the bar with a pain in my chest so intense, I can barely breathe. I'll get over it. I always do.

33

———

MICK

Shit! That was a train wreck. I came here to talk to her. I needed to tell her about the damn expired condoms. I started to, but she didn't give me a chance. Maybe if I hadn't tried to do her against the side of the building. I also wanted her to know I missed her. Because I have. I've missed her like fucking crazy. The drive back home is going to suck. I'll spend the entire time reliving what just went down at the bar. Fuck! What the hell just happened back there? Did she just break up with me? Can I call it a breakup? No. I can't call it a breakup. We weren't a couple. But we were, in a way. It felt like we were a couple at her launch party. And at my Halloween party— until we weren't. Fucking Lauren.

She has feelings for me? I guess I knew that. Veronica McGonigall is not the kind of girl who just hooks up with a guy. She's girlfriend all the way. She's right. I'm not for her. Did she say that? That I wasn't for her? Or was I just summarizing her words? Jesus, I'm going insane. Maybe if I talk it out with someone besides myself, it'll help. I hit the phone button in my car. I know it's late, but she'll be up. She's always up late studying or doing whatever med students do.

"What the hell, Mick. It's late," Emily grumbles. "Where are you? Are you in your car?"

"I knew you'd be up. Can we talk? I'm on my way home from Goblesville, Indiana. I went to see Roni."

"Roni? I had a feeling this was about a girl. Why is she in Indiana?"

"What do you mean you knew this was about a girl?"

"The only times you want to have a serious talk with me is to talk about a woman. Spit it out. What'd you do?"

"First of all, that's not true. I talk to you about all kinds of shit. As for me, I didn't... Yeah, I did. I fucked up."

"Mmm-hmm, girrrl." She giggles.

After she stops taunting me, I tell her everything that has happened since the Halloween party.

"You stalked her all the way to Indiana?"

"Yeah, so?"

I hear her pretend to shiver. "You're a creeper, brah."

"I need advice. I need for you to tell me what to do. You're my kung fu master; I'm your grasshopper."

"Jesus, Mick. You need sleep. You're delirious."

"True." I haven't slept for shit this week. "Will you help me? Give me the truth?"

"Okaaay. Here goes. You're a fucking idiot douchebag."

That takes me off guard. That's not what I expected to hear. "And? Jeez. Don't hold back on my account."

"You said you wanted the truth, but you can't handle the truth, dude."

"I can. Just say it."

"Where was I? Oh, yeah. Blah, blah, blah, fucking idiot douchebag. Okay. I've caught up. Mick, you know the answer already. I don't need to tell you what you already know. You want the girl, but you're scared shitless. That's all thanks to that cun—to Lauren."

I hear Emily clanking dishes in the background as she speaks. "That bitch doesn't deserve one more minute of your time. She's a stain on your life, for sure, but a stain that will eventually disappear. But by keeping all of that hate and anger inside of you, you're missing out on something that could be fantastic and real and forever. Roni is cool. She's funny and super pretty. Not to mention that she seems to put up with your shit. Or she did. Apparently, she got smart and dumped your ass. She deserves to be treated better by you, big brother."

"I know."

"Plus, you're obviously attracted to her. I mean, the deal in the bedroom. You were so freaking loud. I'll never be able to unhear you, dude. Gross."

I chuckle.

"Not funny. I'm serious. I've got PTSD from that." She sighs. "You want my advice? For real?"

"Yeah."

"Get your head out of your ass, pull up your big boy pants, and go get your girl. She's that forever kind of girl every guy needs. She's one you hang onto with both hands. If you don't, you'll lose her, and you'll literally regret it for the rest of your pathetic life."

I nod. She can't see me doing that, but it's okay. She's right. I know all of that. I've known all of that for a while. I just wasn't ready to accept it. I've gotta get ready, though. "When I picture my life moving forward, she's with me."

"So you had your answer already. You were just too chick-enshit to admit it?"

"Pretty much. Now the question is, will she take me back?"

"No, the question is, what's your play gonna be?"

"My play?"

"Yeah, your play. It needs to be a grand, enormous gesture.

I'm talking huge. Jeez, Mick. There's nothing worse than an old guy who can't commit."

"I'm not old. I'm twenty-seven."

"Yeah, but you're almost thirty. O-L-D, old."

"I'm not...." The highway I'm on is dark. I haven't seen another set of headlights for thirty miles. Just as I hear her spell out old, I catch something moving in my peripheral vision. I've forgotten all about my phone call just as I make contact with something enormous and brown.

"Fuck!" I shout.

"Mick?" Emily's voice sounds frantic. "Mick? You there? Jesus, say something, Mick!" Panic has set in, and now she's screaming. "Mick!"

I feel my body being slammed forward, right, then left. My world is spinning around me, glass is breaking, metal is scraping and crunching. Then nothing.

34

___

RONI

I'm woken up by the sound of ringing. It won't stop. Am I hallucinating? I lift my head up from my pillow as I hear my name being called from downstairs.

"Roni? Telephone," the voice yells from a distance.

I sit up too fast, and my head spins. My head is splitting but not from drinking. I stuck to cola all night. This is a headache brought on by a good old-fashioned crying jag.

"Roni! Telephone," my dad yells again.

I peer at the clock and see 12:03 a.m. illuminated in bright red numbers.

Damn. I've only been asleep for half an hour. I slowly lift my body from my bed. Still dressed in last night's outfit, I drag myself off my bed. Lumbering to the top of the stairs, I call down, "Dad? Who is it?"

In his deep, raspy sleepy voice he says, "Hell, I don't know. Just get down here."

I stumble down toward the wall telephone. It's so old, it's not even cordless. It still has the curly, yellow plastic cord attached to it. Like so many people, my parents use their cell phones for everything, but they like to have a landline "just in case."

I take the phone receiver from my dad. "Hello?" I say tiredly.

"Roni? This is Emily."

"Emily?"

"Yeah, Emily Flynn," she says hurriedly.

What the hell? "Mick's not here." *Why is she calling me? At my parents' house. On the old yellow wall telephone.*

"I know. What time did he leave?"

"Why? What's going on?" I'm starting to wake up because I can hear the fear in her voice now. "Emily? What's wrong?"

"He had an accident. Or I think he had an accident."

"An accident?" I screech. "Is he okay?" My breathing picks up.

"Listen, I need for you to think."

"What? How can I help?"

"I was talking to him on the phone when he wrecked. It was after eleven. Close to eleven thirty. What time did he leave you?"

Leave me? "He came to the bar at...." We hadn't been to the bar very long, maybe twenty or thirty minutes. My sisters and I went out late after their kids were in bed. They picked me up just before ten. "I think he was there around ten fifteen or ten thirty."

I hear her muffled response like she's talking to someone else. "So that means he'd been on the road for about an hour."

"Emily? What's going on? Is he okay?"

"We don't know, Roni. I heard him yell, and then all I could hear were the sounds of a crash. Then nothing. I called 9-1-1 but couldn't give them his location, so after a Google search, I found only one McGonigall in Goblesville, Indiana. Thank God it's you."

"What can I do?" I look over at my dad who is standing nearby with his hands on his hips, looking worried.

Emily's voice changes to a deep masculine voice. "Roni? It's Hank. I need for you to think. You know the roads better than any of us. How far would he have gotten in about an hour?"

I've made the trek so many times that I should know approximately where he'd be if he drove without stopping. I can't think. "An hour out?" I mumble. "Dad? Mick. They think he had an accident an hour out. Where would he be?" God, I'm numb.

My dad takes the phone from my hand gently and speaks into the receiver. "This is Roni's dad. No matter which highway he took, he'd be close to Plymouth, Indiana."

But which way would he have taken? I tune out my dad as he talks to Hank. He could have taken Highway 30 up to Interstate 90, or he could have taken Highway 31. "Dad? Which way would he have gone?" I interrupt him as he talks to Hank Flynn.

Dad holds one finger up as a sign to wait.

"Yeah, okay. We'll head out now. Give me your cell number," my dad says to Hank. "We'll leave in five minutes and let you know when we get close to Plymouth." He pauses to listen, then ends with, "Talk to you soon."

Dad hangs up the phone. He reaches out and squeezes my arm. "Put your shoes on. Grab your coat."

"What's going on, Dad?"

"They aren't sure where he had his accident, so you and I are taking one route to Plymouth and Hank and Emily are going to search the other. They've been on the road for thirty minutes. Hank's going to alert the Plymouth police to be on the lookout for an accident. Let's go."

I race to the foyer and see a pair of Mom's shoes. We wear the same size, so I slip them on and grab my coat off the hook near the door. I run upstairs to grab the keys to my rental car.

The overwhelming need to vomit hits me like a Mack truck. "It's my fault."

I move as fast as I can to the one and only full bathroom. *Please let me get to the toilet.* I push the door open, and just as I'm opening the lid to the toilet, it comes out like a torrent. Once I'm done retching, I flush the toilet and grab a cloth from below the sink. As fast as I can, I clean myself up and rush out the bathroom door.

Dad is waiting for me by the front door with two bottles of water and a thermos of coffee. He's dressed in his work boots and heavy-duty Carhartt gear. As a former volunteer fireman, he knows about search and rescue. I only hope he doesn't need to utilize those skills. He's big and tall, and he's always been my hero. I feel the tears burning the back of my eyes, but I can't get emotional. "Let's take my car. It's got a full tank of gas."

He nods and takes the keys from me. I'm too emotional to drive. Besides, I'm a better lookout than he is. I know what Mick's car looks like. "We're taking highway thirty-one up. I'm going to drive as fast as I can. Okay?"

I nod to him as I open the passenger side door. I slip in and buckle up, then squeeze my eyes closed as I feel the car lurch forward. "Did you tell Mom?"

"I left her a note."

"Okay, good."

We drive in silence for the first twenty minutes. My hands are fisted around the bottom of my coat, and I haven't moved. I'm tense and scared. "It's my fault, Dad."

"How do you figure?"

"Because he wouldn't have had an accident if he hadn't come to see me."

"That logic is problematic."

I roll my eyes. The car is dark, so I know he can't see me.

"Don't roll your eyes at me, young lady."

That surprises a small laugh out of me. "I didn't." I sigh. "Yeah, I did. I know it's not logical to take the blame here, but he has been trying to get in touch with me all week, and I've just ignored him."

"Why's that, dove?"

My parents both call me "dove." It's their nickname for me. My sisters didn't get a special name, and I like that. A lot. "It's complicated."

"How so?"

Jeez. He's not going to let this go. He asked for it... "Well, I met Mick at a bar."

Dad groans.

Ignoring his response, I continue. "He's a bartender."

He groans even louder now. It makes me smile. I laugh. "Well, he manages a club downtown."

"That's better than just being a bartender."

"Anyway...." I explain how we met, how we became friends, how we became more than friends—ick, not the specifics. I told him about his deal with Lauren and why I'm home.

"Wow, Roni. That's a lot to take in. Why was he here tonight?"

"He missed me. He wanted to see me, but for all the wrong reasons. I made him leave."

"He drove here to see you, and you sent him away?"

"He didn't come to tell me he loved me or that he wanted to be my boyfriend or anything. He was just, you know...."

"No. Why was he here?"

"Seriously, Dad! You're going to make me say it?"

"Say what? I'm the one who's confused now, dove."

"You asked for it. He was horny. Okay?" *There! I said it. Fast.*

"Oh. *Oh!* Well, that's not a bad thing. Right?"

I choke on my sip of water from my bottle. "What?"

"Well, he came all this way to see you. You must be special to him."

I smile. Of course, he sees the good in all of that. "Dad, that's not okay. Like I told him, I'm not a 'hookup' kind of girl. I'm girlfriend material."

"Obviously! You're too special to just be used for... you know." Now he's getting in over his head. "So, how do you feel about him?"

"I care about him. I like him. I probably love him. But none of that matters now. I said my peace, and now it's over."

"You think it's over?"

"Yep. He doesn't want a relationship—not one with me, anyway. He doesn't want kids, and I want kids."

"I know. I want that for you too, but don't count him out just yet. You really are special, Veronica. I'm not just saying that because I'm your father. You're smart, beautiful, and kind."

"You're supposed to say those things. I just hope he's okay." I feel the burn of tears behind my eyes and don't try to stop them. "What if he's n-n-not okay?" I stutter. My tears turn into sobs.

Dad places his hand over mine and squeezes. "He'll be okay. We'll find him and make sure of it."

35

RONI

As we drive, I reach for my hair nervously. It's like a phantom limb. I keep thinking all of my hair is still there. My attempt to think about something as mundane as my hair is short-lived when my dad says, "Okay, dove. We're about ten miles from Plymouth. Time to keep an eye out for anything out of the ordinary. This section is very wooded. It's possible he hit a deer or other animal. Emily didn't think she heard another car, but she's not sure. My guess is deer. They're everywhere this time of year."

He slows the car down to about half the posted fifty-five miles per hour speed limit. While I want him to go faster, slower means I can scan both sides of the road as he drives. We're silent as he crawls along.

"Wait! What's that?" I say, pointing to a limb lying across the road.

"It's just a limb. It's been windy today."

"Right."

Dad continues to move past the limb when I see the body of a large buck, antlers partially on the highway, the rest of his large body on the edge. "Dad!"

"I see it. I'll pull over, then we'll need to get out and look around. Are you going to be able to do that?"

"Yes, of course. Just pull over."

He stops about ten feet from the carcass, and I jump out of the car. It's gotten colder overnight, so I wrap my coat around me tightly. Dad reaches his hand out, and I place mine in his grasp. He's such a great dad. He knows I'm scared. We walk to the spot of the fallen limb and Dad crouches down. "Skid marks. This could be it. Are you sure you want to...?"

"Yes! I'm sure." We both peer into the wooded area. There's a deep ditch at this spot on the highway. It looks like it goes down about twenty feet, but it's hard to tell because it's pitch-black. Dad pulls out a flashlight from his work pants, clicks it on, and shines it down into the ditch.

I gasp and then let out a gut-wrenching cry. "That's his car, Dad. That's it!" I pull my hand out of his and start down.

"Roni! Wait."

"No, you call 9-1-1 and Hank. I need to get to him."

I sit down on my ass to slide down to the car. There's no risk of it going any farther down because his mangled car is pressed up against a huge tree. I hear nothing coming from the car, and that scares me to death.

How long does it take me to get to him? Seconds? Minutes? But when I reach the back end of his car, I stop. What if he's...? No! I can't think that way. I slide my hand over the side of his vehicle, gingerly stepping over broken tree limbs, glass, and other debris. The driver's side window is open, shards of glass everywhere. I pull myself over to it and peer inside.

"Oh, God. No! Mick!" I start to cry and hear myself scream, "Dad!" Mick is unrecognizable. Covered in blood, I can see he's got cuts on his face, and his body is being pressed between the dash and the seat. Something shiny catches my eye. The clasp from the seat belt is dangling next to the open window. "Oh, Mick. No seat belt? Why?" I lean into the window as far as I can to listen for something, anything. Whimpering, I whisper, "Mick?"

Dazed, I don't remember much after that. The next thing I do remember is my dad helping me back into our car as lights flash everywhere. People are yelling and working frantically. I open up my car door and step out as a gurney is being brought up from the ditch.

"Mick?" The first thing I notice is his face is not covered by a sheet. That's good. I remember hearing him breathing, barely. Next, I see his leg is encased in a puffy casing. I can't see his upper body yet, but I make my way over to him, dodging police and firefighters as they work. I see Dad talking to Hank, and I catch a glimpse of Emily. She's walking alongside the gurney talking to one of the paramedics, but I can tell she's been crying. I speed up my pace to get to her. "Mick?"

"Roni!" Emily says as she wraps her arms around me. "He's alive." She pauses and quietly adds, "Barely."

"Okay," I reply absently. I look over at him and gasp. He's still covered in blood, and now he's hooked up to bags with tubes and wires. "Where are they taking him?" I'm so numb I can't figure out what to do or say or even think.

"Plymouth Medical Center," says Hank as he walks over to us. "They'll assess him there and then Life Flight him to Chicago."

"Life Flight him? Oh, God. This is all my fault." The tears start up again.

"Shhh, Roni. This is not your fault," reassures Hank. He pulls me into a tight hug and kisses the top of my head. "It was an accident. Pure and simple. He'll be okay. He's strong and healthy. He'll be okay."

I get the feeling he's saying that as much for himself as he is for me. I just nod into his big chest. I have to believe him. There's no other choice. The sirens start up and startle me.

"We'll meet you at the hospital. Emily's riding in the ambulance, so she'll be sure to find us to let us know what's going on, Roni," assures Hank.

Dad wraps his arm around my shoulder. "Let's go, dove. We'll follow the ambulance."

By the time we get to the hospital in Plymouth, Mick is already in the Emergency Unit. Dad asks the receptionist if we can go back, but they inform him it's for family only. She points us to the waiting area, and we sit and wait. And wait. After what seems like days, Hank steps out and scans the room.

When his eyes land on me, he makes his way over. "Okay. Well, he's stable." He runs his hand through his hair. "He's unconscious, but the doctor thinks that's a good thing because of his head injury. He's got a compound fracture on his right leg that they have set temporarily and splinted. He'll most likely need surgery, but they want Northwestern to make that call. His right arm is injured as well, but not severely. They've got that stabilized, and now he's ready to transport."

I let out a squeak. I knew he had hit his head. I saw it for myself. I can't recall seeing his airbag. "Didn't his airbags deploy?"

"No. The paramedics reported that they didn't. If they had, he probably wouldn't have the head injury." Hank sits down next to me. "He may have a few broken ribs too, but the biggest concern is the head injury and if there's any swelling of his brain."

"What happens next?" my dad asks.

"The chopper is on its way. As soon as they land, they'll load him up and head to Northwestern Memorial in Chicago right away. Emily is going to fly with them as support since she works at Northwestern Memorial. The sooner they get him there, the better. This is a good hospital, but they just aren't able to give him the level of care that he needs. So, do you know where Northwestern Memorial is, Roni?"

"Ye-Yes," I say, clearing my throat. "Should we go there now? Or can I see him?"

"They won't let you back there right now, Veronica."

"Oh. Okay." I know I'm not family, but that hurts. I need to see him. I need to tell him I'm sorry.

"Let's hit the road, dove. We can stop for some coffee and get a head start. How does that sound, honey?"

A tear drips down my cheek, but I ignore it. I clear my throat again. "Good. It sounds good. We'll see you there, Hank. Right?"

Hank reaches over and squeezes my shoulder. "Yep, we'll see you there. I'll be right behind you guys."

36

RONI

The drive to Chicago seems to take a week even though it's only a two-hour trek from Plymouth. Dad and I listen to the radio as he chats about mundane things like Chicago sports and his job. I know he's only doing that to help keep my mind off of everything. Just as we pull into the edge of the city, my phone chimes. I don't recognize the number, but I know it has to be about Mick. *Please let him be okay.*

"Hello?"

"Roni? It's me, Emily. Where are you now?"

"We just pulled into the city. We're on Lake Shore Drive heading north. We should be there soon."

"Hurry. Okay?"

I gasp as fresh tears start pouring out of my eyes. "Is he?"

"No, he's stable. He's been in and out of consciousness, and he keeps saying your name."

"My name?" I squeak.

"Yes. That and... well, he's agitated, and that's concerning the docs here. Just drive safely and let the receptionist in ER know you're here. They'll send you back as soon as you get here."

"Okay." I turn to dad. "He keeps asking f-f-for me, Dad," I sob.

"I'll get you there as quick as I can, Roni." Dad presses down on the accelerator, and I lurch back at the new speed.

"Thanks, Dad."

He smiles at me and then turns his eyes to the road. In record time, I look up and see the large sign indicating the Emergency Unit of Northwestern Memorial. Dad pulls up to the entrance and stops. "Go ahead, Roni. I'll park the car and sit in the waiting area until you come out."

I hesitate. I don't like leaving him alone.

"Go on. I'll be okay. I'll get a cup of coffee and call your mom. She'll need to be updated."

"Okay." I lean over and kiss his cheek. "You're the best dad in the entire world. You're my hero," I whisper.

Dad gives me a shy smile. "Thank you, dove. I love you. Now go see your fella."

I laugh at his use of "fella." "I'll see you in a few." I jump out of the car and jog into the ER. It's a busy place. People are everywhere. Some are injured, some sick, and others are just waiting with their loved ones. There's a big difference between our small hospital in Plymouth and the one here. I maneuver my way through the crowd to reach the information desk.

"May I help you?" asks a tired-looking woman.

"I'm looking for someone who was brought in on Life Flight. They told me to tell you when I got here."

"Name."

"Mick Flynn."

"No, sweetheart. Your name?"

"Roni. I mean Veronica McGonigall."

The woman clicks away at the computer, then pauses. Then she clicks again. "I don't see anything here about that. You're going to need to take a seat."

"But...."

"Next!" she shouts.

There's nobody behind me. "Ma'am, I was told—"

"To. Sit. Down," she says curtly.

I turn to the waiting area and search for an empty seat. It's then I see my father walk in. He looks around and spots me. His expression says "confused." I walk over to him and tell him I'm supposed to sit down.

"Text Emily. Let her know you're here."

"Good idea."

Me: We're here, but they won't let me back there.

Emily: Jesus. Fecking idiots. I'll be right out. Are you in that hellish waiting area?

Me: Yes.

"She'll be right out." Before I can even sit down, Emily is throwing open the ER doors and looking around. She's wearing blue scrubs like she's working. I lift my hand and wave as she motions me toward her. I head her way, but my dad stands still, not knowing what to do.

"You too, Dad," she shouts. She turns to the woman at the reception desk and says something.

The woman sneers back at Emily but says nothing.

Ignoring that interaction, Dad and I follow Emily into the large and chaotic Emergency Unit. "He's back here, Roni."

We follow her down a long corridor, then take a left turn. Emily stops in front of a large opening in the wall. When I look into the room, it's a sea of Flynn's. I think every one of them is here. "Hi," I say weakly. I notice Hank isn't standing among them. He must still be on the road.

All eyes turn to me. There are several smiles, a few relieved expressions, and one scowl. Yep, Jennifer is here. *I thought she and David were splitting up.* Dad is standing behind me with his hand on my shoulder. "This is my dad, Jeff."

"Hi, Jeff," says everyone at the same time. It makes me giggle.

"How is he?" I ask nervously.

A tiny woman walks toward me. I'm going to guess this is Sarah Flynn, Mick's mom. "Hello, sweetheart. I'm Sarah. I birthed most of them." She points her thumb back to the crowd. "You must be Veronica." Sarah smiles broadly and reaches out to shake my dad's hand. "Sarah Flynn. Pleased to meet you, Jeff. Thank you for finding our son."

"You too," Dad says tiredly. The poor man has been up for twenty-four hours now.

Sarah turns back to me. "Now, Mick is still in and out of consciousness. He hasn't opened his eyes, but the physicians here say that's normal. He's been asking for you, so we've gotten permission for you to go in and see him."

"Oh. Okay. Now?"

"Yes. Now. Walk with me." She takes my hand and leads me down the corridor. "Sweetheart, it's nice to finally meet you."

"You too, Mrs. Flynn."

"Sarah. Please. Mick told me all about you."

"He did?" I squeak that out. "Why?"

She gives me a sly smile. "We both know why."

"I don't. I really don't."

"Uh-huh. Here we are, dear." We're standing in front of a beige curtain that hangs floor to ceiling. "We're all going to grab something to eat and have a family meeting while you're in there. So if the waiting area is empty, we're just downstairs. Okay?"

"Okay. Thanks, Sarah." I find the opening in the curtain.

When I walk in, I'm shocked. I know I saw him at the accident, but this is overwhelming. He's lying on the bed, covered by a white sheet. There are tubes and wires all around him and attached to his arms and chest. I walk around to the side of his bed that is free of beeping and whirring machines. Thankfully, he's been cleaned up, so the blood is gone. The closer I get, the more physical damage I see. His face is covered in cuts and the start of bruising. His nose has a white bandage running over the bridge. He must have broken his nose. His lips are swollen and cut, and there are Steri-Strips on his forehead that act as stitches. The most significant injury is on the right side of his head. They've shaved off a large section of his hair, and the gash that extends from his forehead back about four inches has been stitched with traditional sutures. The sheet covers the rest of his body, so I can't tell what else he endured. I think I'm glad about that.

I lean over him, so I can speak to him. "Mick? It's me, Roni. I'm sorry I made you leave last night. It's my fault."

Just then, his breathing starts to sound labored, and I can see the heart monitor is showing more activity, but it's almost like he's getting upset. His body stirs slightly. "Shhh, it's okay. You're going to be fine." I attempt to reassure him, but it's not working. *Shit, I'm upsetting him.* "Mick? It's okay." I reach out and slide my hand under the sheet, searching for his hand. When I feel it, I notice that he's chilled. I slide my hand into his and grasp it, running my thumb over his palm and wrist. I feel a slight squeeze from his hand, and he seems to calm.

I stretch out awkwardly, so I can grab the one and only chair in his room while still holding his hand. I slide it next to his bed so I can sit and hold his hand. I talk some more. "Your entire family is here. My dad came with me too." I continue to rub my thumb over his hand as I try to think what else I can say when I hear a sound come from him.

In a low, raspy murmur, I hear my name. "Roni?"

"I'm here. I'm here," I say, leaning over him.

"The baby," he mumbles.

The baby? Who is he talking about? "Katie? Are you talking about Katie? She's fine. Don't worry about that."

"Our baby," he mutters again. His head is turning from side to side as I watch him get agitated again.

The only baby he could be talking about is his baby with....

"Roni. Love."

I'm taken aback. Did he just say he loves me? I wait to hear what he says next.

"Love.... Lauren," Mick says more loudly. "Lauren."

Does he want to see Lauren? I can't believe he'd want to see her, but maybe.... It's hard to know what he wants. Right now, he needs my help. I squeeze his hand one more time and say into his ear, "I'll be back, Mick."

I stand and turn to leave when I hear, "No! Lauren." This time it's clear and much louder.

I'm doing my best to hold my emotions in check. The thought of him wanting to see her right now is devastating. Surely what I said last night didn't upset him enough that he'd want Lauren again. Would it? I hold back the tears and leave through the curtain. Breathing in and out to keep myself calm, I make my way to the waiting area. It's nearly empty except for one person. Jen.

When I walk in, she walks toward me tentatively. "How is he?" she asks, sounding sincere.

"He's still unconscious."

"They said he might be out for a while. They're confident he'll wake up, though." She reaches out like she wants to comfort me.

She really does seem sincere, worried. Maybe she regrets everything that happened? Who knows. I feel like I need to tell her. She knows him better than me. She knows Lauren. Dammit, I wish Emily were here. Screw it. I need to tell someone. "He was asking for Lauren."

With a look of pity on her face, she slides her palm down my arm. "Of course he was. He still loves her, and she loves him. They're meant to be together, hon," she simpers and then sighs. "You should really just accept that, Roni. There's no point in you hanging around. I mean"—she looks at me from head to toe—"you look terrible, tired. You should go on home and leave this to his family. There should only be family here now."

I choose to ignore her comments. Arching my brow, I start to speak but she interrupts. "I know what you're thinking, and I *am* family. David and I are working things out. Why else would I be here?"

I nod but don't respond to her question. She's right. I'm tired. I need a shower and some clean clothes. Numb, I pull my nearly dead cell from my pocket and text my dad.

Me: I'll be outside the ER entrance when you're done. I'm ready to leave.

Looking back at her, I notice for the first time that she looks like she's ready to go lunching. She's wearing a dress with four-inch heels. Ugh, I guess I do look terrible compared to that. Sighing, I ask, "Will you let them know I'm running home to shower and change. I'll be back."

By the time I make it outside into the chilly air, I get a reply.

Dad: Be there in a few minutes.

I lean against the rough brick exterior of the hospital and close my eyes. It's then everything hits me. Mick nearly died because of me, and he wants to see Lauren, not me. I look up and see my dad exiting the hospital. He looks over at me and gives me a look only a parent can give. It's filled with love and concern.

I walk up to him and wrap my arms around him and sob. "He... he didn't want me, Dad. He w-wanted Lauren." I cry so hard I feel nauseous.

And like a good father, he wraps his big arms around me and holds me until I'm all cried out.

37

———

RONI

By the time Dad pulls my rental car in front of my apartment building, Mom is sitting on the curb in her car. Stepping out, she reaches into the back seat for something. My luggage. Mom was kind enough to pack up my things.

"Hi, Mom," I say tiredly.

"How is he?" she directs the question to Dad.

"Stable. Still unconscious, but they think he'll be okay. He'll need surgery on his leg, I guess. But I didn't get any more information about that."

"Thank goodness," Mom says with a sigh.

Dad turns to me. "Sweetheart, are you going to be all right if I head home?"

"Of course," I say with a fake smile. "I'm exhausted. I'm just going to get cleaned up and rest for a bit before going back." I wrap my arms around him again. "Dad, thank you so much. I love you. You mean everything to me." I feel the burn of tears but resist. There shouldn't be another drop left for me to shed.

I feel him hug me tighter. "You know you're my favorite, right?" he whispers in my ear.

That makes me giggle. "Thanks, Dad. I always knew that."

He chuckles with me, and we let each other go. I hug Mom and watch them pull away from the curb.

Clutching my suitcase and overnight bag, I trudge into my building. I look to my left at the staircase. I almost always take the stairs so I can at least claim that as exercise, but I don't have it in me today. I walk forward and press the up button on the elevator. I hate this thing. I've been stuck on it more than once, and it makes some really awful noises when it's moving up and down. But, today, I'm going to risk it. Once the old death trap opens up, I step in. The doors shut slowly; then I feel it lurch upward. I pull out my house keys and wait. A few long minutes later, I'm on the third floor. I grab my bags and drop them in front of my apartment. Unlocking the door, I slide it open and use my feet to kick my bags inside. Leaving them by the entrance, I lock up and lumber into my bedroom. I walk to the side of my bed and fall face-first onto the soft mattress. So tired. I just need a few minutes. A fifteen-minute nap is all I need. Then I'll get up, shower, grab a sandwich, and head back to the hospital.

I'm woken by sounds. And they aren't the sound of the alarm. They're sounds coming from my neighbor's apartment. A television? I lift my head up and feel the drool that has gathered beneath my face running down my chin. "Gross." I lean against my wall and do, in fact, hear the low hum of a TV. I look around my space, trying to remember how I got home. It's then I remember Mick's accident and the events of last night. I peer at the clock on my nightstand. "It's five o'clock?" I slept for over four hours? Shit! I only wanted to sleep for a few minutes.

I jump out of bed and race to the bathroom. Flipping on the light, I wince at my own reflection. "Holy hell." I look like utter shit. Not only that, my heart is beating at double time thinking about Mick. "I should have been there with him. Shit!" Undressing quickly, I reach over and turn on my shower. The fastest way to feel normal again is to shower. I work fast to wash my hair and body. Grabbing my towel from the bar next to the tub, I dry off and speed walk naked into my bedroom. Since everything I took home is dirty, I dig through my drawers for some old leggings and a T-shirt. "Might as well be comfortable. It may be a while before I get home again. Okay, stop talking to yourself. I sound like a crazy person." Yep, I said that aloud.

Once in my kitchen, I start a pot of coffee, grab a travel mug, and go in search of my cell phone. Finding it on the entry table next to my keys, I plug in my dead phone. I look around my living room to take it all in. It seems like it's been weeks since I've been home, but it has only been one. The last time I was here, Mick was sitting on my love seat. I close my eyes at the memory. I wish things had ended differently for us because I think I was falling in love with him. Hell, who am I kidding? I was in love with him. Am. I *am* in love with him. But it's not in the cards for me. Not with someone like him. No, it'll need to be someone safe, boring. We'll have two point five kids, a dog, and a cat. The thing is, it's got to happen soon. My biological clock is ticking like a time bomb.

My eyes scan the room and end up on my answering machine, circa 1999. It's flashing furiously at me. If you count the blinks, it'll tell me how many messages I've got. It's flashing continuously. Hitting the Play button, the automaton says, "You have twenty-two messages."

"Twenty-two messages?" The only people who call me on my landline are people from work, telemarketers, my doctor and dentist offices, and my parents. I let the messages play as I make my way back into the kitchen. There are several messages from Mick from early in the week. How did he get my landline? Deb and Martha from P&P have called numerous times. There have been some hang-up calls. People just don't like to leave messages these days. There are two quick messages from Bill's assistant,

Gloria. She wants me to call her back. Surprisingly, there are three messages from the man himself. In the most recent, he asks me to call him on his personal cell phone. I grab a notepad and pen to jot down the number. I'm surprised. To my knowledge, only Gloria has that number.

As expected, there are telemarketing calls and one wrong number. But the last two calls are disturbing. The first is an angry male voice who says, "You are a fat, fucking bitch." Then they hang up. The final call on my old machine is a woman—an angry woman. Her lovely message for me is, "You're a fat slut. I hope you get what's coming to you."

"Okaaayyyy. Nice," I say aloud. It's strange, but the guy sounded like Chris Smith and the woman sounded a lot like Trisha Kepler. I save those, shaking off the final calls, and look at Bill's cell number. I decide to call him as I make myself a peanut butter and jelly sandwich for the road. I pick up my landline and dial. Unlike Mom and Dad's, mine is cordless. After two rings, Bill says cheerily, "Roni? Is that you?"

"Yes, this is Roni. I, uh, got your message."

"Terrific! I'm glad you called. I'd like to sit down and have a chat. Would you be amenable to that, Roni? Does tomorrow work for you? Ten? My office?"

"What's this about?" I know it's about my job, but I have to ask.

"Can we talk about that tomorrow morning? Say ten?"

"Sure, but can we make it closer to noon?" I don't know what's happening with Mick. Noon seems like it could work.

"Great! I'll look forward to seeing you. Thank you for calling me back, Roni."

"Sure. See you tomorrow." I hang up my phone and breathe deep. What did I just do? Hell, I might as well see what he wants. I can be away from Mick for an hour, right?

A loud growl from my stomach sounds, reminding me I

haven't eaten for hours. The last morsel of food I consumed was dinner before I went to Smitty's. I finish my sandwich and wrap it in a baggie, pour myself coffee to go, and turn off my pot. Curious if my parents made it home safely, I pick up my phone and give them a quick call. When I finish the call and am reassured they made it home safely, I go in search of my shoes and that old college sweatshirt I found a couple of weeks ago. Grabbing a large messenger bag, I toss in the book I'm currently reading, my laptop, my eReader and some M&Ms I had stashed in my nightstand. With my bag packed for the hospital and coffee in hand, I stop near the door where I see my phone has come back to life. It looks like I've missed some things. Important things. There are a bunch of texts from Emily Flynn and Hank Flynn and voice messages from Emily as well. I click on the text icon and see that most of them are from around the time I left the hospital.

Emily: Where are you?

Emily: Where did you go? You just disappeared.

Emily: Mick keeps asking for you.

Me *and* Lauren.

Hank: Roni, it's Hank Flynn. Where are you? Call me when you get this.

The rest are similar, but I can tell that Emily's seem to be getting angrier.

Emily: Jesus. WTF, Roni. Mick needs you!

Emily: Some friend!

Her last two texts make me wince. I am his friend. "I should have never taken a nap. Crap." Besides, I did what he asked me to do or what I thought he wanted me to do. I told someone he wanted to see Lauren. I know he was pretty much unconscious, but I had to assume he meant what he said. Did I do the wrong thing again? I look at the voice mail icon and feel dread. I hate voice messages. I click to see two messages from Emily; one from around the time I left and one from about thirty minutes ago.

I click on the message from earlier. "Roni? It's Emily Flynn. Where did you go? Jen said you just walked out of his room and out of the ER without saying a word."

That's a lie.

She continues, "He's still asking for you. Maybe you just went to grab something to eat. We're all going to be here, so come back as soon as you get this. Okay. See you."

My finger hovers over her second message. I know it's going to be a bad one. I should just rip the Band-Aid off. I press the message and listen.

"Jesus, Roni. Where the fuck are you? Mick needs you. He's more and more agitated. Lauren was here, and he nearly coded, but the entire time he kept saying your name. Fuck! You don't deserve to be his friend, Roni. Friends don't leave like that." I can tell she's crying into the phone. She sniffles and then adds, "If you get this, please come back to the hospital as soon as possible. They've moved him to a regular floor. He's in room three eleven." She hangs up.

I'm in shock. I don't deserve to be his friend? I was a friend when I left. Or I thought I was. I suck in air and realize that I don't deserve to be his friend. I should never have left his side. I don't want to see any of the Flynn family right now. They probably all hate me. I should let that go, though, and think of Mick.

I grab my bag but forget the coffee on my small table as I run out the front door. Luckily, I still have my rental car. "Shit! I still have my rental car." It was due back today. I'll call them in the morning and pay the late fees. I hop in, start it up, and I'm off only minutes after getting Emily's angry voice mail.

38
___

RONI

Finding a parking spot at Northwestern Medical Center is a combination of luck and fortitude. Oh, there's a pinch of evil in there too. The trick is stalking people who are walking out of the hospital. I find one such woman as she makes her way from the main entrance toward the parking lot. I weave in and out of the parking spots keeping one eye on her and one on driving. With luck, I'll get to her spot before anyone is any the wiser. I snort out a laugh at this whole thing. Mick would think this was funny too. I feel like a damn spy. Finally, I see taillights flash from someone hitting their keyless entry. The woman I'm stalking is close by. I sit and watch her get into her car, start it up, and then nothing. I wait a good ten minutes before she finally pulls out, which pissed off quite a few people who wanted the same spot, but I wasn't about to move and lose this spot.

I pull in and jump out of the car, click my locks, and jog toward the main hospital entrance. I walk directly to the elevator and hit three. My feet fidget as the box ascends. I feel my stomach flip and flop around, and it's not pleasant, like I might be sick. Nerves. I'm nervous to see Emily and the rest of the family, and even more nervous to see Mick. When the doors open to Mick's floor, I see a pair of restrooms on the opposite wall. I dash toward the women's and make it to the toilet just as I start to retch. The only thing I've had today is water, two bites of my PB&J, and half a cup of coffee. It's painful, to say the least. Once my body decides it's done, I splash cold water on my face and wipe away the drops and drips with a paper towel.

I exit the bathroom in search of room 311. *Be brave, Roni.* I lift my head, pulling my shoulders back. Half the battle is looking strong. The third floor is quiet. Since it's after seven o'clock now, most of the visitors must be gone. His door is ajar. I don't hear any voices. Should I knock? I err on the side of caution and tap lightly on the door.

"Come in," says a woman's voice.

Sarah. I push the door open and walk down a short hallway into a relatively large room. I see Sarah first. She's sitting in a recliner next to Mick's bed. She's the only one in the room. It makes me wonder where the rest of the family is hiding.

"Oh, hi, Sarah. Where is everyone?" *Sarah's the only one here?* It makes me feel only slightly less terrible.

Sounding curt and very formal, Sarah says, "Oh, hello, dear. Everyone went home to shower and rest. We figured we'd need to work out a schedule for staying with him." She nods toward Mick.

"I just heard Emily's messages. My phone was dead."

"Well, I'm glad you're finally here. They've given him a healthy dose of pain medication, so he's out like a light." She gives me a small smile.

"Can I explain?"

"No need. It's none of my business."

"Please?"

"If you need to tell me, then I'll listen."

I tell her about Mick's words, about him asking for Lauren. I also tell her about my conversation with Jen and how I accidentally slept four hours. I honestly didn't mean to throw Jen under the bus. Who am I kidding? Yeah, I did. She lied to Emily, and I needed to set the record straight. Sarah remained silent as I finished my side of the story. Her expression, which started off as stiff, was now tense.

She slaps both legs with her hands and stands up. "Well, that's just terrific."

I'm sensing sarcasm.

"Jennifer Flynn is the antichrist."

I let out a shocked laugh. What else can I do? "The antichrist?"

"The flipping antichrist. Now I'm confident she's the one who called Lauren."

As soon as her name is mentioned, Mick's monitors start beeping. Sarah walks over and touches his arm. "Shhh, it's okay, baby boy. Roni's here."

He calms down, and his machines return to normal.

She whispers, "Lauren was here today. She marched right into this room and announced to all of us that Mick wanted her there. We were shocked, to say the least, because he's been unconscious since you found him. I'm pretty sure she isn't telepathic. I suspected Jen was the culprit." She sits back in her chair. "Lauren walked over to Mick and leaned down and announced her presence." Sarah rubs her palms over her tired face. "He started to jerk about, nearly pulling out his IVs. His monitors were going crazy and, I swear, the entire floor of medical staff ran in here. We were shuttled out fast. It took them half an hour to get him stable."

"Needless to say, my children got rid of her. I could tell by the look on Jen's face she was shocked. Hell, I'm not even sure why Jen was here. David filed for divorce this week."

"She told me they were working it out."

This time it's Sarah who snorts out a laugh. "Not a chance. Especially after he hears about the crap she pulled today. She's gonzo."

Gonzo?

Sarah stands up from her chair. "Well, they said one person could stay with him tonight. I think it should be you, Roni."

"Me?"

"Yes. You. He's been saying your name all day. The doctors think it's just a matter of time before he wakes up, and I think you should be the first person he sees."

"I'd be happy to stay. Are you upset with me? Because I left?"

"No, under the circumstances, I get it. Besides, you need your rest. You won't get a lick of sleep in this place. But next time, don't trust Jen. She's the—"

"Antichrist. I'll remember."

Just then, an orderly walks into the room with a rolling cart. "Time for Michael's vitals."

"See?" she whispers. "They're in here every twenty minutes. Don't get me wrong, I'm glad. I want the best for Michael. You just won't get any rest." She pats my arm. As Sarah gathers up her things, she leans over and kisses Mick on the cheek. "See you in the morning, Michael. I love you so much, but I'm gonna let your girl take care of you now." She turns and gives me a tight hug, and then she's gone.

I take a good look at Mick. In some ways, he looks worse than he did this morning. He's pale and looks almost frail. I don't like it. My Mick is strong and charismatic. Pushing the chair closer to the bed, close enough to hold his hand, I sit and lean my upper body onto the bed. I rest my head beside his hip and rub my fingers over his palm and wrist again.

"I love you, Mick," I whisper. It may be the only time I get to tell him.

Yeah, I know he can't hear me, but I wanted to say it out loud. Next, I tell him about all of my phone messages, even the creepy ones. I also tell him about my meeting with Bill set for the next day that I may have to cancel if I'm needed here. I pull my phone out of my purse and bring up my Kindle app, deciding to read to him. I keep a selection of books on there in case I'm ever waiting for an appointment or a bus. Since it's between *Fifty Shades of Gray* by E L James and *Harry Potter and the Prisoner of Azkaban* by J K Rowling, I choose the latter. I smile outwardly thinking of my choice. I wonder if he's read any of this series of books. The Potter series is on my top ten list of favorites. I set the phone on the bed and begin to read. "Chapter one, the Owl Post." I sigh, leaning my arms onto the bed. "Harry Potter was a highly unusual boy..."

I'M awoken by the sensation of touch. I feel a finger running over my hand and palm. I blink my eyes and realize that I'm facedown on the side of a bed. Mick's bed. And he's touching me. I lift my head quickly and see that he's awake. His eyes are open and looking right back at me.

"Hey, baby," he says in a raspy, dry voice.

"Hey, yourself. How are you feeling?"

"Like shit." He tries to laugh but winces. "I hurt everywhere. What happened?"

"You were in an accident. You hit a—"

"Deer. I hit a big-ass deer."

"You did. You've been unconscious for—" I look up at the wall clock. It's two in the morning. "—over twenty-four hours."

He blinks at me a few times. It's obvious he's still out of it. "Seriously?"

"We were worried about you. Your family has been here all day. But they only let one person stay with you overnight."

"And you volunteered?"

"In a way." I look sheepish. "It's a long story. I'll tell you about it sometime. Right now, I think I should call a nurse in to check on you."

"Yeah. That would be nice. Everything really hurts. Do you think they could give me something?"

I press the call button attached to his bed. "Probably. Let's ask." When a nurse answers through the intercom system, I say, "Hi there. Mick's awake. He's in a lot of pain."

"I'll be right in," the nurse says excitedly.

While we wait for the nurse, I grab my phone and send a text to Emily and Hank.

Me: Mick is awake. Will you let your mom and dad know?

I wait for a response from either or both of them, and it takes only minutes.

Hank: Thank fuck. I will. How is he?

Me: Good. Sore, but he remembered a bit about the accident.

Hank: That is good news. Tell him we'll see him tomorrow, will ya?

Me: Sure.

I don't get a response from Emily right away, but eventually she replies.

Emily: Thanks.

That's it. Just "Thanks."

His door slams open, and two nurses race into the room. One is about my age and another one closer to my mom's age. "Oh, dearie, are we glad to see you awake, Michael Flynn!" They both smile brightly, and the younger nurse giggles. The older nurse introduces herself first. "I'm Gladys, and this young'un is Maddy. She's a nursing student from the university."

Mick gives them a weak smile and winces. "Everything hurts."

"It's probably time for another dose of morphine. Let me check the orders, and I'll be right back," says Gladys. "Maddy will take your vitals." She turns to Maddy and says, "Go easy."

Maddy nods and takes the blood pressure cuff from the wall. "I'll be careful."

After Maddy has determined his blood pressure is high and so is his temperature, Gladys returns with a syringe filled with clear fluid. "I'm gonna shoot this right into your IV, honey. It'll only take a few minutes for you to feel better. Okay, sweetie?"

Mick nods and watches her shoot the morphine into a special opening in his IV tube.

"Would you like some water? Crackers?" asks Maddy.

"Water," Mick says in his raspy voice.

"Be right back," the young nurse says as she sprints out the door.

I smirk as she leaves. Even beat up and bruised, the ladies are running all over themselves to please him.

Gladys is straightening up his area, tucking him in gently. Mick has leaned back onto his bed. "It's working already." He sighs.

"That goes right into your bloodstream; that's why it works so fast."

Mick smiles a dreamy smile at Gladys. "Did you say your names was Betty? 'Cause that's cool. It's old fashioned."

"Well, it's Gladys, but it is old fashioned. I was named after my—"

"Betty, have you met my girlfriend? Betty, this is Veronica. Veronica, this is Betty." He snorts to himself. "Betty and Veronica? That's an old-timey cartoon." His eyes shoot skyward, and his left arm rises to point at the ceiling. "Look!" he shouts. "There are pixies flying around. Cool!" he says, smiling.

I giggle at him. "Is that normal?" I ask Betty—I mean Gladys.

She chuckles. "Everyone reacts differently with pain medication. Some get angry, some get sleepy, and some act like they're intoxicated. My guess is our Michael is going to be fun to watch." She chuckles again.

"Betty? Isn't my girlfriend pretty?"

Girlfriend? Oh, right. I'm a girl who is his friend.

"Yes, she—"

"I looooovvveee her sooooo much."

He loves me? Yeah, like a friend.

"Well, that's nice." She smiles at me. I know I must look surprised because Betty—er, Gladys adds, "Does she know you love her?"

"Shhh, I haven't told her yet," he slurs.

Gladys laughs again. "I think she knows now."

"She's not my usual type, you know, Betty. She's bigger than the girls I generally date."

"Uh-huh." Gladys looks at me with sympathy in her eyes. She's not a small woman either. She's going to get why I look a little hurt.

"Don't get me wrong. Veron... Veron... Roni is stacked," he says, holding his hands out front to show the size of my breasts. "She's got it in alllll the right places."

"Well, that's great news, Mi—"

"I want to take care of her and the baby," he says, interrupting Gladys again.

The baby?

"Oh, congratulations! I didn't realize you were expecting."

"I'm not," I interrupt the train wreck that is Mick Flynn's conversation. I'm not pregnant!

"You coooouuuullldd be," he sing-songs.

"What?" I say too loudly.

"Yep," he says, emphasizing the "p." "Expired condoms. Emily says there's a teeeeeeny, tiny chance I knocked you up."

"Emily knows?" *Emily knows before I know?* "You talked to Emily about this before you spoke to me?"

"Of course. She's my best sister, and she's gonna be a doc—" He hiccups. "—a doctor."

"But—"

"Shhhhhhhhh," Mick slurs again. "It's gonna be fiiiinnne. I'll take care of you both," he says sleepily. "I've got it alllllll figured out."

I stare at Mick as he drifts off to sleep, then look at Gladys, and I can tell she wants nothing more than to back out of the room as fast as she can. Before she can dash away, Maddy returns with water and crackers. "He's asleep. Just leave those on the tray table and let's scoot. More patients to see after all."

Yep, she wants out, and she wants out *now*. I don't blame her. I want to leave now too. I could be pregnant? And Emily knew before I did? My first instinct is to punch Mick in the jaw, but I can't hit a man when he's down. No, I'll wait until he's all better, and then I'll punch his lights out. My second instinct is to flee. That's usually what I do, but I can't leave him here alone. I'm already on Emily's shit list, so I wouldn't want to make that situation worse than it is already. Not that I should care. Jeez. I could be pregnant? I lean back in the hard recliner, close my eyes, and think. We had sex almost eleven days ago. I've thrown up a couple of times, but that doesn't mean anything. There's been so much going on in my life, so many changes, it'd be natural for me to get anxious, which could make me nauseous. It's way too soon for that to be caused by pregnancy.

Right?

I pick up my cell phone and see that it's at only three

percent again. I only charged it for a short time at home, so it makes sense that it's about to die. I'll have to research morning sickness when I get home. I lean back again and think about the Halloween party and the time at my place. He wore a condom both times. Can expired condoms be that unreliable?

I reach for my phone again and remember it's nearly dead. "Damn it." I lay my head back, and without trying, my eyes flutter closed and I'm off to sleep. It's a restless sleep, but I'll take what I can get.

MICK

I blink awake and attempt to acclimate to my surroundings. It shouldn't take long. The staff around here has been waking me up every half hour to check my vitals and ask me question after question. I'm sure they're gauging my concussion symptoms. I know I've got one. My head hurts like someone hit me with a hammer repeatedly. Bright lights hurt, and I feel nauseous. I haven't gotten sick or anything, but I suspect when I have to move around, I'll feel the need.

Honestly, what hurts the most is my leg. They told me I broke the right leg and messed up my arm. They also told me I cracked my ribs; plus, I've got internal and exterior stitches on the right side of my head. I know they shaved some of my hair off because I've touched my scalp and felt nothing but skin. Yay. I should probably be freaked out by the loss of hair, but I really don't care. I was getting sick of long hair anyway, so this is my chance to shave it off. I know the ladies dig the hair, but I only care about one lady, and something tells me Roni will be okay with it. She doesn't like me for my hair. At least I hope not.

I open my eyes and look down at Roni. She cut her hair. I forgot about that. I touch her soft locks and run my fingers through it. She's sexy with this style. I keep running my fingers in and out of her hair until she wakes up. When she lifts her face, I see the telltale signs of sleep. She's got creases on her left cheek from sleeping on the crumpled sheet. Sleep is in her eyes, and she looks groggy.

"You awake?"

"Yeah," she says in a sexy morning voice. I could get used to hearing that in the morning. "Coffee. I need coffee," she moans.

My cock twitches at the sound, and that makes me happier than I can tell you. I've still got my dick, and it still works.

I blink awake with my face planted on the side of Mick's bed again, this time with a hand running through my hair. I don't remember moving around, but I suppose it's possible.

"You awake?" he asks.

"Yeah. Coffee. I need coffee." I can't do anything else until I get some java.

"Your hair is so soft," he says sleepily.

I lift my head off the bed and smile at him. It's then I remember everything he said earlier when he was under the influence. Wow, he was under the influence. Maybe he was just hallucinating and none of it is true. A sense of relief washes over me, and I give him a real smile. "How are you feeling?"

"I'm in pain. I don't think that stuff they gave me worked."

"Oh, it worked."

"It did?"

"You don't remember?"

"Remember what?"

"You got really chatty after the morphine kicked in."

"I did?"

"Oh yeah. You said—"

I hear footsteps, then Gladys steps in holding a tray with water, clear soda pop, crackers, and Jell-O. "Are you hungry, young man?" she asks cheerily.

"I... a little. I feel like sh—like crap."

"I'll check to see when you can have another dose of morphine. In the meantime, I want to see those sutures."

I excuse myself while the nurses check his stitches and change his gown. "I'm going to run down and grab something to eat. I'll be back in a few minutes."

I walk to the elevators and press the down button. I haven't eaten for hours and hours. I feel like I might pass out, actually. The hospital cafeteria is abuzz with activity. There's a grill where they're preparing pancakes and eggs. I avoid that area and head straight to the coffee station. I grab the biggest cup available, and as I'm about to fill it up, I stop. What if I am pregnant? I know for a fact that caffeine is not good for a baby. Groaning, I look over at the pot that reads Decaf. I need the real stuff, damn it. I spy some hot tea bags and wonder if those would be okay. Deciding they have to be better than coffee, I open a pack and set the bag into my cup. Pouring hot water over the top, I stare down at my cup as the tea steeps in. "This will have to do for now. Until I know what the hell is going on, anyway." I inhale the steam and wish it was the delectable aroma of coffee.

Next, I march toward the tall glass refrigerator, open the door, and pull out a prepackaged yogurt, a small cup of fruit, and a bagel with cream cheese. After checking out, I return to Mick's room to see him sleeping again. I sit down in my chair and look at my food. I work quietly to open up my packages and dig in. I'm literally shaking from hunger. I pop open the fruit cup and watch as Mick's eyes open up.

"Could you have gotten a quieter snack, woman? Can't you see I need my beauty sleep?" He chuckles, wincing once again.

"Sorry. I'm hungry. I haven't eaten much since Sunday."

"What day is it now?"

"Tuesday."

"You haven't eaten for two days? Roni, you need to eat. It's not good for you."

"I know. It just didn't work out that way. I'm eating now, see?" I say, holding up my yogurt. "The breakfast of champions."

Sighing, I watch him attempt to move around on his bed. He winces as he grumbles, "I can't sleep or get comfortable."

"Do you want some crackers?"

He shakes his head.

"Jell-O?"

"Nope. Not hungry."

"You're uncomfortable and you're not hungry." I look around the room, trying to think of ways to help him. "I'd read to you again, but my phone is dead."

"You read to me?"

"I did. Harry Potter," I say, holding up my phone.

"I love those books," he says sleepily. His eyes slide shut as he winces in pain.

MICK

"Dude! You're alive!" shouts Keith.

I'm literally shocked awake. Normally Keith is the quiet one, but I guess he's excited to see me. He stomps over to my bed and grabs my hand to shake.

"Holy fuck, Keith. That hurts. Be gentle." I wish I were kidding, but I'm not. I need some more pain meds.

"Oh, shit. Sorry, Mick. I was just so glad to see you awake."

I look over and see Roni getting ready to eat her food. She looks tired. I don't think either of us got much rest last night.

"No problem, man. When is everyone else descending on this place?" I ask as I attempt to move to a more comfortable spot on the bed. I raise the back of the bed up and yelp when the pain hits me.

"Soon. Emily is on her way right now, and everyone else will be here later. You need something for pain, man?" Keith asks, looking concerned.

Before I have a chance to answer, there's a knock and a stunning woman just slightly older than myself steps into the room. "Hello, I'm Clarice Brookes, your orthopedist. I came to talk to you about the plan for your recovery." She walks up to my bed and pulls back the sheet.

She proceeds to tell me more about my compound fracture in my lower fibula. There's also a hairline fracture in my right arm. I've still got a splint on my leg due to swelling, plus they want to be sure the wound was cleaned out and free of infection before they perform surgery. But, according to her, the Brunette were reset at Plymouth Memorial and everything seems to be doing well so far.

"Don't try to walk or put any pressure on your leg whatsoever," Dr. Brookes warns. "We'll assess the situation and decide on the next step, but you need to plan on being wheelchair bound for several weeks, if not longer. Does your home have stairs?"

I've got a shit ton to get up to my place. No elevator in that old building. "Yes."

"You'll need to find a place to stay that's all on one level or has elevator access. If you can't find a place, there are always rehab facilities that will accept you. You'll probably need rehab down the road."

I look at Keith, then at Roni, but without actually seeing them. I'm wondering who has a place like that. Almost everyone I know lives on a multilevel. Emily lives on one level, but her place is so small, I wouldn't get a wheelchair in the door.

Mom and Dad's place could work, but Dad would need to build me a ramp up to the front porch, and then I'd have to live in the main room. The only bathroom on the main level is a half bath.

Keith and Hank's places are both out. I'd rather lop off my own limbs than stay with David and Jen. Not that Jen will be around. I just don't want to live with my brother while he's dealing with divorce drama. So, that leaves friends or Roni. Roni's place is all on one level, plus there's an elevator. Sure, her place is small but not so small I couldn't maneuver around in a chair.

I see movement at the corner of my eye. Roni has her purse in her hand. She's making her way toward my door. I interrupt Dr. Brookes, "When are you coming back, Roni?"

"Oh, soon." She won't look at me.

"Soon?"

"Yep. See you later, Keith. Dr. Brookes. Be a good patient, Mick. I'll let Betty know you need more pain medicine," she adds.

Who's Betty?

"Okay. See you later." She steps out of the room, and I get the overwhelming sense that she won't be coming back.

Dr. Brookes takes the hint and quickly goes over her plan for my recovery. In no time, she moves on to her next patient. My mind is racing. I've screwed up so badly—I know I have—but I'm not sure what I've done.

"So, when did you finally wake up?" Keith asks, drawing my attention from the door.

"No clue. Sometime in the night."

"Fuck, Mick. You scared the shit out of all of us."

I focus my attention on my brother because I can't think about Roni right now. "Any news on my car?"

"Toast. It's toast, dude. Dad called your insurance company for you yesterday, and once he was sure you were okay, he drove out to the accident site to oversee the towing."

Fuck. It was a sweet ride, and all paid up. Maybe I should trade up—get a bigger, safer car or an SUV. A family car.

42

RONI

Stepping out of Mick's room, I take the breath I needed. I'm not ready to live with Mick Flynn. I could practically see the wheels turning in his head. While I've never been to any of the Flynn family homes, I know his place has a long staircase leading to his apartment. I also know that mine has an elevator and my unit is all on one level. When he started to turn his head to look at me, I knew I had to get out of there. If it ends up he's got nowhere else to go, I'm sure I'll do it, but until then, I'm going to feign ignorance. I hustle out the door to my rental car. Before I forget, I call the car rental place and extend my rental period for the rest of the week. I race home to shower and change for my meeting with Bill Phillips. I'm going to be late, late, late. I let my hair air dry on the ride to P&P Advertising. I fluff it up with my hands and finger comb it. It's wavy and messy—in a good way. Having short hair is awesome.

I enter the lobby of P&P Advertising right on time. Before I can even announce myself to the receptionist, she says, "You can go right up, Veronica. Mr. Phillips is expecting you." I thank her and make my way to the bank of elevators. When I step on, I see a few people from the office. We smile at each other tentatively.

Standing in front of Gloria's desk, she signals with one finger for me to wait until she's done with her call. "Roni! It's so nice to see you. You look fantastic. I love your hair!"

"Thanks." My hair is good, but I don't think I look good. With little sleep, I feel like utter dog shit, but I keep that to myself. I'm glad I opted for slacks and the light pink cashmere sweater my sisters gave me for Christmas last year. I look professional, but I'm also really comfortable. I didn't want to overdress for this meeting.

"Thanks, Gloria. So, Mr. Phillips wanted to see me?" I say hesitantly.

"Yes! He certainly did. He's on a call right now, but he'll be with you shortly. Just have a seat, and I'll let you know when he's free."

"Okay. Thanks."

Gloria gives me a sincere smile and then turns away from me when her telephone rings again.

Five minutes later, Bill steps out of his office. "Roni! I'm so glad you could make it." He opens his arms out like he's going to hug me. I stiffen my arms in preparation for his embrace, but he just grasps my upper arms and squeezes.

"Come on into my office. Can I get you anything? Coffee? Soda?"

"No. Thank you." He rounds his desk and sits in his swivel office chair. I sit in the chair directly in front of his large mahogany desk. His desk would have taken up my entire office. "What did you need to see me about, Mr. Phillips?"

"Bill. Call me Bill." He chuckles. "You don't mess around, do you, Roni? Okay. Well, I'll cut right to the chase." He leans forward in his chair and rests them on his desk. "I want you back."

I was expecting that, but it's still a surprise. "I don't think—"

"Hear me out, please," he says, sounding desperate. "I made

a mistake, and believe me, I'm not one of those people who likes to admit they were wrong, but I was wrong about the whole mishap after the launch party."

I remain silent.

"In retrospect, I can see why you did what you did. I would have been very upset if someone had come in and taken credit for my work."

I nod. *Where is he going with this?*

"I should have reprimanded Chris for all of that," he says sheepishly.

"Yes. You should have," I say with command in my voice— command that is all bluster.

Bill stands and starts to make his way over to his large seating area. "Come. Let's sit over here. It's more comfortable."

I stand up and follow him. He sits in a large, black leather chair while I choose his gray, wool sofa. These two pieces of furniture probably cost more than all of my furniture in my apartment combined.

"The truth is I realized, fairly quickly, what you do— or, I mean, what you did around here. You were an asset to P&P Advertising and to me. I knew you did good work; I just didn't realize the scope of your talents."

I know that's true. I worked my tail off every day. And not just on my own work.

"Roni, I need you back. EnerSport only wants to work with you."

And there it is. One client complains, and here I am. Bill doesn't want me back. He wants to make sure he keeps his client happy. I suppose that's good business, but it makes me feel used.

"That's the only reason you want me back? To keep Owen McCormick happy?"

"No!" he says, leaning forward. "I meant what I said. I now

know the impact you had on the marketing side of things. It's obvious you are missed."

What exactly is he saying? Did something happen? "What happened with EnerSport to make them unhappy?" I need an answer to that.

Looking embarrassed he admits, "Chris Smith happened."

I chuckle lightly at that. "Yeah, I get that." I worked with him for a year and a half and watched him struggle with simple marketing concepts. Chris also knows very little about market analysis. I have no idea how he got this job in the first place, or a degree, for that matter. Furthermore, what did I ever see in that guy? I guess I thought his self-deprecating way of asking for my help all the time was sweet. I figured he was just using that as a way to talk to me. I snort, and it gets Bill's attention. I was such a stupid fool, and that hasn't changed, apparently.

"What'll it take to get you back?"

"Bill—"

"Please, Roni. Give me another chance."

Why do I feel like we've broken up and he wants to date me again? "I'm just not sure I want to work at a place that doesn't value hard work and dedication."

I've shocked Bill. His eyes are huge, and he's opening and closing his mouth like a fish. "What? I value hard work and dedication?"

"No, you really don't, Bill, and I'll tell you why I feel that way." Okay, you know I'm exhausted and delirious when I get lady-balls. I start to count using my fingers to emphasize these points.

"One, the fact that you reprimanded me and not Chris after the launch party is the main reason I feel this way. Two, you gave Chris that huge office with floor-to-ceiling windows and never even blinked an eye. Did you ever consider that office should go to anyone else?" I didn't want to assume it would go to me. There are other worthy candidates for such a space.

Bill interrupts my list. "What? Chris told me you were afraid of heights and didn't want the big office with the huge windows."

I stare at Bill. "Did you think to ask me yourself? Chris spoke for me, and you didn't question him? That can be number three. Four, Chris is able to pull Trisha from her actual boss and her real work, so he has an assistant of his own. And, five, the only reason I'm here is because a client complained. You never would have asked me back on your own." I'm sure there are more examples, but five is good.

"Wow, you don't like me very much, do you?" he says with sadness in his voice.

"I respect you, Bill. I always have. That is until the launch party. Honestly, Bill, it's thanks to having two weeks off and time to think," *and dealing with Mick Flynn,* "that's allowed me to realize I deserve better." *There! I said my piece.* I lean back into his comfy sofa. A weight has been lifted off my shoulders that I didn't realize was there. I had some pent-up resentment in there, and now it's gone. Well, almost.

Bill's still looking at me with large, round eyes. He's stopped moving his mouth open and closed, but it looks like he's surprised I said all of that. "You're right."

Now it's my turn to look shocked.

"You're right about everything. I've been neglectful when it comes to seeing the inner workings of this company. I had to question my own staff to find out the truth about you and some others in your department. I had no idea the things that were happening there, and I'm sorry for that."

I nod. I'm glad he sees it, but I'm still not sure returning to P&P is in my best interest. Although, I'm nervous about money and I can't go on forever living off my meager savings account. I gasp aloud, and what if I'm pregnant? I'm going to need money. And insurance.

"Is everything okay, Roni?"

"Yeah. I mean yes. It's just been a hectic couple of days."

"Let me offer you this. I'll raise your salary. I'll pay you half again what you were making when you left."

That's not a bad deal, but I'm still not sure it's enough. "I'm not—"

"I'll double it."

"Double it?" I say distantly. I should sound elated, but it's making me dizzy. He really wants me back. "I'll have to sleep on it, Bill. I can't make a decision today."

"I understand. Go home. Sleep on it. But call me tomorrow with your answer, would you?"

I nod and stand. "I will." I reach my hand out to shake his and leave. I wave to Gloria and a few other ex-coworkers as I leave. I press the elevator button and wait for it to open. Stepping on, I turn to push the lobby button when I see two people rush on before the doors close. *Great.*

"Well, hello, Roni," snarls Trisha. "What are you doing here? Come to beg for your old job back?" she snickers.

I ignore her because my first instinct is to punch her in her smug face, but I don't need to be charged with assault today.

"I know why she's here, Trish. I overheard some people talking. Bill wants her back." Chris steps closer, forcing me to move back toward the wall. He's standing so close I can feel his breath on my face. "But you aren't coming back, Roni."

"I'm not?"

"No, you fat bitch!" shouts Trisha.

What is the deal with this chick? I ignore her because I swear Chris is even closer.

"You aren't coming back because if you do, I'll make your life a living hell. You'll wish you were dead."

Jesus. I'd wish I were dead? I stutter, "Ar-Are you threatening me?"

"It's not a threat, fatty. It's a promise," Chris spits.

At that exact moment, the elevator dings its arrival on the lobby floor and the doors slide open. Chris and Trisha walk out like nothing happened. I, on the other hand, am shaking like a leaf. Now I know for sure they were the ones who left those nasty messages on my machine. They're crazy and unpredictable, and I just don't need that right now. I step off the elevator and quickly walk out the front door. I don't look at anyone. I don't wave goodbye. I don't speak as I make my way out to the sidewalk. Before I can give it more thought, I grab my phone and dial Bill's private number.

"Did you decide already?" he asks optimistically.

"I can't do it. I can't work in that environment. It's too...." *Dangerous.*

"What happened? You just left. What happened between my office and now?"

I hesitate. I won't tell him about Chris and Trisha in the elevator. I can't. I'm not afraid of Chris Smith, not really. I just don't want to be that person. They were just empty threats. It'd be my word against theirs, two against one. A fight I'd never win, and that would be detrimental to me when I'm job hunting. I've got to think ahead. I may not be thinking about only me now.

"It's nothing. I just can't do it. Thank you for the offer. I appreciate it, Bill. Have a good day." I click the phone off and walk away from the building. It's too far to walk home, but I want time to think and need the fresh air to get perspective on my disaster of a life. Besides, I'll pass by a pharmacy on my way and can grab a pregnancy test or two, so I can be prepared to take them in a week or so. The idea I could be pregnant is overwhelming me. If it's true, it changes everything.

43

MICK

I wake up slowly. I seem to be sleeping my life away. The last thing I remember is a nurse putting something into my IV. I think it was pain medication. My eyes are still closed because I know there's too much light in my room. I can sense it. Once the fog lifts, I hear voices. It's my mom and Emily, and I hear three words I never want to hear again.

"Lauren was here?" I ask Mom and Emily.

Emily nods and speaks first. "Jen called her. Apparently, you said her name to Roni, so Roni assumed you wanted to see Lauren. She saw Jen out in the waiting area and told her what you'd said. Jen told Roni she should leave because she isn't family."

I scoff, then wince in pain. "*Jen's* not family."

"I know," adds my mom. "Not anymore."

"So, Roni left?"

"Of course, she did, sweetheart. But only to freshen up. She came back later that day," Mom says, looking directly at my sister.

"I know, Mom. Jeez. I feel terrible that I gave Roni such a hard time. I didn't know," admits Emily.

"Okay, I'm confused. What are you talking about? Why did you give Roni a hard time, Em?"

She explains how she was upset with Roni for leaving and for not answering her phone or text messages. She thought Roni was bailing on me. "How is it she was the one who stayed with me last night?"

"After she heard Emily's lovely messages, she came right over. I was the only one here, and I felt she would be the one you'd want to see if you woke up."

I nod. I was glad to see her, that's for sure. I close my eyes, trying to concentrate on the conversation and not on the pain in my body and head.

I feel my mom's gentle touch on my arm. "Sweetheart, do you need something for pain?"

"It doesn't work. Every time I wake up, it's the same."

Emily giggles.

"What's so funny?" I ask, sounding irritated. Pain makes me cranky.

"Dude. You're hilarious when you're on morphine. You don't remember?"

"No." I remember it going into the IV, but that's it. "Why? What happened?"

Mom is laughing right along with Emily.

"Oh, honey. You can't help it. It just made you say some hilarious things."

Mom is sugarcoating, I can tell. "Tell me," I growl, then regret it. It hurt.

"Let me tell him, Mom." Emily sits on the edge of my bed and begins to recount all of the crazy things that came out of my mouth when I was on the pain meds. Evidently, I told everyone I loved them. I named every nurse Betty. I talked about Roni and how much I loved her, and I rambled about the baby and flying pixies.

Flying pixies? When Emily says the last part, I look at my mom. She nods. "Mom?"

"Emily explained the situation. Don't worry, I won't spill the beans. I'll wait until you talk to Roni first."

"Roni doesn't know," I say to myself. "I didn't tell Roni, did I?" I'd hate for her to learn about the condom situation like this.

"Who knows, dude. You were on morphine last night too, so you may have said a bunch of shit."

"When she left, I got the feeling she wasn't coming back. What did I say to her?"

Mom and Emily look at me sadly. "We don't know. We could ask your nurse. Is she still here? I'll go check." Emily hops off the bed and makes her way out the door. In minutes, she returns with Betty.

"Hi, Betty."

She cackles at that. "Sweetie, I'm Gladys."

"Oh, sorry."

"No problem. Your sister said you had a question. What did you want to ask me?"

"Were you in here last night when I was under the influence of pain meds?"

Gladys smiles. "Yes, darlin'. I witnessed that train wreck." She cackles again.

"Did... did I say anything to the girl in the room?"

"Oh, sugar, you said a lot. I think you shocked her."

"Please, tell me what I said."

Gladys recounts everything I said about Roni, to Roni and to Gladys, AKA Betty.

"Fuck!" I say and feel the pain race through my tired body.

"I'll get you some—"

"No! I don't want morphine. Can I get something else? Something that won't make me say things I shouldn't?"

"I'll buzz the doc. I'll see what he recommends. I'll be back."

Gladys leaves, and I stare up at the ceiling. I told Roni I loved her. I called her my girlfriend. I practically told her she was fat but had enormous breasts. But the thing that, I'm sure, got me into hot water with her was the deal with the expired condoms.

"She knows about the condoms," says Emily like she's read my mind.

"Yeah, and she knows that I talked to you about them before I spoke to her."

"Oh, Michael. How could you? What were you thinking? I know you and Emily are close, but you totally screwed the pooch with Roni now," says Mom. She's not laughing.

"I know." *I totally screwed the pooch.* "She's not coming back, is she?"

"I wouldn't," adds Mom. She sounds disgusted with me, and she should. I'm disgusted with me. "So you'd better figure out a way to fix things. Decide what your real feelings are and go from there. Don't say things you don't mean, or she may never trust you. Trust is the key to a good marriage."

"Marriage?"

"Yes. Marriage. Good gracious, Michael. When are you going to pull that handsome head out of your bottom? It's time to be a man and do right by Roni. You love her, and she loves you. What's so hard to understand about that? Sure, Lauren hurt you, but Roni didn't. She wouldn't. I could tell that the minute I met her. She's a keeper. Don't fuck this up, Michael."

Emily spits out the drink of water she just poured into her mouth. Mom doesn't cuss. Ever. I'd love to smile and laugh at her for dropping the f-bomb, but this is serious. I can't fuck this up—again. I've done nothing but fuck things up with Roni since the minute I met her. How could she love me? She should hate me. Hell, maybe she does.

44

RONI

I stroll for five or six blocks in a fog. I should get something to eat since the only thing I finished eating this morning was the yogurt, but nothing sounds good right now. I just want to sleep. I raise my hand to hail a cab when my phone rings.

"Hello?"

"Roni? It's Emily Flynn. How are you?"

"Fine." *What does she want?* "What can I do for you, Emily?" I stand near the street not wanting to deal with a cab while I'm on the phone.

"It's Mick."

"What? What happened? Is Mick okay?"

"Well, he's very upset. Agitated. When are you coming back? You seem to calm him down."

"I'll come now." Hanging up the phone, I raise my arm to catch a taxi. That's when I remember the rental car. The one I parked in the ramp closest to my old office building. "I'm an idiot." I turn on my heel and walk back the way I came but this time I don't doddle.

When I walk into Mick's room, it's filled with his family. Hank and Sophie are there along with Beth and Emily. Sarah

Flynn is sitting in the one and only chair in the room, and Mick? Well, Mick is happily eating a fruit cup and something resembling pudding.

What the ever-loving hell? "Mick? Are you okay?"

He looks up at me with a huge smile. "Babe! You came back!"

"Of course, I did. Emily called and told me you were having problems."

He looks at Emily, then at his mom, then back at me.

Sarah jumps in, "Roni, honey, we just wanted you to come back. He's worried about what he told you last night when he was under the influence." She leans into me to whisper, but no joke, Sarah Flynn cannot whisper. She whisper-shouts loud enough for the rest of the patients on this floor to hear. "He wants to talk to you about the condom situation."

I turn to Mick so fast it makes me dizzy. I grab the foot railing on his bed for support. "Are you kidding me right now, Mick? Your mom knows? Did she know before I did too?" I shout.

By now, every Flynn has their eyes on me.

Mick says, "Can you all leave us alone for a minute?" Without a word, they all scatter like rats on a sinking ship. "Babe, let me—"

"No! Let *me* explain. I do not appreciate your family knowing my business before I do. This conversation should have happened between the two of us. In private. It's personal. It's none of their business right now, Mick!" I'm panting now.

"Babe, come on. You need to take it easy—"

"Do *not* tell me to take it easy, you asshat. How would you feel if I kept something like this from you, but I told everyone else?"

Mick's face changes from something jovial to something

pained in one second. He does know what that feels like. Lauren did it to him.

"This is my life we're talking about. I'm going to have to deal with this on my own if I'm pregnant. I can't trust you to... to...." I'm lightheaded. I've gotten myself so worked up I feel—

MICK

"Roni? Roni!" Fuck, she's fainted or passed out. "Mom! Hank!" I shout as I press every single one of the buttons on my bed. I can't get out of my bed because I'm practically attached to it thanks to my leg. Not to mention my catheter is hooked up somewhere too. I lean over the bed as far as I can and see her eyes. They are closed, and she's as pale as a ghost.

"Michael, what's...?" Mom says as she runs into the room and sees Roni on her back at the foot of my bed. "Oh, goodness, what happened?"

Before I can reply, a nurse and an orderly run in. "What happened?" the nurse asks.

"I don't know. She was talking; then she wasn't. One minute she was standing there, the next she was falling backward onto the floor. I think she fainted. She hit her head." *Fuck. She's hurt.* "Help her, please," I whine. I feel the burn of tears and wetness on my cheeks. "Help her," I croak.

In less than five minutes, they've gotten a gurney into my room and are lifting her onto it. She's still out. Her head hit the terrazzo floor hard. There was no blood, but fuck.

"Mom? Can you get someone to get me out of my bed? I need a wheelchair." I wipe away a stray tear.

"Honey, you can't be moved."

"Mom, help me get out of this bed! I've got to go with her."

Nodding, Sarah Flynn marches out into the corridor. I know she'll get it done because she's, well, she's Sarah Flynn. Sure enough, an orderly, a nurse, and a doctor all walk in. Yeah, that sounds like the beginning of a bad joke.

"This isn't a good idea," says the doctor on duty.

"I'm going with her. She could be pregnant with my kid. I need to know she's okay."

Without words, they lower the side rails on my bed, grab my catheter bag, and pull the only remaining IV bag filled with antibiotics out from behind me. It hangs on a hook at the back of my chair. Next, I'm lifted out of bed and placed in a chair that props up my leg. I'm not gonna lie, getting moved into the chair hurt like hell, but it's worth it if I can be with Roni.

The orderly wheels me out of the room and down the hall. "Where did they take her?"

"To the ER."

I remain silent on the trip downstairs. Hank follows close behind with his phone to his ear. We're ushered into the internal waiting area, hoping to get the word that she's all right.

"Her parents are on their way."

"You called them? How did you—"

"We exchanged numbers when you had your accident. I thought they should know."

I agree. They should know.

46

———

RONI

I wake up feeling like I'm on some sort of amusement park ride—and not a good one. Whatever I'm riding on is rolling down a long hallway, weaving in and around people and furniture. Nausea hits me like a ton of bricks. I turn to my side ready to vomit, but nothing comes out. Dry heaves are worse than anything. I heave and choke, attempting to get whatever evil is in my stomach out. A woman I've never seen before places a kidney-shaped bowl under my mouth. I plant my face into the bowl and heave several more times. Bile is the only thing that comes out, but the bitter, sour taste is enough to make me sick again. I lay back on the gurney and watch as I'm rushed into the emergency room. I concentrate on figuring out what happened to get me in here. I close my eyes and think. I remember the cab ride to the hospital. The Flynn family was in Mick's room. His smiling face, and then it hit me. I was yelling at him. I was furious.

I can't seem to muster up the anger right now. I know it'll return eventually. The thought that every Flynn knows about the condoms is so embarrassing. "God, Mick. You're such a tool," I murmur.

Surprisingly, a doctor enters my curtained off area in only minutes. "So, Ms. McGonigall, is it?"

"Yeah."

He brings his hand up to me like he wants to shake. I lift my arm to him.

"I'm Dr. Bigalow. It's nice to meet you. I understand you took a fall upstairs."

"I-I don't remember. I was talking and then nothing."

"A witness believes you fainted. Is there a chance you're pregnant, Ms. McGonigall?"

Jesus. Did Mick put him up to this? I groan loudly. "Yes. There's a slight chance. But the truth is, I haven't eaten very much lately. I'm hungry." *Or I was.*

"Fainting can be caused by hunger, so that's certainly a possibility. When was your last period?"

Shit, he's not going to let this pregnancy thing go. "I don't know, two weeks ago, maybe more? Look, I'm tired and hungry. So...." Maybe he'll take a hint and bring me some food. Real food. No yogurt or pudding.

"Well, let's hold off on food until we know what we're dealing with. I'm going to run some tests just to be sure."

Sure? About what? "Isn't it too soon for a pregnancy test?"

"With an over-the-counter test, yes. Blood tests should give us a result much sooner, sometimes eleven days is all we need. We'll take some blood and see what your hCG levels are now. We've got a state-of-the-art lab here in the hospital. They'll do the lab work tonight, so we should have news tomorrow.

I have mixed emotions about this. I'd like to know, but part of me just wants to go home and wait it out. I don't need the entire Flynn clan descending on me, asking about the results. This should be a private conversation between Mick and me.

"We're going to get you checked in because I'd like for you

to stay overnight for observation. You're not showing any concussion symptoms right now, but we need to be sure."

"Great," I mumble. *How am I going to pay for this? I lost my insurance the minute I quit my job.*

I lay in my bed watching the medical staff work on me. They've put me in one of those awful hospital gowns and drawn blood. When they've done all the poking and prodding they can do, I'm wheeled up to a regular room.

After I'm lifted onto a slightly more comfortable bed, the nurse arranges my bedding and brings a tray table over. "The doctor has ordered you some food. It should be here shortly."

"Thank God." *I'm so hungry I could eat hospital food.*

Turning on my television, I lay back and tune into a comedy channel. *Laughter is the best medicine.* An orderly enters my room with a food tray. Yay! It's only got things like clear soda pop, crackers, Jell-O, and you guessed it, pudding. I don't care. I eat everything on the tray. I sigh deeply, rest my head on a firm pillow, and close my eyes.

"Roni?"

I open my eyes slowly and see Mick Flynn rolling into my room in a wheelchair. *The man looks good even in that state.* His hair is half shaved, he's bruised and scratched up, but the only thing I notice are his eyes. He looks sad and scared.

Pulling his chair up close to my bed, he asks softly, "Are you okay, baby?"

It's literally impossible to stay mad at this man. I smile at him. "Yeah, I'm fine. They just want to observe me overnight to make sure I don't have a concussion. I've got quite a goose egg on the back of my head."

"I bet. You hit the floor hard. Look, Roni. I'm so sorry."

"About which part?" *There are so many right now.*

"Let's start with the night of the party."

Let's not.

"I'm sorry I treated you so badly that night. I'm sorry you found out about the condoms the way you did. I tried to get in touch with you all week. I wanted to see you, talk to you, but I really wanted to let you know about the condom issue."

I nod. I know I wasn't responding to his texts and messages. I wasn't ready.

"When I came to see you at the bar, I started to tell you, but you were mad at me. You didn't let me finish."

"Hey—"

He holds up his good hand. "No, I'm not blaming you. I'm just telling you why it took me over a week to tell you."

Sighing, I look down at my hands, then up at him. "I'm sorry too. I may have overreacted back in your room." I hold my fingers up, showing an inch. "Just a tiny bit. I have a right to be angry with you about the fact that your family knew before I did."

"Only Emily knew. My mom found out about it when Betty told me what I'd said to you. She was in the room."

"Your entire family probably thinks I'm a raging bitch. Another Jen."

"No, they don't. You're not a bitch, Roni. You could never be a bitch. You had every right to be upset. I had no idea Emily lured you here, telling you I was having problems. I also had no idea Mom would blab—wait, yes, I did. My family cannot keep a secret. I should have warned you about that."

He has warned me. The only one he trusts is Emily—or the only one he used to trust. She may have blown that with him. She certainly has with me.

"Well, you need to rest, baby. I'll—"

"They drew blood. A pregnancy test. I'll know tomorrow."

"Oh. Right. Good."

"What are the actual odds I could be pregnant from an expired condom?"

"According to Em and Google, it depends. Expired condoms can get dry and crack or tear easily. The latex sort of breaks down. If there was a tear in one of ours and you were at that time of month, ovulation or whatever, it's very possible."

Shit. Was I ovulating then? "Did the condom break?"

"I didn't pick it up and look. I should have, but I didn't realize that's what I was looking for. It's still in your bathroom trash can...."

"I think I'll just see what happens tomorrow. It's sort of too late to worry about that now, don't you think?"

"Yeah. Let's just see what happens tomorrow. For now, I'm going to head back to my room so you can get some rest. What if I call your room from my room later?"

I giggle at that idea. What a pair we are, both of us hospitalized. I nod. "Yeah. That sounds good."

"I'd give you a kiss if I could get any closer to you."

I slide out of bed and place my feet on the cold floor. Leaning over, I kiss his lips gently. He reaches up one hand to slide around the back of my neck. Pulling me in closer, he deepens the kiss.

"I'm really glad you're okay, baby."

"Me too. I'm glad you're going to be okay too, Mick."

"We are quite a pair, aren't we?" He chuckles.

I nod, leaning back over for another kiss, but feel a wave of light-headedness hit me. I sit back down on my bed and close my eyes.

"Okay. Get back in bed. You just turned white as a sheet. I'm going back to my room. I'll call you in a while."

I slide back under my sheet and watch him roll out the door. Relieved that we've cleared the air, I shut my eyes and fall fast asleep.

47

———

RONI

"Roni?"

"Dove? She must be exhausted," my dad murmurs.

I blink open my eyes and see my mom and dad leaning over me like I'm a science experiment. "Hey," I say huskily. "Why are you guys here?"

Mom says, "Hank called your father. He thought we should know."

"Are you pregnant, Roni?" asks my dad stiffly.

"Dear Holy Mother Mary and Jesus," I groan. "I'm going to kill Mick Flynn."

"Oh, Mick didn't tell us. Hank did."

"Well, if I weren't terrified of him, I'd kill him too." I let out an exasperated breath. "In answer to your question, I don't know. They've taken blood to see if I'm pregnant. It's early, so it may not say for sure."

"Roni," Mom sounds like she's about to lecture me, "you need to be more careful."

"We used condoms, Mom. I guess they were expired."

They both blink down at me like they aren't sure what to say to that.

Are they picturing...? Nah. I can't go there.

"Does Mick know?" asks Mom because my dad wouldn't be caught dead talking to me about birth control.

"Know what?"

"About the expired condoms?"

"What! Of course! They were his condoms. He didn't tell me until the other night while he was under the influence of morphine. Otherwise, I probably wouldn't know now myself, Mom."

"I'm confused," Dad says, rubbing his forehead.

"You and me both, Dad. You and me both. You should go down and ask Mick to explain. This is all his fault. He should be the one getting the Spanish Inquisition right now."

"Oh, Roni. Give your dad a break. He's beside himself with worry and the desire to punch Mick in the nose. But, Jeff, you should go down and read him the riot act. He needs to make our daughter an honest woman."

"No! No! No!" I shout. "Do not pressure him into doing something he doesn't want to do. I couldn't stand the idea that he feels forced into being with me. Please? Dad? Don't."

"All right, dove. I'll go check on him, but I won't say anything, even in jest. Just don't get upset. We're here for you. Can I bring you anything while I'm gone?" asks Dad.

"Yes! Food! More food. All kinds of food. Lots of it."

Dad chuckles and leaves my room. "I'm on it, dove."

I turn to look at Mom and know what's coming. "Now, Roni, tell me everything."

So, I do. I tell her about the Flynn's, the possible baby growing in my belly, Mick's words when he was under the influence of pain meds, and my fall.

"Well, the only thing we can do is wait on the test results," agrees Mom.

"Yep. That's all we can do. Well, we can eat. I'm still so hungry, Mom."

"I'll send Dad out to get something yummy. How's that?"

"Good idea."

We sit and watch some *Real Housewives* on the television and wonder how shows like this ever got on the tube. They're almost as bad as the Kardashians.

48
____

MICK

"Mick?" I look up and see a man standing in my doorway. He's about my dad's age but bigger by at least two inches. He's got silver hair and tan skin, which makes me think he works outside. Yeah, he reminds me a lot of my dad.

"Yes?"

"I'm Jeff McGonigall. Veronica's father."

I lean up, attempting to show respect, but I can't. I raise my left hand to shake his. "Good to meet your, sir."

"Call me Jeff, please. So, how are you feeling?"

"Good. Well, not bad, considering. Have you seen Roni?"

"Yes, I was just up there. She seems to be feeling better, considering...."

Uh-oh, Dad sounds pissed. I think I know what this is about.

"So, you used expired condoms with my daughter?"

Yep. I knew it. "Yes, sir. I believe so. It was an accident. I never—"

"What? You'd never want to have a child with my daughter?"

I've hit a nerve. Dad is going on the defensive, and I could end up getting a beatdown. "No, that's not what I was going to say. Roni's amazing. Any man would be lucky to have her."

"Uh-huh."

"On the same token, I would never have tricked her into having my baby—not that I would mind if she were pregnant. I care about Roni. A lot. I see us together for the long haul. I'm just not sure Roni feels the same about me."

Her dad scoffs. "She loves you. She told me when we were out looking for you the night of your accident, but don't tell her I said that. She'll kill me."

I laugh and smile big. *She loves me? She loves me!* "I won't tell her, sir—I mean, Jeff," I say with a smile that reaches from one ear to the other. "The trick now is to convince her I feel the same about her. I don't think she's got much confidence in me. My track record with her is not very good."

"Just be steadfast and true. That's all any woman wants. She wants to know you'll stay true."

That makes sense. Trust is really what he's saying. She needs to trust me. "I'll do what I can. I'll do what she wants. I'm at her mercy, really." I've got real work to do on that front. First, I told her I'd help her get that asshat from her work. Next, I friend-zoned her. Then, I screwed her and possibly knocked her up all under the guise of friendship. Yeah, I've got work to do.

Jeff chuckles. "We are all at the mercy of our women. It's really true what they say, 'Happy wife, happy life.'"

There's that damn reference to marriage. I should run screaming at those words, but a wife? Roni Flynn? Veronica Flynn? It sounds good. Real good.

I watch as Jeff checks his phone. "Well, son, duty calls. Roni needs some food. Apparently, she's very, very hungry. Her words, not mine." He chuckles.

"Thank you for feeding my girl, Mr—uh, Jeff."

"She was my girl first. Don't forget that." He pauses. "Don't tell anyone, but she's always been my favorite," he whispers conspiratorially.

"I can see why." I'd like to elaborate about her bitchy sisters, but it's best not to press my luck. "See you soon. Thanks for stopping by."

Jeff lifts his hand to say goodbye. "Yep. Get well, Mick."

I nod as he exits my room. He's cool. I bet he and my dad would get along well. They're cut from the same no-nonsense cloth.

49

RONI

"Are you ready to hear the results of your blood test?"

Mom and Dad look at me as I look up from my dry toast, bland tea, and oatmeal at Dr. Bigalow standing in my doorway. I'm supposed to be released from the hospital later this morning, so I'm not surprised to see him. The announcement of my pregnancy test results did shock me, however.

"Well, I think Mick should be present. I want him here. Can we go down to three, so you can tell us both at the same time?"

Dr. Bigalow looks at his watch. "Give me twenty minutes, and I can meet you there. What's his room number?"

"Three eleven."

"All right, see you there. I'll get an orderly to wheel you down."

"No need. I can walk."

"It's hospital policy. You must go down in a chair."

I grumble but agree to the stupid chair. I wish I could put on some clothes. When my nurse comes in, I tell her the plan and ask for my clothing. She opens my tiny closet and pulls out my slacks and the pink sweater I was wearing. My underthings are in a plastic bag. "Need any help getting dressed?"

"Nope. My mom can help. Thanks, though."

Dressed in my meeting clothes and socks, I sit in the wheelchair waiting for the orderly to return. "Mom, Dad? Do you mind waiting up here? I think it should just be Mick and me right now."

"Of course, honey," says Mom.

Dad smiles. "We'll wait right here. Call us if you need us."

"Thanks."

The orderly takes me down to Mick's room. When we roll in, I notice he's alone. It's shocking, really. "You're alone?" I ask, surprised.

"Hey, baby!" Mick gives me his best smile. Well, all of his smiles are pretty great. This one is special, though. I get the feeling he's really happy to see me.

The orderly leaves me and tells me to call the nurses' station when I'm ready to go. I take that opportunity to get out of the chair and walk to Mick's bed.

"Hard to believe, I know, but I told them all to get on with their lives. Shockingly, they did as I asked. I'm sure they'll start to trickle in later. I'm due for surgery in the morning."

"You are? Your leg?"

Mick reaches out to me with his right arm with the new cast. He takes my hand in his and runs his thumb over my palm. "Uh-huh. They're going to need to put a pin in my leg and make sure it's cleaned out. So far, no sign of infection, so they want to get the wound closed up. The sooner that happens, the sooner I can leave. I'm getting sick of this place." He chuckles.

"I know. I've only been here one night, and I'm ready. Can I get you anything?"

"Just a kiss," he says sweetly.

I know I shouldn't, but I want to kiss him too. I lean forward and brush my lips over his. He opens his mouth slightly, and his tongue touches my lips. My god can he kiss. The man is sex on wheels even in the hospital. His good arm rises, his hand sliding into my hair. He pulls me closer to deepen the kiss. I was the one in charge, but he's now taken control. His kiss becomes almost frantic.

"God, Roni, I've missed you so much."

I look down in his lap and see his erection. "Apparently," I snicker.

"All you have to do is walk into the room for that to happen," he says, pointing to his crotch.

I giggle again. "Good to know, Mick."

"You should climb up on the bed with me, baby. We could snuggle."

"And by snuggle do you mean have sex?"

"Yes. Definitely. I know I've got some broken Brunette, but the most important one is still in working order." He winks.

"You're such a pervert. Jeez." I laugh out loud.

"But I'm your pervert, so you're going to have to get used to it."

That does it. I throw my head back and laugh so hard it hurts. "I missed you too. I've missed our friendship."

"Friendship? Is that all I am to you? Your friend?"

Fun time over. Now it's getting serious. "Mick, I'm—"

We're interrupted by a swift knock on the door. Dr. Bigalow marches in and says, "Ready?"

I blink at the doctor and then at Mick. I pull one of his blankets up over his lap in a lump to disguise his little tent. "One second, Doc." I turn to Mick. "Dr. Bigalow is here to tell us the results of the blood test, Mick. I wanted him to tell us together."

"So, you haven't heard the results yet?"

"No."

"Can I say something before you read them, Doc?" Mick asks.

Dr. Bigalow nods.

50

MICK

"Roni, I don't care what the results are because I want you to be my girlfriend. If you aren't pregnant, I'll be disappointed because the more I've thought about it, the more I love imagining you and I having a kid together. You'd be a great mom."

She smiles at me, and I see the start of moisture in her eyes. I continue, "If you aren't pregnant, I'm going to hope we are someday—soon. But no matter what this is, I want to be yours, Roni. Just yours. You and me—a couple. I'm not saying we need to get married right away, but I like the idea of that. I like the sound of Roni Flynn. I love the idea, actually."

A lone tear runs down her cheek. "Mick. I—"

"I love you, Roni McGonigall. I'm sorry it's taken all of this"—his eyes sweep around the room—"for me to come to my senses."

"Mick, I've... I've caught feelings for you too."

He laughs. "You've 'caught feelings' for me too? Jesus, Roni, you crack me up. I'm going to go ahead and assume you feel the same about me. Caught feelings?" He laughs again. "I'll wait until after the doc has read the results, then I'm going to insist you clarify that statement."

I nod, and we both turn our heads to Dr. Bigalow who looks irritated. "Are we ready now?"

"Yes," we say simultaneously.

"Let me preface this by saying that you'll want to have another test taken in a couple of weeks, but this preliminary test does show low levels of hCG in your blood."

We both continue to stare at the doctor.

"You're pregnant, Veronica. Congratulations," he deadpans.

We turn and look at each other. Roni looks terrified, and I've got the biggest smile on my face. It almost hurts, but I'm so fucking happy. "Roni! We're having a baby together—you and me. How do you feel?"

"Honestly? Shocked. Scared. Nervous. Nauseous. Did I say scared?"

"Yes, you did." I chuckle. "I'm scared too, baby. But this is such great news. I really hoped you were pregnant."

"You are kind of cavalier about all of this, Mick. This is a big deal. This is life-altering stuff."

"I can't wait to tell everyone. I hope it's a girl. No, that's not true. I don't care as long as she's healthy. Or he." *I'm rambling.*

"Okay, wait for a second," she looks at me angrily. "I want this to stay between the two of us until we know for absolute sure I'm pregnant and we know the baby is okay. Can you keep a frigging secret from your family? From Emily?"

"Of course. Yes. I know what you're saying. It can be between us until we're in the clear. They're going to ask, though. What should we tell them for now?"

"That we have to wait a couple of weeks before we know for sure." It's the truth, so....

She looks at me like she doesn't believe me. The truth is I'm usually the only Flynn who keeps everything secret. The fact that I'm excited to spread the word only reinforces how I feel about Roni and our baby.

"So, should I move into your place or do you want to move into mine. Oh, hell. It'll have to be your place until I can walk. I won't be able to get a wheelchair up those metal steps." *Rambling again.*

"Mick, I'm not ready for all of that. I'm not ready to live together. I need some time to regroup and think about all of this. This is such a huge thing."

I must look surprised because she backtracks. "I'm not saying I don't want to live with you eventually. I'm just saying for the time being, I've got to let all of this sink in."

I nod. I know what she's saying. I've had over a week to get used to the idea that I could have knocked her up. She's only had a couple of days. "At least admit that you love me too," I say smugly.

"I'm not ready to do that yet either."

"Your dad already told me, so you're just stalling."

"My dad? My dad told you I loved you?"

"Yep." I pop that "p" again. "So, it's out there. Just say it."

"No. I'm not going to say it right now. First, I'm going to kill my dad. Then, I'm taking a nap. I'm tired."

She stands up from the edge of my bed and turns to leave the room. I know she loves me, and I'm an ass about it, but part of me is hurt she won't say it. "I love you, Roni."

"I... I'll see you later. I'm getting released soon, so I'll come down here before I go home to change. I'll be here for your surgery tomorrow too."

"Okay, babe. I'll call you shortly," I say sadly.

That fucking hurts. My heart feels like someone stabbed me with a fork. I know she loves me. I just know it. She's got to.

Damn, I don't like being on the other side of this. I'm usually the one who can't commit. This sucks. I just need to remember what Jim McGonigall said, "Be steadfast and true." I can certainly do that. I can show Roni I'm in this for the long haul. And unlike Lauren, I know Roni will be steadfast and true too.

51

RONI

"Home sweet home." The doctor finally released me right after telling me to "take it easy, don't do any strenuous exercise, don't return to work for a week, eat healthily, and call if you have any questions." I laugh to myself because that's all very easy to do. I don't have a job. Check. I don't exercise anyway. Check. I'm tired, so I'll just lie around. Check.

Hungry again, I open the fridge to see it full of healthy choices like milk, yogurt, fruits, and veggies. After they wheeled me back to my room, I told Mom and Dad the news. Now, before you chastise me for telling my parents and not letting Mick tell his, it's because... well, mine won't tell anyone and mine live three hours away. I wanted to be able to tell them face-to-face. Okay?

So, anyway, Dad drove me home in my rental car while Mom stopped at the grocery store on the way here in their car. She bought me everything a pregnant woman would need for the next month. I open the cupboard and see several new boxes of cereal. I pull out the box of Honey Nut Cheerios and the half gallon of skim milk. Cereal sounds so good right now. Mom's a genius. I make myself a bowl and return to my living room. I settle into the chair that used to be in my office at P&P and sigh. Cozy in my chair, I eat. From the corner of my eye, I see my answering machine flashing. I count three messages.

I stand and walk over to hit play. "Roni, it's Bill Phillips. Can you please give me a call on my personal number?" He lists off the number again, and I hear the next message.

"Roni, it's your mother. I'm just calling to check in on you. We're still on the road, but I keep wishing you'd have let me stay overnight. Remember, you promised me you'd just lay around your place for the next day or two. Call me as soon as you get this. I'm worried."

The third message is a hang-up. I don't have caller ID, so I can't tell who it was. It's probably just Mom trying to catch me again.

I call my parents first. Surprisingly, they're still jubilant about the pregnancy news. "Remember, I told Mick he couldn't tell anyone, so please don't let on that you know. Okay?"

Dad chuckles. "I don't blame you, honey. They're quite a gossipy group. I've only known them a day or two, and I figured that out." Dad pauses, then adds, "You're going to be a wonderful mother, dove. Just wonderful." He sounds emotional, which makes me emotional.

"Dad," I murmur. "Thank you."

"And your young man is going to be a wonderful father. He loves you, Roni. He told me so."

"That reminds me. You told Mick I love him?" I say, sounding annoyed.

"Oops, sorry, honey. It slipped out. Forgive me?"

"Yeah. I forgive you. Geesh, Dad."

Dad laughs into the phone. I hear Mom giggling too. I must be on speakerphone.

It's then that the weirdest sensation rolls over me. Contentment. Happiness. Fulfillment. I love my parents so much. I already love this baby, and Mick? Mick Flynn loves me. It hasn't sunk in just yet. Mick Flynn loves me. Something equally as warm hits me. I love Mick Flynn right back. He needs to know. I'll tell him tomorrow—before his surgery.

Grabbing my cell phone, I call Bill Phillips back. "Roni?"

"Yes. I just heard your message. What did you need?"

"I've got another proposition for you."

Wow, Chris must have really screwed up for Bill to work this hard. "Another proposition?"

"Hear me out. I'd like to offer you the same money—double what you were making."

"Bill—"

"Let me finish, please, Roni."

I wait in silence.

"Same pay and you work exclusively with Owen McCormick and EnerSport."

"But—"

"The other part of that is you can work from home. I'll pay for whatever you need to set up a home office. I'll pay for your internet and for a business line to be added to your telephone. I want you back, and we both know Owen wants you back."

"I'm just not sure, Bill. It sounds great, but at some point, you'll require me back in the office. I don't think I can do that."

"Chris and Trisha no longer work for P&P."

"What? Why?"

"After you refused the job so quickly, I had a feeling something happened between my office and the street. You sounded frightened on the phone. I had security view the video footage from the time you left my office until you stepped out the door."

"Footage?"

"From the elevator."

"You saw?"

"More than that. I heard."

"There's audio?"

"Yes. We don't advertise the fact that there's surveillance in places like the elevators. And this incident is the exact reason why. I saw the footage in the elevator, Roni. I heard what they said to you. I heard the threat. I had no idea they were like that. I knew a few things but was shocked to hear how they spoke to you. They will not be in this building anymore."

God, they're going to blame me. They'll think I snitched on them. I just hope they'll leave me alone.

"One other thing that may help sweeten the pot. Apparently, Martha never completed your paperwork related to your resignation. Which means you haven't quit, technically. We'll just call it a paid leave of absence. You still have your health insurance and—"

"I'll do it!" *I still have my insurance? That's flipping amazing.* I touch my stomach and smile. That's one less worry. One less *big* worry. My baby has insurance.

"Wow! Excellent. I'll have Gloria call you tomorrow to set up the delivery of your new computer and anything else you may need. Make a list. You'll need a scanner, copier, and printer, no doubt. Just make a list. We'll get you whatever you need to get back to work."

The question is where will I put those things in my tiny apartment? I'll just have to rearrange and purge. It's been a while since I've done that anyway.

"Great. Thanks, Bill."

"Do me one favor, though. Call Owen McCormick in the morning and let him know you're back and will start to work with him after you're all set up. Will you? He's driving me nuts." Bill chuckles.

"I will. Can you email me his contact information again?" I give him my private email address and hang up. "Oh, my gosh! This is so perfect." I pat my stomach and speak to my peanut. "You and I are set, little one. No matter what happens with your daddy, we're going to be okay."

52

———

MICK

Getting prepped for surgery is nerve-racking. I had a tonsillectomy when I was young and had my wisdom teeth removed, but other than that, I've never gone through something this complicated.

My family is here, but I've been waiting on Roni to appear. I called her last night, letting her know when I'd be going into surgery. She's only got a few minutes until they wheel me downstairs. At that moment, I see a beautiful blonde walk into my room.

"Finally," I sigh with relief. "I was afraid you wouldn't make it."

"Sorry. Traffic was crazy. Are you nervous?" she asks tentatively.

"Yes. Even though I know what to expect, it's still scary. Not gonna lie."

She walks over to stand next to my bed, leans the front of her legs on the mattress, and places her hands on the bed rails. "I know, but I read up on your procedure last night, and I know you're going to be fine. It's a piece of cake," she says, snapping her fingers.

"I know. I know. I just think I need a kiss to help me get over these nerves."

Roni giggles, and I love the sound. "A kiss, huh? That's what's going to get you through this? You're such a playah, Michael Flynn."

"Not anymore." I look at her with a serious expression. *I mean it. Not anymore.*

She stops laughing and leans down to kiss my lips. "I love you, Mick Flynn. Playah or not."

Our lips meet, and I feel a sense of relief rush through me. I pull back. "Thank God, Roni. I can't stand the thought of you not loving me. My heart would break into a million pieces if you didn't." I blink as I look up at her.

"Well, it's true. I love you. You're going to have a successful surgery, and you'll be good as new in four to six weeks."

"Four to six weeks? You really did read up on it, didn't you?"

"I did. I learned that an open fracture is a surgical emergency. Antibiotics are started as soon as possible in the emergency room." She points to my one and only IV. "The next steps in controlling the risk of infection are to cleanse the wound and remove as much contamination as possible from the skin, soft tissues, and bone. This procedure is called debridement and irrigation and is typically performed in an operating room. Depending on the severity of your injury, you may require several debridement and irrigation procedures."

"Did you memorize something from a medical journal?"

"Google. Same thing." She giggles again.

"They have been working on cleaning the wound every day. Now I know why. Thanks, baby. Now, kiss me like you love me."

She leans down and kisses me with tongue and everything. I'd laugh out loud if my dick weren't hard as a nail. "Better stop or you're going to have to give me a hand job. Ooh, or better yet, a blow job."

"And the pervert is back. Just hurry up and get done with surgery. We can talk about a hand job later." She winks as she squeezes my hand.

When they wheel me out of my room, my family are all standing on either side of the hallway like I'm some type of celebrity. I quickly grab my blanket to pool around myself. I refuse to let my mom see me in an aroused state. "Jesus, Flynns. Go sit down. This is all so weird. But not you, Roni. I want to look at you before I go under the knife," I say dramatically.

She leans down and kisses me softly. "You're going to be fine, baby. I'll kiss it all better when you get out."

Fuck, I'm getting hard again. "Shh," I whisper. "Damn you, woman. You're seriously gonna have to take care of me in the elevator down to surgery if you keep that up."

Laughing loudly, she says, "See you soon, Mick." She squeezes my hand, and they roll me away. *Please, God. Let me live through this. My girl and my baby need me.*

I WAKE UP GROGGY. Bright lights are overhead, and I hear the hustle and bustle of busy people around me. The sound of voices around me gets clearer the more I blink awake.

"Michael, what's your last name?"

"Flynn."

"What day is it?"

"Thursday?" I'm really not sure. This week has been a blur.

"Good. You're in recovery, Michael. Surgery went well. The doctor will be in to speak to you in a few minutes. She's already talked to your family and your wife."

"Wife?"

"That's what she said. Rest easy. I'll be back in a few minutes."

My wait is just long enough for me to remember things. I had surgery on my broken leg. A leg I broke in a car accident. I'm married. I'm married?

"Michael?"

I look up and see that sexy doctor from the other day. I try to give her my sexy look, but she laughs. I guess I lost it when I got married. *Shit*. "Am I on morphine?"

"Yes, we've given you morphine for pain. It should kick in shortly.

"No. Crazy on morphine," I slur.

She ignores me and tells me about my procedure. "The surgery went exceptionally well. You can plan to start moving four to six weeks from now. From there, you'll work with a physical therapist to get back to 100 percent."

"One hundred percent," I repeat.

"There was no damage to ligaments, so there's optimism that you'll be ready in time for physical therapy in four to six weeks, barring complications. The Brunette did rupture the skin, so infections are possible. We'll keep a close eye on that."

"Rupture," I mumble.

I catch her laughing again, and I don't like it. I scowl at her. "Roni."

"We'll get your wife in here soon. We'd like for you to wake up a bit more."

"No! Roni!" I shout.

"All right. All right. We'll get her. Sit tight."

"Tight. Sit." I try to raise my upper body from the bed, but a bunch of hands stop me.

"No, no, no. Lay still, Michael."

53

RONI

After Mick's surgery, he went to stay with his parents. I meant what I said when I told him I needed space. I wanted time to get back to work and mentally prepare for the baby. It's worked out well for him because his mom has doted and spoiled him rotten. He complains that she's smothering him, but I think he secretly loves it.

Sarah took him to a salon to see what they could do with his hair since a large section of the right side had been shaved off in the emergency room. He just wanted to have Emily shave it all off, but his mom wouldn't have it. The result was, well, fantastic. The hairdresser cut his hair in a men's fade with the top of his hair in a longer faux hawk. It seems impossible that he could be better looking than before the accident or the haircut, but he does. He's even sexier.

The first few weeks, Mick was wheelchair bound, but it wasn't long before he was fitted with a super sci-fi looking boot. They didn't want to encase the wound in a cast for fear of infection after surgery. Sam, his personal Uber driver, takes him everywhere. It's kind of hilarious.

Thanks to Sam, Mick comes over almost every evening. He spends his days going to physical therapy, going to his follow-up doctor appointments, and going in to work for short spans of time. He's not bartending yet, though; he's only doing the managerial things until he's out of the boot.

My mornings are spent working on the EnerSport account and my afternoons are filled with baby prep. We've had two appointments with the OB-GYN. I am in fact pregnant, and the baby is doing well. We heard the heartbeat at our first ultrasound, and that made us both cry. He's so happy—almost as happy as I am.

When we told our families about the pregnancy right before Christmas, everyone was thrilled. Mick and I celebrated the holidays with both of our families, but Christmas Eve was just the two of us at my place. We ordered from my favorite Thai restaurant, watched some old Christmas movies, and exchanged gifts. I bought Mick a few silly things like a Gryffindor scarf from Harry Potter. He loved it. I also bought him a great book on starting a small business, and the last thing I purchased for him were two baby onesies. The first said "I Heart Boobies (Like my Daddy)," the second said, "I have the Best Dad in the Whole World." The first one made him laugh, the second made him cry. I did well.

His gifts were thoughtful too. He bought me a gift certificate for a fancy spa to get "the works." He also bought me some cute maternity clothes that I'd already pointed out to him. He added some sexy pregnancy lingerie into the mix. *Men.*

The last thing I opened came in a small light blue box. Tiffany's packages are very distinctive. At first, I was worried it was an engagement ring, and when it wasn't, I was disappointed. Not gonna lie. The truth is, I'm not ready for that yet. What he did buy me was a rose gold Sprinkle necklace. It's stunning and tasteful. I haven't taken it off since I opened it. Our first Christmas as a family was perfect. I hope they're all like that.

We didn't go out for New Year's Eve for obvious reasons, but Sarah had a celebration for us and for Sophie and Hank on New Year's Day. They finally announced Sophie's second pregnancy right before the holidays as well.

It was the first time my entire family met Mick's entire family. Sarah and my mom got along perfectly. It's almost like they were long-lost sisters. Dad fit in perfectly with the Flynn men too. They have a lot in common, what with them all being big and manly. I snort at that thought. My dad is sweet and kind, but when provoked, he's just as alpha as Mick and his brothers.

My sisters have been acting strange since I told them about Mick and me. At the party, they were polite but not super affectionate. Instead, they seemed to be fixated on newly single David Flynn. They spent most of the get-together chatting him up while their husbands watched the kids. I'm curious how they pulled that off, but I think their spouses were careful not to cause a scene. It was obvious, thanks to their scowls, they weren't happy about the flirtations between Frankie, Gloria, and David Flynn.

The rest of the time, Mick and I have spent relaxing and planning. When Mick isn't at work or at physical therapy, he works on his bottled drink idea, Mick'sology. I've done very little work on it myself. My role has been to show him how to research the industry, the markets, do a cost analysis, work with a graphic designer to come up with a label and packaging design, and to speak to potential manufacturers.

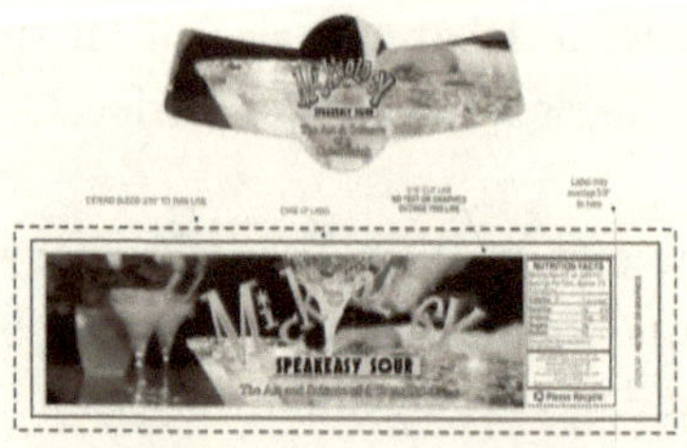

AFTER SIFTING his way through the government rules and regulations relating to the sale and production of alcohol, he decided the best way to get started is to work with a company that already manufactures and bottles alcoholic beverages. He's made incredible headway in only a few months. The graphic designer has come up with a cool label design, and after presenting his findings and plans to Hank and David, they've decided to invest in his product.

He's developed four drinks, the Speakeasy Sour made primarily with brandy and rum and a few secret ingredients, the Purple Urple made with grape vodka and lemonade and a few secret ingredients. Do you see a trend in the secret ingredients? The third drink called Fire in the Hole has Fireball whiskey, apple juice, and a twist of lemon, and, you guessed it, secret ingredients. I know. It sounds weird, but I'm told it's delish. The last drink he wants in his initial batch is called Sweet Sensation. It's a fruity and sugary concoction that includes coconut milk, pineapple juice, and rum.

"You're well on your way to becoming a drink mogul, Mick," I say to him one evening.

"You did all the work, babe."

"No, you did the work. I just pointed you in the right direction." He deserves all the credit. It's amazing to watch him because he's so passionate about his ideas. I wish I could say I've tasted his drinks, but since I'm several months along now, it's a no-no.

We've developed a bit of a routine since his accident. Like I mentioned, he comes over to my place almost every evening. We eat dinner together. Sometimes he cooks, sometimes I cook, and the rest of the time we have food delivered. It's amazing how well we sync up at home. He'll eat just about anything, so it's usually lady's choice.

He likes the same pizza toppings as I do and the same Thai dishes. At least, I assume he does. It could be Mick just trying to be nice. He doesn't even say anything when I eat the same number of pizza slices as he does. Actually, he doesn't seem to notice. I haven't dated a lot of guys, but the ones I did date took a keen interest in my food choices and portion sizes. I hope this is the real Mick, not just Mick trying to win favor.

My growing baby bump doesn't seem to faze him. If anything, it turns him on. He rests his hand on my abdomen, rubbing it absently when we cuddle up on the couch. I love it. It lulls me into a sleepy state as we sit on my couch watching television. Since my company has paid for my high-speed internet, I've added more cable channels and a movie channel. We started watching *Game of Thrones* together, and now we're hooked.

The best part of that is when the characters on the show get passionate, so does Mick. As soon as they start at it, his hand moves from my belly to my breasts. His next step begins with kisses on my neck, face, and then my lips. We've been making out like teenagers almost every night. It's becoming increasingly more difficult to keep my hands to myself. Nobody told me that getting pregnant meant you're horny twenty-six hours a day.

Ladies, it's true. I want to hump the man every chance I get, but I'm afraid of hurting him, so I've turned him down every time our necking sessions have turned into more. I've used my hands and mouth on him, and he's done the same for me. I don't think he should be straining himself like that yet, even though he's told me repeatedly that he's okay. Frustrated but fine. I know how he feels. He swears his doctor and physical therapist said it was okay to have sex. I'm just not so sure.

Tonight is one of our nights to cuddle in front of the TV, and we decide on pizza from Giordano's. In my opinion, they make the best Chicago-style pizza. There are a bunch of great restaurants, but this one is my favorite.

"Do you like your pizza, Mick?"

"Yeah, it's good."

Okay, something is bothering him. "Is everything all right? I can tell something is wrong."

He drops his pizza onto his plate and sets it on my coffee table. Turning to look at me, he looks cross. "Roni, I'm fucking dying."

"What?" I screech.

"Not dying, dying," he says, running his hands through what's left of his hair. It doesn't matter how long or short his hair is, he's still hot as sin. "I need you, baby—to be inside of you. I'm ready. The doc said it's fine. We can take it easy. We'll be safe. I've even thought about the best position for us, so you don't have to be concerned."

He's figured out the position for us? Oh, jeez. That's humiliating. Is it because I'm getting bigger and he's afraid I'll hurt him?

I know my expression is telling because Mick says, "This is not about you. I was just trying to make it so you won't worry about me hurting my leg. Damn, woman. I'm seriously going to die if you don't fuck me."

I set my plate on the table and turn to him. "I feel the same way, Mick. I'm dying for you too." I slide my oversized T-shirt over my head. I'm wearing a white cotton bra that I bought at the maternity store. My breasts have grown so much in the last month I had to bite the bullet and get new bras.

"Holy hell, Roni! It's not possible, but I think your tits are even more spectacular." He slides his fingers over my rounded stomach, then up to cup my breasts. His right hand moves to the center and unsnaps the front closure of the mammoth maternity bra.

My breasts pop out like escaped convicts.

"Jesus, woman," he groans. His head moves down to suckle on my right breast.

It's so sensitive I nearly come from just that. I make a noise that I've never made before. It's a cross between a moan and a squeal.

He takes my noises as encouragement and reaches down and lifts his own shirt off. He still looks perfect. How can a guy eat junk food for three months and still look that yummy?

It's my turn to taste. I lean down and lick each of his nipples as I run my fingers down his tight abs. My right hand moves down to cup him through his sweatpants. Hard as steel—my man is very turned on.

He grabs my hand and lifts it over my head, then goes back to work on my nipples.

I squirm and wiggle all around. "Mick. Let's go into my bedroom."

"No, I want you right here."

While I no longer have my love seat, the sofa I found on clearance isn't very deep. If he expects us to lay down on this thing together, he's crazy. There's no way.

Mick stands up and slides off his sweatpants and boxer briefs. His long, thick erection juts out, so I'm eye level with his gorgeous cock. Yeah, cocks aren't the prettiest things, but Mick's is stellar. He sits back down on the couch. "Take off your clothes, baby."

He's so bossy. It makes me nervous. I stand up and slide off my leggings. It's the first time I've been completely naked with him since we found out about the baby. We've had parts of our clothes off, but not everything.

"Jesus, Roni. You're incredible. You look beautiful all round with our baby."

I smile down at him and wait, not sure what he wants me to do. He pats his lap. "Straddle me."

"No."

"Straddle me, Roni."

"No, Mick. I'm too.... I'll hurt you."

"You won't hurt me. Trust me."

I remember what Jen said about Mick liking his women on top. We tried it, and it didn't work. He got frustrated and nearly lost his sexual mojo. "We tried this once, and it didn't work. I'm too big."

He blinks up at me. "What are you talking about?"

"The night after the Halloween party. I wanted to try being on top because.... Well, anyway, it didn't work."

"Because why?"

"Huh?" I decide to play dumb.

"Because why, Roni?"

"I overheard Jen talking on the phone. I think she was talking to Lauren. She said that you liked to have your women on top and that I was too, well, too big and you'd just have to do me from behind so you wouldn't have to look at me."

He blinks up at me, staring into my eyes and saying nothing for a long, long time.

"Mick?" I whimper.

"First of all, Veronica," he says—I've noticed that he only says my full name when he's extra bossy or irritated—"never believe a word that comes out of Jen's mouth. The truth is, I really hated it when Lauren was on top because that's the only way she ever wanted to do it. She liked to be in control, and I'm not into my woman being in charge in bed. In life, we're equals. In bed, I'm the boss."

Why did that make me wetter?

"As for that night and us trying that for the first time? I was tired. I wanted you badly, but I just wanted to sink into you and get lost in you. I could tell you were having a hard time navigating, and I was attempting to move us along to the fucking part of the night." He chuckles. "I'm sorry I was a dick, babe. You make me so crazy, and I need you every time I'm with you. I need you now. So do as I say and straddle me."

I can't believe it, but he's still hard as a rock. He must really need a release. I sigh and walk toward him. He reaches forward and places his big hands on my waist and pulls me toward the sofa. I set one knee on the outside of his right leg and the other over his left until I'm open to him.

"Slide closer to me."

I scoot up until my breasts are pressed up against his chest and face. We're nearly eye to eye now. He touches me all over my body. His hands slide up both arms to my neck, then into my hair before gliding down to my breasts, where he runs his fingers over my sensitive nipples. The sensation hits me, and I feel his cock press into my inner thigh. One hand moves to my belly, and his fingers spread out to hold it like a basketball. I like it. It feels like ownership. His right hand moves farther down to brush my clit. I'm dripping wet. I can feel my wetness between my legs as I move over him.

"Lift up just a bit."

I place one hand on the back of the couch and the other on his broad shoulder. I sit up on my knees and watch as he uses his hand to move his cock to my entrance. "Sit back down. Slowly."

I lower myself, feeling him enter me. "Oh, God, Mick," I moan. I'm anxious to get the rest of him, so I sit down fast.

With a harrumph, we're completely entwined. "Jesus, Roni. I've never felt anyone bare before. It's amazing. I never want to wear a rubber with you again. You hear me?"

"Yeah, I hear you."

"Jesus, I've missed your pussy so much. I want to do it like this ten times tonight and twenty times tomorrow to make up for lost time."

I giggle and lift up again using my upper thighs and arms, then slide down again. I literally squeal at the feeling. "Mick. God. You feel so fricking good. Help me. I want to go faster."

He places his hands under my ass, helping me rise up, then uses my waist to push me back down while he thrusts upward. We pick up the pace until I'm bouncing up and down.

"Don't stop. Fuck, Roni. Your tits are mesmerizing," he says as he presses his face between the girls. "Don't stop. Ride me. Fuck. I'm gonna come."

I feel him lose it inside of me, and it takes me over the edge. It's the longest, most amazing orgasm I've ever had. I don't want it to stop. I pump up and down on him until he starts to laugh.

"Stop, babe. I need rest."

"Wow, Mick. That was incredible. I loved doing it like that. I want to do it like that again, okay?"

"Me too. I just need a few minutes to recoup, then we can."

"Awesome." I stand up, watching as his come runs down the inside of my thigh.

Mick watches it flow down my leg. "That's the fucking hottest thing I've ever seen. If you weren't already pregnant, I'd make sure you were tonight, Roni," he says, giving me a heated look.

I feel my legs get wobbly again with just a look. I smile coyly and move into the bathroom to clean up. "Best sex ever," I whisper to myself.

54

———

MICK

I watch as Roni exits the bathroom and strides toward me. She's completely naked and sexy as hell. I love her new-found confidence and her body. It's growing more round every day, and I can honestly say that there's nothing more beautiful than a woman carrying your child. Nothing.

"We need to talk, Veronica."

"You know? I've noticed that you call me Veronica when you're extra bossy or serious." She laughs.

"Well, it's because we need to have a serious talk."

"Uh-oh."

"Knock it off," I say, laughing. I watch as she dresses in her leggings and an oversized shirt. I've got my sweatpants on again but left my shirt off. I'm hoping for round two soon. I pat the couch next to me. "I think it's time for us to talk about our living situation."

"Our living situation?"

I ignore her need to repeat what I'm saying. "I think we should live together." There. I've said it.

"Oh, Mick—"

"Don't turn me down, Veronica." *Yeah, I do say her full*

name when I'm extra serious. "You're three months along. You told me you needed time and space, and I've been giving you that."

She looks at me like I'm full of crap. So, yeah, I've come over almost every night since I became more mobile. She's got her days to herself, at least. "I know. I'm here a lot, but it's not the same as living together."

She nods as I continue. "I love you, Roni, and you love me. We both love this little baby." I place my palm on her belly. "It's time to think ahead. I want us to be a family when she arrives."

"She?"

"Well, he or she. It'll take us time to find a place that we can afford together and still be large enough for our future family."

"Future family?"

"Yeah, I want a bunch of kids. Don't you?"

"Not long ago, you told me you'd never have a child, a family, or a serious relationship. I find it hard to believe that this leopard"—she points to me—"has changed his spots that much."

She still doesn't trust me. "I know, Roni. I gave you a bunch of mixed signals. That didn't have anything to do with you. It was me and the fact that I was clinging to all the bad shit with Lauren. It wasn't fair of me to lump you in with that, with her. Besides, Roni, things changed. My attitude about all of that changed the minute I realized you were my person."

"Your person?" Roni's been extra emotional lately, so it's not surprising that comment gets her all misty-eyed. She cries at commercials for dog food one minute, and then she's completely dry-eyed the next. I can't keep up. Mom told me to expect the unexpected with a pregnant partner, and I guess she's right.

I add fuel to her emotional fire by adding, "We all have one person we're supposed to be with, and you're mine."

She's looking at me like that's the sweetest thing anyone has ever said to her. By the tears flowing down her cheeks, I know she's touched. "You... you're my person too, Mick. I felt that way the first night at the bar. It was so easy to talk to you. I thought it was just lust, though," she says earnestly.

I chuckle at her comment. "Look, babe, it's not like I'm proposing." I know she's not ready for that, but the look of hurt on her face makes my chest constrict. I attempt to rebound. "Unless you want to get married. I'm ready when you are."

"No. I'm not ready for that." She sighs. "I guess we could talk about it."

"Well, I may have asked around about possible places we could move in together. Big enough for the three of us."

"Uh-huh. Of course, you have," she grumbles skeptically.

"Yes, and there's a place in Edgewater." Edgewater is where Hank, Sophie, and Katie live. "My dad and brother bought an old Victorian there. They're fixing it up with the intention of flipping it. They either want to sell it or rent it out."

Roni looks thoughtful. "Edgewater is getting better. I've driven through there a few times. Being close to Sophie and Katie would be nice. Oh, and Hank too. What's it like? And don't tell me you haven't seen it because I know you."

"Yeah, I've seen it. I stopped by last week. They're just about done with the place. It's perfect." I pull out my phone to show her some pictures. "I've got before and after photos in there. Keith sent them to me."

The before pictures show the exterior of a run-down old Victorian in drab white. The front porch is in such bad shape it looks like it could crumble to the ground. The inside was slightly better when they started. The original woodwork was intact, including built-in cupboards on either side of a fireplace and built-in cabinets in the formal dining room. The original kitchen was a mishmash of old and new cabinets and appliances from the 70s. I swipe through the pictures and show her the kitchen now.

"Wow, it's really nice. I love the cabinets in the kitchen. It looks like they tried to make it look appropriate to the period and style of the house."

"They did, but it's all updated. New everything. They added a three-quarter bath on the main level and renovated the one upstairs, so it's got a big bathtub and a shower now. They used tiles from that time period and fixtures as well. It's nice. There are three bedrooms up—"

"Oh, that's good. One for us, one for the baby, and we could use the third one for an office. If there's room, we should have a bed in there for guests. We'll have people visiting once the baby is born."

Am I dreaming? She's actually considering this?

"But it's got to be really expensive. That's an up-and-coming area, so I know prices are rising."

"Well, the thing is, Dad and Keith bought it at auction way under market value. Dad said they'd sell it to me for the price plus their cost to renovate."

"Sell you? Just you? I don't like the idea that it would be just your house. I wouldn't feel like I had vested interest. You could just kick me out."

"Jesus, Roni. What kind of man do you think I am?"

"That's just it, Mick. I have no clue."

I'm silent as I limp into her tiny galley kitchen. I'm now wearing a boot-type cast on my lower leg, so getting around is much easier. I should just stay silent because what I'd like to say will piss her off. I practice some deep breathing before I say a word, walk back out to her living room, place my hands on my hips, and speak my mind.

"I get it. We had a rocky, confusing start. So, let me set you straight. You asked what kind of man I am, Veronica?" Yeah, I did it again—said her full name. "I'm the kind of man who protects the people he loves. I'm the kind of man who would die to protect you and our little one. I'm the kind of person who is loyal to a fault. I'd never cheat on you because it's not in my DNA to do anything that deceitful." I step closer to her, so she can see my eyes. "I'm the kind of man who loves you with my whole heart, baby. I spend my days working hard, but I think about you constantly. And not because I knocked you up. I thought of you constantly when it was just you and me. I'd try to think of shit to text you just so I could talk to you. You're the most beautiful, most sexy woman I've ever known, and I want to be with you. I've told you before, when I picture my future, you're standing next to me. That's the kind of man I am."

She's crying again. See, emotional. "Mick," she sobs. "That was so sweet."

"I wasn't trying to be sweet, angel. I'm glad you think so, though. I wanted to tell you to pull your head out of your gorgeous ass and embrace this thing between us. It's good. It's the best I've ever had. You're the best I've had, and I'm not just talking about sex. Although, sexually, you're the best I've ever had too."

"I am?" she asks, shocked. "But—"

"But nothing." I walk to her, sit down next to her, and pull her onto my lap. I speak in a whisper close to her ear, "You've got the sweetest pussy I've ever had. So snug and warm. You hug my cock like I was made just for you."

When I look up at her, she's breathing hard. Her eyes are dark and dilated. She brings her hands up to hold my face in place and kisses me like it's her job. I jump right in, and so does my dick. She makes me fucking hard as granite in seconds. I slide my hands under her shirt and pull it off.

"New rule. You're naked whenever we're home."

Roni giggles. "If I'm naked, so are you."

"Not a problem." I lift her up, so I can slide my sweats down to midthigh. I pull her leggings down but can't get them past her knees without her standing up. "Bedroom, now."

She hops off the couch, and we race, literally, to the bedroom.

I beat her there, but I wait for her near the bed. "We're going to use my bed in the new place. It's a king size and there are slats in the headboard. I'll be able to tie you up, and I can't fucking wait for that."

Giggling again, she lifts her knees onto the bed. I swat her bare bottom as she climbs up, then use my hands to stop her from moving too far in. I want her ass on the edge of the bed. "Stay there, Veronica."

I move in behind her and guide her hands to the headboard. It sits high on the wall, so she's kneeling, but her upper body is upright. I move in behind her and place my hands over hers before leaning down to kiss her neck and suckle on her ear. "Are you wet for me?"

"Yeah," she says breathlessly.

"Show me."

Without any guidance from me, she slides her hand to her entrance and draws out her moisture. Her fingers glisten. "Taste us." I came inside her earlier, and that memory is making me crazy. She takes her fingers into her mouth and moans. "Jesus, let me taste."

She leans down and takes more. I grasp her hand and slide her fingers into my mouth. "Mmm, we taste perfect together."

"Mick?"

I wait for her to continue, but she doesn't. "Yeah? You want more, babe?" She nods as I slide one hand down into her heat while the other plays her nipple like I'm plucking an instrument. She's using her hips to move with me. I slide two fingers inside, and with a loud moan, she thrusts her hips down onto my fingers. "That's right, fuck my fingers, Roni. Jesus, you're so fucking sexy."

I slide my hand out of her and use it to guide my cock into her wetness. Finding her opening, I slide in slowly but then stop. I've got to get a grip. I swear I could come right now.

"Mick. Please."

"Please what? Tell me what you need."

"Fuck me. God, fuck me so hard. I need your cock."

My wish is her command. I'll fuck her into next week. She takes my cock like a champ, pushing back as I thrust forward. I know I'm hitting her in the right spot when she comes without warning around me. Using both hands to hold her bouncing tits, I play with her nipples, squeezing and teasing them. The pressure of her pussy as it undulates around me takes me over the edge. I come inside of her and suddenly feel exhausted.

"Best. Sex. Ever," I pant.

"Best. Ever," she repeats, exhausted.

We fall onto our sides in the same position. I'm still inside her, and I've got no plans to pull out anytime soon. I love her around me. We fall asleep just like that, and it's perfect.

55

———

RONI

I wake up with a stream of light shining in my eyes. When I feel the bed move behind me and large arms wrap around my waist, it's then I remember that there's something different about this morning. My first instinct is to jump out of bed and get dressed, but I don't listen to my first instinct this time. Instead, I wrap my arms over his and fall back to sleep. When I wake up the second time, I'm alone. I roll over to the spot Mick slept on and touch the bed. It's cool.

I peer at my clock and see that it's almost eleven thirty in the morning. "Jeez, I slept the day away." I pick up my phone to see a text from Mick.

Mick: I get off work at 2. Meet me at 1333 Granville Ave. At 3.

Me: What's there?

Mick: Our new house. Well, what I hope is our new house. Meet me there, and we can talk about it.

Me: Okay. C U there.

I make myself a cup of decaf. I know, why bother? But I'm so used to the taste of coffee first thing in the morning, I had to keep it up. I shower and change into some clean black leggings and a maternity tunic. Here's something that surprised me—maternity clothes are cute. Who knew?

At two thirty, I exit my apartment, lock my door, and take several steps toward the elevator. That's the moment I hear a voice. "Well, well, well. If it isn't Fatty McGonigall."

Shit. I'm facing away from her, so she can't see my look of shock. I turn slowly to see Trisha *and* Chris leaning against the wall. "What are you doing here?"

"We came to see how you were doing. Heard you got a sweet deal from Bill. What'd you do, blow him?" asks Trisha.

"Jesus, no. That's just... ick." *He's old enough to be my dad.*

I shake my head to get the image of naked Bill Phillips out of my head. I know this is not a good situation for me to be in right now. From the look on Trisha's face, it's obvious she's angry. The slight twitch of her right eye gives me a sense of foreboding. I'm alone, defenseless, and pregnant. As casually as I can, I place my keys between my first and middle finger, essentially making a weapon. Facing them, I focus on my surroundings to assess my options if things escalate. I'm about six feet from the steps down. However, I'd have to walk past them to reach them. My apartment door is at my right, but I'd be vulnerable while I took the time to unlock my door. The elevator is behind me and about four feet away Even if I could somehow press the elevator call button, it would take too long for the cranky old elevator to make its way up.

"Roni, we need to talk." Finally, Chris grows some balls to speak.

"What about?" I ask, trying to act casual.

"About what a fucking cunt you are," spits Trisha.

"Trisha, stop," says Chris, holding a hand up in front of her face.

Jesus, what is her deal? I look at her and say, "What did I ever do to you?"

That wasn't my best idea because her slight twitch has turned into a full-blown face of rage. She's a deep red color, and she bares her teeth like some kind of wild animal. Trisha lunges at me so fast I don't have time to prepare myself. At that moment, I hear the ding of the elevator and quickly look back to see the doors opening slowly. Looking back at Trisha, I see her coming for me, her long nails spread out like claws. As she reaches toward my face, I step back, turn, and make a dash for the elevator just as the doors open wide enough for me to get through. With one foot over the elevator threshold, I lunge forward, hoping and praying the door shuts in time. It doesn't. My body is pushed forward and down, probably due to the fact that Trisha has somehow jumped on my back like a monkey onto a tree. She doesn't weigh all that much, but her momentum sends me crashing to the ground nonetheless.

Pain radiates through my head as it makes contact with the hard floor of the elevator. The pain flares from there to my face, arm, and then my ribs as she furiously punches me. When she jumps off me, I think it's over. But then she just starts to kick me. The only thing I can think to do is curl into myself to protect my stomach to shield my baby. "Stop!" I feel like I'm shouting, but it's hard to breathe. The hits to my side aren't helping. I try one more time. "Stop, please..." *I'm begging you.*

56

MICK

I wake up with my head facedown on a bed covered in a white sheet. People are moving around me; there are voices speaking softly. When I lift my head, it takes me a few seconds to realize I'm back in the hospital, but this time, I'm the one keeping watch over someone else.

Roni is in the hospital bed, sleeping. I slide my hand over hers and gently squeeze. I recall the events of last evening and wince. I've tried to push the memories out of my head, but they just keep rewinding. I'd been waiting at the house for almost an hour for Roni and sent her several text messages asking where she was to no avail.

Then, I'd gotten the call from Emily. "You need to get here. Now."

"Here? Where? What's going on?"

"It's Roni. They just brought her in. It's not good."

"Not good? What the fuck happened? I've been waiting for her. Emily? Tell me. What the fuck happened?" *Jesus, what happened?*

"Don't drive. Are you with someone?"

"Yeah, Dad and Keith."

"Get one of them to drive you. I'll talk to you on the way. Call me when you're en route. I'll know more in a few minutes."

I'd raced around the house in search of either of my family members, spotting Dad first working on an upstairs bathroom. "Dad! Something happened to Roni. Emily called. Can you take me to Northwestern?"

He'd literally dropped everything and raced past me and down the steps. I ran behind him. When we got out into the open, I sped past him to his truck. Wrenching the door open, I slid inside just as Dad was doing the same. Cranking the car on, he peeled out of the driveway and onto the street. I pressed the call button and waited for Emily to answer. "Come on, Em. Answer."

"Hey. You on your way?"

I pressed the speaker button because my hands were clammy and I couldn't grip the damn thing. "Yes. Now tell me!" I shouted at her because I couldn't help it. "Is she okay? What happened?"

"She was assaulted."

"Assaulted? What? By who?" *What the fuck?*

"We don't know the entire story, but apparently it happened right outside her apartment door."

"How bad is she?" My voice was quieter. I guess I thought if I asked nicely, I'd hear what I wanted to hear.

"She's sedated. Beat the hell up."

"The baby?" The sobs started then.

"Jesus," my dad muttered.

"She has several broken ribs and lacerations." She pauses. "We're worried about the baby, though, Mick."

"Oh, fuck." I bawled like a little bitch. "My girls."

"Calm down, Mick. We've got her stabilized. Get here. I'm in ER room three. Text me when you park. I'll wait for you at the door."

"Okay." I turned to my dad. "Hurry, Dad. Please?"

I felt his big Silverado pickup lurch forward and watched as shit zipped past the window. I don't know how long it took; it felt like days and like five minutes. He pulled up to the emergency entrance, and I jumped out before he fully stopped and ran into the building. I sent Emily a text and waited by the door. She must have been waiting too because the doors opened immediately. "Come on. This way."

I beat Emily to the room, pulled open the curtain, and stopped in my fucking tracks. She looked dead. She was so white I could have sworn she was a ghost. "Roni?"

"Go in and sit with her. Hold her hand. Talk to her. She was mumbling a few minutes ago."

I couldn't move. It was hard to believe she was even alive. She has bruises on her cheeks and cuts on her forehead and chin. I walked closer to her and can't help noticing bruising on both arms. I lifted the blanket off her legs and nearly choked. It seems no part of her is unscathed. I set the blanket back down gently. Moving over her, I looked down at her face. Even battered and bruised, she was still the most beautiful girl I'd ever seen. "You're going to be okay, baby. Emily's on the case." I ran my finger over a spot on her arm that wasn't injured, then placed my hand on her head and ran my fingers through her hair.

When she moaned, I stopped. *God, I'm probably hurting her.*

Her eyes fluttered open. "Mick?" Her voice was raspy, pained.

"I'm here, love. I'm here."

"The baby," she whimpered, and I saw her breathing escalate. "The baby?"

"Shh, you're fine, angel. Don't worry. You're going to be

fine." I didn't know what else to say since Emily hadn't updated me.

"I didn't think fast enough." A sob escaped her, so pained it broke my heart. "Our baby. I hurt her because I didn't think."

"Shh." I lean down so I can be close. "You did all the right things." Hell, I don't even know the story, but I'm positive Roni did what she had to do. "You're already a great mommy, Roni." Oh, shit. I felt the emotions sweep over me, but held it in. "It's all going to be fine. Just rest. I'll be here."

"Don't leave me, Mick."

"I won't. I promise. You're going to be okay, Roni. You and Peanut are going to be okay." I said that as much for myself as for her.

She sounded so damned worried. Did they say something to her? I watched as her eyes fluttered shut. Holding her wrist, I gently ran my fingers over her pulse point. I did that for what seemed like hours. At least until Emily and Dr. Lansing finally came back. They were able to wake her enough to ask her questions about the pregnancy. Things like morning sickness and when she last ate. The doc ordered an ultrasound just to be sure the baby was unharmed. He was more concerned about the fact that she was having heart palpitations. Something I didn't know was happening.

"Let's get the ultrasound ordered up, okay? Then we'll talk about your injuries."

When Roni asked the doctor if they caught them, I blinked. "Caught who, Roni?"

"Chris and Trisha."

"Why would they catch Chris and Trisha?"

"It was Trisha."

"Excuse me?" I looked at Emily. "Did you know that?"

She pulled her phone out of her back pocket and shot off a text.

"Did you text Hank?"

"Sure did." Her phone dinged. "He'll be here within the hour."

Our attention turned back to the doctor as he ran through what they knew so far. "Roni?"

"Yes."

"Can you bear with me while I talk you through this?" Dr. Lansing asked.

"Yes."

"Okay. I'd prefer not to do any X-rays on you, as it is a risk to the fetus. We've evaluated your injuries and believe you have several broken ribs. There's really nothing we can do for that. It's painful, but we'll just have to wait until those heal. You have multiple lacerations and deep bruising. We've cleaned the wounds and administered antibiotics to prevent any infection. You'll want to be sure to apply an antibiotic ointment several times a day. You're not showing signs of a concussion, but again, I think we should keep you overnight to be sure. After that, you should have someone stay with you to keep an eye on you and help you until you're able to get around. Do you have anyone who can stay with you?"

Is this guy for real? "Yes. I'm her fiancé. I'll be staying with her. Every night." I emphasized the last two words. *Every damn night for the rest of our lives.*

"Right. Well, let's get that ultrasound ordered up. Once we determine everything is fine as it relates to the baby, we'll get you up to a room for the night. Sound good?"

"Yes. Thank you, Doctor," Roni said softly.

When Em and the doc left, I sat next to my girl. "You doing okay?"

"He was right about my ribs. They hurt."

"I know." I run my fingers over the top of her hand just as Hank peeks through the curtain. "Roni? Mick? Can I come in?"

"Do you mind if Hank comes in, Roni? I want you to tell him about Chris and Trisha, if you can."

She nodded. "Yeah. What I can remember."

I watched Hank's face the minute he got a look at Roni. His jaw clenched and his eyes turned into slits. He was in cop mode. Not only that, I suspected he remembered when Sophie was brought in after an incident with a coworker. "Hey, Roni. How you doing?"

"Could be better," she rasped.

"No doubt, sweetheart. Emily sent me a text. Are you able to talk about this?"

"It was Trisha and Chris."

"Who are Trisha and Chris?" Hank asked, looking at me.

"She works with them."

"Used to. They were fired. They blame me." She groaned in pain when she attempted to adjust herself in the bed.

I stand, trying to figure out how I can help her. "Babe, do you want me to get someone?"

"No. I'm okay."

"All right. I'll get more details about them later. Tell me what happened today." Hank requested.

"I was leaving the apartment."

"Where were you going?"

I decided to answer that one. "To see me at Dad's Edgewater property."

"Yeah. I was leaving. As soon as I had my door locked, I heard her voice."

"Trisha's?"

Roni nodded. "It wasn't nice. She called me something." She closed her eyes. "Fatty McGonigall."

"What?" I said too loudly. "Jesus. I'm going to kill them."

"Not now, Mick. That's not helping." Surprisingly, that came from Roni.

"Fine."

"Then they asked me how I got my job back. I'll spare you on their crude words."

"Roni, if you can, tell me what they said. I'll need it for my report." Hank instructed.

"They asked me if I blew my boss to get the job." Her face is scrunched up in disgust. "He's like a hundred."

I chuckled at her comment, but she was not laughing. "Sorry."

"Then what happened, Roni?" My brother is so good at this shit. So calm, his voice soothing. I could see how he gets confessions out of people.

"I knew I was in a bad situation. I tried to figure out how I'd escape from them if I needed to. They were in front of the stairs and the elevator was behind me. As I was doing that, Chris said he just wanted to talk. Then Trisha called me the C word, yada, yada, yada."

I tried not to laugh, but she was sounding more like the Roni I love.

"Then, I asked her what I did to her. You know, to hate me so much. It was the wrong thing to say because she lunged for me with her long nails out like an angry cat. She was going for my face. When the bell rang for the elevator. I saw the doors open from the corner of my eye. So, before she could scratch my eyes out, I turned and ran for the elevator. But..." Her eyes started to glisten with tears. Turning to me, she told the rest of her story. "By the time I was going through the door, she was on me." She placed her hand on her stomach. "The la-last thing I remember, Mick, was praying our baby would survive." A sob escaped her as I walked to her. "I'm so sorry, Mick. What if...?"

I brought my arms around her in an attempt to hold her without hurting her. "Shh, it'll be okay, honey. Don't go there. Everything is going to be okay, baby. I promise."

I felt her nod against my neck, but she said nothing. I kept myself wrapped around her until her breathing evened out. She had fallen asleep. I turned and saw Hank texting. He'd already started working her case. "What do you know?"

"Chris is the one who called 9-1-1. He gave his name to dispatch, but they were gone by the time paramedics arrived."

"What does that mean for him?"

He shrugged. "He may only get a slap on the wrist, but he didn't stick around. As for Trisha, hopefully Chris will testify against her." Sliding his phone back into his pocket, he states. "I'm out. I'm going to track them down. I'll let you know when I find them. In the meantime, let me know how she's doing," he said, nodding toward Roni. "And the baby. Let me know that too."

I turn to Roni, "I'm going to walk him out. I'll be back in a minute, okay?" She nods and winces again. I need to see if she can have something for pain.

I follow Hank out of her room and down the hall. At the door, he slapped me on the back. "She's a keeper, Mick. She'll make you happy. Like Sophie does for me. Congrats, man."

"Thanks. She's already made me the happiest person on the planet, Hank."

"Good, little bro. You deserve it." I smiled at his back as he disappeared through the drapery.

57

RONI

At some point in the night, I was moved from the emergency ward to a room on one of the floors. Don't ask me which one. I've been sleeping so much I don't really remember much of anything except for the news that the baby is okay. Shortly after I was settled into my room, the ultrasound tech arrived, rolling in a portable machine. She inserted a camera in my vagina. It was a strange sensation, but it didn't hurt. When we saw our baby on the picture, the tiny thing was squirming around inside me. We both nearly fainted. Then when the volume was turned on, we heard a swish, swish, swish sound.

"That's the heartbeat," the tech said.

When I heard those words, I nearly had a full-on crying jag on the spot until I saw how relieved and happy Mick was. He actually did have a full-on crying jag. God, he's so sweet. He loves this baby as much as I do. I'll never doubt that for a second. We watched in awe as the tech told us all about our little peanut. She captured images for us to take with us. I suspect Mick's going to blow it up billboard size and hang it on Michigan Avenue. He's such a proud papa.

After the doctor checked out the ultrasound, he told us that it all looks healthy. I was released several hours later with a list of duties a mile long for my handsome caregiver. David picked us up in his big SUV to drive us to my place. When we walked into my building, Mick attempted to pick me up, but I waved him off. "My ribs hurt. I can walk as long as we go slowly. Besides, I'm too heavy."

Halting in his spot, Mick looks at me warily. "Veronica?"

"Yes."

"If you ever say another negative word about your weight, or if you insinuate I can't carry my woman when she needs to be carried, or you get upset when you think someone is going to lift you for any reason, I will tan that luscious ass of yours. It'll be so red you won't be able to sit for a week. I promise you. Do you understand what I'm saying to you, babe?"

I peer at him with huge doe eyes.

"Do you understand? Because I mean it, Roni. I mean it with every fiber of my being. You aren't heavy. You are perfect."

I start to scoff.

"Roni," he warned. "I mean it."

"Okay, Mick." That was an awkward conversation. The good thing? It distracted him from trying to lift me up.

When we reach my door, he looks down at me. "Keys?"

I open my purse and pull them out. Taking the keys, he lets us inside and pulls me straight into the bedroom, demanding I get into bed to rest.

I scoot up on the bed and lean my back against the headboard, then giggle. "God, that was so exhausting. I could sleep for days."

"You hungry?" he asks, ignoring my little joke.

"Yeah. I'm thirsty too."

"Be right back." He limps out of my room, and when he returns, he's got a bottle of water, a banana, and a yogurt from my fridge. I wasn't kidding; I'm really exhausted. My eyes are heavy, but I can see him set the food and water on the night-stand. I feel the warmth of my blanket being pulled over me and the bed beside me dip. He's lying down with me. I like the sound of that.

"Roni? Wake up, Roni."

I hear his voice but will myself to stay asleep.

"Babe, you need to wake up for a while."

"Noooo," I whine.

"Just for a bit. You need to drink some water, honey. You've been asleep for hours. Let's get some food in you so you can take your antibiotics."

As I watch Mick work, I ask, "Have you heard anything from Hank?" I hope they've at least talked to them.

"They're in custody. Chris's account is the same as yours."

"And Trisha's?"

"She's lawyered up and blaming you and Chris."

"Me?" I squeak. "What'd I do?"

"She says you attacked her."

"What? That's ridiculous."

"It is. Hank's hoping Chris will plea out and work with the DA to get Trisha."

"Me too. She's scary crazy. She shouldn't be out in the real world. She'll kill someone."

"Maybe she already has."

I blink, thinking of everything we've just said. I need to call people. "I need to call Bill."

"I already did. I used your phone yesterday to call him. I also called Deb and Martha."

I blink at him. "Should I be mad about that?"

"Should you be mad? At me?"

"No. I'm sorry." I shake my head. "Of course not. What did Bill say?"

"He said he felt terrible, responsible. He also offered to pay for your attorney's fees."

I gasp. "Seriously? Heck, I just may hold him to that."

"You should. It'd probably ease his guilt. Now, eat this, babe."

I look at the plate Mick's holding and smile. "Mac and Cheese? That's one of my favorites. My mom makes the best. Where'd you get that?"

"From me, dove," a voice says from the doorway.

"Mom? When did you get here?"

"Dad and I arrived about an hour ago. I'm so sorry we couldn't get here sooner. Mick assured us you were doing okay, but we rushed through chores to get here as soon as possible. We're staying for a few days too. Mick's letting us use his place."

I smile at Mom, at Mick, then at my dad as he peers at me above Mom's head. "Hey, kiddo."

"Hey," I say, trying to hold back the tears. "I'm really glad you're here."

IT HAS TAKEN me two weeks to feel normal again. Not only am I attempting to get over the injuries from my assault, but I'm also dealing with morning sickness. It should be ending any day now because every book I've read about pregnancy promises that it will stop by the second trimester. That was like two weeks ago. Enough already!

Since I finally feel human again, Mick and I are going over to the house in Edgewater that his dad and brother have been renovating. They own Flynn Construction and do all types of building projects, from large commercial buildings, to new homes, and doing flip renovations like this Victorian home we're going to see today. They are now completely done updating the home. Mick has shown me pictures of the place, and it's amazing. It went from nearly needing to be condemned to move-in ready in only a few months.

I finish up my work for the day and decide it is time to get dressed. Yeah, working from home has made me extra lazy when it comes to getting dressed. My commute is five seconds, and I wear pajamas to work now. Not that I'm complaining. It's been great, but I get stir crazy. Bored. I'm bored. So bored. That's why this outing to the house in Edgewater is thrilling to me.

Mick unlocks my door and walks into my apartment at exactly three o'clock. Yes, Mick has a key to my place. It just makes the most sense. He's here all the time anyway. "You ready, Roni?"

"Yep." I grab my purse and meet him at the door. Leaning up, I give him a quick kiss on his sexy lips. "I can't wait."

Mick grabs my hand and pulls me to him. It's his turn to kiss me. His is longer and passionate. He doesn't mess around when he kisses me. "Let's go. Dad and Keith are meeting us over there."

Mick's brand-new SUV is only down the block, so we hop in and take off. He was determined to get a safer vehicle after his accident, but he also wanted it large enough for a family. Damn, he's sweet.

Edgewater is the neighborhood east of mine. It's evident from the style and size of the homes there that it was once a wealthy area. Years of neglect have left it in need of people like Declan and Keith, as well as Hank and Sophie, to inject some much-needed love and money into the area.

Mick chatters on about his day at work, about a new bartender he hired that's driving him crazy already. I giggle at him when he rants about the new ones. He's not very patient with them, but they almost always turn out to be great bartenders. He does an excellent job teaching them, and he enjoys that part of his job. The second half of our drive, he talks about the company he's working with to manufacture his drinks. David and Henry have paid for the initial batches, and he's researching test markets. It's all coming together. I don't think he realized how long it actually takes to get something like his product on the market. From start to finish, it could take him over a year to really get it on any store shelves.

Mick stops talking in midsentence and looks at me. "We're here."

I turn my head to see the most beautiful house I've ever seen. I really mean it. "It's perfect," I say with a gasp. "Mick, it's perfect."

"I know. But let's go inside and take a look."

He runs around the car to open my door, reaches in, and helps me out of the car and onto the curb. There's a driveway and a new one-car garage on the property, but there are still Flynn Construction vehicles and equipment around. Mick said they were doing some landscaping since it seems spring has arrived earlier than normal.

We step onto the covered, wraparound porch on the front of the house, which is now painted a light shade of blue-gray. The gingerbread work above our heads and along the wooden railing has all been restored and painted with a dark plum color that contrasts beautifully with the cream of the railing and window frames. They've added hanging baskets of flowers on the porch and placed some wicker furniture to stage the space.

"Is the furniture included, Mick?"

"You like it?"

"I do. It's really perfect."

"We can ask them about that, okay?" He pulls the screen door open and knocks on the wooden front door painted dark plumb like the other woodwork. There's old bubble glass used for the window in the center of the door that looks like it's been there since the house was built. Mick knocks again but then just turns the knob and walks in. "Dad? Keith?"

"Back here," yells one of them.

We step in, and a beautiful wooden staircase catches my eye first. On the left is the formal living room with a fireplace as the focal point of the room. Wooden built-in cabinets with glass doors flank the hearth. The woodwork matches the staircase and other trim around the entire space. We walk through the living room, into the formal dining room. There's an elaborate built-in dining hutch and buffet in the same wood, but the glass on the lower cabinets is made with stained glass. It looks original too, but it's been restored.

"My goodness, Mick. Your dad and brother do amazing work, don't they?" I say in awe.

"They do. Come on. I think they're in the kitchen."

We step through a swinging door, and I gasp. The kitchen looks like it belongs in a magazine. It's primarily white except for the countertops. Those have a mix of the same gray-blue of the house with a vein of plum running through. The backsplash is made of white subway tile, and the floor looks like hardwood, but Mick says it's ceramic tile. You can't tell.

"Declan and Keith, it's incredible."

"Thank you, Veronica. We're glad you like it," says Mick's dad with a chuckle. "Want to buy it?"

"I do! How much?" I've never asked how much it was. I was afraid to know. Now, I'm afraid because this is my dream house, and if I find out it's too much, I may cry.

"Once you two finish your walk-through, we'll sit down and crunch some numbers. Sound good?"

"Yes." Mick grabs my hand and pulls me toward the staircase.

The upstairs is just as amazing as the downstairs. The

bedrooms are a decent size even after they added larger closets to each room. These old houses were notorious for having tiny closets. There's also laundry hookups on the top floor, which is great when you've got a baby. The bathroom is spectacular. There's a huge whirlpool bathtub and an even bigger walk-in shower with three showerheads. The one on the ceiling flows down like rain.

"Mick, I'm scared to find out how much this place is because I want it."

"I do too. Let's go look at the yard, and then we'll talk to Dad and Keith."

The backyard is a work in progress. The landscapers are working today, cleaning out the flowerbeds and setting up pavers. There's a new deck on the back, but the thing that catches my eye and literally makes me cry is the children's play-house. There's a swing, a slide, a jungle gym, and a play house with a door.

"Oh, Mick!" I exclaim. "It's so perfect."

He taps my tummy. "Dad bought that for us. For you, actually. He thought you'd like it."

"Y-Your dad bought it? But this isn't even our house yet."

"It will be," interrupts Declan. "Now, let's talk."

When we sit down with Declan and Keith, they have a spreadsheet showing us the purchase price of the house and their expenses plus labor. I'm glad they aren't going to lose money on this place. I've brought the information from the bank about how much house Mick and I can afford together. It's surprisingly high. Part of that is due to my new and improved income, but still.

When it's all said and done, they are only asking $459,900 for the house, which is about two-thirds what the bank said we could afford.

I say, "We'll take it."

All three Flynn's laugh loudly.

Mick's dad slaps him on the back and then pats my hand gently, saying, "Good. I'm pleased."

"When can we move in? Oh, and how much more for all of the furniture?"

Keith takes this question. "You can move in at the beginning of next month, after you close with the bank. We should be done with the landscaping and a few last-minute things inside by then. We'll get a list of the things we bought to stage the place, and if you want any of it, you can just pay us our cost. Sound good?"

"Yes!" I turn to Mick and smile so big it makes my face hurt. "We have a house, babe!"

He slides his hand over the back of my neck and pulls me in for one of his kisses. "We do. Congratulations. Dad, Keith, can you give us a second?"

"Sure thing," says Declan.

I turn and watch as the guys get up and leave. When I look back at him, he's on his good knee, holding a small, square box. It's light blue just like my necklace. "Mick?" I say shakily.

"Veronica."

I giggle at that. "Uh-oh."

He chuckles. "Veronica McGonigall, I know I've told you many times that I love you. That I loved you the second you attacked me in that taxi."

I giggle and snort at that. "Mick! I didn't attack you."

"Please don't interrupt. I'm trying to be romantic. Plus, my leg is killing me."

"Oh, babe. Get up."

"No. Now shush. Now I have to start over. Blah, blah, blah. I love you... yadda, yadda, yadda. Oh yeah, now I remember where I was."

I'm giggling through his entire proposal, and it's perfect.

"Veronica Minerva McGonigall, did you know that 4,153,237 people got married last year? Not to cause any trouble, but shouldn't that be an even number?"

I throw my head back, knowing that was a joke. Again, this is the perfect marriage proposal for us. It's so very us.

"One more try... Veronica Sue McGonigall, I love you with all of my heart. You and our peanut have made me the happiest man on the planet. That's quite an accomplishment because, when you met me, I was the most miserable man on the planet. You complete me."

I laugh again.

"I know it's a movie line, but it's true. You're my person, and I'm yours. I love every single thing about you, but my favorite is definitely your tits. Just sayin'."

"Mick! You're ruining it," I admonish, but I don't mean it.

"No, my favorite part of you is your heart. The second thing is your mind, and the third thing is that I know what an amazing mother you'll be. Be my wife, baby. Marry me?"

I've stopped laughing but haven't stopped smiling. "I know you wanted to add tittage in there at the end, but you were smart to leave it off the list," I say with a smirk.

It's his turn to laugh. I take the blue box from his hand and pop the lid open to reveal the most delicate and beautiful rose gold solitaire diamond I've ever seen. It's the same gold as in my necklace.

"Mick, it's perfect." I smile down at him. "Yes. Of course, I'll marry you. I love you so much, Michael Flynn."

"Thank fuck!" He sighs in relief. "I was scared shitless you were going to say no."

I take the ring from the box and hand it to him. He slides it onto my left ring finger. I wrap my arms around his neck and pull him in for a kiss. "Thank you. Your proposal was perfect."

58

———

RONI

"Roni, put that box down. Now!" shouts Mick.

I stand from my stooped position to see eight Flynn's and a McGonigall—each with their hands on their hips. "I just wanted to help."

"You are helping. You're telling everyone where to put the boxes, babe. You aren't supposed to be lifting anything."

"Look at Sophie; she's doing as she's told," Henry adds, pointing his thumb backward.

We all turn to see Sophie clutching a large box meant for the upstairs bathroom. "Yeah. I see that," I say sarcastically.

"Sophie, goddamn it. Put that box down!" Henry races to her to grab the box out of her hands.

I know why they're worried. I'm about four and a half months along in my pregnancy, and Sophie is about a month more than that. Neither of us should be lifting anything. I just feel terrible that everyone is lugging all of my junk. I should get over that and go back to directing traffic.

We closed on the place three days ago and lined up the movers and lots of help for today. The weather is warm and sunny, and everyone is excited for us. Almost every Flynn family member showed up bright and early to help us. Emily had to work at the hospital, and Beth is over at Sophie and Hank's place watching Abby and Katie. She'll switch places with Sophie soon, so she'll have a chance to be part of the moving day fun. Mick even enlisted the help of one of his cousins I've never met before. I'd heard him talk about Ernie Flynn, that he was a twenty-four-year-old computer genius and into comic books, so when I pictured Ernie Flynn, I saw poly-ester pants and a pocket protector. I felt sorry for poor, short, stout Ernie Flynn.

I could not have been more wrong. It seems impossible, but I think Ernie Flynn wins the prize for best-looking Flynn ever in the world. In my eyes, no one is as gorgeous as Mick, but this guy is competition. He's about six foot four with bigger muscles than Mick or Hank. His hair is dark auburn and cut short. He's clean-shaven, so I can see his strong jawline. His eyes are the same Flynn-blue as the rest of the clan, and his mouth is full and always smiling with perfect white teeth. He's funny and charming and nice. Very nice. I sigh just thinking about him. Yeah, I've got a crush on him. I should be careful because he brought his best friend along with him, and it's obvious, to me at least, that she's got feelings for him. He seems to be clueless, though. Typical.

Mary Clair Hammer could be my shorter, nerdier sister with her dirty blonde hair cut short and blunt at her chin. Her black-rimmed glasses are bottle-glass thick. The poor thing must be blind as a bat. The glasses do nothing to hide the freckles covering her nose and cheeks. She's a cute girl—woman, I guess. She's the same age as Ernie, so she's a cute woman.

They've all been calling the poor girl MC Hammer and singing "Hammer Time" all day long. Her face turns a bright crimson whenever the Flynn's sing another MC Hammer song, but she says nothing. Ernie seems to enjoy the way they tease her as he joins in the fun. I've been watching her, and I really want to say something to them all, but she and Ernie have been besties for several years. I'm sure she's used to it.

The rest of the moving crew includes my mom and dad. Neither of my sisters could get away, claiming they had "family responsibilities." I think I'm actually relieved they aren't here, to be honest. I don't think my sisters are very happy for me—for us. At least that's how it seems.

As I make my way around the new house, I feel a tug on my arm. Mick then grabs my hand and pulls me into the new three-quarter bath just off the kitchen and shuts and locks the door. With my back against it, he leans down and kisses me sweetly.

"You need to be careful, babe," he says, giving me another gentle kiss. "Our peanut needs for you to take it easy. There are ten plus people here who want to help. You're stressing them all out with your attempts to carry shit. Let us do it. Okay?" He does his signature move, sliding his hand to the back of my neck to pull me closer to him.

I lean in for my own kiss, but mine isn't so sweet. The man turns me on even sweaty and tired from moving all day.

He continues his lecture. "'Cause if you can't stop lifting shit, I'm going to have to spank that luscious ass of yours until it's hot pink."

I sputter at his last thread. "Mick! You wouldn't?" I know he would. He loves to add spanking to the bedroom fun. I like it too—in small doses. I'm not crazy about having a hot pink bottom. "I'll be good." I wink.

"Promise?" he asks with a smirk.

"I—"

Mick slides both hands up under my old Rolling Stone T-shirt and moans. "Your skin is like silk." He molds his hands over my enormous breasts. "Baby," he purrs. He slides his head underneath the shirt so his mouth is right over my bra.

Pulling down the cups, he licks and sucks on my sensitive nipples.

"Mick! What are you...?" I can't remember what I was going to say; it feels so good. I'm super turned on right now, but when he starts playing with my breasts, I'm suddenly focused. "Don't stop, Mick. Please." We literally have ten people wandering around our new home, carrying our stuff, and we're in the bathroom making out like teenagers. Well, more than making out.

"Mick, don't stop. I think I can come from just your mouth on my tittage."

He snorts out a laugh against me, and I feel him shaking with laughter. He wraps his arms around me, squeezing me. Next, he kisses my left breast, then my right one. He pulls his head out from under my shirt.

Whimpering, I say, "Why'd you stop?"

Smiling the most amazing smile, Mick says, "I love you so fucking much, Roni. You make everything so much better. I'm the luckiest bastard that ever lived."

"Awe, that's sweet," I say sarcastically. "Now, get back under my shirt and finish what you started." I pull my shirt up to reveal myself.

Mick groans and dives back in.

"Yessssss," I hiss.

59

MICK

She left me hangin'. I made her come just by playing with her super-sensitive nipples. Once she was finished, she slid her bra back in place, pulled her shirt back down, turned, and unlocked the door and away she went.

"Damn it, woman," I mutter under my breath. I stay back in our bathroom, willing my hard-on to calm down. "Damn it."

When I finally make my way out, the last few items are being removed from the truck. Roni is being true to her word. She is standing inside the house, telling people where each box and piece of furniture needs to go. Having her direct everyone is a big help. Because of that, we won't need to move boxes around as we unpack. They'll already be in the right room. I walk through the house to get a feel for the amount of work left to do. In the kitchen, my mom is on a step stool placing plates and other dishes into cupboards.

Mom suggested we set up one bathroom, our bedroom, and the kitchen on this first day. After that, the rest can be unpacked as needed. She's nearly done with our kitchen. Sandy is working on the upstairs bathroom, and Emily has already put our clothes in the closet and made the bed. We'll be able to sleep, eat, and shower now.

After everything is unloaded, we order pizza as a thank-you for everyone's help, and Em brought beer and soda because she said you can't have a moving party without beer. I agree. I half expected my family to hang out the rest of the night, but they could tell Roni was dragging. She seems to get tired fairly quickly now. I find her dozing at her computer throughout the day. In the evenings, when we relax on the sofa, it takes only a few minutes before she's snoring into my chest.

Now that we have our new home, we'll be spending a lot of time unpacking all of these boxes while also decorating the baby's room. Since we don't know the sex, and we don't plan to find out before the birth, the walls are already a soft gray. Roni wants yellow accents to go with the animal theme like Katie's room. She loved the idea of having all sorts of cute animals all around his or her space.

Her sisters are throwing her a baby shower at our place in the next few months. We've registered for things we'll need at the local baby store, and now all we need to do is decide on a name. According to Roni, this baby is a boy. She claims to have had several dreams where the baby's sex is revealed.

I think that's just hokum. You can't just dream up the sex of the baby. Women! We each have a list going of possible baby names, but we're having a hard time agreeing on anything. It doesn't help that all of Roni's suggestions are ridiculous. See for yourself.

Roni's baby girl names:

- Hermione
- Luna
- Minerva (of course)
- Ginny

RONI'S BABY BOY NAMES:

- Harry
- Severus
- Neville
- Viktor
- Seamus

ARE YOU SEEING A TREND THERE? They're all names from the Harry Potter books. There are a few of those that could work, like Seamus. Seamus Flynn has a nice ring to it. But the rest are terrible. Since it's going to be a girl, I prefer to stick with those names first. My favorite girl names include: Scarlet, Rebecca, Sydney, Penelope, and Harmony.

When I mentioned Harmony, Roni spit the apple juice she was drinking all over herself and me. "Oh, hell no. Harmony Flynn? That's way to hippy for me. And Scarlet? I like that name, but it rhymes with another word that I could just hear being chanted on the playground. You've got to think about that, Mick. Kids are cruel."

I guess she's right, but if she's using those rules, then Minerva is definitely out, as is Neville, Severus, Viktor, Luna, and especially Hermione. When I mention that, she cackles with laughter. "You thought I wanted to name our baby Minerva?" She laughs so hard the tears fall down her cheeks. "Jesus, Mick, you must think I'm a complete idiot." She cackles again.

"How was I supposed to know? One minute you're laughing, the next you're crying. Then you're mad at me for hours because I forgot to put the butter away. I can't win."

She stops laughing and smiles sympathetically. "I'm sorry, babe. I know my emotions are all over the place. I'll be serious about the names now, I promise."

After that, she provides me with a revised list of names. Hmm.

Roni's revised "serious" baby girl names:

- ~~Hermione~~
- ~~Luna~~
- ~~Minerva (of course)~~
- ~~Ginny~~
- Penelope
- Sydney
- Lainie

RONI'S REVISED "SERIOUS" baby boy names:

- ~~Harry~~
- ~~Severus~~
- ~~Neville~~
- ~~Viktor~~
- Seamus Michael (still like this one)
- Declan Jeffry (FYI: Not D.J.—I don't like using initials for baby names.)
- Finnegan

"BABE. Finnegan Flynn? Finn Flynn? Are you crazy?"

She giggles this time. "It's adorable."

"No. Just no. Now, I do like the idea of using a family name.

What about using my grandfather's name and your dad's like the middle name, if it's a boy."

"That all depends on...."

"On what?"

"Your grandfather's name. It's not something weird is it?"

"No! His name was Calum. It means dove."

She gasps, and I swear a tear slides out of her left eye in seconds. "Dove? That's what my parents call me. I'm the only one of the girls who has a nickname. I... I love it, Mick. My dad is my hero."

I smile at her, but my heart hurts. I want to be her hero, but I know what she means. My dad is mine too. "Calum Jeffrey Flynn if it's a boy? CJ for short?" I added the last part to annoy her. I saw the note.

"Yeah. I love it."

"Okay, if it's a girl—"

"It's a boy, Mick. Get used to it."

I laugh because she's convinced it's a boy ever since she had the dreams. "Well, let's have one ready just in case."

"Fine. What was your grandmother's name?"

"Morag."

That one makes Roni cackle again. "Morag? No way. Wait... what does it mean?"

"It means princess."

"Oh, that's so sweet," she starts to tear up again.

See, emotions run the gamut with this woman. "We can just call her Princess all the time. I like Lainie from your list. I Googled that one, and it means light."

"Really? Oh, I love that one. Lainie Flynn. It sounds perfect. What about Lainie Morag Flynn?"

I love hearing my name attached to anything to do with Roni. Soon, she'll be Flynn too. "It sounds perfect, baby." I reach out and wrap my arms around her. "We did it. We've got our names."

"Promise me you won't tell your family. I want the sex and the name to be a surprise. Besides, if we say the names now, they'll tell us if they like them or not. If they don't like them, they'll pester us to change them. So, deal?"

"Deal." She's right. They're relentless. When Hank and Sophie found out it was a girl, they told everyone the name. There were a few grumbles about it, but he told them in no uncertain terms that the name was set and to "shut the fuck up about it."

I pull her onto my lap. "Now, let's seal that deal with a good ole fashion fuck."

She giggles, which turns into a full-on belly laugh.

"I was serious."

That makes her laugh even harder. "Mick Flynn, you're a pervert." She continues laughing.

Since I'm not kidding in the least, I run my palm over her thigh to the juncture of her legs, then rub my thumb over her center.

She stops laughing immediately and moans. "Damn, you don't play fair."

"I never claimed to play fair. Now, walk that sweet ass of yours into the bedroom and strip for me. I want this baby name deal sealed nice and proper."

"You're serious?"

"Fucking serious. Now go," I say, swatting her behind.

She jumps off my lap and quickly walks to our bedroom.

"Strip!" I yell out behind her as I pull off my shirt and unzip my pants. I'm already rock hard thinking about sinking into her. My girl gets me so hot. When I get to our bedroom, Roni is crawling onto the bed on all fours. She turns her head and smirks.

"My girl wants it from behind today?"

"Yeah, Mick. I need you." She crawls up farther into the bed and grasps the headboard. "Hard," she adds, looking back at me again.

Fuck! I climb up behind her and run my fingers between her legs. She's soaking wet.

"Mick. Now. I need you."

"As you wish." I line myself up and thrust upward. Jesus. She takes my breath away. So hot and wet. "I'll never get tired of this sweet pussy, Roni," I whisper in her ear. "Best fucking pussy I've ever had, Roni."

"Mick," she whines. "Shut up and fuck me harder."

"Yes, ma'am."

60

 RONI & MICK

Roni
Living with Mick Flynn on a full-time basis is amazing. I love how we are together. We get along so well it should probably worry me, but it's never been hard for us. In retrospect, it seems impossible that it happened at all—that our friendship evolved into this incredible love affair. But it has. I should probably thank Chris Smith. If it weren't for him, I would never have gone into Chrome alone to drink away my sorrows. I would never have talked to Mick and confessed, and I would never have kissed him in that taxi. According to Mick, that kiss was the hottest kiss he'd ever had and made it hard for him to forget me. I know I wouldn't have forgotten about him, ever, kiss or no kiss.

Speaking of Chris Smith, he did in fact make a plea deal. With Chris's testimony, Trisha was sentenced to a minimum of two years in prison for assault and as part of that agreement she has mandatory anger-management counseling. I really hope she can get the help she needs, and I also hope to never see her again.

. . .

Mick

Living with Roni is better than I could have imagined. I've lived with other people before—hell, Lauren and I were practically living together—but it was never like this. My mom is right, there is nothing better than being in love with your best friend. Roni and I talk about everything. We argue, we laugh, and we make love. She's turned me on to Thai food, and I've turned her on to the Cubs. We have fun relaxing on Sunday mornings; then we head to my mom and dad's place for Sunday dinner. She loves my family, and they love her.

Watching our baby grow inside of her has been the most amazing and cathartic experience of my entire life. Sure, she's been moody, but she's also been sweet and sexy and cuddly too. There have been weeks at a time where she's felt like crap. Others when she was so exhausted she couldn't get much done, and weeks where she's felt exhilarated and fulfilled. It's probably the same for all women, but that doesn't matter. The past nine months of baby time has been worth all the ups and downs.

We're due any day now. Actually, the baby is overdue, but I try not to say that out loud because being pregnant during the hot summer months has not been fun for Roni. My kid is pretty big. According to our last visit, our bundle of joy is over eight pounds now. It's hard to say if that's the actual weight, but they're sure he or she is going to be big. They've talked about a C-section, but Roni wants to wait to make any decision on that. It may come to that though, so we need to be prepared. We have another appointment with the OB-GYN today, so we'll know more then.

At the appointment, Roni can't get comfortable in the hard-plastic chairs at the OB-GYN's waiting area. Why wouldn't they have nice fluffy chairs for all of these expectant mothers? After way too long, we're finally called into the exam room.

There's the standard equipment along with an ultrasound machine in the room. They take Roni's blood pressure, and there's concern on the nurse's face.

"Roni, I'm going to have you lie down on your left side for a few minutes. Then I'll take your blood pressure again, okay?"

"Why?" I ask. "What's going on?" They're starting to worry me.

"Her BP is slightly elevated. Lying down on her left may help bring it down a bit. We'll see. I'll get the doc in here, so she can talk to you about it." The nurse scoots out the door quickly.

"Is that bad? The blood pressure?" I ask Roni.

"I guess."

The ultrasound technician comes in next. We've had several of these, so we know what to expect. She measures the baby's weight and length again.

"Well?" I ask the tech.

"You'll need to wait for the doctor. She'll read the results and be in shortly."

"Damn it," I say impatiently.

"Don't worry, Mick. It'll be okay."

But it's not okay.

"Veronica? Mick? How are you today?" asks Dr. Chandler as she comes into the exam room.

"Good," replies Roni.

"Well, let me just tell you what we think is happening." The doctor pauses, and it makes me even more nervous. "Your blood pressure is high. That's a concern. The baby measures much larger than the last visit. We're going with over nine pounds now. You may not be able to deliver vaginally. With your blood pressure, it's not ideal."

"What are you saying, Dr. Chandler?" asks Roni with a look of terror on her pretty face.

"I think we need to do a C-section. Tomorrow morning at the latest."

"At the *latest*?" I choke. "Is everything okay? Is Roni okay?"

"Mick, it's going to be okay. Whenever the blood pressure goes up, we like to expedite delivery so it's safer for mother and child."

I run my fingers through my hair and start to pace around the room. That is until I look at my girl. Fear. There's real fear in her eyes. I walk to her and take her hand in mine. "Listen to the doc, baby. She's done this a million times. I'm sure this is common. Right, Doc?"

"The high blood pressure is not uncommon. You don't have preeclampsia, but we don't mess around with high BP. The fact that your baby may be over nine pounds is less common," she smirks. "You should probably blame this guy for that," she jokes, pointing to me.

"Yeah, his mom said he was humongous." Roni laughs.

"Okay, let's get you scheduled for tomorrow morning. How does that sound? Are you ready to have a baby?"

We look at each other, and I smile first. "Yeah, we're ready. Lainie Flynn is about to be born."

"You mean Calum Flynn, don't you?" says Roni.

I squeeze her hand and say, "I don't care what we have as long as you're both healthy."

Tears appear out of nowhere again, and Roni sobs quietly as the nurse schedules the birth of our humongous baby.

The following morning, with every Flynn and almost every McGonigall in attendance, we welcome our son, Calum Jeffrey Flynn.

It's a Boy!

Born August 4th at 9:51 a.m.
9 lbs 4 oz -- 22 inches long

Mother and child are doing great, and daddy Mick has never been more proud.
Now he just needs to get Roni down the damn aisle. Stay tuned...

61

ONE YEAR LATER...

Me: Roni?

Roni: Yeah?
Me: We're getting married today.
Roni: So I've heard.
Me: I wrote this for you... There once was a man from sprocket...
Roni: Mick...
Me: Seriously, I wrote this all by myself.

THE NIGHT you kissed me in that Uber was the best night of my life.

Or so I thought until the night I had you for the first time. That was even better.

The morning you gave me a son seemed like nothing could make my life more perfect except for today. Today you're going to marry me, and I finally feel complete.

Roni: ...

Me: Roni?

Roni: I love you, Mick. So much. Thank you.

Me: I love you too. Now, let's get hitched, woman!

Roni: You just had to go one step too far. LOL. At least you didn't talk about my tits.

Me: Damn, hang on. I'll Google a good poem about tits...

Roni: Don't you dare.

Me: See you soon, baby.

Roni: ;)

"Will you take this woman to be your lawfully wedded wife?"

"Hell yes!" I shout. "Finally!" I wrap my arms around Roni and kiss the hell out of her.

It took me a damn year to get her to walk down the aisle. Roni used one excuse after another to delay this thing. First, it was her wanting to lose the baby weight. Then, she wanted to wait until our son was old enough to be a part of the ceremony and remember it. Yeah, like a one-year-old is gonna remember anything but the cake he's going to eat later.

The final excuse was the last straw for me. She wanted to wait until this next one was born. No. Can. Do. We're pregnant again. This time, it wasn't an accident. I had every intention of knocking her up again. Being a dad is the best thing I've ever done in my entire life, besides being with Roni, that is. She's amazing, and knowing we're going to add to our family makes me feel blessed in ways I can't even describe.

The crowd around me starts to laugh. My wife is smiling and laughing too. Holding our little guy in her arms, we finally tied the knot in our beautiful backyard. My brother David is officiating our wedding. He volunteered to become ordained just for us. He's changed a lot since his divorce. He's noticeably happier, for one. For another, he's in love with Jen's complete opposite. Thank fuck.

My entire family is here, along with cousins, aunts, uncles, and nieces... only nieces. We've got the only Flynn boy so far. Roni's sure this one is a boy too. I learned the first time not to question her thoughts on that matter, so we'll just plan on welcoming Seamus Declan Flynn into the world in about eight months. But don't tell my family. They can't keep a damn secret.

Roni's family is here too. Even her sisters decided to show up this time. What is the story there? She gets no support or love from her siblings. Her parents are wonderful as they dote on our son.

Our son. He's a perfect blend of the two of us. He's sweet and cuddly like his mom, and at times, ornery and surly like his dear old dad. He's got blue eyes and blonde hair, and he's smart as a whip. I'm not just saying that because he's my kid. He's genuinely smart. He started to crawl at eight months, and by the middle of the ninth, he was running, much to our chagrin. He keeps us moving, that's for sure. Roni's still working at P&P Advertising. She works the majority of the time from home but does go into the office one day a week. Her client list has expanded from EnerSport to include a few others. She's content with her job and her life, I believe. That's what she tells me, anyway.

My drinks are on local store shelves. We haven't gone national yet, but we will in the next year. I've got my first four drinks for sale, and we're working on four new flavors. You'll have to wait to find out what those are later. I'm still managing Chrome too. I only work during the day or on nights when someone blows off their shift. Otherwise, I'm home every night with my family. It's fucking perfect. My life is fucking perfect, and it all started with a kiss.

Roni: Hey, Mick. Here's one for you.

Me: Uh-oh. Yeah?

Roni: A man pulls up to the medical clinic, leaving his wife and kids in the car, and races inside. "We're leaving on vacation, and my wife says I need to be vasectomized immediately!"

The doctor is surprised but makes the guy happy. Snip, snip, and it's done.

The guy shuffles back to the car and gingerly lowers himself back into the driver's seat.

"So, are you vaccinated, then?" asks his wife.

Me: **groan** You suck, Veronica.

Roni: Oh, babe. You wish.

BOOKS BY KAYT MILLER

The Palmer Sisters

Lainie

Agatha

Sadie

Cortland

Keely

Violet

Molly

Standalones

The Art of the Game

The Virginia Chronicles

One of a Kind

The Portrait Painter

Game Changer

Bedhead

It's All Thanks to Santa

Coming Soon: Farm Boy

Coming Soon: Redhead

The Flynns

Out of the Blue

Mick'sology

Vested Interest

The Importance of Being Ernie with Bonus Book The Importance of
Being Kennedy's

Quirky Girl

For a complete list of Kayt's books, visit:

Kayt's Website: kaytmiller.com

ACKNOWLEDGMENTS

Thank you to Virginia from Hot Tree Editing for editing this book from start to finish.

And an extra special thank you to Becky at Hot Tree Promotions for your advice, expertise, and her positivity.

And to my beta readers. Your feedback is essential to this process. Thank you!

Many thanks and adoration to Colleen Galligan for re-designing the The Flynn series for me. She read the books twice to get them just right. Thank you, Colleen!
You can reach her at: galligancolleen@gmail.com

<3 KM

ABOUT THE AUTHOR

How did it all start? Well, I love reading and one day I was searching for a book. A book about a certain type of woman and a specific kind of man and I couldn't find it so, I wrote it. I called it Game Changer and it couldn't have been a more appropriate title. It changed my life in many ways. While my real job is teaching young people, my fun job is conjuring up characters and situations to write about.

My goal, as a writer, is to write stories that relate to all of us, to make readers laugh and maybe cry sometimes. I hope my readers can escape into a fantasy, one that's actually possible. Sure, some of the stories could be dubbed "Insta-love" stories but that's okay. I fell in love with my husband pretty damn fast and with my daughter the second I saw her. So, it's a thing, I swear.

Please Follow Me on these social media sites. Following on BookBub to learn about special book deals.

I love hearing from you!

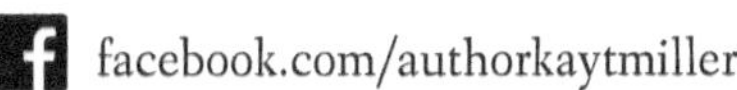

bookbub.com/profile/kayt-miller

THANK YOU!

Thank you so much for reading Roni and Mick's story! When I start a story, it begins with an outline, notes, and lots of crazy thoughts running through my head. When I actually start writing, the characters take over, leading me through the story like they're holding my hand —guiding me. The process is exciting and cathartic. With that said, I hope you enjoy the story.

If you did, please go to my website, www.kaytmiller.com, and join my newsletter so you can be the first to know what's coming up next. And...

Please, leave a review!

REPLACE WHAT-IFS AND SHOULD-HAVES WITH FUCK-YEAHS AND NO-REGRETS.

Chapter 1: David

You see that quote right there? For as long as I can remember, it's been my mantra. Well, that one plus these: No regrets. Win at any cost. Only the strong survive. Those philosophies have served me well in the ten years I've worked at Ingot Investment Management—or IIM for short.

I started here, right out of college, at the bottom at IIM as a business analyst. That was a coup in and of itself; at that time, the job market was in the tank. My boss, Lester Ingot, took a chance. He said he "saw something in me" and went with his gut. Lester Ingot is a guy who always goes with his gut. It's what made him rich, and in my case, his gut didn't let him down. I moved up to investment banking associate much faster than the average new business analyst. Two years later, I was an associate, and by age twenty-nine, I was promoted to director and have been in this job for four years. But now, with my latest deal, I've got my fingers crossed that I'll finally be promoted to vice president.

Hell yeah! Fuckin' VP! It'd be a major accomplishment for me, and it's happening today. I know it. I *feel* it. Because the big guy upstairs—no, not *that* big guy; I'm talking about Lester Ingot—has decided to throw a little party to celebrate the shit ton of money I just made for him—and for myself.

From my corner office, I can see caterers setting up a bar and loading the conference table with food. Lester's cheap as hell. He's got the first penny he ever made; I'm sure of it. So when he shells out money for a bar, I know this party is a big deal. All kidding aside, this could be it—the day that Mr. Ingot finally moves me upstairs to the executive floor. My dreams would become reality. Shit, I'm so stoked. I've been waiting for this for ten fucking years.

And I could use a dream come true at this point in my life. The last few months have been a fucking nightmare. Anyone who says divorce is easy is full of shit. Of course, maybe my divorce was worse than most. No maybe about it. My ex is the spawn of Satan who is also the greediest person I've ever met. That could be why my divorce experience has been *hell*. Pure and unadulterated hell. Thankfully, the divorce was final two weeks ago, right before the huge payoff from this investment. I can't help but smirk when I think about Jen's reaction when she hears about this bump in my bank account. She'll be pissed, and that makes me smile. The woman was relentless. She wanted it all, everything I had. My lawyer, an old college buddy, was an ace. He saw through her and played her like a violin. Squeezing my eyes shut, I rub my palms over my face. I need to clear my head of all of that negative shit brought on by Jen. Today, I'm not gonna think about that divorce drama. No, today is all about me and the promotion I've wanted for four years.

Lester's email requested that the staff gather in the conference room at 12:30 p.m. At 12:20 p.m., I stand up and adjust my tie as I move into my en suite bathroom. After checking my hair in the mirror, I wash my face and brush my teeth. I take a leak, zip up, smooth my shirt down, and shake my arms out at my side. "Fuck, I'm nervous," I say to the guy in the mirror.

"What are you nervous about?" a feminine voice says from my office.

I stick my head out, "Shit, Cassie, you startled me."

She giggles. "You're talking to yourself like a crazy person in there. Everything is going to be perfect. You're going to be patted on the back, congratulated, and hopefully, we'll be promoted." My assistant is beaming at me and holding up a tie. "This one doesn't have a coffee stain on it, David."

I look down and see a small spot on my light blue tie. I'll be damned. The woman has eyes in the back of her head.

"Besides that," she continues, holding up the replacement, "this is your lucky tie."

"True." The tie's pattern is the Flynn family tartan. It's brown and orange with a tiny bit of blue in the plaid. This tie has never let me down. I wear it whenever I need something to go my way. If I need good juju, I put this baby on. I pull off the stained tie and throw it aside. Knotting my lucky tie, I grin at Cassie. "Thanks, Cassandra."

"You're welcome. Now,"—she stands with her hands on her round hips and nods at me and my tie—"you'd better get out there." She places her hand on my back and gently pushes me out the door. "Don't drink too much. You start to ramble after your second one."

I nod, heading toward the door, but she's not finished.

"Don't eat anything with garlic in it."

I nod again.

"Watch out for mustard. I can picture you with a big blob of yellow on your white shirt." She frowns. "On second thought, don't use any condiments or eat any of those little sausages in sauce that you love so much. Don't eat anything from a toothpick."

"Yes, dear," I say with a smirk. Honestly, I give her a hard time, but I don't know what I'd do without her; I would be completely lost in more ways than I can count.

"Go get 'em, tiger," she teases.

"Grrrr." I laugh. "Thanks, Cassie." I pause at the door. "You're coming, right?" Cassie hates office parties. I've found her hiding in the corner on more than one occasion during office celebrations. If I didn't insist, she'd stay at her desk instead of joining us.

"Of course, I'll be there. I heard they're having baby quiches. Plus, there will be cake. You know I never skip cake."

She means it. She does love cake. Cassandra Darrow is, well, what is the politically correct way to describe it? Full-figured? Plus-sized? No! Curvaceous! That's a good description. She's definitely curvaceous with her wide bottom and enormous ti—um, breasts. Shit, you'd think, since I used to be married, I'd be able to describe a woman's body more eloquently, but I guess I can't. One thing I can say clearly is that Cassie is nothing like my ex-wife, Jennifer. They're complete opposites, and I'm not just talking about their different body types. Cassandra is classy. She does everything tastefully. She's graceful and articulate, and she's smart as fuck. Maybe that's not the right word. Genius. The woman is a fucking genius. So, yeah, Cassie's the complete opposite of Jennifer. Jennifer's only flashes of brilliance occur when she wants something. Then and only then is she creative, manipulative, and devious as fuck.

Don't misunderstand. Cassie is more than brains—she's a

beautiful woman too. Her long, dark brown hair looks like a curtain of wavy silk. In the morning when she comes into work, her hair is down. But by midmorning, she grabs a hair doohickey and winds it up into a complicated coil and attaches it—somehow—to the back of her head at the top. She always wears classy clothes too. At the office, she wears dresses or pencil skirts with pretty blouses and heels—always heels. Even the few times I've seen her in jeans, she's wearing stilettos. It's a good look. A *very* good look.

Cassandra's pale skin is flawless and looks like china—or is that porcelain? Yeah, porcelain. She wears very little makeup. She doesn't need it. Her eyes are emerald green, and she's got thick, dark lashes. Above her full lips, Cassie has the hottest little beauty mark. I love that little spot. It looks just like Marilyn Monroe's trademark spot. I've wondered what that little mark tastes like.

Shit. She's my assistant. I can't think of her that way. Besides, she's not my type.

Cassie's been with the company as long as I have —ten years. We went through orientation together, sitting next to each other during a long-ass week of meetings and training videos. If it weren't for her and her ability to make the tedium of the process fun, I'd never have made it without falling asleep. The two of us hit it off right away, and by the end of the week, we were good friends and have been ever since. I may even go so far as to say she might even be my best friend except that spot is reserved for my sister, Sandy. Or it used to be. I may have said it already, but I'd be lost without Cassie. Even if I did say it already, it's worth saying twice.